MULLIGAN

BY

MICHAEL CORRIGAN

"Mulligan," by Michael Corrigan. ISBN 978-1-62137-251-6.

Published 2013 by Virtualbookworm.com Publishing Inc., P.O. Box 9949, College Station, TX 77842, US.

Manufactured in the United States of America.

BOOKS BY MICHAEL CORRIGAN

Confessions of a Shanty Irishman

The Irish Connection and Other Stories

Byron

The Filmmakers

A Year and a Day (a grief journal)

These Precious Hours

Mulligan

FOREWORD

An Irishman's Perilous Journey by Tony Bucher

Mulligan tells the story of an Irishman's odyssey from strife and starvation in Ireland to an expansive but deeply troubled American landscape. It comes to us from an Irish-American writer deeply versed in the folk memories of previous generations.

Author Michael Corrigan explores extraordinary characters and themes from history within the modest narrative structure of a single man's life journey. Our protagonist, Michael Mulligan, drifts across landscapes of poverty and war his entire long life. It is a world where people conceal their identities and are not who they seem to be, and where life and death struggles between close and bitter enemies dominate the stage.

Corrigan was raised in San Francisco's Mission District in a house facing Dolores Park. That house sheltered three generations of Corrigans from 1914 onwards. The household was dominated by his immigrant grandparents from Ireland. About his grandfather he writes: "Like so many of his countrymen, Thomas was a laborer. They were not college educated, though the collected works of Shakespeare sat on the shelf. Our clan worshipped labor unions ('better to rob a bank than cross a picket line'), the One Holy Irish Catholic Apostolic Church and the Democratic Party." The house was also "a crowded, noisy place with the excitement of music and talking and a love of language," where every member had to tell a good story and be able to handle a good argument. The old gals in John Huston's film of James Joyce's novella *The Dead* "were just like my grandmother and her sisters."

Corrigan gained an appreciation for higher forms of argumentation through Irish literature. He says "I loved the rebellion Joyce showed with language," and the artistic creed he declares through Stephen Dedalus in *Portrait*: "I go to encounter for the millionth time the reality of experience and to forge in the smithy of my soul, the uncreated conscience of my race."

The Irish of those days used to "play it close to the vest," and were secretive about a lot of things. All of a sudden a certain "Uncle

Pete" might show up at the house from the mines in Butte, Montana, and suddenly there's an uncle no one ever bothered to mention. Memories of bad times in the old country would come out in odd bits of conversation, which a young Corrigan assimilated piecemeal. There is this scene from *Confessions of a Shanty Irishman*:

"Eat your corn beef and cabbage,' Grandfather would say at the table, 'or the Black and Tans will be after getting you.'

'Who are the Black and Tans?' I asked, imagining dual-colored monsters.

'Half police and half army—and English,' Grandfather added.

The very word—English—stopped all conversation."

Corrigan's stories are the product and the extension of his growing up in that world. He has authored *Confessions of a Shanty Irishman, The Irish Connection and Other Stories, These Precious Hours, A Year and a Day*, and now *Mulligan*, a novel covering one man's life from famine ravaged Western Ireland, the coffin ships, to San Francisco, Gettysburg and finally—the return to the land and people of his birth.

Mulligan addresses the drama of struggle and survival in war and peace in a foreign land, of a man declared an outlaw in his own country. His story spans years of trauma for the Irish people—of famine and pestilence in a nation colonized by an imperial neighbor against whom direct resistance was futile.

Here Corrigan describes the deeply troubled landscape of mid-19th Century west Ireland: "Mulligan then rode through the open Irish country, seeing mud huts with bare floors and half naked children running around in the cold drizzling weather. He saw women washing clothes in the river, and everyone had a small potato garden while cattle grazed in the fields."

Young men called the Whiteboys take secret oaths of resistance in the hills and fields to settle scores and fight for freedom. They are deeply hidden among the population, bound by secret ties, ever present, yet stoutly denied. Young Michael Mulligan encounters them during an act of gruesome revenge against a landlord who has killed Mulligan's father.

"Are you Whiteboys?'

'Whiteboys?' Both men laughed. 'They don't exist, lad.'"

Mulligan's path takes him out of Ireland on a long and perilous journey, first to Canada with a forbidden love, where he encounters one of the many tragedies that are to mark his long life. So many times Mulligan must cope with illness and death, and the painful separation from those he loves. Again and again he loses someone precious to him, or leaves them behind: a dying or lost lover, a little son.

There are moments to savor as he moves forward in his long journey, including an adventurous evening in the old streets of San Francisco. Searching for a missing actor, Edwin Booth, Mulligan wanders the foggy, sinister streets, fights alley thugs, and encounters spirits from a dimly sensed netherworld offering eerie guidance.

"Michael Mulligan saw blurred colored lights through the fog and heard tinny piano music. Newspapers referred to Sydney Town as a dangerous district run by Australian thugs called Sydney Ducks. The images were strong: brothels, taverns, gambling casinos, cutthroats, and the whorehouses of Chinatown using young women kidnapped in China. The few visiting miners who had actually struck gold soon found themselves drunk and robbed, some beaten nearly to death, and some waking up to service on a ship at sea."

Soon enough Mulligan finds himself in a fight, and his fighter's skills prove true as he saves a drunken Edwin Booth from being shanghaied.

"The short man advanced. Michael Mulligan saw the derringer and swung his night stick, cracking the thug's right wrist. Mulligan then slashed across his forehead with the blade, blinding him with his own blood. Kicking the derringer away, Mulligan reached up and pulled Booth from the wagon.

'An adventure,' Booth yelled."

They encounter the supernatural during their escape:

"Then he saw the pale figure floating toward them through the cold mist, the face old and white, the features caught in a frozen grimace. Mulligan had seen him on stage and it was the very image of Junius Brutus Booth himself, revisiting foggy streets. He heard the fear in Edwin Booth's voice.

'Father? Look where he comes!'"

The ghost of Booth's father envelopes the pursuing thugs and Mulligan escapes with the young Edwin.

His journey leads further onward from the streets of San Francisco to the field of battle, where he emerges as a skilled deliverer of death as a Union cavalry officer in the Civil War. Here he performs a deadly mission with great skill:

"Michael Mulligan selected a target, an anonymous Rebel soldier beginning the climb. He had a young face and held his rifle before him. Mulligan heard the lieutenant's low voice: 'Prepare to fire.'"

He observes and is permanently marked by the human leavings in the horrible aftermath of war.

"The soldier with the gangrenous leg was unconscious. They had placed him on a door, and two men held him while a doctor sawed off his leg. Amputated legs and arms lay in a pile near a tree."

After many years Mulligan finally returns to Ireland as an old man. He is reunited with his past and finds reconciliation with the world he had left behind, bringing to conclusion the many years of exile, violent trauma, and gritty survival that marked his entire life.

A fitting end comes for him from the supernatural world:

"Though blind, Michael Mulligan could see shapes and shadows on the periphery, and when he raised his head, he saw suddenly clearly an old woman in black coming toward him, her face partially hidden by a hood. Leaning down, she pulled back the sides of the hood, revealing a young beautiful face.

'Michael Mulligan. Hello, my dear one.'"

Home at last, his wandering comes to an end.

The reader experiences through these stories how an Irishman from the era of 19th century famine and rebellion finds reconciliation in his native land after many years of American exile. It is a deeply rewarding journey.

Tony Bucher is a columnist for The Irish Herald newspaper and a native of San Francisco.

AUTHOR'S NOTE

"The Famine," "Edwin Booth," "The Celtic Cross," and "The Plantation" were published in earlier, different versions. A friend suggested I write a novel incorporating more stories about Michael Mulligan, 19th century Irish freedom fighter, Union cavalry officer, theatre producer and adventurer. The ill-fated romance of an Irish stable boy and the elegant English lady is a familiar one. So is the tale of an Irish freedom fighter labeled a criminal and forced to flee Ireland.

It's a sad history for the Irish who escaped the famine made worse by England only to fight on both sides in the American Civil War. At Fredericksburg, the Union and Confederate Irish brigades faced one another. Michael Mulligan's story spans a period that includes the Irish famine, the American Civil War and Custer's Indian campaign. He is a character out of a picaresque novel, perhaps, a warrior nomad seeking eventual peace. Filling in the gaps before, between and after the original four stories took some research, but proved an exploration.

So Irene, here is your book. I hope it works on many levels.

I must thank Alison Quaggin for her criticisms and editorial suggestions regarding this manuscript.

THE PAVEE BOY

THE THEATRE COMPANY HAD just performed for an attentive gathering of lords and ladies on the dock of Cove Harbor in Cork. Many of the wealthy travelers gave generously for the performance. After the actors removed the flags and dismantled the stage, Tyrone Mulligan's young daughter, Maggie, found a strange boy hiding in the prop wagon. The boy, thin and filthy, wore a devil's mask and held one of their stage swords. She screamed. The boy dropped the fake sword as other actors seized him, dragging him before director Mulligan. When they ripped off the mask, Tyrone saw a handsome but underfed urchin with uncut brown hair. The boy's dark face showed desperation, but he didn't resist as they pushed him forward. He stumbled, smiled, and then took a mock bow.

"Just what the hell do you think you're doing?" Tyrone said. "You scared my little girl."

The boy said nothing.

"He's one of those thieving tinkers," an actor said. "Those people work the crowd when we do our shows."

Tyrone Mulligan asked the boy to step closer. "Are you a tinker?"

"No, sir. I don't know nothing about no tinkering."

The boy's accent was thick, the words garbled.

"Do you pick pockets?"

"Never. I'm a gentleman, sir." The boy took out a wallet and tossed it to an actor. Some company members laughed. The boy shrugged and made a face like a mugging clown. "I'm a Pavee," he told them. The accent was on the second syllable. "We just like to travel, sir."

"Were you planning to steal one of my props?"

"No." The boy smiled. "You need them. I saw you performing in Galway. I says to meself, 'I wanna join that troupe.'"

"Join us? Speaking that bog Latin of yours?"

"I can learn proper English, sir."

"What's your name and age?"

"Michael Dunne, sir, born at midnight ten years ago."

"Midnight, eh?"

Later that night on a camp above the harbor, Tyrone asked the company members what to do about their stowaway child. "Take him on or have done with him?"

"He comes from a race of thieves," a lead actor said. "Travelers. And those Irish Gypsies are violent. They could attack us."

"Thomas Connor, we could use a child actor. He just needs to be educated," Tyrone said. "He might even help us."

Tyrone found the boy sitting by a fire eating ravenously. Maggie watched him, her eyes round and focused on the boy's rapid gulping. "You're a pig," she said, the firelight catching highlights in her blonde hair.

"Michael Dunne?" The boy looked at Tyrone. "My company is afraid your tribal relatives will show up and cause trouble."

"Father won't care if you slip him a few coins."

"He would sell you?"

"He might if I don't help him."

"Help him do what?"

The boy didn't answer.

"You have a mother?"

"She ran away."

"I see. And you want to act on a stage?"

"Yes."

"And you think you're a good actor?"

"We are taught to act from birth. And I know horses."

Michael Dunne liked Tyrone's lined face and long silvered hair; it was the face of an artist—a kind man.

"We do religious plays during Easter," Tyrone said. "The Wakefield Cycle plays from Adam and Eve through the crucifixion. You have any religion?"

"Roman Catholic," he said. "But wherever we land, we like to blend in."

A woman in the troupe laughed. "Blend in? With those wagons of yours? Those clothes? A language no one can understand? Blend in?"

"You play any musical instruments, Dunne?"

"Well sure. Guitar. Fiddle. Tambourine. All tinkers or Gyppos as you call us play some instrument. We are entertainers. We are the Walking People."

"And pickpockets," an actor said. "The piker will get us in trouble. Send him back, Tyrone."

"Send him back where?" Tyrone looked at the boy, so frail and tough at the same time. A distant lighthouse marked the bay full of anchored sailing vessels. "Dunne? You can stay the night."

The next morning, they left Michael Dunne behind and rode to the next town for the first of many lucrative cycle plays performed on church steps. The Catholic Church encouraged their performances but Protestant Churches censored the plays, omitting references to the Pope. Large crowds came to watch. In the summer, they had Comedia del Arte shows, and even an occasional Moliere or Shakespeare.

Tyrone Mulligan didn't expect to see the boy again. He did notice some Travelers in the audience and suspected they were picking pockets. As they performed the temptation of Eve and the seduction of Adam in the Garden of Eden, Tyrone saw Michael Dunne riding up to the plaza on a beautiful young horse, the boy riding bareback with only a bridle. He was surrounded by three men, one of whom led the horse away. An older man slapped the boy, knocking him down. Then the burly man disappeared.

The show ended and the crowd applauded. Tyrone's musicians began to play and sing while another passed a hat. This was when spectators often discovered missing purses. Tyrone watched as Michael Dunne got up and took off his broad-brimmed hat, walking through the crowd collecting money for the troupe. As they were about to camp for the night, Tyrone and Michael Dunne spoke again.

"Why are you here, boy?"

"I cleared everything with me da. I can travel with you."

"Is he the one who hit you?"

"Don't know who that was, sir."

"Your father won't come after us?"

"No. I am one less mouth to feed."

"And why should I take you on?"

"I think you could use me." The boy picked up a fiddle and played passably well. "I can take your last name, if you like. Maybe people might recognize Dunne as a Traveler name. They do hate us, you know. I got kicked out of school when a boy asked to read my fortune and spit in my hand. I hit him pretty hard."

"Your people are known as thieves. In one town, we were blamed when spectators couldn't find their purses…and we didn't make any money."

"We're taught young that we have permission to steal," the boy said.

"Permission? From whom?"

"Jesus Christ."

Tyrone blinked, looking at the boy's dirt streaked face. "Explain that."

"When Jesus was nailed to the cross, the Pavee Travelers stole the last spike so the Romans couldn't drive it into the Savior's throat. Our Lord could speak his last words. After that, Jesus gave us permission to steal."

At first, Tyrone was stunned. Then he began to smile.

"What an amazing story," he said.

Michael Dunne remained silent. Maggie came into the circle of firelight and openly stared at him. "You smell bad," she said.

"I do need a wash," the boy said. "Sometimes me da makes us run naked in the rain."

"Am I supposed to pay your father when he shows up?"

"No need. I gave him a new horse," Michael Dunne said. "Beautiful young stallion, he was. Da was pleased...with the horse."

"Where did you get it?"

The boy put down the fiddle.

"I stole it," he said.

Tyrone shook his head, laughing. "Why do you want to leave your people?"

"Because I was taught to travel...even from them."

In the morning, Tyrone introduced Michael Dunne as a new member of the company.

"From now on, he wants to be listed as a Mulligan."

For five years, Michael Mulligan performed with the traveling troupe, sometimes playing in England and France. They performed in parks, city plazas and on cathedral steps. Occasionally, he saw Travelers working the crowd. When not on stage, he would approach them and curse in Shelta, the Pavee language. They would look surprised and back away, some calling him a traitor to his people.

"All the same, if my father tries to hit me again, I'll break his neck."

One afternoon while collecting money from a crowd at Ballyshannon, a tall old woman with white hair dropped money into his hat. She smiled at him.

"Glad to see you've found a home," she said.

"Who was that?" Tyrone said, after the woman left.

"A nice lady who fed me lunch when I briefly went to school."

Tyrone Mulligan didn't inquire further. He was pleased with Michael Mulligan's skill as an actor and musician, and he learned quickly, even losing the Traveler accent and grammar.

Tyrone also noticed how Maggie now looked at Michael. One day he caught them kissing by the river.

"You cannot marry an Irish Traveler," he told her. "He has no nationality. And no matter what he's left behind, he can't marry outside his nomadic tribe…his people."

"He's not a Traveler anymore," she said. "Father, he's one of us. And we don't exactly have any nationality either. We are traveling actors. We are nomads."

"He's fifteen. You are fifteen. You are too young. He is like a brother to you!"

"But he is not my real brother."

"True." Tyrone considered Michael Mulligan his son and felt guilty that a union between his daughter and the adopted boy would matter. "All the same, I don't approve."

"Maggie is like a sister to me," young Mulligan later told him.

"For how long?"

They played in Oxford. It was a town of wide boulevards, impressive ancient buildings and thick moving crowds of families and students. Statues stood on ledges between the massive windows of the Oxford Academy. A large audience arrived to see *Romeo and Juliet*, starring Maggie and Michael; the young actors created a passionate heat on stage with Tyrone playing the Friar. Mulligan's recently breaking voice now projected with a lyrical tone: "How silver-sweet sound lovers' tongues by night, like softest music to attending ears!"

A young actor named Edgar played Tybalt. Their fight scene was unusually realistic, and sometimes Tybalt seemed reluctant to die, savagely fighting Mulligan as Romeo. The English crowd cheered the young star-crossed lovers and wept when they died. After the show ended, Mulligan confronted Edgar.

"You try to hurt me on stage, again, I'll run you through."

Edgar remained silent, glimpsing Juliet's décolletage as she escaped back stage. Then Tyrone made an announcement.

"We are going back to Ireland, but I have arranged for Michael Mulligan, who is now my legally adopted son, to take classes at the university."

Maggie began to cry. Michael Mulligan protested.

"I want to stay with you…and the company. Why can't Maggie take classes?"

"They don't take women students."

"I won't go," he said.

"Don't waste your life on us," Tyrone said. "You will have more choices after the university."

"This life was your choice," Mulligan said. "And it is now mine."

When Tyrone touched the whip to the horse and they pulled out of Oxford, Michael sat next to him, with Maggie in the wagon. They crossed the River Thames. "I made arrangements for you to enroll at a later date," Tyrone said. "I still have some authority."

"Where do you get this power with the university?"

"Money. Their library needs to expand." Tyrone laughed. "I was once part of that academic life, and yet I prefer doing this."

"So do I. Don't send me away."

"I won't, but you *must* not break Maggie's heart. I don't want her to die young like her mother."

"Don't speak for me," Maggie said.

Mulligan stared ahead at an ornate enclosed bridge over the road. Perhaps he was meant to travel roads like his forebears.

"Many of my people die young."

"Which people?" asked Tyrone.

In Ireland, Michael Mulligan and Maggie took long walks after the shows, but they were followed by Edgar who didn't hide his contempt for young Mulligan. Often, Michael Mulligan extended their walks and hid from Edgar who found himself out of breath and even lost.

"That ratty old Edgar wants me, and my flesh crawls whenever he brushes against me," Maggie said. "He calls you a thief behind your back."

"But I am a thief. One day, he may take a long swim."

"And one day, you may regret not staying at Oxford."

"How long would I last? I'd be sent down, I'm sure."

They passed a grove of trees. Mulligan took her hand and kissed her. Maggie responded. She took a deep breath.

"Maybe we are doing the wrong thing," she said.

"We probably are," he told her. "We can wait."

"Maybe we can't," she said. Maggie pulled him into a grove of trees. They embraced kissing in the thick brush. Michael Mulligan pulled apart her blouse.

On his sixteenth birthday, the troupe performed in Galway before the Spanish Arch. Michael Mulligan was playing a song on the guitar when he saw a group of Travelers working the crowd. He finished the song, and while the play continued, walked up to the men, speaking to them in Shelta.

"Stay away from these people. They are actors—they need what money the crowd can give them."

"So do we...and why ain't you with your people?" a man said to him.

Another man grabbed his arm. "Michael Dunne? Is that your last name? Dunne?"

"Yes."

"Your father's dead."

"Dead? How did he die?"

That night, Michael Mulligan told Tyrone that he was leaving the company but would return. He quickly explained.

"Some English guards hired by a landlord attacked my father and others at their camp. My father was killed. I have to return with my people."

"They are not your people anymore," Tyrone said.

"Am I part of your people? My father was shot like a dog."

"Were they camping on the landowner's estate?"

"Yes. The English seem to think Ireland is theirs to rule."

"But those people were camping on another man's land."

"They are nomads—that's what they do. They didn't deserve to die at the hands of those robbers." Michael Mulligan felt his heart racing. He knew it was dangerous to join his former people. "I must act," he said.

Maggie confronted him. "If you leave, we'll never be together again."

Tyrone walked away. Michael Mulligan met the girl's eyes. "I will always want to be your friend, Maggie."

"Friend?"

He saw tears forming in her eyes before she bolted from him. That night, Michael Mulligan saddled his mare while Tyrone and Maggie stood waiting. Edgar watched from a distance. The evening air was warm and still.

"Come back, Son," Tyrone said. He gave Michael Mulligan money and shook the young man's hand. "You know what will happen if you get revenge?"

"I do. Don't worry."

He kissed Maggie who had stopped crying. Tyrone looked away and then walked toward the wagon where Thomas Connor watched, leaning against a wheel.

"May you stay safe," Maggie said.

"I will, Maggie."

"Maybe it's just as well, Michael."

"I'm sorry if I hurt you."

"I'm sorry, too, but maybe it just wasn't meant to be."

"I'll come back."

She took his hands and kissed him gently on the cheek. "Good-bye."

Then Maggie walked away, and for the first time, Michael Mulligan felt misgivings about leaving. Thomas Connor stopped Mulligan before he mounted his horse. He had the kind of angular face that could be handsome or ugly depending on his expression and makeup, or the angle of light.

"Take care of yourself, Boyo," Thomas said. "And do come back. We need your talent, even if you will take all the romantic roles I want."

The two men embraced. Moments later, Michael Mulligan was riding toward the road. Other members of the company waved and wished him well. He heard Edgar shout "Good riddance" as he left. Within a mile, he caught up to the Traveler wagons and fell in behind them. That night around the fire, Michael Mulligan felt disconnected: he was among them but not really of them. He heard the details.

"They just rode upon the camp firing their guns. Your father was shot running."

"Who owns the land?"

"An Anglo Irishman named Nathaniel Burke. He hires landlords who rent to farmers."

"We must kill Burke," Michael Mulligan told them.

"No—the soldiers will be waiting for us. They know who we are."

"They don't know who I am. My name is now Michael Mulligan, the son of Tyrone Mulligan, a former professor at Oxford. Perhaps this Lord Burke needs a groom for his horses. I will enter his employment, and the first chance I get, cut his throat."

Bartlett, an older man and the leader of the Travelers, suddenly broke into a wheezing laugh.

"First of all, it's the landlord who shot your da. And you're gonna kill an Anglo Irish Aristocrat? Hah! They'll hang you."

"They have to catch me first," said Michael Mulligan. "And you must *never* acknowledge me as one of yours."

"You don't sound or look like one of us, no more," Bartlett said.

"What is the name of the man who shot my father?"

"John Boyle. He's a fat landlord working for Lord Burke. I feel sorry for his horse. Sure, but he was afraid we'd steal his cattle or potatoes."

"Was that your plan, then?"

Bartlett didn't answer.

In the morning, he found the secret place where the Travelers had buried his father. Someone had placed a statue of the Virgin Mary over the grave. He stared at the fresh mound of dirt, feeling little compassion for the man who gave him life. His father had beaten him once for not helping to rob an old woman.

"What ails you, lad? While we work in her barn, you're supposed to visit the house and steal her jewels. She must be rich."

"I couldn't find nothing," he told his father.

"You're an idiot or a liar!"

Then his father struck him and Mulligan remained passive. He couldn't tell his father how the kind old woman chased off some boys who were taunting him for being a Traveler and then invited him in for milk and beef stew. His father would not understand. Despite the memory, he felt a deep outrage. Though he had left his father and the Irish Traveler culture, someone had to pay.

That night, Michael Mulligan took a room in an inn near the Burke estate. It was late when he joined some farmers sitting at the tables, drinking. They watched him without meeting his eyes.

"Any work around here, gentlemen?"

They looked at each other, workers with callused hands and red faces.

"Work? Sure, you can work yourself to death for whoever owns the land…or you can rent out little plots yourself. Just pray the potato crop is good. I'm sick of potatoes, meself, but I'd rather starve than end up a slave in the workhouse."

They laughed and drank more. An emaciated man stared at Michael Mulligan.

"Who are you and where are you from, lad?"

"Michael Mulligan. I've been traveling with some actors."

"I've seen their shows. Just watch your purse with them Travelers."

"Thieving tinkers," another man said, lifting his mug. "They'll rob your crops and then you can't pay the rent. Then you starve."

"I heard about the recent troubles."

They were staring at Mulligan, the men suddenly alert.

"And who told you about recent troubles?"

A drunk with a goatish beard seized Michael Mulligan's arm. "Are you an informer? Ireland is plagued with them."

"Let him go," another man said. "Burke was on trial recently. Of course, nothing happened." The man stared at Michael Mulligan. "Can you read, Mulligan?"

"I can read, sir."

"The name is Reilly," the man said. "Burke defended his landlord who was simply protecting his land. Burke got acquitted and Boyle got off free." There was a sudden silence. "I better be quiet," Reilly said.

"And why not acquit Boyle?" someone said. "He did the right thing, even if he does work for a landowner. I'd like to shoot the lot of them tinker bastards."

Mulligan felt color coming to his face as the men chuckled and drank.

"Boyle sure ain't after starving to death."

"I have to leave, gents," Reilly said. He regarded Mulligan. "You may need other means of employment than playacting. What else do you do?"

"I know horses."

"Maybe Lord Burke will give you a job on his large estate. You can train his horses for the annual fox hunt. You won't have to break your back to feed him and yourself." He drained his glass. "I need another drink," the farmer said.

"Let me buy a round."

"Well, our little actor friend has a few coins."

They drank together.

"I'd like to buy this Boyle a drink," Michael Mulligan said. "He deserves it."

"Boyle won't drink with us," Reilly said. "He gets to collect rents while we live in mud huts."

When the tavern closed, the farmers left except for one.

"It's a conacre system, Mr. Mulligan. You don't get money. You get a small patch of ground in exchange for labor. You eat what potatoes you can grow. Your labor keeps the landlords and landowners rich."

Michael Mulligan sensed a subdued violence in the thin wiry man. Though young, his face was lined with deep wrinkles. His voice had a rough edge.

"You're not exactly loyal to your master, are ya?"

"I am not. And sometimes we strike back. Do you understand?"

"I think I do," Mulligan said.

That night, Michael Mulligan lay in bed. He could find where John Boyle lived, though he knew Boyle was armed and probably had guards. There was the wiry man to consider.

The next day, Mulligan rode through the open green country, seeing mud huts with bare floors and half naked children running around in the cold drizzling weather. He saw women washing clothes in the river, and everyone had a small potato garden while sheep and cattle grazed in the fields. Michael

Mulligan noticed a gaunt woman tending her small garden. She waved at him.

"You seem pretty rich to be riding that nice horse," she said. "And don't you look pleased with yourself? A knight in shining armor."

"I'm just looking over the land."

"Not a landlord, I hope."

"No."

"You want something?"

"You have too little to share with others. You speak Irish?"

"God no," the woman said. "The English took our language years ago." She stared at him, touching a strand of brown hair visible from under a head band. "My man will be out working the fields until dark. Perhaps you'd like to come in for tea." A small naked boy ran from the hut, chasing his half naked screaming sister. They ran around a corner. "Food is so high," she said. She unbuttoned her blouse of coarse cloth. "I *do* have tea. Come in, my handsome young man. Don't mind the children."

"Where's Mr. John Boyle?"

"Who cares where that evil Boyle is? I'm sick of his palaver. Sometimes he wants to collect rent in personal ways. You know what I mean?"

"Yes."

"Don't want to lie under that fat carcass."

Michael Mulligan dismounted. He reached in his pocket and gave some coins to the emaciated woman whose cheeks had a sunken look. "Where does Mr. Boyle like to take his drink?"

The woman quickly pocketed the coins. "That sot will drink anywhere. He likes Galway. There's a tavern near the Spanish Arch." She touched the top of her breast. "You want nothing, young man?"

"No. You've been very helpful." He mounted his horse.

"I thought you were English at first. If you need a bit of excitement, come visit."

"I'll remember that. Good day, ma'am."

Michael Mulligan rode to Galway and found a tavern near the Spanish Arch. The River Corrib flowed into the distant bay, and there were many swans. Police watchmen and occasional

English soldiers passed in the street. One officer saw his horse tied to a post and addressed him.

"Sure, that's a fine horse, young man." He pronounced it 'harse.' "I would love to know where you got such an animal."

"I breed and train horses," Mulligan said. "I've been saving money to attend Oxford, one day."

"Oxford?" the young constable was clearly startled. "And what Irishman goes to Oxford, may I ask?"

"A smart Irishman. I even have a letter of acceptance. Would you like to see it?"

"No. I suspect anyone with that kind of tall tale is probably telling the truth. There are a lot of wealthy land owners with stables around here. What's your name?"

"Michael Dunne."

"Dunne?" A British soldier passed in the street. "Soldier! This Irish boy is going to Oxford," the policeman told him. "What a dreamer."

"Oxford?" The soldier laughed. "Just what we need: an educated Irishman. You're not running with any outlaw gangs, are you?"

"I just work the stables, sir."

"These so called Levelers have been a problem," the soldier said.

The policeman agreed. "We used to call them Whiteboys. After terrorizing local landlords, they were." Both men glared at Michael Mulligan. "You are well fed, young man. That means you're either a criminal or an aristocrat. I've yet to meet an Irish aristocrat, especially with the name, Dunne."

"There are some wealthy Irish Protestants living in Belfast," the soldier insisted. "Our own Lord Burke is well off."

"You are right," the constable said. "Superior stock, he is."

"I'm just enjoying our lovely country, gents," Michael Mulligan said. "Maybe I should cultivate an English accent."

"Spoken like a criminal," the constable told him.

"And what is your name, officer?"

"Officer McConnell."

Michael Mulligan also wanted to ask the policeman why he was insulting a fellow Irishman but he remained silent. The two men walked off. Michael Mulligan knew he would need papers for identification, or else wear ragged clothes. Then he saw a huge fat man leaving the tavern, staggering toward a waiting carriage. The man had a round face and a beard that ran over his cheeks and under his nose, exposing a double chin. As Michael Mulligan approached, he heard the footman say, "Climb aboard, Master Boyle, and we'll take you home."

Boyle grunted and boarded the carriage, settling himself, the wheels sagging. Michael Mulligan walked over to his horse and mounted, following behind as they traveled along the bay. The carriage turned off on a narrow muddy road and continued into open country with many green hills and fields of uncut turf. Mulligan wasn't sure what he would do since he didn't have a weapon. The carriage disappeared around a bend, and when Mulligan turned on the narrow trail, he saw the road blocked by a tree. He heard shots, and the driver slumped forward. Moments later, a man wearing a white shirt and pants rode alongside the carriage and fired inside. The door opened and Boyle stumbled outside clutching his stomach. He fumbled for a gun and then his huge bulk collapsed on the muddy road. The man on horseback pointed his pistol once more at the cursing Boyle.

Mulligan was about to turn his horse when another man in white appeared beside him, leveling a pistol at his face. "Who are you?"

"Michael Mulligan, sir."

"And who is Michael Mulligan?"

"I work with a traveling theatre troupe."

"Why were you following Boyle?"

"He killed my father."

"And why did he do that?"

"He was a Traveler, sir."

"Squatting on Boyle's overpriced land, eh?"

The second man lowered his pistol.

"And what were you going to do, lad?"

"Kill him…but I don't have a weapon."

"So I see. You were going to choke that fat thief?"

"I wasn't sure."

"Take my gun. Shoot him. Gwine. Do it."

Michael Mulligan took the pistol and rode toward the first gunman. It was the wiry man from the tavern.

"He wants to avenge his da," the second gunman said.

"Do ya, now? Go ahead."

Mulligan stared at the laboring Boyle, struggling to stand. A red stain spread on his silk shirt. Boyle's fearful eyes were wet with tears.

"Do you know who I am?" Mulligan said. "You killed my father."

Boyle met his eyes. "Them Travelers was squatting on private land. I have to collect rents and deliver profits or I end up in the workhouse."

"You shot my father who was unarmed," Mulligan said. He aimed the pistol.

"No, please," Boyle said. Mulligan hesitated. Then they saw blood gushing from Boyle's mouth. His eyes stared ahead, suddenly empty of light, and Boyle's fleshy body slumped and rolled into a reddening puddle. The second gunman took back his pistol.

"Looks like you don't need to shoot the fat son of a bitch," said the man who fired the first shots. "I think Boyle's death will send a message to Burke and his greedy landlords." The assassin regarded Mulligan. "You better leave and get rid of the horse. They'll assume you stole it. Or maybe you are rich?"

"No sir. Who are you?"

"Meskill. If you tell police or soldiers what you saw, we'll find you and kill you."

"And if you want to join us," the second man said, "our people are not hard to find."

"Are you Whiteboys?"

"Whiteboys?" Both men laughed. "They don't exist, sir."

The two men rode away. Michael Mulligan looked at the body of Boyle lying in the muddy water, and then rode toward Galway. The same police constable who questioned him watched as Mulligan galloped through the narrow cobblestone streets and out toward the edge of town. Mulligan knew the theatre troupe would be performing in Dublin. Then Mulligan rode toward the wharf looking for a stable. He found one near the landing dock with three scarecrow-looking men sitting on chairs in front of the stable door. They drank from bottles of whiskey. Mulligan dismounted. The sitting men wore their caps pulled low, their eyes in shadow.

"Do you know where I can find the stable owner?"

"Why do you want to know?"

Mulligan regarded closely the bone-thin men drinking and watching him with lidded eyes. After a moment, he spoke again.

"I want to sell my mare. She's lovely but it's time to part."

Another man spoke up. "You got a horse to sell, eh?"

"Yes."

"I could sell you a donkey."

"Mick, you don't got no donkey."

Mulligan asked again. "Is the owner about?"

The third man stood up. "Did some English landowner send you to collect rent?"

"No." Michael Mulligan was surprised at their hostile tone but smiled at the men. "I just want to sell my mare. I won't be needing her." He playfully slapped the horse on the rump. The men looked at one another.

"You want to buy his mare, Paddy?"

"I can't afford a horse," Paddy said.

"There's a lot of things you can't afford."

They laughed.

"I can't afford a wife, either."

The standing man said in Irish, "That little bugger don't need a wife. He's got his mare."

"Or maybe he's getting fucked by an English landlord."

The three men laughed again. A fourth man appeared in the doorway.

"*Poke ma hoin,*" Mulligan said.

The men were surprised to hear Irish.

"Our little fake Englishman speaks our language," said the standing man. "He told us to kiss his ass."

"That's right, Dickie."

Michael Mulligan observed the three men, so weak and sick looking, as though they had recovered from a ravaging fever. "Gentleman, I don't know why you hate me but—"

"What shite," Dickie said. He took a drink from his whiskey bottle. "Anyone riding his own horse who looks well fed is a thief or an informer working for the police."

"I am neither. Now stand aside or I'll shove that bottle up your ass, Dickie."

For a moment, they stared at him. Then all three men advanced. Paddy took out a small knobby club and swung at Michael Mulligan's head. Mulligan stepped back and Paddy stumbled to the road. Mulligan kicked him once in the ribs and then saw the other two men drawing knives. Mulligan grabbed the fallen man's club. The man in the doorway called out.

"Stop, for God's sake. Let the man state his business." He pushed the three derelicts down the street. "Go away—now!"

"We'll be waiting for you," Paddy said, pointing at Mulligan.

"*Slan*," Michael Mulligan said. "Good bye. Enjoyed our chat."

The three men staggered around a corner.

"Sorry for that. I'm the owner. My name is Daniel Bailey."

"Michael Mulligan…and I have a mare to sell."

Bailey examined Mulligan's horse.

"I haven't bought a new horse in some time. Got cheated, the last time. Come in."

The large barn smelled of fresh hay and manure. Michael Mulligan looked at the rows of horses in stalls and noticed one sway-backed horse with missing teeth and prominent ribs.

"He looks ready for the butcher…if he'll take him."

"He looked good when I bought him. Nice coat, had all his teeth, full body."

"There's a way to get that effect," Mulligan said. He suspected Bailey bought the horse from a Traveler. "A certain plant with water swells the flesh over the ribs. There's oil for the coat, and even fake teeth made from rock salt. Doesn't last a day."

"You know a lot about horses, then?"

"I grew up around them."

Bailey had a young sun-burned face and a watchful manner.

"What was wrong with those men outside? Why did they attack me?"

"You looked too healthy and rich. You had a horse to sell. They're out of work and drunk all the time. It will be the workhouse, soon, where they'll become slaves for some watery mush and a place to sleep."

"Times are terrible," Mulligan said. "You have some nice horses."

"I'd appreciate your professional assessment, Mr. Mulligan."

Michael Mulligan examined each animal and found Bailey had a healthy stock of work and saddle horses. He gave an assessment of each animal.

"You have saved me an expensive visit from the horse doctor," Bailey said. "So you are selling that mare?"

"Yes. She's a lovely animal, but I am traveling by boat."

They quickly settled on a price, though lower than what the horse was worth.

"I'd offer more but I have fewer customers."

"I understand."

"Mr. Mulligan. I sell horses to the local landowners for riding, fox hunting and occasional racing. I may go into the thoroughbred racing business. Those horses are expensive, however."

"And so beautiful. Irish thoroughbreds thrive on Guinness."

"Never knew that. If I start a stable for race horses, you may want to come back and work for me."

"I would like that, Mr. Bailey."

"I don't like the English but they do love horses, don't they?"

They shook hands. Michael Mulligan caressed his mare, speaking to her in Irish. Then he bought a ticket on a boat going to Dublin. On the way to the pier, he saw the three scrawny men, sitting on a bench, drinking. Mulligan took out some coins and threw them on the ground.

"Have a drink on me, boys. Drown your worms."

They dived on the coins as Mulligan continued toward the dock. Bad weather delayed the boat for a day. In Dublin, he took a room for a night and the next morning, walked to Trinity College where the troupe was performing a comedia piece for students. Walking onto the campus square, Mulligan saw the stage and the raised flags. He noticed that Maggie and Thomas Connor were missing. After the final bow, Tyrone saw Michael and motioned to him. He named a place near the college. "Meet me there. Something has happened."

As Michael Mulligan left the green college grounds, he saw Edgar watching him. In a small tavern, his adoptive father, still wearing his clown makeup, sat across from him. Patrons sat drinking at the tables, and tobacco smoke filled the room.

"You need to leave, Son."

"Why?"

"There was a killing of a landlord in Galway. A sheriff has been asking about a Michael Dunne wanted for questioning. I told them there was no such person. Still, there are informers everywhere."

"I didn't kill the landlord," Mulligan said.

"Do you know who did?"

Michael Mulligan didn't answer.

"I have a contact at Oxford who can act as a mentor. They will remember my name since I taught Latin and English. Stay at Oxford and study for a year. That is all I can afford unless you get a scholarship. I doubt the authorities will look for you there."

"I have to leave?"

"For now."

Tyrone searched his face and Mulligan could see he was grieved.

"Son, Michael, you need to get out of Ireland. The Levelers have been killing landlords in these violent times. The authorities may connect the dead man to your father since the police know your real name."

"Mulligan is my real name."

"They may find that out as well."

"They'll find a lot of Travelers named Dunne." Mulligan held Tyrone's eyes. "You're sending me away?"

"I have to. We'll meet again." Tyrone pressed his adopted son's hand. "Son? There is something else."

"I noticed. Where are Maggie and Thomas Connor?"

"They eloped. Married they are."

"Married? I guess that eases one of your worries."

Tyrone closed his eyes and gently touched his forehead. "I'm sorry about what I said." He looked at Mulligan. "It was quick. I am embarrassed to say this, but I suspect my daughter is with child."

"With child?"

There was a long silence with a question between them never asked.

"Thomas Connor moves fast."

"Perhaps. Edgar isn't too happy with the elopement—and what has he got against you?"

"I don't know. Maybe he's just angry that I'm a better actor. He could inform on me."

"I don't think he's that bad."

Michael Mulligan regarded the man who had raised him for six years and taught him about English and Shakespeare and the stage. In the gaslight, his face seemed older with the layers of makeup. Tyrone glanced out the tavern window. The streets of Dublin were always busy, but he didn't see any police or soldiers. Then he faced Michael Mulligan.

"Tomorrow morning, meet me at Kingstown Harbor. I'll have a ticket and money for a suitable wardrobe. You can stay with a friend in Oxford until the next term begins. I can send more money depending on our season, and you might get work at the stables. By God, Michael, avoid any fights." Tyrone suddenly smiled through tears. "And one fine day, if I don't get too old, we can work the stage together."

"One fine day," Michael Mulligan said.

They embraced. Moved, Michael Mulligan walked out the back door while Tyrone Mulligan left through the front and walked back to the college where the actors were breaking down the outdoor stage. For just a moment, Tyrone wondered why he had left the comfort of Oxford University to work as a street performer. There was no Globe Theatre left standing, but perhaps the Swan of Avon was to blame for Tyrone's nomadic life in the theatre.

Edgar stopped him when he returned. "So where is the great Michael Mulligan?"

"I sent him back with his own kind. We'll have a company meeting tonight about the future of the company."

"I guess the constables shouldn't know he became a Mulligan."

"That's right. I hope we have no informers here—right, Edgar?"

Edgar lowered his eyes. The next morning on the windy dock, Tyrone Mulligan again embraced his adopted son.

"I think you'll make a difference in the world, someday."

"If they don't hang me first."

"It's best we not write for a long time."

"That will be hard."

"But necessary. I'll be following your progress, Son."

Michael Mulligan took Tyrone's hand. "Good bye, Father. I'll never forget the day you let me join the troupe."

"Nor I." There was an awkward pause. "Good bye, son— and good luck. If we don't meet again, this parting is well made."

Tyrone briefly wondered if they would ever meet again. Then Michael Mulligan boarded the ship bound for Liverpool. Rain was falling, and Tyrone hoped Michael Mulligan's ship would navigate past the treacherous Dublin harbor waters where so many ships had come apart or run aground on the rocks.

THE BLIGHT

AT FIRST IT WAS a mist coming in from the Atlantic that covered Western Ireland, but soon they could smell a sickening rotting stench. It was only when the Irish farmers tried to harvest the potatoes that they realized a fungus was turning the potatoes black. To avoid the smell, Lady Maria Burke started riding her horse in the fields where the sheep and cattle grazed. Devlin, the landlord, warned Lord Nathaniel Burke that something was killing the main source of food for their farmers. Devlin was a short stocky man with a red face and dark facial hair that gave him stubble even when he shaved. Lord Burke was in his mid-thirties, a tall thin man with short hair combed forward and no beard. His eyes were pale and Burke rarely smiled except when sketching plants and flowers, his hobby.

"Don't they have potatoes stored?"

"They do, but they won't keep past nine months."

"I'm sure the next year's harvest will keep the buggers fed. Nothing else is affected? Grain? Cattle? Sheep?"

"No Sir," Devlin said. "Everything else is fine."

"Rents are collected?"

"Yes."

"Taking the lady of the house for a ride?"

"Later this afternoon, Master Burke."

"She gets bored easily. I'm expecting Lord Sterling for tea this afternoon. Alert the servants."

"I will."

"That will be all, Devlin."

"Very good, Sir."

Devlin left. Outside on the main house, workers were adding Greek Doric columns for either side of the massive door, and installing new wide windows, as well.

When Devlin found Maria Burke in the stable, she was already mounted on her black gelding. Maria Burke had a classic small but pretty English face, as if sculpted by a major portrait artist. Maria Burke was overdressed to ride and didn't relish riding side saddle, the common if impractical fashion for women equestrians. There was something in her eyes that bothered Devlin, but he could never identify it: perhaps the expression held a latent defiance, even when she was polite and deferred to her strict husband.

"I won't need you, Devlin. I just want to get away for an afternoon."

"Very good, Lady Burke. Watch for rain."

"Can nothing be done about that awful smell?"

"Not likely, Missus. It will have to go away on its own."

"Will the tenant farmers be all right?"

"They can take care of themselves. They're a tough lot."

Clutching her fashionable hat, Maria turned her horse toward a distant hill. The elegant Lord Sterling passed her on the way in, tipping his hat. He placed a scented handkerchief to his nose. Lady Burke imagined her husband enviously watching the red-lipped, handsome Lord Sterling riding up to the house, posting gracefully. For Lord Burke, riding wasn't his skill, though every member of his class was expected to ride well—for fox hunting, general pleasure, racing or polo.

In the mansion, the two aristocrats faced each other having tea. Burke liked the sweet resonance of Lord Sterling's voice and his precise formal speech. Family portraits adorned the walls.

"I am considering a move to Belfast," Lord Sterling announced. He loosened his white silk cravat. "I am evicting all the Irish farmers, even the ones not behind on their rent. Of course, many of them are sickly and may die anyway, but I do think it would be better to just pay outside farm workers. We have many excellent farmers in Scotland."

"It might be costly."

"True. Frankly, Lord Burke, I find one major problem with Ireland."

"What is that?"

"The Irish. No offence."

"None taken, my Lord."

"I know you have English blood and you're not a Papist...so I'm told."

"I am not a Papist," Burke quickly said. He could see Lord Sterling studying him. "I think Cromwell was right. Kill the Catholics."

Sterling nodded. "If this blight comes back next season, I do believe we must flee this cursed country. I like Belfast, and Paris, of course. I *can* stomach the French."

"Oh, the French have good wines...and some good art."

"Indeed. What I fear," Lord Sterling declared, "is that we'll evict these filthy Irish—but we'll still have an Irish storage problem."

"Irish storage problem?"

"We can evict them, but they'll still be *here*. I am even willing to pay their passage to America or Canada. Deport the brutes."

Lord Burke deliberately lifted his eyes to the ceiling. "You are a coldhearted man, Lord Sterling."

Sterling laughed, lifting only his upper lip, and then quietly sipped his tea. "Am I? I suppose I am. I try to be tolerant. I don't know what smells worse, the potato blight or the foul Irish shanty towns. I struggle to be patient, but these Irish famers breed like rabbits. They understand nothing but a whip. They seem to know only one crop, the potato. No wonder they are often desperate, starving or drunk."

"Well, it is true—in point of fact—that we control the beef and grain products."

"Who else? We have the Act of Union, Lord Burke. England expects little Ireland to provide food for her citizens. Of course, disease could kill the bloody Irish off."

"Disease will threaten us, as well."

"That is correct, my dear Lord Burke. The answer is for us to become absentee landowners. Your landlords can handle these unpleasant affairs. Actually, some Irish brutes are good at collecting rents. Let them handle any Whiteboyism."

"Are they coming back?"

"I've heard some rumblings. They don't frighten me." Lord Sterling smiled over his tea. "Will we see you at the Galway races?"

"Of course. I may one day enter a horse myself."

"Splendid. The Bailey Stables are the best. I discovered that some Irish *can* talk to horses." A maid watched them from a distant corner of the room. Lord Sterling lowered his voice. "Tell me, have you bedded any of your Irish maids?"

"I'm a gentleman," Lord Burke said.

Lord Sterling found this amusing. "I discovered one of my landlords was paying a young widow's rent. I investigated and she was quite lovely for an Irish girl. Now she works for me. Very talented," Sterling said. Then he stood. "I must be off. Say hello to your lovely wife. I love those dark green eyes, the pale skin—very English. I hope the stench doesn't suffocate me on the way home. Do take care, Lord Burke. I recall your father, Lord Wesley Burke, a splendid Englishman."

"A great man, indeed, Lord Sterling."

"You will fill his boots, I'm sure," Sterling said, and left.

The following planting season, the blight returned and the entire potato crop perished. In addition to the sick smell of rotting potatoes, Irish families clogged the roads heading toward Cove to emigrate, some to North America, some to England. The dreaded workhouses were now packed. People died in the very roads, and everywhere, evictions increased.

"It is pretty desperate," Devlin told Lord Burke. "Sick and dying buggers everywhere. What are you orders, sir?"

"Evict those who can't pay or work. I am also considering something else."

"And what is that, Master Burke?"

"I think we need to start buying breeding stock for race horses. I would like to do that and get out of farming all together. Tomorrow, I'd like to visit the Bailey Stables in Galway. Alert my wife. She may welcome the news."

Devlin did not find Lady Burke in the stable as she had already gone for a ride. It would be harder now to avoid the death smell across Western Ireland or the sight of so many starving or sick people.

The next afternoon, they rode a coach to Galway and visited the stables of Daniel Bailey. He sold quarter horses, saddle horses and recently, thoroughbreds, some imported from Arabia. As Lord Burke and Devlin walked with Bailey through the stables, Maria Burke approached the track and watched the grooms exercising the horses. Then she heard a pattern of thudding hooves and saw a young man astride a large brown thoroughbred stallion racing down the track, the rider using only a bridle and small saddle, leaning forward, his taut buttocks high as they galloped past Maria, the horse and rider caught in a moment of terrific motion. Maria caught her breath. The young jockey reined in the stallion with strong hands and took him on a cantor toward the stables. He glanced at the elegant red-haired young woman watching and nodded once. Then he was gone. Maria turned to another horse groom—a black man.

"Who was that?"

"His name is Michael Mulligan. He sure does know horses," the man said, a slight British accent to his speech.

"Does he race them?"

"Oh no, he's too big. You need a smaller man for a race jockey, but he can take them for a run. Thoroughbreds are easily spooked, ma'am. They're big and strong and dangerous if you don't handle them right."

Maria watched the rider, now dismounted. He wore form-fitting brown pants and black boots.

"He's Irish?"

"The horse?"

"The rider."

"I believe so. He might be a little English too. I think his father was some sort of theatre man."

"Theatre? I see."

Maria saw her husband and Bailey talking, and a moment later, Mulligan joined them. Maria could tell, even from a distance, when her husband was annoyed. He had a way of crossing his arms and standing erect. Bailey put his arm around Burke and they started toward the stable housing the brown stallion. Then Maria saw her husband struggling for breath, Burke's mouth forming a circle as he sucked air through his swelling passageways. She walked quickly toward them.

"Are you all right, Master Burke?" Bailey was genuinely concerned.

"It may be the awful smell of dung," Burke said, wheezing. "Or hay. I get sick around horses."

"He has asthma," Lady Burke said. She tried to avoid looking at the tall horse groom.

"Well, you better stay away from the barn," Bailey said. "Are we agreed on the matching pair and the price?"

Nathaniel Burke sucked in another breath, his breathing growing shallow. "Yes," he said. "Send them to my estate."

"We can have Mr. Mulligan or Sam take the horses to you."

"Who is Sam?"

"He's the Negro gentleman."

Nathaniel Burke managed a choked raspy laugh. "So I have a choice between an Irishman and a Negro? The Irish aren't worth much, but I'll take the Irishman," he said. "Come along, Lady Burke."

"You know," said Bailey. "Mr. Sterling and Mr. Perry also are planning to breed and raise thoroughbreds. You'll be in good company."

Nathaniel Burke stopped and glared at Bailey. "The gentlemen known as Sterling and Perry are not to be addressed as 'Mister.' They are both Lords. And I am Lord Burke, as well. Good day, sir."

As he took Maria's arm, she managed a glance at the Irish groom. His expression startled her. He was observing her husband, not with curiosity or malice, but with a focused calculation. Though without judgment, it was unpleasant. She nodded to Mulligan.

"See you soon, I presume."

He glanced at her; his observation felt like an appraisal, as though she were a breeding mare. To her surprise, Maria felt no discomfort.

"Tomorrow will be fine," he said.

They walked toward the carriage, Nathaniel Burke panting, sucking sir into his aching lungs. Maria held him and a footman helped Burke into the carriage.

"I better watch the horses from a distance," he said.

The carriage pulled away. Thinking of the Irish stable hand, Maria suddenly remembered a drawing of a shark, and the cold eyes that had neither love nor hate—the eyes of a predator.

"You were a tad rude to Mr. Mulligan," Maria said. "I believe Mr. Bailey and Mulligan are both Irish."

"Are they, now? Then they have to know their place."

As they pulled away, Daniel Bailey shook his head.

"So our Mr. Burke is a 'Lord,' is he? Maybe he's forgotten he's Irish."

"Protestant Irish are different," said Mulligan. "They think they are English. That's because they kiss so much English ass."

Bailey laughed. "Well, we sold him a matching pair of thoroughbreds. And he can use that horse for stud service."

"I'd like to be a stud for his wife."

"What else do you do with a beautiful woman like that married to a cold cod fish like Sir Burke?" Bailey glanced at Mulligan. "That nasty little man came by, today. If he is what I think he is, be careful. The so called Levelers are getting quite bold, lately."

"And the Irish farmers are paying higher rents and working longer hours. Or they're facing eviction to starve in the road. This failure of the potato crop is serious business. Our countrymen are dying."

"All the same, be careful. No one has forgotten what happened to the landlord, Boyle."

"Good," Mulligan said.

"I don't want police or military men paying me a visit, Mulligan."

"Nor I."

"You are the best trainer I've ever had. You should do well in any horse country."

Michael Mulligan turned and walked back to the stable. He wanted to feed and wash the stud and mare that Nathaniel Burke now owned. Mulligan did not want to think about his father shot by John Boyle. Since Boyle was dead, there was no reason to attack Lord Burke. Still, he knew Burke owned and controlled his landlords, and he knew that soon the landowners and landlords would become targets themselves. The poverty and repression of the Irish demanded a response, and Michael Mulligan suspected it would be bloody.

The next day, he took a wagon with the two thoroughbreds tied behind and following, though occasionally they would stop and resist him. He got out and talked to them in Irish, and the horses calmed down. He hoped the mare would accept the stallion when she went into heat. It was a long trip and as he rode, a small wiry man with a wrinkled face and sharp but cold eyes suddenly jumped into the seat beside him.

"Well, Mr. Michael Mulligan is going to visit his Anglo Irish master."

"That I am," said Mulligan.

"This could be good to for us. Be polite. No threats or insults to the poor misguided man."

"But I am polite, Mr. Meskill. By the way, what kind of an Irish name is that?"

"Symbolic of the old Celts. You can call me Sean. Is that Irish enough for you? Perhaps Lord Sterling will soon have need of your services. Until then, good day."

"Wait."

"Yes?"

"I will never harm anyone's horses…not even the most evil of landlords or landowners."

"Of course not, Mr. Mulligan. We are at war with England and oppressive landowners, not livestock."

"We might be better off with some political organization."

"Agreed, Mulligan. *Sein Fein*. Ireland for ourselves. We need a free state with our own government, our own police force, our own military. *Slan*."

Sean jumped from the wagon and Mulligan proceeded toward the Burke plantation to deliver the two horses. The main house with its Greek columns was impressive. A stout man was standing in front and motioned him toward the barn.

"You must be Mulligan."

"I am."

"You don't look like a Nigger." He laughed at his joke. "Devlin's my name. I'm the landlord, here. You don't need to bother Lord Burke."

"That's just fine."

Michael Mulligan could feel Devlin watching him. He led the two thoroughbreds into their stalls and gave them a rub down. Then he asked Devlin for oats.

"I don't know if Lord Burke has any oats at the moment. We have hay, Mulligan."

"These are thoroughbreds, Devlin. And you may appreciate this. They could take a little dark beer with their food."

"They are Irish horses, now," Devlin said.

"My husband always has plenty of beer," a female voice said. They saw Lady Burke who had entered quietly. She had removed her bulky cage crinoline and wore a comfortable, closely fitting dress. "And we can certainly provide oats."

Devlin bowed. "My lady."

"Where are you from, Mr. Mulligan?"

"Well, my parents were English, but my father died and my mother married a man named Mulligan. I took his name."

"Your accent is neither Irish nor English," Maria said.

"The product of both cultures."

"Where did you grow up, Mulligan?" Devlin said.

Mulligan met Devlin's eyes.

"Does it matter?" said Maria. "Mr. Mulligan, I'd like to show you my horse."

Mulligan smiled at Devlin and followed Lady Burke to the stall where she kept her black gelding. It was a small but fast, well groomed horse.

"Looks healthy enough to me," Mulligan said.

She watched his hands as he ran them along the sides of the horse, and then smiled when he put a carrot in his mouth which the horse nibbled until it disappeared.

"I wonder if I should buy a stallion."

"Perhaps—but only if you can control a wilder animal."

"I'm sure I can."

"Would this be for stud service?"

"For pleasure," Maria said.

"I can inquire into it."

Maria found herself blushing. "Please do."

"Now—if you need anyone to look after your horse…or the thoroughbreds, please send for me."

"I will," Maria said.

Devlin suddenly pushed between them. "Shall I walk you to your wagon, Mr. Mulligan?"

"My pleasure, Mr. Devlin. Nice to know Lord and Lady Burke are in good hands."

As Mulligan drove the team away from the house, Devlin grinned at Lady Burke and said, "If he had English parents, I'm the next King. I bet he was raised in a saloon."

"So Mr. Mulligan is a man of mystery, Mr. Devlin? Sounds intriguing."

Maria walked back into the house. Devlin watched her leave.

The next day, Mulligan was summoned for an audience with Lord Burke. Once again, he rode up to the spacious house, this time on a golden palomino from the stable. He passed Devlin who watched him, grinning. Inside the mansion, an English servant girl wearing a black gown and white muslin apron brought him some tea which he drank out of politeness. Nathaniel Burke, dressed in fashionable riding pants and coat, entered the room, wide with a high ceiling. On the wall hung a wedding portrait, a seated Lady Burke wearing a billowing dress, Nathaniel Burke standing behind her, staring ahead stoically. Lord Burke and Michael Mulligan sat on straight-backed shiny chairs facing each other.

"Mr. Mulligan, Maria tells me you are from English stock. Is that true?"

He saw the man studying him carefully. "Not completely. I am Irish as well. I hope I got the best of both."

"So do I. There's nothing wrong with being an Anglo Irish. You are educated?"

"Oxford...but only for a year."

He could see Burke was impressed. "You are a Protestant?"

"Of course," Mulligan said. "No Popery for this Irishman."

"You approve of the Act of Union between England and Ireland?"

"Absolutely, Lord Burke. The Irish can't manage the island alone."

For the first time, Burke laughed.

"Prime Minster Peel is creating an Irish police force."

"We'll need the peelers for order, Lord Burke. The horses are settled?"

"Yes. Mr. Mulligan, I would like it if you would come here once a week to examine them, exercise them, and I suspect Lord Sterling will want his mare bred. Perhaps you could also teach me and the lady Burke how to ride. My allergies aren't so bad outside."

"It would be my pleasure, Lord Burke."

Mulligan stared at the pale conventionally handsome man who was indirectly responsible for the death of his father. For just a moment, he imagined taking out his hidden knife and slicing Lord Burke's throat. The elegant noble would bleed to death silently on the rug while Mulligan rode away. He was still riding away when Lady Maria entered the room.

"Mr. Mulligan."

She held out her hand. Mulligan kissed it.

"I do hope you visit more often. In addition to riding lessons we both need, perhaps you could join us on a fox hunt."

"It would be my pleasure," Mulligan said. "The sport of nobles."

Devlin appeared in the doorway. "Lord Burke, an Irish Constabulary officer is here. There seems to be some trouble brewing."

33

"Irish Gypsies?"

"No. Lord Sterling's landlord has been stabbed."

"My word. Send the constable in."

"I'll leave you," Mulligan said. "Contact me."

"Yes. Here, something for your pains."

Lord Burke gave Mulligan two gold coins.

"Thank you, sir."

He walked past Devlin and the policeman he had met in Galway years before. The constable, hair turning gray, nodded to Mulligan and then stopped. "You! Young Man?"

Mulligan turned. "Yes?"

"Have we met?"

"I don't think so," Mulligan said.

"He's with us," Maria said.

"Very good, then. He seemed familiar."

The officer was still watching him when Maria left the house and walked with Mulligan toward the nervous palomino. "We hope to see you soon, Mr. Mulligan."

"You will, Lady Burke."

"Maria, please. It is such a long ride back. Why not spend the night?"

"I have a town nearby where I can stay the night. Another time, Lady Burke."

"I pass my time reading romantic novels, I'm afraid."

"Are they any good?"

"Diverting. Although romantic books are entertaining, I don't really believe in love at first sight as the novels suggest. Elegant ladies getting ravished."

"Pretty unrealistic," Mulligan said.

His eyes lingered on her a bit too long. Maria suddenly turned away. Then Mulligan mounted his horse and rode toward Galway. In the twilight, Mulligan noticed the many small farms and huts and the empty potato bins. The rotten potatoes left a stench that lingered, and he saw families staring across the field where wheat grew to feed the English. Herds of cattle grazed in the distance, and sheep dotted the green hillsides. The bucolic scene jarred with the image of so many famished peasants.

A tall thin woman appeared on the road and blocked his path. Mulligan reined in the palomino.

"Sure but that's a fine circus animal you got, sir."

"It is, though we're not in a circus."

He saw her children dressed in ragged cotton pants and thin shirts, standing along the road. They didn't smile or play. He didn't see a father. Down the road, some men were carrying a body from a hut to place in a cart.

"The potato bin is empty. I need money, young man, to buy food for my children. Can you help us?"

"Sure but I can."

Michael Mulligan gave her a gold piece. The thin woman began to cry. "My God," she said. "My husband will think I did something sinful to get it."

"Buy food and don't let him know…if you can."

"I need it, no matter what he thinks. I know Devlin will soon be demanding rent. Can't work if you're hungry. We may use some of this to take a boat elsewhere."

"The fare is cheap."

"It is if you sleep and stay on the deck in all weather. But— it may be better just to escape Ireland. God bless you, sir."

Mulligan waved to the starved-looking children and rode on. He left the road, but even on the higher ground, he saw so many marching victims of hunger, and he could smell the death scent left by the unseen blight that killed potatoes but nothing else. Unburied bodies lay in ditches. In the distance, he saw a caravan of wagons filled with Irish Travelers. They were migrating from Ireland. For a moment, he was tempted to follow them.

If the potatoes failed a third year, the devastation would be complete, and Mulligan wondered if the English would notice. When he arrived in Galway, he lay in the barn, sleeping with the rich smell of horses. Occasionally, he dreamed of Lord Burke's wife. She was watching him, smiling, and slowly removing her many layers of clothing. In another dream, he was lashing Devlin with a bullwhip, thrashing the man for beating a horse.

In the spring, Lord Sterling said good-bye to his Irish mistress and walked toward the stable for an evening ride. At least the sullen widow had finally returned his smile. The house had seemed unusually quiet as he left. He stopped when he saw a strange wiry man holding his horse.

"Do I know you, fellow?"

"I'm your new servant. May I give you a leg up?"

Sterling turned to his Irish horse groom, recently recruited.

"Shoo that horrid little man away, will you please?"

The stable hand said, "Of course, your majesty," and pointed a pistol at Lord Sterling's face. His horse reared with the gunshot. In a muddy pig sty, authorities later found torn clothing, a skull with a bullet hole, and one of Sterling's riding boots with a foot still in it.

That summer, Mulligan attended the Galway races with Lord and Lady Burke. The races were dedicated to the memory of Lord Sterling, shot to death in Belfast by a person or persons unknown. Though unsettled by Sterling's murder and the fact none of Lord Sterling's servants heard the shot, Lord Burke enjoyed watching his horse in a close race. Mulligan had trained him well. Many wealthy English and Anglo Irish attended the races, though the stands were empty of workers and farmers. The population had dropped rapidly, even as dead bodies increased and the workhouses overfilled. Occasionally, Maria glanced at Mulligan and he nodded, once furtively touching her fingers. In brushing against each other, she whispered, "I can't stand this." They knew Devlin now watched them constantly and almost caught them kissing.

It had happened one afternoon after Michael Mulligan took Lord and Lady Burke on a ride. Nathaniel Burke had suffered a sudden asthma attack so they returned home where servants boiled water for Lord Burke to inhale the steam. Michael Mulligan took the horses to the stable to remove the saddles and wash and rub them down. With each riding lesson, he had been aware of Lady Maria Burke watching him, though their eyes rarely met. Occasionally, they moved close to each other. While rubbing down the horses, he heard her voice calling his name. She was standing in the door. Mulligan followed her to a room where grooms often slept. There was a narrow cot by the wall, and the room smelled of tack and leather and horses and horse dung. She faced him and after letting down her hair, calmly began to undo her low-cut blouse. He felt himself trembling.

"Maria? What are you doing?"

She seemed surprised at the question.

"We've been watching each other. Don't you think it's time?"

"Yes," he said. "But we could get caught."

"Not today," she said. He saw her firm breasts.

"You might get in trouble with the likes of me."

"I know. It will be scandalous." She looked at him. "Take off your clothes."

Michael Mulligan nodded. He reached for his long dressage whip.

"Hold this," he said.

Maria fondled the whip as Mulligan slowly undressed.

Shortly after the summer horse races, Daniel Bailey informed Mulligan he was moving the stables to Dublin.

"It's a necessity for business. Come with me, Mulligan."

"I need to think about it."

In the early fall, Devlin evicted remaining tenants after the blight had returned. Lord Burke had gone to Dublin on business, and one afternoon, Lady Burke saddled and mounted the powerful brown stallion and rode into the nearby mountains, finding a lake in a grove of trees. She saw the hobbled palomino. Lady Burke was panting as she dismounted and found Michael Mulligan bathing in the cold lake waters. She stripped off her clothes and plunged into the water. They embraced, kissing.

"At last," she said. "This separation is killing me."

"And me," Mulligan said. "I want you."

She kissed him again. "And I want you." Then he carried her naked and dripping body to the waiting horse. He mounted bareback and lifted her up.

"What are you doing?"

Moments later, she faced him, sitting on his bare lap as they rode down the rutted and furrowed path, bouncing on the horse, their two bodies joined as one. Maria threw back her head and cried out in ecstasy.

Later, they lay by the lake, a soft breeze blowing over their drying bodies.

"What are we going to do, Michael?"

"I don't know, Maria."

"Bailey is moving his stable to Dublin and Lord Burke is moving us to Belfast."

"He won't divorce you?"

"Never. I almost feel sorry for him. He's a product of his time and his culture."

Mulligan grinned and kissed her. "And so am I. Many cultures."

"I shall learn about them all."

The next day, Devlin and his new band of regulators surprised some Irish peasants running off Burke's sheep; they rode down upon them, shooting one farmer in the back. Lady Burke was calmly reading by the fireplace when Devlin returned.

"Oh, it's been bad day, Lady Burke," he finally said, without being asked. "Women crying. Men cursing me. Dead bodies in the ditches. Young thugs threatening me. We had to kill a man, today, another Irish thief."

"You killed a starving man?"

"It wasn't me. It was Oliver, my new helper. He's a cockney brute, but very good with a gun and his fists. Still, I feel sad. This famine is killing so many of my people."

Lady Burke forced herself to meet Devlin's eyes.

"Your people? Well, if you feel so guilty, Devlin, maybe you should find another line of work."

Devlin stared at her, grinning. "You'd like me to leave?"

"It's up to you."

"How is our handsome Master Mulligan?"

"I assume he's fine. Why don't you ask him when he moves in, today?"

"Oh yes, Lord Burke gave him a job and a room in the stable. That's a good place for him."

"He loves horses."

"And that's not all."

Lady Burke put down her book. "What does that mean, Mr. Devlin?"

"The servants are talking, ma'am."

"Oh really?"

Devlin took some steps toward her and Maria watched him, feeling the first touch of fear. "Stay where you are."

"Oh, I know my place, ma'am. It's just that one day, I thought I heard something in the barn and I know the master can't even walk in without wheezing and breaking out. What is going on? I thought to meself. Peeping through the window, my God, what do I see?" Devlin began to gesticulate and mug in a theatrical manner, pursing his lips. "My dear Lady Burke—such a refined lady as yourself, and with a common stable boy? Glad our poor maids didn't see what I saw."

"Take your filthy story somewhere else."

"Oh, I'll keep quiet, ma'am. For a price."

"You dare blackmail me, you low dog!"

"A dog, am I? Mulligan is a fraud and a liar. He's a bloody blight, himself. His real name is Michael Dunne. Used to be one of them thieving Travelers, he was. Heard it from an actor he used to travel with. And that's not all. I suspect he's running with them Levelers, the murderous Whiteboys who killed Sterling. If I talk to the peelers, I won't be surprised if Mulligan is arrested and hanged."

"Get out."

"I will. And I'll be quiet, ma'am, for at least a week. Perhaps we can make an arrangement."

Maria felt a sudden wave of nausea. "I have no money to give you, Devlin."

"I don't need no money. Root of all evil, you know. I'm a reasonable man. Maybe you can wear out your knees with me."

Lady Burke picked up the hot poker and advanced on Devlin.

"Let me tell you something, Devlin. My husband won't believe your vile gossip...and you better be careful these so called Levelers don't come after you. People are dying all over Ireland—some of them thanks to you!"

Devlin smiled showing black teeth. "That's a possibility, ma'am."

They heard Lord Burke's carriage pulling up in front.

"I'll be in touch, Lady Burke."

Devlin left. Lady Burke clutched the poker. A moment later, Lord Burke entered the room, happy and smiling.

"I think I got a good price on the Belfast home of our dear departed friend, Lord Sterling. We can move the horses, there. Devlin and his men can watch the farm. They're moving into the cabins and the huts abandoned by the farmers."

"You mean the evicted farmers?"

Lord Burke caught her angry tone. "They didn't pay the rent or do the work." He peered closely at her face. "Is something wrong, love?"

"I want you to fire Devlin. He's a pig."

"Has he been too familiar with you?"

"He has."

Lord Burke took her into his arms. "Now, now, my sweet girl. I know Devlin is a crude man, a rough one, for sure, but we need men like him to run the plantation...especially when we're gone." He pulled away and gently touched her cheek. "Don't cry, precious. I'll talk to him."

Lady Burke walked into her room. A moment later, she emerged in tight riding pants and boots.

"Where are you going?"

"I just want to take a ride."

"You shouldn't dress in a man's pants."

"It's more comfortable."

"But it shows off your womanly figure...and we do have Devlin and his rowdy men about. Maybe you should take Mulligan with you if he has arrived."

"Good idea, my love."

"I can't keep him when we move."

"No, you can't."

Lady Burke walked to the barn and saddled the gelding. She didn't see anyone.

"Going for a ride, my lady?" She turned. It was Michael Mulligan unloading his tack and possessions. "I think I'll like this stable for a home."

"Come join me. There are a lot of rough men, about."

"There are."

"And one of them knows about us," Lady Burke said.

When they rode out together, Devlin and Oliver stared at them. Oliver was a large man with a gap in his teeth and thick muscular arms. Mulligan waved to both men as they headed toward the open field.

"Ballocks," Oliver said. "What gall."

Burke suddenly appeared. "Mr. Devlin, could you come in here, please?"

Devlin walked toward the house.

Lady Burke and Michael Mulligan found a grove of trees and sat on a wide black rock, looking over a herd of grazing sheep.

"Devlin is out to get you," Maria said. "And he will probably tell my husband about us." Mulligan remained silent. "What should we do?"

"I don't know."

He was watching Sean who had stopped to talk to the lone sheepherder. The news of the desperate raid had spread.

"A man was shot to death here," Maria said. "By one of Devlin's men."

"I know," Mulligan said. "Oliver, the cockney."

"How did you know that?"

"We know everything.'

"Who is we?"

"I can't tell you." Mulligan watched Sean walk away and jump into a wagon. Mulligan knew other men were inside the wagon. Then he looked at Maria. "It's best you don't know too much about me, Maria. I haven't always told you the truth."

"I know more about you than you think, and so does Devlin."

"He must have an informer."

Maria suddenly felt like crying. "Oh wonderful. The man I married is a vain, vile little man who fancies himself some kind of British Lord. The man I am in love with will probably be hanged as an enemy of the crown."

"And who's to blame? For me, it all started with a man named John Boyle."

"Boyle? I know that name."

"One of your husband's landlords who killed my father, very much like Devlin's regulator killing that man, today."

"Did you kill Boyle?"

"No."

"Lord Sterling?"

"It doesn't matter."

"It doesn't?"

"Maria, we have two choices. We can run off...leave the country. That means I abandon my brothers here...and the cause."

"The cause?"

"The cause of a free Irish state and the destruction of people like Devlin and—"

"—my husband?"

"Yes." Mulligan looked away. "I'm against violence," he said. "I think it will destroy all of us, but I'm not sure if the Irish have any other choice. You are an upper class British lady and have every right to view me as an enemy."

Maria stroked Michael Mulligan's face. The horses were grazing nearby.

"What is the other choice?"

"That you stay with your husband and I continue with the rebellion. I will be a fugitive from the law and the military. They will be coming after me, Maria, so you will have to let me go. Therefore, if that's what we decide—"

"We decide?"

"Yes—and we better decide today."

They rode in silence back toward the Burke mansion.

That night, Lord Burke took Maria to his bed. They lay together, Maria wearing a long white slip. A dying fire in the fireplace and candle glow lighted the room. Burke's painting of tulips adorned an opposite wall. Facing the large bed, a formal portrait of Lord and Lady Wesley Burke stared down at them, their eyes gleaming in the flickering light and shadows.

"I talked to Devlin, today. I warned him about being too familiar with you. He seemed to understand."

"Really? What else did he say?"

"He seems to think Mr. Mulligan is too familiar with you...but he'll investigate and report later." Lord Burke chuckled. "I thought it was quiet amusing, myself."

"Why's that?"

"I can't imagine a refined English lady of your breeding and intelligence under the protection of a lord and landowner taking an Irish stable hand seriously. Certainly he's better looking than the rest of his kind, and he knows horses, but really—what a preposterous thought. So, if you see Devlin spying on you and Mulligan, don't be alarmed."

"He's always spying on me. Did you know they shot an Irish farmer to death, today?"

"Yes. His pack of ruffians was running off my sheep. We have to control these people, starving or not. I suspect if the crops fail again, next year, they'll all be gone." Maria laid her head back on the pillow. "I see I'm making you sad. Perhaps I could make you feel better."

He snuffed the candles and touched her under the sheet, running his hand up her leg.

"I don't feel well," she said.

"I understand. You're tired. You've been stressed. All these sick Irish peasants and the murder of Lord Sterling by those barbaric revolutionaries." He moved against her body. As his hand moved up her thigh, Maria knew he would find her unaroused. "We should think about a little Burke," he said. "I need a male heir."

"Nathaniel?"

"Yes?"

"I feel tired, tonight." Maria sat up. "Maybe I could do something for you. Why don't you just relax and lie back and let me do all the work?"

She reached out with her hand and touched him under the sheet.

"My goodness," he said.

Before he finished, Nathaniel Burke rolled on top of her, forcing his way inside. Maria closed her eyes against the pain.

"I don't know where you learned that trick, but you need to conceive," he said, just before he went to sleep. A strong wind was blowing outside, shaking the large house and rattling the windows. Maria stared at the ceiling in the darkness, feeling apprehensive but excited. She had made her decision.

A week later, Maria left a message for Devlin instructing him to meet her after dark in a grove near the house. Devlin was excited, and left his cabin at midnight. He noticed the carriage was missing, and two of the horses, but Maria's black gelding remained in the stall. Devlin knew he could convince Lord Burke that all was well with his wife. Devlin walked through the low brush, holding up his lantern. Then he stopped, staring ahead at a shape on the ground. He lifted the lantern and shined the light on a man's dead face. Oliver lay against a tree, eyes bulging, a red line around his throat where he had been strangled with a wire. Devlin cried out, even as the lantern suddenly went dark. A moment later, someone put a hand around his mouth and whispered, "You are a traitor to your people, Devlin. Let Oliver be a warning to you—and to others."

Devlin tried to break free but something struck him behind his right ear and he went out.

THE FAMINE

DEVLIN WOKE LORD NATHANIEL Burke after midnight
with news of the lovers departing, and Nathaniel quickly called
his guards, desperate hungry men who would kill for pay. In a
time of plague, a landowner needed protection. Standing in
flickering light, facing the armed men holding lanterns and
smoking torches, he gave orders.

"Michael Mulligan has kidnapped my wife, Maria, I'm sure
for ransom. They are probably heading toward Cove Harbor in
Cork." He could not see their hooded faces in the shadows but
Nathaniel Burke imagined them smirking. "Find them and bring
her back."

"What about Mulligan?" Devlin said. "One of my men is
dead—strangled, he was. I bet Mulligan's a bloody Whiteboy."

The other men reacted to the name of the secret assassins.

"Bring him here alive and we'll hang him. If you can't take
him alive, shoot him!"

It began to rain. The men mounted their horses but
Nathaniel chose to stay behind; it was too dangerous on the
roads. He found his pistols in the house and loaded them. In a
dream, that night, he caught the guilty pair on the road and

watched as his men hanged the arrogant Mulligan pleading for mercy. Maria shrieked with terror and guilt. Nathaniel awoke just as he was about to rape Maria, frigid and cold from the start. In the morning, the English maids, busy and well fed, avoided his eyes.

"Elizabeth!"

The maid approached him, her eyes lowered.

"Yes sir?"

"Your mistress has been kidnapped."

"Oh my Gawd, sir."

"I believe the culprit is Michael Mulligan, the stable groom." Elizabeth said nothing, her eyes lowered. Burke noticed the swell of her breasts. "Do you know anything about it?"

"Oh no, sir."

"You never saw them…intimate?"

"Gawd no," Elizabeth said. "But he was a rough one, he was."

"Soon—he'll be a dead one!" Lord Burke gazed up at their wedding portrait. "I want that painting taken down and burned."

"It will be done, sir."

Elizabeth left him, and he wondered if he caught a lewd spark of amusement in her eyes. Fortunately, his wife had proved barren so they had no children. A new wife might bring him a son, he thought, a wife less squeamish about the sick and dying peasants. When the potato crop continued to fail, there remained plenty of food for Nathaniel Burke and his fellow Anglo Irish landholders. Irish exports of beef and grain brought money so they would recover from the lack of rents, though unknown men had killed his former landlord, Boyle, dumping his body on a muddy road.

They won't kill me, he thought to himself.

But planning for future good fortune didn't erase the humiliation Nathaniel Burke felt over his young bride of three years running off with the darkly handsome Irish inferior. Devlin's men never found them at Cork, nor did Burke ever hear of the coffin ships sailing to Grosse Isle east of Quebec City. One night, he walked with a pistol to the stable and found Maria's black gelding in the stall.

"She loved that horse, didn't she?"

"Oh sure," Devlin said. He wiped his nose.

"Which one did Mulligan prefer?"

"All of them, sir. But the lady loved that one, yessir."

"Really?"

Nathaniel Burke lifted his pistol and fired between the horse's eyes.

———————

It was a blustery day when Captain Seers of the good ship Providence prepared to depart from Kingstown and sail for Quebec. The harbor had been built to help navigate the treacherous Dublin waters. Thousands of desperate Irish were escaping the famine ravaging Ireland. The captain would have preferred healthy captured Negroes to these ghostly Irish, some of them too weak to walk the plank. Then he saw the striking couple waiting to board. According to the ledger, she was Maria Burke, an elegant English lady and her personal servant, a ruggedly handsome man who signed himself as "Michael Mulligan, horse trainer." Captain Seers observed them board the ship. He also spied a group of men in cotton pants and white shirts watching from the dock, their eyes betraying nothing. The captain was curious about the station of this wealthy aristocratic woman who had no reason to flee Ireland. Mulligan carried her bags and tipped his cap to the captain and his crew.

"He's wanted," the captain said to his wife, Isabel, who always traveled with him.

"Wanted, yes, but by whom?" Isabel asked. "Besides her, of course?"

Captain Seers heard one of the crew address Mulligan in Irish. For the first week, Maria and Mulligan remained locked in their cabin. Passing sailors heard their loud lovemaking inside. Occasionally, the lovers walked the deck staring at the open sea, talking quietly to each other, the sun bright on her copper-colored hair.

"Who are you?" Maria asked, smiling. "Really?"

"I was born an Irish Traveler."

"We were taught to hate them in England."

"Then I became a traveling actor. Then I became your stable boy," he said, kissing her wrist. "Your sweaty groom."

"Tell me more," Maria said, blushing.

"I'm the man who stole you from a tyrant."

Maria turned away. "That you did. We can never go back."

"I know." Michael Mulligan studied her classic profile. "Are you afraid?"

"Yes. A little." She faced him. "You know, Nathaniel Burke was very attractive at first. Like me, he was English but born in Ireland. He had wealth and position."

"And Irish slaves."

"We called them servants…including you."

"Sure but you'd rather be back at your old plantation?"

Maria frowned. "I'd rather die."

Maria remembered the gradual change in her husband, the sudden cold looks, the long hours of his absence while she sat alone in her beautiful rooms, and then his travel restrictions, and warnings about starving peasants in the roads. He welcomed the famine for it might clear his land of the filthy Irish, but the bony creatures that appeared at the farm frightened her. Nathaniel allowed Maria to take riding lessons with Michael Mulligan whom he trusted with his horses.

Now they were at sea.

"Michael?"

They felt the ship move under them.

"Yes?"

"Those men who took the horses and carriage. Who were they?"

"My boys," Mulligan said.

"They spoke in Irish. I couldn't understand what they were saying—but they sounded angry."

"And sad."

Maria was thinking about the men clustered in an alley by the stable when the captain appeared.

"A word," he said. "Watch those scurvy Irish below deck. Who knows what disease they're carrying?"

"We will," Maria said, smiling. Captain Seers glanced at Michael Mulligan.

"No offense, young man," he said. "I know you're Irish."

"Yes I am," Mulligan said. "But they *are* a filthy lot, and I'm always ready to serve."

He made an elaborate bow. Then Maria and Mulligan continued along the deck while the captain followed them with his eyes.

"Maria? Those men were old friends," Mulligan said. "*My* people. They think I've betrayed them by leaving."

"Have you?"

He didn't answer but instead kissed her. She returned the kiss.

"We had to escape," she said.

The lovers had little choice. Maria knew the level of vengeance Lord Nathaniel Burke would take; it was only a matter of time before Devlin reported them making love in the stable or Lord Burke found them together in a green field.

"Michael Mulligan is good with horses," Nathaniel told her. "But when we leave for Belfast, I'll send him away to starve with the others."

"As you wish," Maria answered.

As the potatoes turned black, hunger struck and more people died, the lovers finally escaped along a dark road to Dublin, Mulligan driving the horses that knew his touch. Mulligan was personally spooked by the terrible silence that covered the land. They passed bodies lying along the moonlit road, and slept briefly in the carriage. Finally, they saw the harbor and the ship that would carry them away from Ireland.

Maria could feel the eyes of the captain and crew watching her as they boarded the ship. On deck one afternoon walking alone, Mulligan observed a frail Irish girl sitting against the side of the ship; when he saw her bright glittering eyes, he gave her some water and a piece of cheese. Later, he brought her bread from the captain's table. The girl's health seemed to improve as they crossed the Atlantic. Other Irish families came up on deck to cook what food they had over small fires, using portable brick-lined ovens. He saw a small group of Irish Travelers walking the deck, but decided not to approach them; they were from a different clan and ignored Mulligan. A few had sheep and pigs in a pen. The lead colored sea seemed unusually calm.

"What's your name?" Mulligan asked the bony wraith.

The girl rolled her yellow eyes, glaring at him. "Patricia. Yours?" He told her. "And your Missus is English? A refined lady?"

"English and some Irish," Mulligan said.

"Bet the English part counts more," Patricia said, grinning, clutching a loaf of bread with bony fingers. She reached out and touched his fine silk shirt. "I bet you taught the lady how to ride." She cackled.

Mulligan recognized something secret and knowing in the girl's eyes. Mulligan saw the same suspicion in the eyes of Captain Seers. Though Maria and Mulligan passed themselves off as an elegant English lady with her Irish male servant, anyone could see the secret glances between them, the suppressed mirth and sudden blushes, and imagine the fierce carnal embraces in clandestine places—the sudden release of covered breasts, Mulligan himself like a prize stud as Maria's cuckolded husband sat in his mansion studying figures and sums or sketching tulips, his private hobby.

In the captain's cabin, Isabel's gaze probed the elegant composure of Lady Maria Burke as she discussed celebrated English novels at dinner.

"Jane Austen has polish and style but lacks passion," Maria said. "Everyone lives in an elegant house and has such good manners."

"Her confrontation scenes have passion enough. It's a pity Jane Austen died so relatively young," Isabel said.

"That *was* sad," said Maria.

"You came from County Roscommon?"

"Yes, Captain Seers."

"There's a closer dock in Cork. Why take a ship from Dublin?"

"Dublin's a lovely city," said Maria. "Still full of life, even now."

"Exciting," agreed Mulligan, usually quiet. "And you have a bigger ship."

"But why travel to North America?" asked Isabel. "Surely you can still run the estate in Ireland."

Maria sipped her wine and smiled, though they saw a flash of anger in her eyes. "Right now, the estate is in capable hands."

"Irish farmers are dying and the English don't care," Mulligan said.

"I've heard," said Captain Seers. "Tell me, do the so called Whiteboys still exist?"

Maria was puzzled. "Whiteboys?"

"It's a secret Irish society," the captain said. "They kill landlords."

"The Whiteboys are a myth," insisted Mulligan.

"They also kill deserters," the captain told them. "Once you join them, you can't leave. If you do, the Whiteboys will dump your eviscerated body in a ditch."

"My dear husband, really!" Isabel poured more tea. "Is there a Mr. Burke in this picture?"

Maria glared at the older woman's moon face across the table. "Nathaniel Burke. He died of cholera."

"Pity," the captain said. "Of course, it's none of our business. We used to transport an African cargo. Now Irish."

Maria nodded to Mulligan who replenished her wine.

"But we're *not* going to Boston," the captain continued. "We're going up the Saint Lawrence River to Quebec. It's another journey to Boston."

"True." Maria glanced at Mulligan and smiled. "Actually, we eventually want to settle in San Francisco. We were anxious to leave so we took the first ship out."

"The English press is full of the famine news," Isabel said. "It must be terrible. Dead bodies unburied. Starving peasants. People living in bogs. Really."

That night, Michael Mulligan dreamed of his adoptive father and a traveling troupe of actors performing in pastures and on street corners, and he saw the Gypsy Irish and their covered wagons and heard the language they spoke. Mulligan saw English soldiers firing on the people. He woke up in darkness, listening to the ship's noises. As Maria slept, he was back in an alley outside Dublin with four men; one of them had pulled a knife.

"You can't leave the brotherhood," he said in Irish. "As a Whiteboy, I have a right to kill you."

"Do it, Sean," Mulligan said. "But spare her."

Thomas Collins, the oldest, pulled the wiry Sean away. Thomas had missing teeth and fingers and his back was crooked from years of brutal work.

"She's a lovely girl," he said. "But you'll be leaving your country. Your people."

"Nathaniel Burke's hunting us."

"We could hide you."

"We killed Devlin's man. We could kill Burke," a third man said.

"Then the British will send in troops. We can't kill too many or they'll know who we are." Mulligan pushed his way out of the alley. Maria was looking down the narrow street for him. "I'll return."

"For what?" Sean said. "To die?"

Two soldiers passed along the cobblestone street. On the horizon stood the Martello Tower. Thomas suddenly took Mulligan's hand. He saw tears in the old man's eyes.

"You'll come back," Thomas said. "Sure but that is a lovely team and carriage."

"Take them and vanish," Mulligan told them. "Good-bye, Thomas. *Slan*."

"Run to your fecking English whore," Sean said. "I hope she dies."

"Don't say that," Michael Mulligan said, "or I'll kill you."

"Kill me? You better be always looking over your shoulder, Mulligan."

Lying in bed, Mulligan could still feel his anger as he shook each man's hand except for Sean's and then ran toward Maria; somewhere street musicians played as they walked quickly over a bridge and took a train heading toward the quay and the waiting ship.

They could've killed me, he thought. *And they may yet.*

Maria stirred and rolled against him. He felt his hunger stirring and gently rolled on top of her, the ship lifting on the swells. The world vanished when he came inside her. Later as they lay together in the cabin, Maria traced her fingers along Mulligan's bare chest.

"Would you have killed my husband?"

"Gutted him like a pig."

"And then the British would have hanged you, and placed me in an asylum. This is better," she said. "A new life in a new place."

Michael Mulligan sat up and looked out the porthole at the sea. Once again, he was a refugee. "Farewell, Ireland," he said.

Nathaniel Burke never discovered what happened to his wife and her lover or that his unintentional revenge came at sea. Though Mulligan had washed carefully before making love in the cabin, Maria caught the deadly ship fever. One day she stopped eating, and Mulligan felt her dry hair. A red rash covered her skin, and she stared at him from the bed, her eyes glowing.

"I think I'm deadly sick, Michael."

"You'll get better," he said.

By the time the Providence arrived, the bay was filled with filthy bedding and floating corpses thrown overboard. Many people below deck were sick or dying. Captain Seers had a fever, and when the authorities examined the crew and passengers, they officially diagnosed ship fever or typhus, and quarantined the ship. Isabel was exiled from the island but vowed to come back and take her husband's body home if he died. A nurse ordered Mulligan to leave though his mistress would remain in quarantine. Holding Maria's hand, Mulligan refused.

"You're healthy. Move along. The woman is very sick and she stays."

"I'll work on the island," he said. "You need help. I want to stay with her."

The supervising doctor named Douglas agreed, knowing more migrant ships filled with dying people were on the way and they had little help. Mulligan's first job was to clean out the Providence; they opened the hold and a stench arose, as from a swamp at the bottom of the ship. Behind an iron grille in a long wooden vault, Mulligan found the body of Patricia, her staring eyes like jelly. When the bodies had been dragged out by hooks and the sick helped to huts and shacks on the island, Mulligan saw another gleaming ship full of happy dancing people, blond and blue-eyed, singing German songs and staring with a startled surprise and even mirth at the victims from the Irish ships. The German immigrants went ashore and on to Canada for a better life. Mulligan went to work among the sick and dying, many lying in their own filth. He could do little but clean and feed victims and dig graves in the island's hot miasmic atmosphere.

In the crowded hospital tent, Maria Burke grew weaker and could barely take water, but her face was still pretty as she talked of going to San Francisco, the bright shining city of hills on the Pacific Ocean. "A primitive outpost," she murmured. "For a new life."

"Yes," Mulligan said.

"I want my pretty little black horse."

"We will send for him," Mulligan said. "And the stallion."

"Yes—and we'll ride on the beach."

Mulligan sponged her body and dropped water onto her dry lips. He had rejected Dr. Douglas's prognosis of death, but one afternoon after calling out his name, Maria's moist eyes gradually turned flat and hard, her face going still. He lifted Maria in his arms, sobbing, cursing a God he didn't believe in. He didn't hear the doctor enter.

"For God's sake, man," Dr. Douglas said, "she's gone. You're holding a corpse." Mulligan didn't respond. "I'm sorry. We also lost the captain, I'm afraid."

Dr. Douglas touched him lightly on the shoulder and quickly left. Michael Mulligan looked down at Maria's dead face, a dark despair washing over him as a void opened. Then he felt another worker's hands gently pulling Maria's body away.

"We have to move quickly," a woman's voice said. "Please."

Mulligan bought a plot in the churchyard near the hospital. He did not want to bury her in the open field where hungry dogs scavenged. It rained as they lay Maria Burke's body in the earth, resting in a simple plain coffin. The rain did not alleviate the foul swamp smell and heat.

"Are you a Catholic or a Protestant?" a priest asked.

Mulligan glared at the clergyman.

"Neither. I'm a Celtic pagan."

"What religion was the woman?" the priest demanded.

"She was a Protestant, of course. Just say a few words and have done with it."

After an angry silence, the priest said a quick prayer. He caught the fever and died a week later. Isabel returned with a note from the mayor of Quebec and took her husband's body aboard the cleaned Providence. Five crewmen had died, replaced by Canadian sailors. Before the Providence left the crowded harbor with more immigrant ships arriving, she met with Mulligan.

"I'm sorry about Maria Burke. I'll bury my husband at sea." After a pause, she asked, "Do you want to return to Ireland? We'll stop in England, first, until the famine ends."

"I can't go back," he said, knowing Nathaniel Burke's men would be waiting, and his own people whom he abandoned.

"I didn't think so. Can you make a new life here?"

"I'll make one in San Francisco."

"Good luck to you, then."

Mulligan watched the single ship sailing back down the Saint Lawrence River. With the constant work among the fever victims, including doctors, he didn't have time to grieve Maria. In October, the Saint Lawrence River froze blocking Irish ships. Grosse Isle closed.

Mulligan took what money he had left plus some from Dr. Douglas and rode with a wagon train following the California Trail west. He made repairs on the wagons and stared at the endless prairie wondering why he had survived. It seemed to him he might travel an endless road for the rest of his life, and he would carry the same emptiness. Work was one answer to fill those long years ahead. Gold had been discovered in California and thousands invaded in search of riches. Mulligan understood the futility of greed but also knew the miners would need services he might provide. He knew horses and carpentry.

One day, he paused on a San Francisco beach watching an elegant woman and her husband riding horses through the surf and he remembered Maria Burke and the hot secret places where they made love and their final personal journey across the Atlantic Ocean to freedom and a life together that never came.

EDWIN BOOTH

LOOKING OUT THE WINDOW of San Francisco's Powell Street hotel, Michael Mulligan saw the fog rolling in. It was thicker than the sinister mist that enveloped Ireland, bringing a fungus that killed potatoes and starved millions of Irish people, altering their history with a plague. He turned away from the window and the Powell Street hill. Laura Keene paced the ornate hotel room, seeming to float across the floor in her cage crinoline. Her long auburn hair hung in ringlets.

"We leave for Australia in two days, and Edwin Booth is missing."

She still had a trace of a British accent in her speech.

"He's probably out drinking," Mulligan said. "Like his father, it's the Booth curse."

"What if he gets intoxicated in Sydney Town? He could be shanghaied."

"He'll get to Australia before you do...only as an involuntary sailor, not an actor."

Laura Keene fixed her eyes on him. "That's not amusing," she said. "At your request, I watched him, I acknowledged his young talent, I admired his Richard III at the Metropolitan

Theatre, I liked his face and voice, and though he wants experience—doing Hamlet at 19 is absurd— I couldn't deny his potential and hired him..."

"As always, a good business decision, Mrs. Keene."

Again, he confronted that famous stare and heard the edge in her voice.

"I am not Mrs. Keene *or* Mrs. Luft. I became Mrs. Taylor but now I am *not* a wife, I am Laura Keene, actress and stage manager, and my most promising actor is out *drunk* somewhere."

"He's still in mourning for his father."

"How *long* will he mourn? It's been over two years. Junius Brutus Booth was great but a trifle old fashioned and though I regret he's gone, this grief is—"

"Unmanly?"

"Yes."

"I'll look for him."

Laura Keene sat on a chair near the window. For a moment, she could have been playing one of her melodramatic heroines from a light comedy.

"Thank you for your assistance, Mr. Mulligan. Take Mr. Anderson with you. He's also a good actor so keep him safe."

At the door, Mulligan paused.

"It was courageous for you to come to San Francisco. Most successful actors would stay in New York."

"It was a business decision. There's money to be made here with all these promises of gold. It's a good place for women to start a business, and not just brothels. James Stark said Australia was also lucrative for theatre companies. Now find that wastrel buffoon. Sober him up and *do* be careful."

"I can defend myself."

"No doubt, no doubt," Laura Keene said, watching the tall Irishman whose past was obscure, but whose talents were evident. He carried an air of danger with him that might have made him a magnetic actor, but he loved producing the theatre arts and had brought Junius and Edwin Booth to San Francisco. When news came that the famous veteran actor had died traveling back East, it was Michael Mulligan who sent the letter to Edwin Booth's traveling company in Grass Valley. The young novice actor who had kept his father sober for performances was now getting drunk himself.

In the hotel lobby, Mulligan saw a female guest reading a new book by Thoreau called *Walden or Life in the Woods*. Two men in frock coats and top hats were arguing about the new Republican Party and the dispute over the Kansas-Nebraska act.

"Allowing a vote on slavery means it could spread to the territories," one of the gentlemen said. "And in the north."

"And what if it does? We have Pomo Indian slavery here."

"An end of compromise could mean a civil war."

Mulligan didn't wait for Anderson but left the hotel and walked down Pacific Avenue, the fog still thick with a wet cold he remembered from Ireland. He wore a soft crown brown hat and a sack coat, less formal than the popular frock coat. He carried a thick oak stick from the Shillelagh forest; it was useful for walking and as a cudgel, a long knife concealed in the smooth cane.

Mulligan was fond of the young Booth and saw in his bold youthful attempt at Hamlet a future as an important actor. Unlike his father, Booth's rich voice was quieter, his performances using fewer gestures, and he managed to speak Hamlet's lines as a real person, not a bombastic performer. Perhaps it was the voice that carried the poetry…but Edwin Booth would need experience and discipline. Already, he showed more promise than his older brother, Junius Brutus Booth, Jr.

Michael Mulligan saw blurred colored lights through the fog and heard tinny piano music. Newspapers referred to Sydney Town as a dangerous district run by Australian thugs called Sydney Ducks. The images were strong: brothels, taverns, gambling casinos, cutthroats, and the whorehouses of Chinatown using young women kidnapped in China. The few visiting miners who had actually struck gold soon found themselves drunk and robbed, some beaten nearly to death, and some waking up to service on a ship at sea.

Michael Mulligan passed taverns with names like Bull Run, known for its smell. If Booth had found a tavern on the waterfront, he might be safer…but Sydney Town was dangerous by any standard. Michael Mulligan himself had nearly been shanghaied except for the intervention of another fugitive

Irishman, Thomas Francis Meagher, a political prisoner. Meagher escaped prisons in England and Tasmania and wanted to join the US army. Together, they had fought their way out of a tavern after Mulligan refused a suspicious drink. Mulligan now checked the many dives, and women in white and scarlet low cut dresses called to him from the misty doorways and alleys.

"Hey Irish, I got somethin' for ya."

"Maybe you need a stiff one?"

"Or somethin' that needs to get stiff?"

Michael Mulligan stopped in a bar known as The Morgue. He knew one of the girls, an Irish woman named Mary who looked much older than her 25 years. Men gambled at the tables or drank at the bar, the light low and full of smoke. There was a piano pushed against a wall but no player, tonight. Mulligan knew there were rooms upstairs. He didn't see the two huge men who could appear at any time, ready to throw a drunk out, or lay one out if needed.

"Well, well, it's the famous Mr. Mulligan. Here for a drink? A poke?"

"I'm looking for a young man with dark hair. A boy, really."

"A pretty boy? Thought you liked girls."

Mulligan tipped his hat. "Oh Mary, but I do. You're my favorite."

"I bet I am."

"I need your help." He slipped her a gold dollar with an Indian princess on the head. "This man is an actor, Edwin Booth."

He saw recognition in Mary's blue eyes. "Oh him. The little boy with a big voice. What else he got that's big?"

Mary pocketed the gold dollar and began shrieking with laughter. Mulligan asked again. "Where is he?"

"He fell for the old trick at the Morgue."

"What trick is that?"

Mary seized his hand and ran it up under her skirt. He felt her bare thigh.

"You get five free drinks if you find one girl with underwear. No one wears under garments here, so he paid for all five. Don't fall for that one."

"Where is Booth?"

"He spent all his money, had himself a shag, then two gentlemen escorted him out."

Mulligan put his hands on Mary's still pretty face, staring into her bleary eyes. "Out where?"

"You got a double eagle, Luv? The new $20 gold coin?"

"No, but I can get one." After a moment, Mulligan said, "Mary, I'll owe you a favor. Tell me. Please."

"I think they got a wagon down the street. They can nab about five, ten buggers a night." She touched the inside of his thigh. "So, Mulligan, how about it? Can't leave here without doin' some business."

He gave her another coin and bolted from The Morgue. Outside, a large man blocked his exit. "You need to pay the lady," he said.

Mulligan smiled. "But I did, sir."

Mulligan showed the knife blade in the stick and backed down the street; at the corner, he saw more revelers and a few women but no wagon. Then he heard a rich Shakespearian voice on the night wind.

"It is a nipping and an eager air. A biting air. Or in plain English, it's colder than a witch's tit."

Running toward the familiar voice, Mulligan saw a horse drawn wagon filled with unconscious men. The young Edwin Booth, his hair dark, his body small but athletic, stood up in the cart and played to passing revelers. His frock coat was stained.

"These our actors are not melted into thin air...but collapsed from drink," he bellowed. "Such is Mankind."

A small tattooed man wearing a bowler hat came around and reached up toward Booth. "Shut up," he said. "Sit down and shut yer gob!"

"I have an engagement, sir, in Australia, with the famous Laura Keene."

"Oh, you'll get to Australia," the driver said. Both men began to laugh. Then Mulligan pushed the smaller man away from the wagon.

"He's with me," he said. "Back away."

"Who the hell are you?" the small man said. He had bad teeth and tight curly hair.

"Mulligan," Booth shouted, weaving but still balanced over the sleeping bodies. "Have you met my new companions? Saucy fellows."

The short man advanced. Michael Mulligan saw the derringer and swung his night stick, cracking the thug's right wrist. Mulligan then slashed across his forehead with the blade, blinding him with his own blood. Kicking the derringer away, Mulligan reached up and pulled Booth from the wagon.

"An adventure," Booth yelled.

Mulligan walked around toward the standing horses.

"What is your business, sir?" the driver said. Mulligan could see he was afraid of this sudden apparition on a foggy night. "Don't interfere. I'm armed."

The driver held a whip and reached for a hidden pistol when Mulligan slightly pricked the lead horse with his knife. The animal screamed and bolted forward, the driver trying to saw back the horses as they raced down the street and took a corner, one unconscious drunk sliding to the street.

Pocketing the derringer, Mulligan pushed Booth toward an alley. The bleeding man sat cursing on the street, covering his eyes.

"Once more unto the breech," Booth declaimed. "We need another drink, noble Mulligan."

"We need to get out of here," Mulligan said. "You're in danger."

They began walking toward the bay.

"I was having some excitement," Booth said. "Strong drinks, beautiful girls. You think I'm afraid of those common cutthroats?" They turned a corner on Broadway Street. Soon they'd be walking uphill on paved streets toward the hotel.

"They were going to put you on a boat to China. I'm amazed you didn't pass out."

"You may have something there, Mulligan, my fine Irish lug. I gave my last drink to a toothless old rum head and he dropped to the floor after a sip! I was out the door and these two gentlemen offered me a ride." Booth stopped and stared at a patch of fog taking shape under the street lamp.

"You have an offer not many actors get, young man. If you don't kill yourself, you'll be better than your father, may he rest in peace."

Edwin Booth didn't answer. He still stared ahead with the same gaze he used when the ghost first appeared in *Hamlet*.

"Angels and ministers of grace, defend us."

For a moment, Mulligan thought he was acting. Then he saw the pale figure floating toward them through the cold mist, the face old and white, the features caught in a frozen grimace. Mulligan had seen him on stage and it was the very image of Junius Brutus Booth himself, revisiting foggy streets. He heard the fear in Edwin Booth's voice.

"Father? Look where he comes!"

Mulligan pulled Booth behind him and held up his cudgel.

"Whoever you are, let us pass!"

Mulligan felt the absurdity of swinging at fog. The apparition pointed at the now cowering Edwin Booth, the eyes blazing with an unnatural fire. Booth collapsed sobbing on the street.

"Thou art a scholar, Mulligan, talk to it."

Booth fainted. Mulligan felt a cold rush of foggy mist enveloping them, the old ghostly man staring at him, but with compassion, this time. He pointed to an alley. Seconds later, Mulligan heard a gunshot and his hat flew off. Through the wall of fog, he saw the small man with the bloody face laboring uphill toward him waving a pistol in his left hand, two thugs with clubs following behind.

"You bastard! I'll kill ya!"

The apparition slid down the street toward the running advancing thugs. Mulligan picked up the fallen actor and threw him over his shoulder. He heard echoing screams as he moved down the narrow, garbage-strewn alley, waiting for a bullet to hit him in the back. By the time he reached the last hill, Booth was awake. Mulligan found a bench and sat Booth down. He slapped him.

"You need to walk on your own—now!"

They continued on and staggered into the lobby of the luxury hotel, Mulligan holding Edwin Booth up. A clerk and Junius Booth, Jr. rushed toward them. Booth's older brother was thin and bore a slight resemblance to the elder Junius. "My God," he said, "what happened?"

"He almost got shanghaied. Put him to bed, for God's sake."

"June, my brother. What I have seen. Your hair will stand on end."

Junius and the night clerk walked Booth toward the stairs.

"Wait!" They stopped. "Brother. I saw Father, tonight. I saw his face! Our father is walking still as we saw him in life—tonight!"

Junius looked at Mulligan and then faced his brother clinging to his lapels. "Don't be absurd, Edwin. You need to sober up and rest."

The two men took Edwin Booth upstairs to his room. Mulligan walked to the door and saw the fog had cleared. He heard a rich female voice behind him.

"So you found him?"

He glanced at Laura Keene and nodded. She was wearing a night gown that displayed her slender figure. "I did. Some criminals shanghaied him but we escaped."

Laura Keene listened as he quickly told the story of their night's adventure. "Where's your hat?"

"I believe it was shot off."

Mulligan could see Laura Keene considering his words.

"Thank God you survived," she finally said. "You say you hurt one of them?"

"One fellow may have a scar on his forehead. I could have cut his throat."

"My God, Mulligan. I better inform the police."

"The police? They care little about what happens in Sydney Town. Most of them take bribes."

"I have to talk to someone."

"If you file a report, those thugs will know where to find us."

Laura Keene hesitated. "I believe you're right." She shook her head and Mulligan saw a faint smile. "You are an interesting man, Mr. Mulligan. You have a few criminal instincts, yourself. They say the Irish often confuse the whore with the Madonna and the Madonna with the whore. Is that true?"

"Guilty," Mulligan said.

"Let's have some tea, tomorrow and talk more. You might accompany us to Australia."

"What for? Let Junius be his brother's keeper."

"He can't keep that reprobate scene stealing little bugger from getting pissed."

"What rough language for a lady," Mulligan said with mock horror.

"Bollocks. I've been married and dumped by a cad, had two children, and taken a lover while unmarried. I am also a successful business woman in a man's world. You're a bit rough, Mr. Mulligan, but I could use you. You can be our stage manager and occasionally act some smaller parts, despite that thick Irish brogue."

"I can lose it any time, but I can't leave San Francisco."

"I see. A lady?"

"Perhaps. What about Mr. Luft? He could be your manager."

Mulligan watched her expression change, as it did on stage during turning points in the drama. "He's going to visit his dying wife."

"I see."

"No you don't. We'll meet tomorrow, and you better not go out, tonight."

In the morning, Mulligan found Laura Keene and Mr. Anderson in the plush dining room. He ordered coffee and sat down.

"They'll bring you breakfast, Mr. Mulligan."

"Good. How's himself?"

"Sick as a dog," Anderson said, staring at Mulligan. "I heard your remarkable story. Do you not exaggerate, Mr.

Mulligan? You confronted a gunman with your knife? Scared off horses? Then someone shot off your hat? That's plausible, but do you really want us to believe you saw the ghost of Junius Brutus Booth, revisiting thus the glimpses of the moon? Poor Edwin remembers nothing."

"I don't doubt he remembers nothing. He may have been poisoned. Are you suggesting my story is a lie, Mr. Anderson?"

"That ghost story *is* fascinating," Laura Keene quickly said. "Might even be worked into a play."

"It already has," Mulligan said. "It's called *Hamlet*."

"I wonder what became of those ruffians."

He lightly touched Laura Keene's hand.

"Those ruffians will hunt for me, dear lady."

Mulligan caught Anderson's round face and slightly amused expression.

"I do hope you brought your sword cane, Mr. Mulligan. I hear you Irish are a tough lot, good for a drunk or a brawl—or both."

Mulligan thought for a moment, but knew hitting Anderson in the face would cause serious problems. He took out the derringer.

"One of the cutthroats had this."

The sight of the gun produced the desired effect. Laura examined it with morbid fascination and Mr. Anderson grew pale.

"Heavens," Laura Keene said.

"It looks like a toy. It shoots?"

"It shoots, Mr. Anderson. This is not a prop, but it's deadly only at close range. Usually it takes a head shot."

Breakfast came and they ate in silence.

"Where's June?"

"With Edwin."

"Was he out last night?"

Laura Keene took a small bite of toast and said, "I don't think June was your elusive ghost. It is most strange, however. Edwin Booth wants to talk to you…when he's not so ill. He needs you to revive his memory."

"Listen, Mr. Mulligan, maybe you could take me down to Sydney Town, tonight. I could do some research."

"That is not advisable, Mr. Anderson."

"Why not?"

"You may get hurt."

"I can handle myself in a fight."

"On stage, maybe. Sydney Town isn't a stage set, it's a district infested with depraved people."

Anderson stood up. "Are you saying I'm a weakling?"

"I didn't suggest that, but you could end up at the city morgue."

Laura Keene pushed Mr. Anderson back into his chair. "Let's have some tea, shall we? We have our Edwin, sober and safe, and we are booked to travel to another country and bring them some *glorious* theatre."

Later as Mulligan smoked a cigar on the back porch looking toward the bay, now visible on a clear day, he became aware of Laura Keene standing next to him.

"You are right about Mr. Anderson. He'd faint at the sight of real blood. And just where *did* you learn all those pugilistic skills?"

"I was an assassin," Mulligan said. He watched Laura Keene's face but her expression remained passive. "Don't worry, I only killed Englishmen."

He wasn't sure if he had insulted the actress-theatre manager, but suddenly he heard her strong laugh, loud enough to startle more reserved guests.

"I am relieved to hear that. I sent Mr. Anderson to pack. Reconsider your decision about traveling to Australia."

Mulligan put out the cigar. "Sorry, I can't."

"This mysterious woman of yours—"

"She's not mysterious."

"—came with you from Ireland?"

"No, that was someone else. Maria. She was lovely." Mulligan stopped himself. Laura Keene leaned against the railing and regarded him.

"I've always felt you are something of a tragic character, Mr. Michael Mulligan. Am I correct in that assumption?"

"Possibly."

"You know weapons, horses, and the theatre arts, an odd combination."

"I am an odd fellow."

"You came here on a ship, of course, and you probably escaped the famine which means…you must have traveled on one of those—"

Her voice seemed to run down and she turned away.

"Coffin ships, yes. Maria died."

"I'm sorry," she said. "This is a delicate matter."

"It's all right. I have been spending my time with a domestic servant and potential actress named Emily O'Rourke."

"You have never mentioned her…but I'm happy for you." She walked toward the lobby and then stopped. "Mr. Taylor will be in Australia. I do like his money but not him. I was hoping you could come along and possibly protect me." She laughed again. "Have a delightful morning."

"I will. Good luck in Australia and the Sandwich Islands."

"A lot depends on this tour. Maybe someone should write a play about you.""

Laura Keene left and Michael Mulligan went for a walk. It was amazing how San Francisco had grown since the discovery of gold. New houses were advancing across the sand dunes. Theatre companies flourished, and with prospectors came criminals. The waterfront thrived with schooners and clipper ships landing, loading and unloading, bringing hoards of laborers: whites, Indians impressed into labor, Mexicans, Irishmen, and Italian fishermen to feed the growing population.

Mulligan knew the men he had thwarted would seek him out. He walked toward Telegraph Landing and along a small beach, looking west toward the open ocean. For a moment, he remembered the coffin ship and Maria growing ill, and the feeling of helplessness. He was losing the woman he loved and couldn't stop it.

Emily would prove a needed distraction: a new love in a new city, and now a responsibility since she carried his child.

Mulligan saw a young boy selling papers and bought one. The news carried articles about the new Republican Party protesting the expansion of slavery, and Mulligan read a speech by their speaker, Abraham Lincoln. As he read, a shadow covered the pages. A well-dressed man with mutton chop whiskers and a policeman stood before him.

"Good day, gentleman. If I had my hat, I'd tip it."

The gentleman man produced a hat. Mulligan saw the bullet hole through the crown.

"Is this your hat, Mr. Mulligan?"

"It is. Some unsavory people attacked me, last night."

"So we heard. A man lost his wagon on a sharp turn, the police arrested a pack of sleeping drunks, and one Timothy Kerrigan reported he'd been attacked by three men."

"Kerrigan is a thief," the policeman said. He had a thick Irish accent. "He spells his name with a K and he ain't even a duck, just a common English arse bandit."

The well-dressed man turned and said, "Officer Mahoney, please."

"There were only two of us," Mulligan said. "Am I under arrest?"

"Not at all. Sydney Town is a disgrace, and a certain celebrated actress threatened Mayor Brenham that if any of her actors or workers were threatened or hurt, she'd take her shows elsewhere. She was quiet angry, and she's right, of course. Theatre is big business in San Francisco."

"I agree. With whom am I speaking?"

"My name is John Egan, and I work for the mayor's office. I will need your gun." After a pause, he said, "the derringer?"

Michael Mulligan handed over the tiny pistol.

"Thank you Mr. Mulligan. I anticipate seeing Mr. Booth on stage. A local critic is preparing quite a praiseworthy article, I understand."

They turned to walk down the beach when Mr. Egan stopped. "You might avoid Sydney Town for a spell."

"Oh I will. Too much local color for me."

The policeman saluted Mulligan and the two men walked away. It was then Mulligan saw Edwin Booth, elegantly dressed and walking carefully, the sea breeze stirring his shiny hair when he lifted his top hat at passing women. John Egan and the policeman shook his hand and Booth signed an autograph for Egan. Then Booth turned and walked toward Michael Mulligan. Fatigue and a sense of boyish wonder filled Booth's eyes. He removed his top hat and sat down. The two men didn't speak. Waves broke on the sand.

"The Golden Gate needs a bridge across the bay," Booth finally said.

"Might be hard to construct."

"Yes." Booth saw the bullet hole in Mulligan's soft crown hat. "Michael Mulligan, what transpired last night?"

"You got drunk and two men shanghaied you. I arrived just in time and we escaped. You remember nothing?"

"Very little, I'm afraid. "My brother says I was raving about seeing Father's ghost. I should remember that. He was a forceful man." He looked at Mulligan. "What *did* we see? What did *you* see?"

"I'm not sure. Maybe an old man in the fog. Maybe an imagined ghostly face. Or maybe it was just the fog, itself. There *was* a resemblance."

"You saw his eyes?"

"Yes."

"Did he speak?"

"No."

"Yet it was a kind ghost?"

Mulligan put his finger through the hole in his hat.

"We survived, Edwin. He may have had something to do with it."

"How strange. Rest, perturbéd spirit, rest."

They watched Alcatraz Island in the middle of the bay.

"We can't repeat last night. You are off to Australia to build your reputation, so you better learn a little discipline."

"I will." Booth observed his trembling hands. "By God, I could use a drink."

"It will end the headache, but one day, you may need too many drinks."

"I know that from Father. I think he had a little madness. It may run in our family. I worry about my brother."

"June seems stable."

"My younger brother, John. At 16, he likes to ride his horse on the farm and charge imaginary troops, screaming and firing his pistol."

"Sounds normal to me," Mulligan said.

"Yes—but he's extreme about everything."

As they viewed the blue waters of the bay, women in formal and informal dress passed. "I'm aware that tastes and styles change. My father saw himself going out of fashion, and so will I."

"I don't believe so. You are natural, on stage. Naturalism will always be popular."

"But that's also a style."

"That it is."

Booth watched a family standing near the gentle surf. They seemed overdressed for the beach.

"Speaking of style, Mulligan, I find Dickens great, of course, but his writing is so obvious and melodramatic, at times. I *do* love his bizarre characters."

"You'd play one of his heroes?"

"God no, Mulligan, one of his villains."

"They are always more interesting." Mulligan stood up. "Let's go back."

Edwin Booth got up and placed the top hat on his head. "Perhaps we could have a drop taken on our return?"

They strolled along the waterfront through crowds of passengers, either leaving a ship or waiting to board one. Laborers carried or pushed cargo. Irish Gypsies played rousing revolutionary songs and passed a hat, though Mulligan knew they were lifting wallets, as well. A mounted young man was trying to calm a nervous white stallion, and Booth watched as Michael Mulligan patted the horse on the neck and spoke to it in his native Irish. The stallion settled down. Moments later, the rider and horse were gone.

"You have a way with horses," Booth said.

"I love them."

Mary appeared with a group of women flirting with debarking male passengers. Mary saw Mulligan and waved. He walked over and after a polite bow, gave her a gold coin. Booth was smiling when Mulligan joined him.

"You know that colorful lady?"

"Yes," Mulligan said. "You should be glad I do."

Bands of women in billowing dresses and bonnets sang hymns in front of the more rowdy taverns. On a platform, a potbellied white man in a long black coat and carrying a bullwhip was selling a group of Pomo Indian children between the ages of eight and 12. Dressed in cheap denim, the dark-eyed children watched the crowd, some frightened and some curious. A short Indian man with deep wrinkles and gray-streaked hair stared at the crowd, his eyes empty. The white man had a high-pitched, shrill voice.

"Folks, we have Indian children here ready to be bound over to any miner to work the gold fields. Better hurry, cause that gold ain't gonna be around much longer. How about sixty dollars for a boy, and $200 dollars for a girl. They're great workers, don't eat much, and just need the lash now and then." There was a pause. "Don't be shy, gentlemen. Just give ole' Jake here a fair price and we can start. What am I bid for these Pomo kids?"

Members in the crowd began shouting prices. Jake reacted with mock outrage at the low offers.

"This is appalling," Booth said. "I grew up in a slave state. We should buy these children and free them."

"The slave catchers will find and sell them again."

"I thought slavery was abolished in California."

"That didn't stop trade in native Indians."

"The tribes should fight back."

"They did. Recently, Indians killed two white slavers."

"What happened after that?"

"The army arrived and massacred the tribe."

Booth suddenly approached the white man hawking the children.

"Sir, this is an outage."

Using his actor's voice, Booth repeated his statement and the crowd went silent. Jake regarded Booth; he slowly pulled apart his long coat. "What did you say?"

"I said that this is an outage. You can't sell these children into slavery."

"Slavery? These kids ain't slaves. They ain't black, for one thing. Of course, we don't allow niggers in the state." The crowd laughed. "These Indians are workers."

"Child workers. Sir! I demand you return these children to their families."

The gathered children stared at Booth.

"They have no families," the older Indian said. "They died from disease or were killed by soldiers. Now you better move on."

"You heard the man," Jake said. He touched his bullwhip. "You better move on. Or does the fine gentleman want to take this further?"

Booth didn't move. Michael Mulligan came up and took his arm.

"Let's go. There's nothing you can do."

"Let's start with these beautiful girls," Jake shouted.

The crowd resumed bidding. Mulligan stared at the Indian in charge of the children but didn't speak. Then they walked on. Michael Mulligan and Edwin Booth found an elegant gentleman's club that barred women; affluent men stood at the mahogany bar or sat on the plush upholstered chairs, smoking and discussing serious issues over drinks. Booth and Mulligan stood at the bar, staring into an ornate mirror.

"No more than two drinks, Booth. Then it's home to the hotel."

"Home? An actor is always homeless. After that last display of human kindness, I need at least three drinks."

"Laura Keene will kill me."

"Come now, Mulligan. You're not afraid of anything. I was hoping you'd beat that ugly slaver."

"It wouldn't accomplish anything."

"That old Indian fellow is a traitor to his people." Booth ordered and drank a whiskey. "Why did you leave Ireland, Mulligan?"

"Three reasons: a woman, a famine, and I was being hunted."

"Hunted by whom?"

"An Anglo Irish tyrant whose wife I stole, and a group of vigilantes who killed English landlords. I left their organization so they marked me for death. They considered me a traitor," Mulligan added.

Booth met his eyes in the mirror. "Michael Mulligan, Irish marauder from the Emerald Isle. Someone should write your story into a play."

Mulligan swallowed his whiskey and nodded. "Laura Keene thinks so."

"What happened to the purloined wife?"

"She died."

"I'm sorry."

Before Mulligan could speak, they heard cursing and saw two men fighting. A large man appeared and pushed them apart. "You'll not fight here," he said.

One of the combatants felt blood on his nose and disgusted, left for the wash room. The other young man addressed the other guests, clearly disturbed.

"How can anyone vote on whether or not to accept slavery? It's evil," he told them, "but President Pierce has signed into law an act that will precipitate a war between the slave holders and the abolitionists in the territories and eventually—even the country." The men in the tavern remained silent. "If so, I'll fight for the North."

"And I'll fight for the South."

It was a deep voice with a southern accent. The gentleman turned to face a seated guest with long white hair.

"Some might call that treason," the young man said.

"I'm from Virginia," the older man continued. He wore a broad brimmed white hat. "My slave is my property to take anywhere in the country, including the territories. If we have a civil war, I will fight for my state of Virginia!"

There was a murmur of voices. They suddenly heard Booth's rich voice, elevated slightly to draw listeners with its commanding edge. He confronted the gentleman from Virginia. "Sir, I am Edwin Booth of Maryland. I am from the south, but I am also an American. I denounce slavery, and if President Pierce has opened up the purple testament of bleeding war, I will support a Union free of slavery...always!"

He lifted his glass. A few guests cheered. The man from Virginia said nothing, holding his drink, staring at Mulligan and Booth.

A FAREWELL

CHRISTMAS DAY AND MICHAEL Mulligan stood on the San Francisco pier with his five-year-old son, John, holding the boy's hand and waiting to board a ship for Panama. From there, he would cross the isthmus to the Atlantic and another ship traveling to the east and eventually Washington, D.C. It was an usually clear sunny day. Gathered pelicans flew overhead. Patrick and Elizabeth Maguire stood behind them, ready to take the boy into their care when his father left. Ship crews were lowering the gangplank for boarding passengers. Michael Mulligan squatted down and addressed his son.

"Son? John. I have to leave to help a friend, a General Thomas Meagher. I'm going to train his horses. You like horses, John?"

"Yes."

"He's the general of a cavalry unit with the Irish Brigade and he thinks that with the election of a very kind man, Abraham Lincoln—"

"He looks like a monster," the boy said.

Mulligan laughed. "You might be right, John, but we think there will be a civil war when he takes office, and so I am going to join the US Army and help my old friend, Meagher. We have to help our friends. Can you understand that, son?"

The boy looked into his father's eyes. He had light-colored hair and sharp blue eyes, unlike his father, and his gaze never left his father's face. Sea gulls flew overhead.

"Are you leaving me, dad?"

"Only for a short time," Mulligan said. "Then I'll be back. If civil war breaks out, it can't last long, and who knows, maybe those folks in the south will accept Mr. Lincoln. Then I can be transferred here—to San Francisco. Then I can be with you."

"How long will you be gone?"

"Not any longer than it takes. How long can I be away from you?" They felt a cold breeze off the bay and Mulligan saw the beginning of tears in his son's eyes. He embraced the boy. "I'll never leave you for long," he said. "I will write every week."

"You're leaving me?"

"Only for a while. I love you, my dear boy."

Looking at his son, Mulligan remembered the nurse putting the new born infant in his arms and the doctor walking down the hall toward him, something frightful in his eyes. Then the doctor was saying that the boy's mother had suffered a hemorrhage, something about an attached placenta, and that they couldn't stop the bleeding. Michael Mulligan felt for the second time the devastation of a brutal loss.

The boat whistle sounded. A man was calling on the assembled passengers to board. Michael Mulligan faced the Maguires. Elizabeth was wiping her eyes. Patrick Maguire nodded and gently lifted John up, holding him close. John held out his arms to his father.

"Daddy, don't leave me."

"I'll come back, Johnny. I'm your father, I love you and I'll come back."

Michael Mulligan took out a toy sun and pulled it in half. He gave one half to John.

"You see this? One day, I'm going to return and give you the other half, and we'll be together, again. I love you!"

"Michael, for God's sake, get going."

A Farewell

John Mulligan began crying and Michael Mulligan kissed his son, and then walked quickly up the plank carrying a rolled bag. He could hear his son's now desperate screams as the Maguires carried him to a waiting carriage. Standing at the ship's railing, Mulligan watched them leave. It was a moment of despair and foreboding he would carry for the rest of his life.

In a letter sent a month later, Patrick Maguire described how John Mulligan watched the ship from the rear of the carriage, and then cried all the way home.

BULL RUN

NEAR MANASSAS, TWO MEN on horseback viewed the battlefield. In the distance, the red and blue uniforms of the dead Zouave soldiers resembled wild flowers growing on a hill. On the field, Zouave troops picked up the dead and wounded and carried them to ambulances. Dead and dying horses littered the ground. Rain began falling.

"By God," General Thomas Meagher said. "This is terrible. We will need your services more than ever, Mulligan. Jackson and Stuart's cavalries decimated our troops. We need to build a strong Union cavalry."

Michael Mulligan could see it, Washington D.C. citizens having picnic lunches and drinking wine, ready to watch the first and last battle at Bull Run, and then the panic as the Union Army retreated in the July heat, soldiers and citizens alike caught in a crush beneath falling shells, one of which took out a bridge. The Rebels, too exhausted to pursue, had fallen back and Washington D.C. was spared an invasion.

"This is going to be a long war," Mulligan said.

He stopped and dismounted. A young Reb soldier lay on the muddy ground shot through the abdomen, his wounded mare lying by him. Mulligan saw the horse had been hit in the chest by shrapnel. He plastered some mud on the horse's gaping wound. The boy cried for water. General Meagher dismounted and gave the fallen young soldier a drink from his canteen.

"What happened to you young man? What were you doing here, for the love of Christ?"

"Just protecting my capital, Richmond," the boy said.

"And here I thought the capital was Washington."

"Not in Virginia. How's my horse doing?"

Meagher looked at Mulligan who shook his head.

"Not so good," Meagher said.

"If I had her back at the stable, I have a compound I could feed her that might work," Mulligan said. "She's lost a lot of blood." Mulligan examined the boy's wound. "And so have you, lad. Let me get an ambulance over here."

"I'm gone. Save my horse."

"I'll try," Mulligan said.

"Who led your brigade?" General Meagher said.

The boy smiled, blood suddenly running from his mouth.

"Why old Stonewall Jackson himself. You Yanks ain't gonna budge him. And Jeb Stuart's gonna follow you Yankees into hell."

The boy stared at them, his face relaxing, his eyes suddenly reflecting light like a flat jelly. The mare began to groan. Other workers had appeared to clear the dead and wounded, including the Confederate dead. Meagher closed the boy's eyes.

"He's right. We don't have the cavalry yet to stop them," General Meagher said.

"We rounded up some fresh horses," Mulligan told him. "But they need to be broken and trained."

"We don't have much time, Mulligan." The mare lay on her side, groaning deeply. "What about the boy's horse?"

Michael Mulligan observed the churned battlefield, his face set in a grim mask. Dead or dying horses disturbed him the most.

"I'll take care of her."

"Don't use a gun," Meagher said. "It might spook the recovery team."

He took a drink from a pocket flask. Another officer with a round face and a mustache passed on horseback. A flock of black birds circled in the hot moist air. Somewhere in the distance, they heard an English accented voice crying out: "Appalling. This slaughter is appalling."

Michael Mulligan gently touched the mare's head, and while he spoke to her quietly in his native Irish, he opened a vein in her neck.

RENDEZVOUS IN HELL

MRS. HENRY WINEBRENNER WATCHED it all from her balcony: first, the brigade of Elijah White and his Rebel "Comanches" holding Hanover citizens at gunpoint and taking their provisions, only to pay with useless Confederate money. Three days later, General Judson Kilpatrick with two Union brigades rode through Hanover, a small man waving his cap at the cheering citizens. Neither General Kilpatrick nor Mrs. Winebrenner knew about Jeb Stuart, the fabled Southern Lochinvar and General John Chambliss now advancing upon Hanover from the south. Suddenly, citizens, ambulances and wagons raced through the smoke-filled streets. Generals Farnsworth and Custer fired from one end of town while the men of Chambliss and Stuart fired from the other, even as the returning Judson Kilpatrick rode his lathered horse into the center of Hanover, the horse collapsing. Artillery at either end of Hanover opened fire and took out Winebrenner's balcony moments before she pulled her daughter inside.

Hours earlier, Michael Mulligan knew none of this as he rode in the rear guard of Kilpatrick's division, stopping when he saw three Rebels camped. He had three choices: shoot them, take them prisoner, or continue on, telling others about their presence in Pennsylvania. He chose the second option because he needed information.

The three men were gaunt, and one didn't wear the gray-butternut uniform. They saw his Spencer repeater and put their hands up, but Mulligan noticed a suppressed contempt and even glee in their eyes.

"One of you will have the honor of tying the hands of the other two," Mulligan said.

One of the soldiers spat and said, "Why sho,' Captain."

The air of the hot June day was still. Then a bullet tore through the chest of Mulligan's horse; he was thrown as the dying animal fell. The men jumped him, taking his weapons; Mulligan broke free and cradled the dying horse's head in his arms.

"You bastards, don't shoot the horse, shoot me!" The horse began kicking and screaming. "Let go, Honey, let go."

One of the men prodded Mulligan with his own rifle.

"Back away from me," Mulligan shouted, tears in his eyes. The soldier was about to fire when they heard another voice: "What the hell is going on? Who shot that horse?"

A mounted young officer with a thick dark beard and mustache rode into the clearing and repeated his question. "Who shot the horse?"

"I did," a voice said.

A tall fourth man holding an old muzzle loader appeared from the thick brush.

"We need horses," the officer said. "That's a Morgan, one of the best cavalry mounts in existence. I ought to shoot you."

The officer dismounted and approached Mulligan who murmured words into the ear of the still screaming horse. The officer didn't recognize the language. Mulligan finally looked up. "Let me have your pistol, sir."

Birds were singing in the maple trees, and the soldiers watched as the young officer considered the request. "Of course," he finally said, handing his pistol to the much taller Mulligan.

Mulligan pressed the bore between the horse's eyes. "I'm so sorry, Honey."

He fired and the horse shuddered once, then lay still. With rifles pointed at him, Mulligan handed the pistol back to the officer.

"Much obliged."

"You called your horse 'Honey'?"

"Yes—he had the color of honey. Beautiful animal." Mulligan saw the rifleman who had fired the shot. "I'll kill you when I get the chance."

"I was aimin' at you, but anytime, Yankee."

As the rifleman approached Mulligan, the officer stopped him.

"Your name, private?"

"Cutpert Cowley."

"You shot a beautiful horse, Cowley. A mistake. Look at ours and then his." He faced Michael Mulligan. "I am General John R. Chambliss, 13th Virginia. My apologies, sir. You are?"

"Michael Mulligan, Union cavalry and horse trainer."

"I will have to take you prisoner, Mr. Mulligan."

Mulligan saw other cavalry coming up the road. In a hoarse voice, General Chambliss barked orders:

"Bury the horse, take the saddle, and get this man a mount." The young general held Mulligan's Spencer. "How does this work?"

"Crank a round into the chamber, cock it, fire."

General Chambliss cranked the lever, cocked it and fired a round into a tree. The gun had heavy smoke. The general cranked a second round but didn't fire.

"This rifle will make cavalry obsolete. Where's your brigade, Mulligan?"

"I don't know, General. I lost them, or they lost me." Mulligan knew General Chambliss recognized his lie. "And where might you be going, General? This isn't Virginia. You have a plantation in Pennsylvania?"

General Chambliss smiled. "Jeb was going to kidnap Abe and his cabinet but got waylaid."

"General Jeb Stuart, the great Knight of the Golden Spurs himself?"

"That would be correct."

"I took a shot at him at Brandy Station…but missed. The famous general *can* ride."

"And your Union cavalry has improved, Captain Mulligan."

One of the soldiers began digging a grave for the dead horse. Honey had served him well; Mulligan turned away.

"And how is Rooney Lee?"

"Shot in the leg. Why?" Mulligan remained silent. He remembered Jeb Stuart with his plumed hat and cape riding with Robert E. Lee's son by his side, but the shot meant for Stuart hit Lee. "Who is your immediate commanding officer, Mulligan?"

"General Kilpatrick."

"'Kill Cavalry' is more like it. He's a butcher. Loves to watch his men die."

Mulligan agreed but chose to say nothing. A soldier brought Michael Mulligan a horse and waited as Mulligan ran his hand along the withers and flanks, seeing the ribs and the sweat and dust from a long hot ride.

"You need to take better care of your horses," Mulligan said.

"We need to do so, and we have little time."

"General Chambliss? Does the prisoner need restraints, sir?"

"I think Mr. Mulligan can ride better without them, soldier."

Mulligan mounted the horse. "And where's himself?" he asked. "General Lee?"

For the first time, General Chambliss avoided Mulligan's eyes.

"Can't tell you that, Mulligan."

"Of course. But the cavalry are the eyes and ears of the army."

Chambliss ignored him. They rode down the road, dust rising from the horses' hooves, the sun hot and the air still. Michael Mulligan knew Lee's army had to be close if the cavalry brigades were present; he also knew General Kilpatrick had a rendezvous with Meade's army near Gettysburg. As they rode along the tree-lined road, Mulligan saw the telegraph wires had been cut.

"You know, Mulligan, I hope the Copperheads in the north convince you folks to quit the war and give us our independence."

Mulligan was about to speak when they heard rifle fire. Another officer rode up and shouted, "Federals down the road, General."

General Chambliss gave orders for his men to advance, and then spoke to the soldier who shot Mulligan's horse.

"Private Cowley. Take him back to the wagons." He looked at Michael Mulligan with genuine sympathy. "I'm sorry about Honey, Mulligan. Splendid horse. If you ever decide to change sides, join us. We have our own Irish Brigade, you know."

"I'm against slavery," Mulligan said.

"A lot of us are. General Lee is against secession. But I'm also against any government that invades my state."

General Chambliss charged down the road, leading his mounted troops toward Hanover and the battle. As dust settled on the wide path, Private Cowley regarded Mulligan. He did not like the man's direct penetrating stare. He had the focused gray eyes of a marksman.

"Let's go, Yank. Don't try anything. If you do, I'll kill you this time."

They turned back down the shaded road.

"I got a bad feeling about all this," Mulligan said to himself.

"Who doesn't have a bad feeling about war? *Et in Arcadia, ego.* Death lives in Paradise."

"Well, well, an educated Reb who knows bad Latin. I don't call this paradise, I call it hell." They could hear the distant guns. "What kind of name is Cutpert?"

"I'm a Manxman from the Isle of Man."

"Jesus, another Celt fighting for traitors."

"You want to fight to free the nigger?"

They heard the second cavalry brigade before they saw them, and then the legend himself came into view: J.E.B. Stuart, wearing his famous plumed hat and cape, long dark beard flying, his saber gleaming in the sun as he led a charge of cavalry—the men giving the shrill rebel yell that made Mulligan think of the avenging Irish

Banshee. Stuart and his men thundered past them raising more dust. Michael Mulligan saw the hunger and desperation in their eyes. Then they were gone around a curve in the road.

"God damn, your fabled knight errant sure does know how to put on a show."

"They know how to kill Yankees," Cowley said.

"But they'll have tired horses."

They rode into a military camp and Mulligan saw a long train of covered Federal supply wagons. Cowley called out to a passing soldier.

"Where's Wade Hampton?"

"Off to reinforce Jeb Stuart," a private said. "Let's hope they don't run into the Army of the Potomac."

"Well, they ran into the Union cavalry."

As they spoke, Mulligan saw a group of gathered infantry with a green flag for a banner. They wore faded gray uniforms, and he wondered if he knew any of these Irish countrymen, now fighting for the Confederacy. They glared back at him, possibly recognizing another Irishman. The two brigades had faced each other at Fredericksburg, and it was bloody. A young dark-skinned boy covered with dust watched them from the edge of camp. Cowley pushed Mulligan into a tent.

"When the generals return, they'll want to know about Meade's whereabouts."

"They'll have to ask my generals. I just train horses, Reb."

Cowley regarded him. "Sorry about your horse, Mulligan. I won't tie you up, but if you try to run, you'll be shot. If we survive, maybe we'll have a shot of Irish whiskey."

Cowley disappeared. Another soldier came into the tent and ate from a can of rations while Michael Mulligan sat in a chair. The soldier was young and thin, a pistol across his lap. Michael Mulligan had a bowie knife hidden in his boot but decided to wait. The soldier, his face dirty and covered with stubble, gulped his food.

"This pork smells bad." He held up a hard biscuit. "Want one?"

Mulligan saw weevils in the hard bread. "No thanks."

"Good seasoning," the soldier said. He laughed. "You like that Chimpanzee you got for a President—Honest Ape?"

The soldier had an Irish accent.

"Yes, I do," Mulligan said. "Where are your people from?"

"Sligo," the soldier said. "Got off the boat and they signed me up right there. Promised me citizenship. Where are your people from?"

"All over."

"One of them Gypsy Irish Travelers, are ya?"

Michael Mulligan felt a strong fatigue.

"Think I'll lie down for a while."

"Sure. Have a rest, Mulligan. We may be dead, soon."

When Mulligan woke up, it was dark and the tent was illuminated by firelight outside. The young guard was asleep, his pistol still in one hand. Mulligan heard arguing outside and the guard stirred. Michael Mulligan looked out the front and saw General Stuart with his long dark beard and powerful bulk, appearing strong even after a battle, a gold clasp pinning his hat topped with a black ostrich plume; next to him stood Chambliss and another general Mulligan assumed was Wade Hampton. They shouted at one another, but Mulligan couldn't hear all the words. Hampton pointed at the wagons, and Mulligan heard a scrap of the conversation.

"Lee is riding blind—and we don't need these supply wagons. It's slowing us down."

"Wade, my job is to get supplies," Stuart shouted back. "Our men are starving."

General Chambliss whispered something in Stuart's ear and they began walking toward the tent. Briefly, Mulligan considered taking the guard's pistol and shooting Stuart when he entered the tent, but rather than risk death, he chose to sit down. General Stuart entered moments later and glared at him with the fearless stare of someone who had witnessed and escaped death many times. Wiping his eyes, the guard stood at attention.

"Were you asleep on guard duty?"

"No General Stuart!"

"I could have you shot, Private Kennedy. Dismissed." The soldier left. "Come with me, Yank."

Mulligan followed Stuart from the tent. Hampton shouted orders and the wagon train began moving. Chambliss nodded to

Mulligan and mounted, waving to his remaining cavalry brigade. A few wounded lay on the ground, and others walked limping into camp, exhausted, some with bloody faces. The ragged young boy watched them from the perimeter and threw rocks at passing soldiers. None of them responded.

General Stuart led Michael Mulligan to a horse tied to a tree. It was a beautiful reddish-brown bay, caked with dirt and dried sweat.

"General Chambliss says you know horses. Examine this animal and give me your assessment."

Mulligan ran his hands over the nervous stallion, patting it, touching it like he would caress a woman, gently feeling with his hands. He whispered a few Irish words into the horse's ear and the horse settled. Mulligan examined the horse's teeth and hooves, picking out dirt.

"It's a fine horse. No laminitis, but you will need new shoes."

"We are short of everything, Captain Mulligan. Food, ammunition, cigars, even horse shoes. I did manage to salvage a few at the Hanover blacksmith shop before Custer and Farnsworth damn near ran over me." Stuart patted the horse. "But you, Virginia, jumped a fifteen foot ditch and we escaped to fight again."

"General Stuart?"

"Yes?"

"Many of you officers went to West Point before the war. You were friends and now you're killing each other. Why?"

Stuart leaned against the horse and met Mulligan's eyes. "We are at war, sir, fighting against northern aggression. That means, I may have to shoot my wife's father and brother who joined the Union army."

"You took an oath to serve the Union Army."

"And now, I am fighting to defend my state of Virginia *against* that army. I have lost General Jackson but must carry on with God's guidance and blessing." After a moment, he asked, "How are you fixed with the Lord, Mulligan?"

"There was no Lord at Antietam," Mulligan said. "Or Fredericksburg."

Mulligan could close his eyes and see wave after wave of the Union Irish Brigade running up a corridor into deadly fire from the Confederate Irish. It was one thing to read about war and another to hear the guns, to smell the smoke and the blood of dying men, to see rows of piled dead on a blood-soaked road.

"The battle of Fredericksburg was our most glorious moment," Stuart said. "All of us were there: Robert E. Lee, Stonewall Jackson, myself, dispensing God's justice." Stuart looked at the men gathering in the torchlight of the camp. "But it was a slaughter for the Federals, especially the Irish." Stuart's eyes lingered on Mulligan's face. "I suspect you'd like a glass of whiskey as your kind seems to crave?"

"My kind? Not now, General Stuart."

"Good. I don't imbibe, though I'm Irish, myself. Now, Captain Mulligan, you have a choice. You can ride with us or I can parole you here and now. I will take your guns and you will be on foot, of course."

"Parole me," Mulligan said.

"As you wish. I suppose you don't know where the Army of the Potomac is?"

"That's your job to find out, General Stuart."

Stuart nodded to himself, caressing the hilt of his saber.

"You ever kill anybody with that thing?"

"No. These are excellent for cooking meat."

"You can't win," Michael Mulligan told him. "You will be defeated and possibly die."

General Stuart's intense stare and measured tone was unsettling. "I don't want to live if we are defeated," he said. "I have shed tears of mourning for too many brothers." Stuart held his eyes. "I hear Abe Lincoln is recruiting Negroes to fight."

"I heard that."

"No white man from the south will tolerate Negro soldiers. We will hang any white officer who leads them."

"Abe might hang a few of your officers, as well. Or enslave them."

Mulligan saw not anger but weariness in Jeb Stuart's eyes.

"You caught me by surprise at Brandy Station," he said. "I will not be surprised again." With a fluid motion, Jeb Stuart mounted his horse.

Moments later, Generals Stuart and Chambliss watched as the last of the wagons moved and the cavalry began its movement to the next Pennsylvania town, Dover. Mulligan could see the deep fatigue in Chambliss's eyes, but General Stuart seemed stronger, his eyes fueled by an inner fanaticism. From Dover, they would march toward Gettysburg.

Unafraid of gunfire, Jeb Stuart's warhorse shied when a dark spirit seemed to spring from the ground: the brown child, half Indian and half black, his ancient-looking face white with dust—the opaque eyes round and unblinking in the glare of the fire and burning torches.

"The great white generals ride out to battle," he said, in an unnaturally deep voice.

"You little urchin, step aside," an officer said. Stuart and Chambliss stared at the boy who kept rocking back and forth, shaking his hands while talking.

"General James Ewell Brown Stuart. Beware the battle of Yellow Tavern. Beware the lone soldier with a pistol."

"I don't plan to outlive the war," General Stuart said.

"How pretty Flora will mourn." The boy made theatrical sobs.

"We all mourn every day."

For a moment, Jeb Stuart imagined his widow, Flora, dressed in black—standing over his grave and the grave of the daughter they had lost.

The child pointed at General Chambliss.

"John R. Chambliss? Beware of Charles City Road."

"Someone shut that monkey prick up," a soldier said

Another soldier fired between the boy's legs. He began swiveling his hips, his eyes raised to the night sky.

"Beware Pickett's charge."

The boy pretended to be shot and pantomimed a grotesque dance of death until General Chambliss motioned with his hand and Private Cowley dragged the child to one side.

"You die tonight, Cowley," the boy screamed. "Down the road you die!"

In the moonlight, the cavalry moved forward on gaunt horses followed by the Confederate Irish Brigade, marching down the dark road and raising again the dry hot dust. Mulligan watched the retreating troops until he was alone. The silence seemed to envelop him. Then he started to walk toward Hanover. Suddenly, the filthy child blocked his path, looking like a demon against the glare and smoke.

"General Elon Farnsworth. Tell him to beware of Kilpatrick."

"We all have to beware Kilpatrick."

"And as for Custer?" The boy laughed harshly. "My people will kill him, the boy general with long pretty hair."

Michael Mulligan began walking.

"You are cursed to live," the boy yelled. He began dancing in a circle and started singing in a croaking voice: "Mulligan, Mulligan, waving his shillelagh, came to fight in the land of the free, died a blind old man bitten by fleas..."

Michael Mulligan continued on foot, following a peaceful moonlit road that led through flowering dogwood trees and farmland, the dead night air still hot. After an hour walking, he heard gunshots ahead. He started running, and then stopped when he saw a dead man beside the road. It was Private Cowley, shot through the left eye, possibly by a sniper. Mulligan searched and found Cowley's bony horse. He coaxed the animal closer, giving him a biscuit, and then mounted and galloped toward Hanover.

When he arrived at Hanover, he saw citizens clearing rubble, many houses blown apart or riddled with bullets. Bodies of Union and Confederate dead lay covered in an open field. A woman with thick white hair was serving porridge to people lining up, including a middle-aged black couple. A bonfire raged in the town square, giving the scene a hellish light.

"Where's the cavalry?"

"They rode out toward Gettysburg, a farming community," the woman said. "I'm Mrs. Henry Winebrenner, but call me Sally. You look like you could use some food, soldier."

"I do, but I need to find the telegraph office immediately."

"The lines are down," Mrs. Winebrenner said.

"Sally? The Armies of the Potomac and North Virginia are going to meet at Gettysburg and I have to warn General Meade. It will be a rendezvous in hell."

Michael Mulligan could already imagine it: thousands of men running into rifle and cannon fire, canister shot destroying marching infantry, and Farnsworth's cavalry following a fatal order by the arrogant Kilpatrick to ride over rough ground against a well-fortified hidden enemy. Even Michael Mulligan could not imagine the Wheat Field and the Union Irish Brigade caught in enfilading fire.

"The telegraph lines are down," Sally Winebrenner repeated. "Eat. Drink some water. I'd offer you a bed but my house got hit by a shell."

Michael Mulligan ate some rich porridge, and then took the tired horse to a stable. He found a man inside.

"My name is Michael Mulligan with the Union Cavalry. I need a fresh mount."

"The cavalry took all the horses, those that Elijah White didn't steal." The stout owner of the stable examined the underfed horse. In the light of the oil lamp, Mulligan's face was drawn and since the war began, the stableman had seen that dead stare before. "This horse is about worn out. I do have a pretty strong mule if you can git that son of a bitch to move."

"I can make anything with four legs move," Mulligan told him.

"Then take him off my hands."

"Thank you."

"Maybe you better get some sleep first."

"I could lie down for a minute," Mulligan said.

In the early morning darkness after fitful sleep, Michael Mulligan rode a mule toward Gettysburg. With the rising sun, he passed a stone farmhouse near uneven ground bordered by a stone wall, too high for horses to jump but low enough to aid and protect marksmen. There were thin trees in the distance. As the day grew warmer, Mulligan approached a ridge and felt the mule slowing down.

"Gwine, gwine, just a little farther, mule."

Mulligan could already see Farnsworth and Kilpatrick laughing as Mulligan, tamer of horses, rode a mule into camp. Then he heard the beating of hooves and turning, saw a Confederate soldier riding toward him. The soldier held up a pistol and commanded him to stop. Michael Mulligan held up his hands, hoping the soldier would see he was unarmed.

"Where's your army, Yank?"

"I don't know, Reb. You tell me. Where's *your* army?

As the rider came closer, Michael Mulligan could see fear in his eyes.

"Stay right where you are! Don't move! You are now a prisoner of General Heth."

For a brief moment, Mulligan saw a bright metal reflection from the ridge boulders. Then he heard a shot and the soldier grunted once, clutching his throat. Mulligan caught the bridle as the dying soldier slid from the horse. Union soldiers waved to Mulligan from the ridge. Up in the saddle, Mulligan spurred the horse to higher ground where dismounted cavalry took positions along the ridge. An officer approached him.

"Lieutenant Marcellus E. Jones," the officer said. "You are?"

"Michael Mulligan, Vermont Cavalry."

"Two enemy brigades are coming this way. We have to delay them until General Buford and General Reynolds reinforce us." The lieutenant stopped. "Where's your rifle?"

"Jeb Stuart has it. Lee's army must be close."

"Stuart *and* Lee? God save us."

They handed Michael Mulligan a Sharps carbine. Then Mulligan was lying on the hill, watching a copse of distant trees. An artillery battalion appeared and marched toward them. The dead soldier lay next to the now grazing mule. As the Rebels came closer, one of the men ran ahead to inspect the fallen soldier. While two soldiers loaded the dead man on the mule, the infantry continued up the hill. Michael Mulligan selected a target, an anonymous soldier beginning the climb. He had a young face and held his rifle before him. Dust and sweat stained his grey uniform. Mulligan heard the lieutenant's low voice: "Prepare to fire."

AFTERMATH

MICHAEL MULLIGAN WOKE UP with a blinding headache behind his eyes, and lifting his hand, felt the bandage on his right temple. He heard a soft female voice.

"You're awake, Mr. Mulligan. I am Abigail Donahue, but call me Abby. Happy Fourth of July."

He opened his eyes and saw a woman's face beneath a nurse's cap. She was young with clear brown eyes and dark curly hair. Mulligan heard muffled screams and groans, and sitting up, heard the pattern of heavy rain on canvas.

"Jesus, where am I?"

"In a hospital tent, next to a farm. You are very lucky. Another inch to my right and that rifle ball would've shattered your skull. You may have suffered a concussion from the fall." She examined his bandage and then his eyes in the light. "Your pupils aren't dilated. That's good. No broken bones. I'd say your body is strong and in good shape. I wish I could give you something for the headache."

Mulligan remembered the fatal charge over rocky ground cut with ditches and tree stumps. They had witnessed two battalions cut down and then, mounted and more vulnerable,

94

made a final slow charge against Alabama and Texas marksmen firing from behind a high wall. Mulligan saw General Farnsworth shot from the saddle. Then Mulligan was airborne, rushing toward the uneven rocky ground.

"Let me out of here," Mulligan said.

"When you feel ready. I have other patients, some not so lucky. We have Confederate soldiers, as well." The nurse gently squeezed his hand. "It's all over, now."

"I have unfinished business, Abby." Mulligan said.

"You are not allowed to threaten enemy prisoners. You are all equal, now, Mr. Mulligan."

"I won't threaten Rebs. I want to shoot General Kilpatrick for a suicidal order."

"Maybe all the generals should be shot." Nurse Abby watched his face and after a moment said, "You know, when you're feeling better, we could use help."

"I've done this work before."

"You must tell me about it."

Abby suddenly left to help a man limping from the tent. He was crying while a doctor led him. "No, please."

"That leg is gangrenous," the doctor said. "It has to come off."

Mulligan lay back on the cot, his head throbbing.

"I'm next," a southern voice said. Mulligan saw a young Rebel solder lying on the next cot. His left arm was swollen and turning black. The young man's face was tinged blue from powder blowback.

"Damn, I can smell it."

"So can I. My name is Mulligan."

"Private Joe Perry, Texas infantry. I was behind that wall when you guys charged us on them pretty horses. I thought it was a damn fool order, myself. You can't manoeuver a horse on that kinda ground."

"No, you can't."

"I think you whipped us, Mulligan." They heard the man screaming outside. "Damn, don't they got nothin' for the pain?"

"Chloroform," Mulligan said. "He's just screaming at the thought of what they're going to do."

"I don't blame him none." The screams stopped, and they heard the heavy downpour. "That nurse is real pretty."

"She is."

Private Perry lay back against the wall, his face pale. "Maybe she can hold my hand."

"She will."

"Think I'd rather lose a leg," Perry said.

Michael Mulligan got up and walked to the opening of the tent. Sheets of rain blew across the rocky ground. He could see men with mules pulling dead horses from the muddy field, and looking toward Gettysburg, Mulligan saw many dead lying in the open areas and near the fences where they fell. Two mules dragged a horse that belonged to General Farnsworth. Mulligan had trained the general's horse; he didn't see his own mount, but remembered standing in the saddle and firing his Spencer at the stone wall before a barrage took them both. Perhaps it was his bullet that hit Perry's arm.

Mulligan stepped outside and felt the rain. The soldier with the gangrenous leg was unconscious. They had placed him on a door, and two men held him while a doctor sawed off his leg. Amputated legs and arms lay in a pile near a tree. Next to the tent was a stone farmhouse. Michael Mulligan began walking across the field, rain soaking him. Mulligan stepped over the bodies of dead Confederate and Union soldiers, stiff and swelling. Many of the dead were barefoot. A man with a large camera prepared to photograph the carnage. Another man was propping the body of a dead Rebel sniper against a rock near Devil's Den. It would make a dramatic photo.

Mulligan suddenly felt nauseated and found a boulder under a tree where he sat down. Closing his eyes, images of the fatal charge came back to him, only it was hot and the sun was blinding. He remembered Farnsworth arguing with General Kilpatrick who called him a coward, and then General Elon Farnsworth saying "I will do it," leading the charge that killed him and many of his men and horses. How many had survived?

Mulligan pressed his fingers to his eyes. He could see General Kilpatrick's arrogant smirk. There was a rumor that Judson Kilpatrick was writing a romantic novel about the conflict. Perhaps Mulligan could blow his head off at an author's signing. He would stand in line with a copy of the book for the great general's autograph.

"Ah General, I love your book, *The Blue and the Gray.* It has the perfume of honeysuckle and magnolias wafting through its pages."

Smiling, the general would look up, pen in hand. Then he would see the shotgun. Mulligan was still thinking about ways to kill the general when he heard someone calling his name. He saw Major William Wells, another officer who led the charge against the Texas and Alabama lines. Major Wells dismounted. He had brown hair and a thick beard.

"I am so glad to see you alive, Major."

"I am glad to see you, Captain Mulligan. Happy Independence Day."

They shook hands.

"You were hit?"

"Grazed my temple, but I'll survive."

"I've been very lucky," Major Wells said. "I marvel that I survived the charge."

"How many did we lose?"

"We had only forty left of General Farnsworth's brigade."

Mulligan cursed. "I will kill Kilpatrick," he said.

"I am writing a report. You can add something if you like."

"I will."

"Tonight, we leave to hunt down what's left of Lee's army."

"General Lee escaped?"

"Yes." William Wells then gave Mulligan a report of all that happened on the third day of fighting. It was the end to a brutal three day battle. "Pickett and two other generals launched an attack up the middle and were destroyed. It was revenge for Fredericksburg. A massacre."

The rain was suddenly lighter and Michael Mulligan watched the photographer shooting photos of the dead strewn on the field.

"I can't say that makes me feel better," Mulligan said.

"I hear even Federals got tired of shooting Rebs."

"We lost General Elon Farnsworth…a good man."

"I just heard that." William Wells took off his cap. "He was a fine officer," he said. "We would have lost more if General Buford didn't secure the higher ground. Can you ride with us, tonight?"

"No. I need more time."

Major Wells embraced him.

"Get your rest, Mulligan. When I come back, you can ride with me. It would be an honor."

"Thank you."

"Close by, there's a little dog guarding some dead soldiers. What a sad sight."

The two men embraced again and William Wells mounted his horse and rode across the muddy field. Mulligan walked toward the farmhouse and the hospital tent. Near the tent, he found a young boy weeping.

"You lost someone?"

"We lost Sallie," the boy said. "I carried the colors of the 11th Pennsylvania, and Sallie ran with me. She hated Rebs, Democrats and women. Sallie didn't come back after the first day of fighting."

"Sallie's a dog?"

"Yes—a bull terrier," the boy said. "She's our mascot. She grew up with the company."

"What's your name, Son?"

"Caleb."

"Come with me, Caleb."

It was behind Big Round Top where they found many fallen soldiers from the 11th Pennsylvania. Guarding them was a pug-nosed dog, starved and dehydrated; the dog bared its teeth as they approached.

"It's okay," Mulligan said. "You've done your job."

The dog made a few weak yelps as Caleb rushed past Mulligan.

"Sallie," he yelled. "Sallie!"

The boy took the trembling dog in his arms. Mulligan poured water from his canteen into the palm of his hand and gave Sallie a drink.

"We'll bury these brave men," Mulligan said.

When he returned, he met Nurse Abby and saw an urgency in her eyes. She touched his arm.

"Mr. Mulligan, I could use your help."

"My pleasure."

Private Perry was lying on the bloody door, and Mulligan could see his fear. The doctor held a saw, his hands bloody. Nurse Abby motioned that Michael Mulligan should hold the man down, even when unconscious. Perry was sweating in the grey light.

"Damn—I'm not ready for this, Yank."

"Whoever is? What hand do you chop wood with?"

"My right."

"Okay, Joe, we have to take off your left arm. You can still play with yourself."

Perry laughed. "That sounds about right."

"Tell me about your girl back home, Joe. And then I'll tell you about the girl I took from Ireland and how I stole her from a bad husband."

Perry started talking about a beautiful woman he knew in Texas who had large breasts and thick blonde hair and on the day they announced their wedding, the governor declared Texas was going to secede from the union. They were at war.

"What was her name?"

"Gloria," Perry said.

"Gloria? That's a pretty name, Joe."

Nurse Abby placed a cloth soaked in chloroform over the young man's face and his voice trailed off. Mulligan pressed on Perry's shoulders as the doctor worked quickly, using two surgical knives, one for cutting tissue and the second for sawing through bone. Perry started screaming and the nurse applied more chloroform. The doctor cut off the arm below the elbow and gave the limb to another doctor; he then sewed a flap over the wound and applied a yellowish amber powder to the site. At one point, Mulligan saw Abby staring at him as he stepped away.

Someone offered him a drink of whiskey which he drank; it made him feel better. Then Mulligan found himself helping the wounded at other hospitals, some in tents, others in churches and farm houses. He followed Abby and another young nurse named Tillie. In Letterman Hospital, they confronted a head nurse named Mrs. Bachman; she was short, fat, with iron-gray hair, and gave orders in a shrill voice. She pulled Nurse Abby to one side.

"Who is that?"

"Mr. Michael Mulligan. He's our new Irish assistant," Abby said.

"Irish?"

Mulligan could feel the head nurse's disapproval, but he was needed to hold down men losing limbs, and for carrying the sick and the dead. The dead numbered in the thousands.

Walking back from Letterman Hospital, Nurse Abby smiled at Mulligan and he could see the appreciation in her eyes. He felt Tillie's admiration, as well.

"You're a good worker," Abby said, "and sympathetic with the sick. I have a male friend in Washington who is kind and compassionate with the wounded. His name is Walt Whitman. You know him?"

"No. Should I?"

"He's a fine poet. He beautifully describes the body electric…he loves life and worships the beauty of women…and men."

"Really, now? He writes in sweet rhymes?"

"No. He doesn't rhyme. It's all free verse. "

"I shall look for his work."

"His book of poems is called *Leaves of Grass*."

They walked on. He suddenly realized Abby was watching him closely.

"Yes?"

"Tell me about your former experience in this gruesome work."

"A place called Grosse Isle. I landed there in a coffin ship after leaving Ireland. Thousands died from ship fever."

"Typhus, I believe."

"Perhaps later I can talk about it."

"You lost someone?" Mulligan didn't answer. "I'm afraid Mrs. Bachman has a prejudice against the Irish, but you will have a private tent. The food isn't great but it's served in the Slyder farmhouse. Poor man. He had such a peaceful life, and now his farm and city have been hit with a disaster."

That night, Mulligan visited Private Joe Perry. He was quiet, lying in the bed, his eyes closed though he was awake. "Good evening, Mr. Perry."

"I got nothin' to say, Mulligan. Except my damn arm hurts...even though it's done gone."

"I'll see if Abby has anything."

"I hate this war," Perry said.

"So do I. You want me to write to your girl?"

"No. That's over anyway," Perry said. "The bitch."

Later that night, Michael Mulligan lay on his cot waiting for sleep when he heard someone knocking on the tent.

"Come in," he said.

It was Nurse Abby carrying an oil lamp. He liked her handsome features in the soft light, and she had loosened the hair that now flowed over her shoulders.

"You might be careful of Mrs. Bachman," he said. "Dangerous to visit an Irishman late at night."

Nurse Abby opened a medical bag.

"An Irishman who needs to have his dressing changed. There's a big danger of infection in these camps, particularly since no one takes the danger seriously." She sat on a stool and undid his dressing. Abby examined the ugly scar along his temple and bathed it with a stinging liquid. Then she applied another clean dressing. Mulligan liked her close presence and the feel of her light but strong fingers.

"Nurse Tillie Pierce finds you attractive, Mr. Mulligan, even if you *are* a bit old for her."

"Forty-three is old?"

"I am sure Mrs. Bachman will be watching you closely."

"I have no interest in Mrs. Bachman. Too ugly."

Abby laughed. "That's not what I meant."

"I know. And I'll have new orders, soon."

Abby met his eyes and he was surprised by the steady focus of her gaze.

"Tell me about Grosse Isle."

Michael Mulligan told her about his escape from Ireland during the famine with the wife of a cruel Anglo Irish landlord, and how they arrived at Grosse Isle, ready for a new life until she took sick. He told her how he buried her in an old churchyard, and then volunteered to work with the sick and dying who arrived daily on the infected ships.

"Her name?"

"Maria. Maria Burke."

"So you stole another man's wife...and she was the one true love of your life?"

Mulligan thought he heard a slight sarcastic tone.

"I thought so. Maybe you can't understand because you've never had a man really love you."

He expected her to blush but she didn't. "Oh I have, Mulligan."

"You haven't saved yourself for marriage, Abby?"

She ignored his comment, and Mulligan felt something secret and unspoken between them.

"Continue your story," she finally said.

Mulligan continued. "I am a wanted man back in Ireland, but someday I will return and kill her evil husband. I will never forgive the English for what they did when the famine hit. It gave them a chance to rid Ireland of the Irish."

"Mr. Mulligan?"

"Call me Michael."

"That's too familiar. I like your last name. It sounds like a stew...good to eat."

"I see."

"You have a lot of anger. It's not healthy, Mulligan. I've learned to cope with my anger."

"What are you angry about?"

Mulligan could not read her expression in the flickering light, her eyes revealing little.

"We can discuss that later. Where did you get that scar in your lower abdomen?"

Mulligan was surprised. "How did you know about that?"

"I examined your body looking for any wounds."

"Abigail Donahue, what would the holy sisters think?"

"My parents weren't religious. I never had nuns in school."

"An Irish girl like you, Donahue?"

"I'm a Scot. I am also a nurse. A body is a body and it has many body parts. You have nothing I haven't seen before."

"When do I get to examine your body?"

Nurse Abby slipped into a stage Irish accent. "Begorra, but for sure, lusty ole' Mulligan would love that." Before he could reply, Abby stood up. "I better go. Nurse Bachman will be prowling the camp with her lantern, searching for drunks and fornicators."

"I got the wound in a knife fight with a jealous Irish Traveler."

Abby nodded with approval. "My, my, Mr. Mulligan, you *are* a dashing rogue. And you are lucky, not only after that cavalry charge, but after the knife fight. A bit lower and you would be unmanned."

"I hurt him more."

"I bet you did. I'm not sure if eunuchs and females share the same indignities: inferior beings with no rights to own property without a man—often weak and undependable—and no right to choose a higher destiny or even to vote."

"Why would women want to vote?"

He felt the sudden heat of her direct stare. "Half the country in this democracy locked in a brutal civil war for the birth of a new freedom can't vote. Does that not seem *ironic*, Mr. Mulligan?"

"Perhaps. Nurse Abby, no need to be bitter."

He waited for her to argue but she remained silent. Then she spoke without looking at him: "Good night, Mulligan. We will talk again. And good work, today. I need a helper with a strong stomach."

Abby left the tent. Michael Mulligan lay back on the cot. Suddenly, her face appeared in the tent opening. "I *am* sorry about your lover, Maria."

Then she was gone.

The next morning Mulligan continued his work with Nurse Abby, tending to the sick and comforting men during the amputations. While exiting a hospital tent, he saw Mrs. Bachman, her piercing eyes like blue seeds in a fleshy face. She handed him a paper.

"Tomorrow, you have a new assignment, Mr. Mulligan. Report to David Wills."

"And who is David Wills?"

"He's an important Gettysburg citizen. You will have plenty of work, believe me." For just a moment, Michael Mulligan thought he saw a malevolent smile on her protruding lips. "You Irish brutes sweat like slave niggers, correct?"

"Absolutely," Mulligan said. "Say good-bye for me to Tillie and Abby."

"You don't need to talk to them. They are silly girls."

"Have you never been a silly girl, Mrs. Bachman?"

"Once. I gave an Irish beggar in Boston some money and he robbed me."

Mrs. Bachman left him. As Mulligan walked toward Gettysburg, he saw Nurse Abby in the distance. She saw him and waved, and was still smiling when Mrs. Bachman shouted an order and Nurse Abby turned away.

The town of Gettysburg had been raked with rifle and cannon fire. Cannon balls were stuck in the sides of some houses. Mulligan met David Wills in a plush lawyer's office. He was a tall man with intense dark eyes, high cheek bones and a thick black beard.

"I have a daunting task, Mr. Mulligan. It is finding, sorting and identifying the dead. It's a gruesome painstaking job. We will have to buy land and create a National Cemetery. I know your division will come for you soon, but until then, if you can help, it will be appreciated. It's a sordid mess out there. Dead bodies still rotting, some with no uniforms or identification. We don't know north from south in some cases. And as Nurse Abby probably told you, there's the danger of disease."

"You do not want cholera," Michael Mulligan said.

"No, we do not. You will have a private room in town and you'll supervise a detail of workers. I admire what your soldiers have done, but at what a cost. Thousands dead, maimed or missing." David Wills held out his hand. "Can I count on you to start tomorrow?"

Mulligan shook his hand. "Yes, but let me stay another night at the hospital tent."

"Of course."

"And one more favor. Transfer that awful Nurse Bachman somewhere else."

David Wills was not surprised. "Frightful woman," he said. "I'll see what I can do."

That night, Michael Mulligan carried a torch and walked around the battlefield. He could smell death. Inside his tent, illuminated with an oil lamp, Michael Mulligan lay on the cot under a sheet and thought about Nurse Abby. He was remembering her eyes and the fullness of her lips when he heard the light knock.

"Are you decent?"

"Beast that I am, I am always decent," he said.

Wearing a long cape, Nurse Abby entered the tent.

"Time to check my dressing?"

"And other things." She pulled up a stool and began to remove his bandage. "You're leaving us tomorrow?"

"Yes."

"It's hard work but necessary. Cleaning up from the aftermath of three days of slaughter."

"I have a private room in town," Mulligan told her.

"I know. Why didn't you stay there, tonight?"

"Maybe I wanted to see you…to change my dressing, of course."

He waited for her to respond but she looked at him with eyes that held private thoughts. Then she examined the fresh scar, cleaning it carefully.

"The famine ended in 1850. What happened after that?"

"I went to San Francisco, worked in theatre, met a woman named Emily O' Rourke, we had a child…and she died. "

"How did she die?"

"In childbirth. A hemorrhage."

Abby listened, her face calm in the lamplight. "I think I know why. And the child?"

"A boy. I haven't seen him since I left. John is eight, now."

"You must see him when this is over. John is cared for?"

"An elderly couple called the Maguires. Why are you asking, Nurse Abby?"

"I'm curious, Mr. Mulligan." She applied a fresh dressing to his head. "Now, do you have any dizziness, problems with balance, nausea?"

"No."

"Good. Do you have nightmares?"

"I have bad dreams, yes."

"I brought something for you. In moderation, it may help."

"Opium?"

"No."

Abby took out a flask of whiskey and handed it to him. After a silence, he asked: "Why are you here in my tent?"

"I hate to admit this, Mr. Mulligan, but I find you fascinating. Most men are rather simple. In fact, I don't really *like* most men, though I need them now and then and hate myself for it."

"Need them for what?"

For the first time, Abby showed her impatience. "Mr. Mulligan, *please* don't tell me you are that naïve or narrow in your view of women."

"Sorry. No plans to find a husband, then?"

She lowered her eyes. "No plans," she said quietly. "I trust you have physical needs?"

"I'm a man," he said. Mulligan took a long swig of the whiskey, feeling it burning in his throat. "You are a remarkable woman, Nurse Abby."

"Why's that?"

"You are…different."

"Yes," she said. "I am different. Sometimes I puzzle myself."

She took back the flask and placed her lips over the opening, taking a dainty sip. "I fear Nurse Bachman will be crashing in here any second."

Mulligan took out his .44 Colt pistol. "Let her."

"No violence, Mulligan. As my friend Whitman says, we need more love."

"He sounds a bit queer."

"He is a bit queer. If Walt were here, he'd probably offer to release some of your sexual tension."

"My God," Mulligan said. He covered his face. "A degenerate."

Abby laughed. "I thought that would disturb you."

"You shouldn't know about such things."

"Shouldn't I?"

She leaned forward and he saw the top of her breasts. Her long brown hair hung loose around her face and over her shoulders. The cape had opened slightly revealing bare thighs.

"Perhaps I better go."

"No. Stay."

He sat on the cot facing her. "I believe Mrs. Bachman thinks I'm a brute."

Abby smiled. "You *are* a brute. I like brutes."

They heard somewhere in the camp a soldier playing a mournful sounding harmonica. Mulligan and Abby faced one another in the lamplight, and Mulligan felt his mouth go suddenly dry. Her eyes were dark, observing him but revealing nothing.

"Do I make you nervous, Mulligan?"

"Maybe you do. Abby? May I ask a question?"

"Ask anything you want."

"Are you wearing anything under that cape?"

"I am." She stood up. "Would you like to see?"

"I would."

Nurse Abby pulled apart and dropped the cape, revealing a thin slip that fell just below her waist. He could see the outline of her small but firm breasts, the nipples prominent, her thighs slightly apart.

"By Christ," he said.

"I saw your naked body, so perhaps it's only fair you see mine. But first—"

She tossed him a packet that held a condom. "Nothing happens tonight without it."

He held the packet in his palm. "I hate these things. I lose the mood. Then I can't even get them on."

"We don't have to do anything, but if we do—I can help you."

Mulligan watched her for what seemed minutes. A sentry was passing by the tent, and they heard a slight wind rising. Abby stood in the glow of the oil lamp and at some point, pulled the slip over her head, dropping it to her feet. Mulligan stared at her small but firm body, the female curves no longer hidden by the ugly baggy uniform. His eyes traveled up her thighs to the triangle of dark hair and then over her breasts until he met her eyes. Abby watched him, neither afraid nor shy, her eyes glowing with anticipation and joy. Mulligan tore open the packet. Then she knelt down and pulled away the sheet, revealing his nakedness. Abby observed his body in the flickering light. Carefully, she took the rubber from his hand and placed it in her mouth. She lowered her head.

When Michael Mulligan awoke, he was lying on bedding on the floor. He reached to his side but Nurse Abby was gone. His fingers closed on a book. It was *Leaves of Grass* by Walt Whitman. He remembered the feel of her body and her strong hands holding his wrists and he recalled sucking on her nipples as she suddenly moaned, her body trembling. Then he felt a release that had been denied so long. It may have been a dream but he also remembered a blobby shape outlined against the tent, but after this disturbing vision, there was only darkness.

He ate with others at the Slyder farm, both Abby and Tillie missing. He was about to leave for the battlefield when head nurse Bachman, wearing a billowing cage crinoline dress, pushed her way into the farmhouse. She blocked Mulligan, screaming in his face:

"I know your game, you filthy Irish! Where's your whore? I'll have you both flogged and thrown in prison!"

"Watch your mouth, Bachman."

Mulligan walked outside and saw a horse drinking from a water trough. Bachman followed him, shrieking in German. Then she switched to English.

"I know what you're doing, and it won't work!"

"I'm afraid it will," a woman's voice said. They saw Nurse Abby standing on the lower step holding a slip of paper. "Mrs. Bachman, you've been transferred."

"You little trollop, you dare talk to me like that? I saw you sneaking out of his tent at 4:00 in the morning!"

"Then lodge a complaint."

Nurse Bachman grabbed the note and read it quickly.

"I think you have work to do, Mr. Mulligan."

Mulligan tipped his hat. "I do. Thanks."

As he walked away, he heard Bachman shouting followed by a loud splash. He turned and saw her struggling to get out of the water trough, but she was stuck, her voice still screaming in German and English. Mulligan walked on. An hour later, he addressed the men Wills had assembled.

"We will separate the dead by state and division, if we can. You will find dead men and body parts with no identification, and those we will separate, as well. Shoot any scavenging pigs. Here are the locations. I know where to start: the 11th Pennsylvania."

Under Mulligan's supervision, citizen details laid corpses in rows. Different units carried the dead to a separate field where they were tagged and prepared for an ambulance. The Union dead would repose in the National Cemetery. The Confederate dead were left on the field to be buried wherever convenient or until claimed. Many of the bodies were decomposing rapidly, the uniforms faded if they had uniforms, and some dead were buried under dirt and rubble. Crows watched them from the trees. As they collected the dead soldiers, Mulligan knew it would take weeks to clear the battlefield of the dead. Some would never be identified.

That night, Michael Mulligan ate in a Gettysburg restaurant recently opened near the house where he had a private back room. The work had drained him, and his headaches were intense. He didn't know how long he could pull dead soldiers from the soggy earth. After a cup of coffee and some wine, he felt better, and then he left the restaurant. He waited on the corner, looking toward the house. He saw Nurse Abby in civilian clothes walking down the street. Mulligan motioned to her. Then he walked around the house and opened the door to his small room; it had a wide bed, a wash basin and a chair. He opened a back door and let Abby in. She was happy and smiling. They kissed and walked quickly to the room. Inside, she stepped from her clothes.

It was a pattern they kept for the next two weeks, the lives they lived by day and by night: passionate carnal moments suspended between the unburied dead and the blood and shit and screams of the wounded. After sex, they would talk in the darkness; Abby told him about her anarchist parents and how she finally found a philosophy she could embrace, the Transcendentalism of Emerson and Thoreau. He told her about growing up as an Irish Gypsy Traveler, sometimes called "tinkers," and about joining an Irish troupe of traveling actors, developing his love of theatre. Later, he discovered his skill with horses.

"And that's how you became the stable boy for this Burke fellow?"

"Yes. I taught Nathaniel's wife how to ride."

"I bet you did. Why don't you ride me?"

Some nights, they paused to read Whitman aloud, and Mulligan marveled at Whitman's American voice, so rugged and free. But mostly in the partial darkness, they spent themselves with furious physical coupling, holding each other, tasting each other, throwing off the sheets by morning. She would leave first, kissing him good-bye. Once he grabbed her and held tightly.

"I love you," he told her.

She pulled away. "Don't say that. We will have to separate, and soon. That will hurt enough. Enjoy my body but don't fall in love."

"It's too late for that."

"We don't have much time."

"I know," he said. "We don't."

She gently touched his face and kissed his forehead. "Mulligan, you poor boy."

Sometimes they met at noon, both of them returning from work and eating quickly, only to work again. At lunch, they tried to avoid too much eye contact. Once he found Nurse Abby instructing a new team of nurses who would be traveling to another battlefield. Mulligan tipped his hat to the young women who smiled at him. Nurse Abby whispered in his ear: "I can still taste you." As he walked away, she warned the nurses about "horizontal refreshments."

The ending came sooner than either expected.

One night, Abby didn't show up at Mulligan's room. Then Tillie was knocking on the door and telling Mulligan that he had to go back to the hospital tent, now being cleared as the remaining patients awaited transfer elsewhere. Mulligan walked into the tent and saw Abby and knew the end had begun.

"Private Perry wants to see you."

"I thought they discharged him."

"They did," Abby said. "But he came back with a high fever. There's nothing we can do."

"Why does he want to see me?"

Michael Mulligan found Private Perry on one of the last beds. Perry's face was pale and he was sweating heavily. Mulligan could see the eyes bright with fever. Nurse Abby put some powder into a drink and gave it to Perry; he managed a smile.

"Bitter, but I feel good." He regarded Mulligan. "Hey, Yankee, I want to dictate a letter to my girl, Gloria Bullock. You write it down and send it general delivery to Palestine, Texas."

Mulligan didn't ask why he was needed over Abby to take dictation, but when the delirious Joe Perry began, Mulligan noticed how Perry's language became inflated and self-consciously poetic.

"Dear Gloria," Perry began. "As golden light shines athwart the sky, I know I'm hearing the black crow of death calling in the Stygian night. I will not live to see your shining eyes, my darling Gloria. I will join the annals that list the names of martyred heroes, soon turned to dust. Just remember that I loved you most of all." Then Joe's voice slipped into a more natural diction. "I love you forever, Gloria. Your man, Joe."

Mulligan wrote down the words.

"Maybe you can add to that, Mulligan. Make it sound real lofty. Then you got to place it in Gloria's hands. You know how bad the mail is with the war."

"I can add lines, Joe," Mulligan said. "But why don't you deliver the letter yourself?"

He heard Joe's laughter rattling in his chest. "Cause I'm dead. Take my hammer to the captain, tell'm I'm done gone."

That night, Joe Perry died of a spreading infection. Abby held his hand.

Outside the tent, Mulligan felt Abby's silence and caught her watching him. She began to cry.

"What's wrong?"

"I got an order to report to the hospital in Washington, D.C. Walt Whitman works there, but guess who else runs that place?"

"Nurse Bachman?"

"Yes. But I am tougher that she is."

"Give me your address. I will find you and we can run off."

"When hostilities cease," Abby insisted. "A cousin in D.C. holds my mail."

"I have only one address…in San Francisco. Please don't share it."

They exchanged addresses and embraced.

"Jesus, when do you leave?"

"Tomorrow." Then he felt her strong hands holding his arms, the eyes large and luminous, boring through him with a fierce urgency. "We must make love one last time—tonight!"

"It won't be the last time," he told her. "It can't be."

And then she was stepping out of her baggy uniform displaying her lovely body in the lamplight, finally lying on the bed and waiting for him to undress. This small wallpapered room would be their final trysting place. Naked, he climbed on top of her, watching her eyes, seizing her wrists. Then he reached toward his pants on the floor.

"No protection, tonight," Abby said. "I want you to come inside me. I want to conceive your child."

"Think about it, Abby. An unwed mother in these times?"

"It's my decision."

"Abigail, I told you I was wanted in Ireland and England. They might find me."

"I don't think they'll arrest you here." He felt her probing hands.

"I'm wanted by a secret society that assassinated English landlords. When I ran off with Maria, I abandoned them. They're called the Whiteboys and they never forget. They could find me and you and *any* of my children."

"I have a few secrets too—so I'll take that chance."

They embraced and he pushed inside her.

She was gone early the next morning and when Mulligan arrived at the tent, Abby had left for the train depot. He ran to the station after giving instructions to his foreman, and found Abby on the platform waiting to board the train to D.C. She saw him, but he couldn't read her expression.

"I didn't want to see you again," she told him. "I felt it would be too painful. But I'm so glad you're here."

She began to cry, and Mulligan felt tears in his eyes. They embraced, kissing, even as the conductor asked all passengers to board. His voice was a flat monotone: "All aboard. All aboard."

"Write to me," Mulligan said. "Please write to me."

"I will. And you write to me."

"After this is over, I will find you, Abby. I will track you down and we'll be together."

"It's a pleasant thought." She held him to her. "I love you, Michael."

Surprised, Mulligan said, "You called me by my first name."

"I did. It feels right, now—because I love you."

"And I love you, Abigail Donahue."

The conductor called again and Abigail Donahue pulled and away and boarded the train. Mulligan didn't see her in the window as the train pulled out. That would have been unbearable. Walking back to the camp, he felt the emptiness described so often in romantic novels, but his pain of separation went deeper.

For the rest of the day, he directed his crew as they found fewer bodies and body parts, most of them unidentifiable, and bones eaten clean and scattered. Mulligan felt himself in a trance. He was still feeling Abby's sweetness on his mouth and feeling her trembling naked body and remembering her cries of love, wondering if he'd ever see her again. Without her, he could never return to their small room. Their melodrama was complete.

An officer waited for him as he left the field.

"Captain Michael Mulligan of the Vermont Brigade?"

"Yes."

"You have new orders," the officer said. "You will join what's left of Kelly's Irish Brigade and travel to New York. There's a draft riot in progress. They are killing citizens and lynching Negroes in the streets. President Lincoln wants order restored."

Michael Mulligan read the orders. "Who is rioting?" he asked.

"The Irish," the officer said.

Mulligan took the train to New York that night. They passed through small towns, some affected by the war. The train was full of Union troops and a few soldiers loudly commented on the irony that they were sending Irish to shoot the Irish.

"I don't like shooting me own kind."

"They're just angry freed niggers might take their jobs."

Mulligan wasn't listening. He was seeing Nurse Abby's face as she appeared on that first morning, her eyes dark and large, her lips full, the smile welcoming him back to health and sanity.

THE FALL OF RICHMOND

SNOW COVERED THE TRACKS as the troop train rolled into Washington D.C. The snow hid much of the dirt and soot of the bustling town, but in the summer, citizens would smell the open sewers. Michael Mulligan saw through the window that Washington was an armed camp, with trenches for sharp shooters and cannons aimed at Virginia. The Confederacy would not risk another bold attack on the nation's capital again.

Michael Mulligan got off the train, carrying a military bag, one suitcase and his Spencer carbine. His blue uniform had faded, and though still a soldier, Mulligan had to present identification to the guards patrolling the station. A young soldier examined his military papers. "Little Phil Sheridan's cavalry, eh?"

"Yes."

"Hear you got Jeb Stuart."

"It was a foot soldier," Mulligan said. "Lucky shot with a pistol at 50 yards."

"The Rebs can't last much longer," the soldier said.

The air was crisp and cold, and Michael Mulligan felt a vibrant festive spirit as citizens and soldiers walked past him.

Perhaps they knew the war was ending, even after the slaughter of Federal troops at Cold Harbor, a southern revenge for Gettysburg. Abraham Lincoln was reelected and the war would continue to its finish.

Passing a store window, Mulligan saw himself. He had lost 15 pounds and his face was more gaunt than he ever remembered. He recognized that hollow dead look he saw in other soldiers' eyes. It did not take many battles or much death to poison a man's sense of inner well-being.

But I am happy, he insisted to himself. *I am going to see Abigail Donahue, the woman I love.*

He did not want to remember that she had not answered any of his letters since they parted at the Gettysburg station a year and four months ago. But then, perhaps they were lost in the mail, and the Maguires never received them at his San Francisco address. If Abby had indeed become pregnant from their last time together, that child would now be seven months old.

On a map, Mulligan found the address Abby had given him that day on the railroad platform. Her cousin's name was John Kavanaugh, and he would know which hospital Nurse Abby worked. Mulligan walked across the crowded bridge over the Potomac and found the neighborhood where Kavanaugh's boarding house sat. A singer somewhere was singing Stephen Foster's "Hard Times" in a rich plaintive baritone:

"There's a pale drooping maiden toiled her life away
With a worn out heart, her better days are o'er
Though her song should be joyful, she sighs every day,
Oh hard times, come again no more.
Tis a song, a sigh of the weary
Hard times, hard times,
Come again no more
Many days you have lingered all around my cabin door
Oh hard times, come again no more."

The voice faded. For just a moment, Mulligan wondered just how hard times had been for Abigail. Mulligan knew she had a tough core. He had seen enough war to create nights of sweat and days filled with terror.

He walked up the stairs and knocked on the door. A tall thin older woman wearing a black dress and bonnet answered.

"And what can I do for you, soldier boy?"

"My name's Michael Mulligan. I'm looking for John Kavanaugh."

Her face was taut and she squinted at him. "John Kavanaugh. Never heard of him, so he didn't board here."

"I was given this address. I sent some letters here."

"For Kavanaugh?"

"For an Abigail Donahue."

The woman scowled. "Now see here, which one do you want?"

"Either. Or both. Actually, I want to see Abigail."

"She doesn't live here either. Sorry."

Michael Mulligan stood on the steps, suddenly feeling alone and isolated. He would soon report to General Sheridan in the final hunt for General Lee. Finding Abigail Donahue had become his obsession.

"Was Kavanaugh a Federal soldier?"

"I don't know," Mulligan said. "Abby is a nurse. We met at Gettysburg."

"Search the hospitals. We got a lot of them."

After a moment, Mulligan looked down the busy street. The sun had come out but it was still cold.

"The house is full, but later I may have a room if you need one."

"I could use a room," Mulligan said.

"I don't rent to soldiers, usually, but I need the money."

"I've also worked with horses and I've worked the theatre."

"An actor visits here sometimes. You can leave your stuff and come back in an hour. I'll see if I can get the room ready. You sound Irish. Are you a Catholic?"

"I know the religion."

"And you say your name is Mulligan?"

"Yes."

"My name is Mary."

Michael Mulligan left to find a tavern. As he ate lunch and drank a beer, he ran through scenarios. Perhaps something happened when Abby returned to D.C. Perhaps her ugly head nurse, Mrs. Bachman, sent her somewhere else. Had Kavanaugh been drafted and sent to the front lines? Was he lost in a battle?

But she never sent me a single letter, he thought. *Perhaps it was only meant to be a brief romance. And she admitted to secrets she never revealed.*

Mulligan also knew he had to write more letters to his son, John, now nine. After lunch, Michael Mulligan visited two hospitals. In the first, they didn't know Abby or Mrs. Bachman. In the second, they knew Walt Whitman.

"I think he's gone to find his brother who was wounded," a nurse said. "I believe there's an Abigail Donahue at the local convent. They had a typhoid epidemic."

He knocked on the door of the convent and a tall stately nun answered. She was in her late fifties and seemed startled when he asked about Abigail Donahue.

"Donahue? How did you know that name?"

"It was the one she gave me."

"*She* gave you? And who are you?"

He told her.

"You're a relative?"

"No."

"Then how did you know her?"

"Well, sister, we worked together. We were…close."

"Close?" He could see the nun's stern and shocked expression. "And where and when was this?"

"A hospital at Gettysburg last July."

"That's impossible."

"Ask her. Is she here?"

For a brief moment, Mulligan saw a change in the nun's eyes. "She passed on, Mr. Mulligan."

He felt something drop inside him. "She's gone?"

"Typhoid fever." Before he could stammer another question, the nun said, "Abigail O' Donahue was a nun serving with us…but we knew her as Sister Anne."

"A nun. I guess I have the wrong Abigail Donahue. Sorry."

"It's understandable."

Mulligan hesitated. "Sister, is it possible another nurse worked here...maybe with the same name?"

"No," the nun said.

He tipped his hat and left the convent. Walking along a street, a newsboy stopped him. He was around 15 with red hair, freckles and green eyes. "Got the latest news, sir."

"I'll take one," Mulligan said.

The paper had the latest war bulletins; General Sherman was beginning his brutal march to the sea, destroying Southern homes and crops. Mulligan saw an advertisement for a New York benefit performance of *Julius Caesar* starring for the first and only time, all three Booth brothers: Edwin, John and Junius. It would be good to see a stage play and meet Edwin Booth, again.

Mulligan watched the newsboy run down the street, hawking his papers and looking too much like the young Irish looter who ran at him in New York brandishing a bayonet on a broom handle. On the same street, a black man hung from a street lamp. There had been that terrible moment when Mulligan lifted his carbine, yelling a warning at the charging youth.

Mulligan remembered his mission. "Abby, where the hell are you?" he said aloud.

At the rooming house, Mary had a room. "It ain't much but it's clean."

"Thanks."

"I found these in the basement. Your name sounded familiar."

Mary held up a small box and inside lay ten unopened letters written by Michael Mulligan to Abigail Donahue. He put the box on a table. "Well, well," he said.

"Guess she never made it."

Mulligan sat by the window and saw the new capitol dome was nearly complete. Perhaps he could check army records for John Kavanaugh. And he could check the rest of the hospitals. There had to be a record of Abigail Donahue somewhere.

That night, Michael Mulligan awoke to the sound of a fire engine bell. A hotel down the street was burning, and people had gathered to watch. He got up and looked out the window at the burning building, wondering if he should put on his military coat and investigate. Many building fires were being started by Confederate sympathizers in the last months of the war. Mulligan then examined his old letters, some stained, wondering if she had even touched them. It was near dawn when he went to sleep.

The next morning after breakfast, Mulligan walked by the burned hotel. Arson was suspected. He continued his rounds of Washington, D.C. hospitals, searching for the elusive Abigail Donahue. Why was she hiding, or had something happened?

Checking the hospitals, he found no evidence of an Abigail Donahue working as a nurse. Each hospital produced a disturbing sight: soldiers in despair, dying or dead, many missing limbs. There were black Union troops now, and the south was running short of soldiers to replace those slain or maimed.

Sitting in the sheltered garden of the last hospital, Mulligan observed wounded men walking by on crutches, or sitting on benches. A nurse sat next to him.

"Is it possible this nurse, Abby Donahue, worked under another name?"

"It's possible, but why would she use a fake name?"

"We are at war," the nurse said. "Maybe she had something to hide."

"While saving lives?"

"Maybe she was hiding from someone."

The nurse left him in the garden. A gold fish pond was frozen over, reflecting barren trees.

Michael Mulligan went to Fort Stevens and registered so that his pending orders could find him. The fort had a wall marked by bullets, and he imagined the recent invasion, President Lincoln himself watching the battle and risking Rebel snipers while former Vice President, Breckinridge, watched from the Confederate lines. In the office, Mulligan read the lists of recent dead and prisoner exchanges. They had a list of dead Rebel officers and he felt sadness seeing the name of General John R. Chambliss. Then he saw another name: John Kavanaugh, Rebel prisoner exchange. Moments later, he sat in an office talking to the Secretary of Military Records. He was a cheerful portly man with white side whiskers.

"I have your record, Captain Mulligan. Why are you a captain? You should be promoted. You'd get a pay raise."

"Thank you. Who is this Kavanaugh person? Why was he exchanged?"

"We got a lot of Irish soldiers being exchanged on both sides. I believe we had a few Kavanaughs, too, except most are spelled with a C. Maybe this Reb couldn't spell properly."

"Reb? He should be a Union soldier."

The secretary lit a cigar and leaned back in his chair. "And why is this certain?"

"I am looking for a woman who I assume to be his cousin."

The secretary considered this answer. "His cousin, eh? You worked together?"

Mulligan explained the circumstances at Gettysburg. The gentleman listened, his face impassive. He consulted the folder.

"You have an outstanding record, Captain Mulligan. Trained horses for the Union Cavalry, survived Antietam, Gettysburg and Cold Harbor. Captured by Jeb Stuart himself and released. Worked with Kilpatrick, Farnsworth, Sheridan and my favorite drunk, General Thomas Francis Meagher. The war is ending. I'm sure of it. Why be connected with anyone...even a lovely woman...who may taint your record?"

"Taint?" Michael Mulligan sat quietly. "I don't understand," he finally said.

"You don't?" The secretary opened his desk and took out a flask. "Drink?"

"Yes."

The secretary poured them a drink. "I shouldn't do this." Then he took out a file and slid it across the desk to Mulligan who read it quickly. Mulligan returned the file to the secretary.

"John Kavanaugh was a Rebel spy in the Union Army?"

"Yes. He was passing on troop locations and battle plans. He faced execution but a deal was made in exchange for some valuable Union officers. I guess Jeff Davis wanted this Johnny Kavanaugh back."

"And Abby Donahue?"

"This Abby Donahue told you she was Kavanaugh's cousin, but we don't have a record of her, not under that name. Maybe she's a cousin or a sister or a mistress. Kavanaugh said he was married; perhaps this Abby was his wife."

"Wife?"

"She served as a nurse, you say?"

"And a damn good one."

"Maybe she felt guilty or was protecting you. We can have relatives on the other side, you know. Even the President's wife has a sister married to a Reb officer."

"Abby never mentioned a husband." Michael Mulligan sat for some time, thinking about what he had read and what possibilities existed. Then he stood up. "Thank you, Mr. Secretary."

"Let it go, Captain Mulligan."

"I don't know that I can."

"You should take my advice," the secretary said. "In the meantime, I'll put in a recommendation for promotion. How about Major? I'll give you a new shirt with the proper stripes."

"Thank you, sir."

"One more point."

"Yes?"

"You are not on duty in Washington so find a place to store your Spencer carbine."

"I will do so. Tell me—do you know something I don't?"

"I do. That neighborhood is known for Confederate sympathizers. Kavanaugh did stay at that rooming house briefly, so your landlady is lying."

"I see. You'll alert me if Abigail Donahue appears?"

The secretary smiled weakly. "Of course."

Walking back to the rooming house with his new shirt and rank, Mulligan saw the newspaper boy and remembered the New York riot and firing the Spencer and holding a dying Irish boy in his arms. The boy was cold and asking for his mother. Blood appeared at the corners of his mouth.

"What's your name, son?"

"John Mulligan," the boy said.

Michael Mulligan stopped at a tavern for a shot of Irish whiskey and a beer. Mary was baking bread when he returned.

He could tell she wasn't well, and moved with difficulty, sometimes catching her breath.

"Any luck, Mr. Mulligan?"

"No. I guess I've lost her. The man she claimed was her cousin is gone."

He could feel Mary watching him, even before he met her eyes. Then she checked the bread. "Is that so?"

"Yes."

"Come to think of it, a soldier named Kavanaugh may have stayed here, but that was over a year ago. Don't know what happened to him."

"He was arrested as a Rebel spy."

Mary stared at him. "Mr. Mulligan. I am from the south."

"I understand."

"But I ain't no spy."

"Never thought you were, ma'am."

"We have a lot of anger amongst our people. We thought God would give us a victory. What happened to Mr. Kavanaugh?"

"He was shipped to Richmond as part of a prisoner exchange."

"They didn't shoot him?"

"No."

She went back to baking and Mulligan climbed the stairs to his room. He suddenly had an idea but it would have to wait until morning. Occasionally he heard footsteps and voices in the hallway, and when going out for a walk, he passed a young ruggedly built handsome man who glared at him as he passed.

"How are you, Yank?"

"I am fine. And you?"

"Couldn't be better. Kill any Rebs, soldier boy?"

"Not recently. You?"

The handsome man laughed, and Mulligan saw a toxic defiance in his eyes. Mulligan still carried the Spencer in a sheath under his coat.

"My President is Jefferson Davis," the man told him.

"My President, your President, *our* President—is Abraham Lincoln."

"Lincoln is a tyrant."

The two men stared at one another when Mary appeared.

"Mr. Payne, you leave Mr. Mulligan alone. He's a boarder."

"The name is not Payne but Powell," the man insisted.

"Be seeing you, Mr. Powell," Mulligan said, and left the building. Another man with a small thin body and a weak chin covered with a wispy beard passed him. As Mulligan walked down the street, he turned and saw Powell talking to the short man. They didn't look at him. Mulligan decided to carry the Spencer, though it was illegal.

Mulligan slept fitfully, that night, hearing storm winds outside. Occasionally he heard noises in the rooming house, and thought he heard someone outside the door, but no one broke into the room. When he left in the morning, he propped a match against his door. Then he walked to the same convent, and this time, a stout nun with a smiling face opened the door. She remembered him from his early visit.

"Sister Helen is a bit rough on visitors...unless they are here to help. I'm Sister Clare. You were looking for someone? A woman who possibly worked here?"

"Yes. I wonder if my nurse friend served the convent under a different name, but decided to take Sister Anne's real name when she left."

Sister Clare watched him, still smiling. "She was running from something?"

"That I don't know."

"Describe her."

Mulligan did so.

"There was a nurse who worked here about two years ago: short, quite lovely, thick curly dark hair, brown eyes. Her name was Ellen."

"And she left?"

"Right after we lost Sister Anne."

"Was she married?"

"Most of our nurses are single. I never heard her refer to a husband."

"And her last name?"

Sister Clare walked to a large ornate desk and shuffled through some note cards.

"Kavanaugh," she said. "Her name was Ellen Kavanaugh."

"Is there a forwarding address?"

"No, but you have her complete *real* name," Sister Clare said.

"If it is the same person."

Mulligan walked to the door.

"I won't ask the details, but good luck in finding her. And take care of yourself. This terrible rebellion has to end, soon."

Mulligan walked through the D.C. streets, filled with large crowds despite the winter weather. Many of the gas lamps were out and the sidewalks had cracks and potholes, except for the dirt streets. Mulligan saw Ford's Theatre; outside were posters advertising Laura Keene and her troupe arriving in the spring to perform *Our American Cousin.* It would be good to see Laura Keene again and talk over their San Francisco days with the young Edwin Booth.

Edwin Booth had just started a run of *Hamlet* in New York.

With a new nation, we will need a new vibrant theatre, Michael Mulligan thought.

Walking toward the boarding house, Mulligan bought a fifth of whiskey. When he entered the building, he heard low murmuring voices, and walking into the drawing room, saw Powell with three other men. They stopped talking when he entered.

"Gentlemen," Mulligan said. "I know we have different loyalties, but I want to say I served as a prisoner of generals Jeb Stuart and John Chambliss…admirable men, both. Noble enemies. Join me in a drink to their memory?"

"Just leave the whiskey, Yank. People like you killed them."

"I understand." Mulligan nodded to Powell and placed the bottle on the table.

"To Jeb Stuart," the short man with the wispy beard said. "Soldier. My name is John. Maybe you can join us another time."

"Sit down," Powell said. He regarded Mulligan. "How's General Sherman, these days? You gonna join his brigade, burning southern homes, stealing southern livestock, killing southern men, raping southern women?"

"The war is ugly for all of us," Mulligan finally said.

Mulligan walked upstairs to his room, passing a young woman on the landing. She smiled briefly. "Mother tells me you've done theatre."

"I have."

"Mr. John Wilkes Booth himself visits here occasionally."

"I know his brother, Edwin Booth. Wonderful actor." He held out his hand. "Michael Mulligan."

"I know who you are. I am Anna," she said, and walked on.

Mulligan saw the match had been knocked down. He entered his room but found nothing missing. Then he walked to Mary's room, and when she answered, he demanded to know why someone broke into his room.

"Anna cleans all the rooms. I'm sure that's it. Anything missing?"

"No."

"You might consider finding another place, Mr. Mulligan. I don't mind you being here, but you're not welcome with my other guests."

"Your guests make policy?"

"No, but they outnumber you."

Mulligan touched his cap with one finger and retired to his room. He slept poorly, that night, the Spencer by his bed and a pistol on the nightstand. Perhaps it was time to rent elsewhere. In the morning, he heard a woman cursing, and then the words: "I won't permit it! I won't allow Nigra soldiers in my house!"

He recognized Mary's voice and was pulling on his pants when the light knocking came.

"Major Mulligan?"

"Just a minute," Mulligan said.

Buttoning his shirt, he opened the door and saw a young black soldier, part of the new Negro brigades. Mary's voice continued: "This is going too far, even for Yanks!"

"Mother, please," Anna said.

"Please what? Africans with guns!"

The squad leader of the colored troops addressed Mary.

"My apologies, ma'am, but we have to escort Major Mulligan," he said. "We are sorry for any inconvenience. We will be gone momentarily."

"Then do your business and get out! I don't even rent to niggers."

The black soldier remained calm as he handed Mulligan his new orders.

"You need to accompany us, Major," he said, his accent white and educated.

"Give me a minute."

In the hall, Mulligan saw three other colored men in uniform, and he heard Mary walking toward her room. He dressed quickly, grabbing his suitcase, military bag and Spencer. As they left the house, he saw Mary and Anna watching him, but noticed Powell and his friends were gone. His orders were clear: report to Fort Stevens, and then join General Sheridan when the weather permitted. Outside, they escorted him down the street.

"Have your boys seen action yet?"

"My boys haven't seen action, no," the leader of the soldiers said. His black eyes were opaque, mysterious, with a latent defiance. "But my *men* will relish any operation against the Confederacy."

"I approve of Negro soldiers," Mulligan told him.

The leader met his eyes and managed a slight smile. "I am glad you approve, Major."

"Gonna kill Rebs for Uncle Lincum," another soldier said. "Yessir."

"I was invited by David Wills to hear Lincoln's speech at Gettysburg," Mulligan said, "but by the time I got ready to listen, Lincoln had finished. I'll have to read it, sometime."

They stopped by a carriage with a colored driver.

"Our duty is finished," the black soldier said. "Good day, Major Mulligan."

"Good day Private—?"

"My name is not important. I have to report back to my white commanding officer."

Michael Mulligan saluted the black soldiers as he boarded the carriage. None of the soldiers returned his salute. They turned and marched proudly down the street. Mulligan would soon be spending most of his time with horses as they ran around a center post or learned maneuvers when facing enemy guns. Mulligan's search for Ellen Kavanaugh would have to wait.

On New Year's Day, Michael Mulligan received his orders; he had to find Sheridan's camp and support his cavalry pursuit of Lee's army.

"You will have a traveling companion," the officer told him.

"Who is that? A soldier?"

"Reginald Taylor, an English journalist. He wants to witness Lee's surrender, which we hope is coming soon. We should take Richmond by spring."

"An Englishman? I hope he can stand hardship and danger."

"We'll see. At least England didn't back the Confederacy."

The officer left and brought back the English journalist. Reginald Taylor was a man in his mid-thirties, medium height, well-dressed, with short brown hair and a trimmed mustache. He liked to smile and had a cultured accent that sounded affected to some Americans.

"I say, old boy, this will be quite an adventure, eh?"

"Yes, I am sure it will. Quite."

"You are Irish, Mr. Mulligan. Oh, of course you are Irish. I hope there's no hard feelings. I am afraid what my nation has done to the Irish people is most appalling."

"Most appalling indeed," said Michael Mulligan.

"Like what your country did and still does to Indians and Negroes."

After a moment, Mulligan asked, "Can you ride?"

"Not really, but I'll have a go. Splendid of you to guide me."

"Do I have a choice? Can you shoot a gun?"

"No, no, my weapon is the pen. I could a tale unfold, Mr. Mulligan."

"Major Mulligan."

"So sorry. Major Mulligan."

"You may need to defend yourself."

Reginald was clearly disturbed. "That will be necessary, perhaps, but most awkward. I am a peace loving man," he said.

"Aren't we all? The Rebs may want to rob and then kill you."

"Oh my," Reginald said. "I abhor violence." After a moment, Mulligan noticed Reginald Taylor studying his face. "I say, you look awfully familiar. Have we met?"

"I don't think so."

They left mid-January, riding toward Virginia with a pack horse. Reginald Taylor loved conversation, and when Michael Mulligan went silent, he filled the void by discussing the history of England and how he admired the rugged American spirit though it was strange that even the late President Tyler backed the Confederacy.

"You know, your Mr. Lincoln offered Lee command of the Union Army?"

"Yes, I knew that. Lee chose to defend his state."

"Extraordinary, when you consider his state was taken over by what we British would call traitors. And yet, I am sure Robert E. Lee is an honorable man. And what brought you to America, Major Mulligan?"

"A coffin ship."

Reginald was quiet for two miles. "Of course, the terrible Irish famine. I'm afraid we British take a black eye for that one. We might have even given support to the Confederacy but for Lincoln's Emancipation Proclamation. England abolished slavery long ago. Of course, we can still enslave people in the colonies."

They rode and camped for two weeks and Mulligan saw Reginald Taylor was rugged enough, despite his insistence on wearing a clean suit and tie.

"You really don't need formal dress out here, Mr. Taylor."

"I know that, Major Mulligan, but we English always feel we must be properly dressed at all times...even in the wilderness."

They rode on through fierce lingering cold. Taylor didn't complain but never stopped talking about endless topics.

"I would like to see your Edwin Booth's Hamlet."

"Someday, Reginald, I may be able to arrange that."

"You are a man of many talents." The horses had slowed to a walk. "I should like to write about you, Major Mulligan."

"Just call me Mulligan." They stopped. "I have a derringer you may want to carry in case we get attacked. There are a lot of roving bandits who are using the war as an excuse to rob and murder travelers."

Reginald shook his head. "I wouldn't know how to use one."

"Simple. You cock it, point the gun and pull the trigger. You need to get close."

Reginald took the tiny pistol. "Amazing," he said. "I don't know if I have that aggressive American nature. I prefer an afternoon at the library. I also tend to be too polite when it comes to confrontations...but Britain didn't become an empire without war and destruction."

They camped that night. In addition to their rations, Mulligan cooked fresh rabbit meat over an open fire. Reginald Taylor's conversations were growing shorter.

"I could sure use a cup of tea, Major Mulligan. I'd die for one."

"How about a bit of Irish whiskey and some water?"

"That might do just as well."

They sipped water and whiskey from tin cups.

"So tell me more about yourself, Mr. Taylor."

"Call me Reggie. Well, I came to America four years ago to write an article about American art and didn't find any. When the Civil War started, I had to cover it. Proper Brits back home may hate America for their revolution, but secretly admire your beautiful open country and wild pioneer spirit."

"Are you married, Reggie? Any children?"

He could see Reginald's expression change. "Yes to both. A lovely wife named Julia and twin boys, Ben and Max. And I *do* miss them. You?"

"I have a son I left behind. Perhaps after hostilities cease."

"Of course. I must say, I believe in a new freedom, but the slaughter of this war is appalling. I was there for the first Bull Run and I witnessed Cold Harbor."

"I saw both."

"Infantry?"

"Cavalry."

"Your General Grant will have to answer for Cold Harbor, someday. It was a bloody tragedy. Why didn't he ask General Lee for a temporary truce to administer to the wounded men...all of whom died horribly?"

"I asked that question myself," Mulligan said, remembering bleeding men lying between the trenches, crying out for water. "Of course, that's an admission of defeat."

"Really? I hope to publish a book about this ghastly Civil War...a cautionary tale."

Mulligan finally went to sleep, trying to suppress memories of the bloated and black corpses at Cold Harbor. He woke up once and saw Reginald writing in his journal by the dying fire. Mulligan listened to the night for any sound of possible intruders. He also hoped Sheridan wouldn't break from his winter headquarters before they arrived. Two men would have little chance if they ran into a Rebel regiment or marauders.

The next morning, there was a break in the weather. They passed a field full of hogs feeding on dead bodies, the uniforms gone, the fallen soldiers forever nameless. Mulligan and Reginald Taylor continued past a meadow where they saw a young muscular black man holding a skull, Hamlet-like. As they passed, the dust-covered man held up the skull next to his dark scarred face and pointed at them.

"What is that black gentlemen doing?" Reginald asked.

"I don't know. Let's keep riding."

Though still cold, the sun was bright on the snow and ice as they rode slowly down a narrow road, slippery in the shade. Reginald was talking about an English poet named John Keats whose fame was rising though he died young and in obscurity when Mulligan silenced him. Reginald stopped his horse. "Problem, Mr. Mulligan?"

"Be quiet."

Mulligan listened to the cold breeze through the limbs overhead and watched the road. Moments later, three armed men rode into view and Michael Mulligan knew immediately who they were.

"Who are those ragged looking chaps?"

Michael Mulligan pulled out his Spencer from under a bear coat and charged toward the three men who were surprised. The man in front called out: "You—present your papers. Union or Confederate?"

For an answer, Mulligan cranked a round into the chamber, cocked the rifle and fired, knocking the lead man from his horse. The other two were raising their rifles when Mulligan rode by, shooting the second man at close range. The horse of the third man began rearing as the rider struggled to get a clear shot at Mulligan, now turning. Suddenly, Mulligan's horse was on the icy ground and Mulligan felt pressure on his right leg. His horse struggled to stand and then limped a few feet. Mulligan's Spencer had slid away. The third man rode up to him, pointing his rifle at his face.

"You shot my men!" Mulligan saw the man's narrowing eyes. "Little slippery, huh? You gonna get kilt, you son of a bitch!"

He aimed the rifle; Mulligan saw the round barrel, thinking this would be his last sight on earth, even as pain tore through his leg. Then he heard hoof beats and a light pop. The third man was startled, staring at Reginald's alert wind-burned face.

"What the hell?"

He looked down at blood spreading just beneath his neck and then swung his rifle toward Reginald, now trying to control his horse. He fired and Reginald's horse reared, throwing the Englishman to the ground. Mulligan stood up on one leg, pulling out his Colt .44. He cocked the pistol and aimed but the third rider was staring ahead, blood coming from the corners of his mouth. He dropped the rifle.

"What the hell?" he said again.

He slumped over the saddle and his horse suddenly bolted toward the trees, a low limb knocking the dying man from his horse. Michael Mulligan felt his burning leg but the bone seemed intact. Then he limped toward Reginald, lying on the ground.

"I say, Reggie, that was what you Brits would call a 'good show'."

Reginald was panting. "What just happened? I believe I shot a man."

"And saved my life. They were thieves."

Reginald's eyes widened. "Like highwaymen?"

"Yes, highwaymen. You'll have to put this in your book, Reggie. Damn! I think I tore a thigh muscle when my horse slipped and fell on me."

"So sorry," Reginald said.

Mulligan's horse was kneeling, and even from a distance he saw the broken front leg. Then he saw Reginald and the blood spreading on his white shirt.

"By Jesus."

"I think that beastly man shot me. I can't move my arms."

Mulligan ripped the Englishman's shirt apart and a saw the bullet hole in his abdomen. He tore a strip of Reginald's shirt and pressed it against Reginald's wound now bleeding profusely. "Stay with me, Reggie."

"Major Mulligan? You may have to write to my wife and children...and *do* publish my journal about this awful war...if you have the chance."

"You'll publish it yourself, Reggie," Mulligan said.

"I hope so. I've always wanted a knighthood."

"You'll get it Reggie, and I'll be there. I always wanted to meet a king."

"Well—it's the queen, actually."

Mulligan saw the light in Reginald Taylor's eyes fading.

"Hang on, Reggie!"

When he died, Michael Mulligan gently touched the Englishman's face. With the Spencer, he limped to a tree, leaning against the frozen bark. He watched the bodies of the three dead highwaymen and Reginald Taylor, his tie still properly knotted, his boots clean, the derringer near his body. Then Mulligan aimed at the kneeling horse and fired once, killing it. He was still lying against the tree when Rebel soldiers rode into the clearing. They pulled up and viewed the scene. One of the soldiers approached Mulligan, his muzzle loader pointed at his face.

"One move and you're dead, Yank. I'll take that carbine."

"Take it."

Another soldier saw the pack horse. "Boys, I believe we got us some provisions."

An officer got off his horse and examined the three dead thieves. He looked at Mulligan who felt his leg swelling. "It appears you spared us hanging these thieves. They killed two of my men after stealing their meager possessions. Who are you? And who's that?"

"Major Michael Mulligan. The dead man with the tie is Reginald Taylor, an English writer."

"Is that so? Well, Mulligan, I'm afraid we are going to take your pack horse and weapons."

One of the Rebels found the Irish whiskey and took a drink, and then passed it around. Others took swigs.

"Captain Reynolds, what about him? Shoot him or take him prisoner?"

The officer leaned down and touched Mulligan's leg. Mulligan cried out.

"I don't know. What *are* we gonna do with you, Yank? Who are you with?"

Mulligan told them.

"General Sheridan? He's as bad as Sherman, burning everything in sight."

"They are ruthless. I have a suggestion, Captain Reynolds."

"And what is that?"

"Surrender to me."

The officer was surprised, and then amused. He laughed and another soldier joined him.

"You are riding into a trap. It is only a matter of time. Surrender now."

The captain leaned close. "We are taking your horses, your guns, and your provisions, and you are telling me and my men to surrender—to you?"

"That's correct."

A soldier led the pack horse away. Another soldier was stripping Reginald's body and Mulligan called out: "Please leave his body alone."

The soldier took Reginald's boots and found the journal.

"That belonged to Reginald Taylor, and now to me."

"I'd like to wipe my ass with it," the soldier told him.

"Leave it be," said Captain Reynolds. He regarded Mulligan. "You're hurt bad?"

"No broken bones but I'll be black and blue for a while."

The captain saw his men passing around the bottle. It was time to depart.

"Mulligan? How did you know those men were thieves?"

"They had mismatched clothing: Rebel shirts, Union caps, and Yankee boots. And I saw their eyes. They were evil men."

"So they were."

Another soldier with a rifle nudged the captain. "Shall I do him in?"

"No." Captain Reynolds regarded Mulligan for a long time. "I can't take you prisoner, since we'll have to feed you, and I don't want to shoot the man who killed the men who killed two of my men. We've had too much killing. I'm not sure we could send you back to Richmond."

"What Richmond? Grant is probably riding through your capital as we speak."

The officer motioned to his men to leave. "We'll see about that."

They heard an Irish voice: "Damn, it's the horse man, Mulligan *na Coppaleen*, Mulligan of the ponies. He was a guest of General Jeb Stuart himself."

"You know this man, Private Kennedy?"

"Yessir. Old Jeb let him go."

"And so will I. Major Mulligan, I'm leaving you with your derringer, two bullets, and some rations. Keep your knife. You will have to limp to the next battle."

"Could you grant me one favor?"

"What?"

"Bury my friend, Reginald Taylor. Leave me his personal belongings. I need to contact his wife and twin boys."

"Granted," the captain said. "Bury the Englishman, Private Kennedy, and let's move out."

"The ground's pretty hard, sir."

"I'm sure you'll find a way to bury an Englishman."

When the unit departed within a half hour, some walking, some riding, they left Mulligan a blanket, his derringer, and rations. Private Kennedy touched his cap in a farewell salute. Mulligan limped to a nearby stream and sat in the freezing water, leaving on his pants and boots, letting the water flow over his waist and legs until he felt numb. Then he hobbled to the place where Reginald Taylor lay buried in a shallow grave and made a crude cross, carving Reginald's name across the top. He added, "English Writer" below the name. The stripped bodies of the three highwaymen lay where they fell, food for wild hogs. Putting Reginald's journal with his bedding, Mulligan started limping carefully down the ice-slick road, using a branch as a walking stick. He had to find Sheridan's headquarters. He could not last long in winter with meager clothing, a few rations, a derringer and a knife. He was most afraid of the cold.

He built a fire, that night, but even with the fire and the blanket, he felt the Virginia winter cutting into him. His right leg felt like a dead limb. When he woke up, the sun was bright, but the air still felt cold and sharp in his lungs. He tried to revive the fire, but could barely move with his bruised leg. Then in the distance he heard gunshots. After eating cold rations, he slowly limped in the direction of the skirmish. By noon, he found Captain Reynolds and his unit in a field. They had walked into an ambush, and though Mulligan saw few hoof prints in the earth, he knew what transpired. Reynolds and his men were sick and starving, some a little drunk, and the Federals decided to cut them down with no thoughts of a surrender. Searching the field he found the body of Private Kennedy, a bullet in his head. Captain Reynolds had taken one to the chest.

As Michael Mulligan observed the death meadow, many blacks converged on the area. They ignored him as they picked through the scattered clothing or searched the bodies looking for anything valuable.

"We'll bury them Rebs later, Cap-'in," an older man said.

"I need to find General Sheridan. Anyone got a horse I could use?"

Moments later, another man brought him a horse they found in the woods. It was Reginald's horse. "You take this and kill more Rebs."

"I will. Thanks."

"Freedom's coming soon," the black man declared. "We are gonna be free."

"I hope so."

After mounting Taylor's horse with great pain and stiffness, Mulligan began riding southwest toward General Sheridan's camp. He rode through a burned-out land, with smoldering barns and houses. He saw no cattle or horses, and began to wonder if the population had disappeared. Was General Sheridan imitating General Sherman's march of destruction? Topping a ridge, he saw a burned house but a barn still standing and rode toward it, hoping to find feed for the horse and a place for shelter. When he entered the barn, it was empty except for roosting pigeons. He gathered bits of hay and managed to break up pieces of ice for water. Mulligan had to move slowly, and he knew that his leg would be stiff for a long time.

He found enough dry kindling and broken wood to start a low fire in the center of the barn, the door partially open. He risked a barn fire, but he needed to warm himself as he ate the rest of his rations, realizing he missed the sound of Reginald Taylor's cultured English voice. He would have to contact his widow, and eventually read the handwritten journal. In the firelight, he glanced at some pages and admired the ornate handwriting and the precise if slightly quaint style. When the fire died down, he closed the barn door and rolled himself in the blanket, choosing a stall next to the horse.

He woke up in the early morning to a low whinny and a mumbling sound. Someone had partially opened the barn door. Mulligan drew the derringer and with the tiny pistol by his thigh, he grabbed the stall and pulled himself up. The door slid open and in the light, he saw a silhouette of a ragged man, but he couldn't tell if it was a soldier from either army.

"We need to get them crops in," the man said. "Need to pick that cotton, yessir."

"Step forward with your hands up," Mulligan said.

"We're here to surrender," the man said. "Yessir. Then we gots to git on home."

The man stepped forward and Mulligan saw the faded Confederate uniform and a face ravaged by hunger, the eyes dark and hollow. Mulligan asked the bony man if he had any weapons.

"No weapons left in this troop. We are marching to the city to surrender. Gonna stand in the light. Let ole' Abe take it all. Yes sir. Cross that River Jordan."

Mulligan pulled on his shirt and hopped closer to the thin soldier, seeing something in the man's eyes, a fading emptiness like an oil lamp with a dying wick.

"I see you're a major. Greetings," the soldier said. He saluted. "We are here to surrender. If I had my sword, it would be yours, Major. Lead the way."

Mulligan looked out the door and saw a double line of ragged men trying to stand, a few sitting by the road. It resembled an image from the Irish famine with people starving to death and collapsing on the country roads.

"Lieutenant Smith is my name. Georgia Brigade."

He saluted again.

"I should salute you, Lieutenant," Mulligan said.

"Got to surrender and go home. Got crops to bring in."

"It's winter, Lieutenant Smith. No crops."

"Oh, we had crops 'til the Yanks burnt them all."

"Lieutenant Smith, could you join your men? I will be right there."

The lieutenant saluted and walked toward the ghostly brigade standing on the road, some barefoot and without uniforms. Mulligan saddled the horse, now hungry, secured his bedding with Taylor's journal, and carefully lifted himself onto the saddle. He rode to the head of the emaciated Rebel troops, some staring ahead at nothing, some watching him with dull eyes. Lieutenant Smith stood at attention.

"Gentlemen," Mulligan said. "I am Major Mulligan. General Sheridan is down the road, and he will give you rations in exchange for surrender. I am hungry, myself. It is some distance, and you must walk just a little more. Lieutenant Smith will lead you and I will follow."

As they marched, the air grew warmer and it began to rain in sudden heavy gusts, hitting Mulligan's face like buckshot from a gun. They walked on, Mulligan trailing on the horse, the bony men marching ahead of him in the blowing rainy mist. Occasionally, one of the soldiers would stagger to the side of the road and fall. Mulligan knew he had to keep moving. Then the sun came out and he was aware of a Confederate officer riding beside him, his long hair and thick mustache blond in the sun, his blue eyes full of shock and outrage.

"You, Yank! What the hell is this?"

Other cavalry appeared, riding along the line and blocking the road.

"I am Major Mulligan transporting these prisoners to General Sheridan, if I can find him. Care to join us?"

The officer was clearly surprised. "Sheridan? Put your hands up!"

"I don't have any weapons," Mulligan lied.

The young officer shouted to another soldier. "Tyrone, guard this man."

To Mulligan's surprise, a light-skinned black soldier in a Reb uniform rode up and leveled his pistol at him. "Don't move, Yankee soldier boy. I'd love to open you up."

Tyrone reached over and took Mulligan's belted knife. "I never thought I'd see a Negro slave in a Reb uniform," Mulligan told him.

The black soldier's handsome face revealed nothing.

"What difference does it make, Yankee...except I gets to carry a gun. That Emancipation Proclamation, which no one read to the slaves, means nothin'. Shit. I'm still a nigger to everyone around here."

Mulligan heard the cracking voice of the Rebel officer shouting at the bony refugees.

"What the hell do you think you're doing?"

As Mulligan and Tyrone rode to the front of the line, Lieutenant Smith stepped forward, holding his hat between claw-like fingers. His hair and face were drenched from the rain.

"We gonna surrender. Then we can bring the crops in."

"You'll do what?"

"Surrender. Then we gonna cross over into Beulah Land."

"Surrender?" The blond officer took out his pistol and shot Smith in the throat. He staggered and fell to the ground.

"Now listen to me, men. I can see you miserable scarecrows are in bad shape. We got a wagon full of rations on the way. You will be fed and given new rifles and you will do your duty. Anyone who talks of desertion will be shot!"

The broken army didn't respond, staring ahead as though drugged or suffering from a high fever. Then the officer confronted Mulligan. "You are my prisoner, Mulligan. You will give me answers or I will personally hang you."

"You didn't have to shoot Lieutenant Smith. The man was starving and ill."

Once again, he saw the slightly mad eyes of the cavalry officer. Then Mulligan felt the singing blow from a gloved hand across his cheek.

"You shut your mouth! Tyrone, take him to the tent for questioning."

"Yes sir, Captain Easy. Let's go, Yank."

Tyrone escorted Mulligan to a large officer's tent in a field. Many soldiers were cooking or cleaning weapons when they arrived. They stared at Mulligan as he passed.

"Got yourself a new Yankee white boy, huh, Ty-rone?"

"Thass right, boss."

"Bet you'll have some fun in the officer's tent."

"We gonna have us a lot of fun, Marster. Maybe I'll visit your tent, tonight, and make some sweet music on that white flute."

Tyrone grinned at the jeering troops as they rode by.

"And just what's so funny, Tyrone?"

"Oh, they know I'm the captain's house nigger, and I gets to entertain. I play de old Rebel songs on guitar. I sings and dances. Yessir, Boss, I'm the dancing Negro." Mulligan felt the powerful gaze on him. "And sometimes I gets to interrogate prisoners...even white folks. They don't like it when they be touched by black hands."

They stopped at the tent and Mulligan carefully dismounted. He winced and Tyrone asked, "Horse step on your foot?"

"A horse fell on my foot."

"Maybe you better let this ole boy here take a look at it."

"So you entertain, *and* do medicine?"

"Sometimes. Can you get that right boot off?"

"I am not sure."

Tyrone turned to watch as Captain Easy approached. Then he glanced at Mulligan.

"You better keep that derringer in your left boot hidden 'til the time's right. Don't shoot until nobody lookin', unless you fixin' to die."

Mulligan didn't respond. He limped into the wide tent. Tyrone sat him down and Captain Easy entered and pulled up a chair. He took out a bottle of whiskey, drank, and then stared at Mulligan with an intense unsettling focus. Mulligan stared back at the face dominated by sculpted cheekbones and a protruding jaw.

"Do I need to tie you up, Mulligan?"

"No. I've been captured twice, paroled twice."

"How did you enter Virginia in the first place?"

"Rode in with a friend, an English journalist named Reginald Taylor."

"No sentries stopped you?"

"No."

"Where is this Limey journalist?"

"He was killed by one of three highwaymen after Reggie shot him."

"And the other two?"

"I killed them," Mulligan said. "Before my horse slipped and nearly crushed my right leg."

He could sense Tyrone standing behind him as the captain leaned forward, his eyes focused and intense.

"Who took you prisoner?"

"Jeb Stuart and John Chambliss near Hanover just before Gettysburg, and after our incident with the three robbers— Captain Reynolds."

"Benjamin Jew Reynolds? Where the hell is he?"

"You'll find Reynolds and his men lying dead in a field northeast of here."

Captain Easy shot from his chair. "Dead? And who killed them—you?"

"I suspect they rode into a Federal cavalry ambush."

"There ain't no Federal cavalry left in Virginia. We wiped you Yankees out at Cold Harbor."

"Maybe you're right, since I never did find General Sheridan's brigade."

Captain Easy took another drink and paced in the tent. "Tyrone, my little boy, you think he's telling the truth? Or are all Yankees liars?"

"I don't know nothing about his business, sir."

The captain stepped on Mulligan's right foot. "That hurt, you Yankee pig, because if you are lying, I'll hang you personally."

Mulligan made no sound. The captain then bolted from the tent and they heard his voice shrieking orders to soldiers outside. Tyrone knelt in front of Mulligan.

"He be mad when he come back," Tyrone said.

"Some Negros were burying the bodies."

"After stealing everything they find? Then he be *real* mad. He'll kill every nigger he find. And then kill the messenger with bad news."

"Not if I kill him first, Tyrone."

"You can call me 'Boy,' it's all right. Let's see that foot." Tyrone slowly pulled off Mulligan's right boot and they saw the black and blue swollen foot and lower calf. He felt for broken bones and then left, returning with cold water. As Mulligan sat in the chair, Tyrone cleaned his foot and lower leg, wrapping it tightly. "Ain't nothin' to do but wait. Drink some whiskey. You need favor that right side for a while."

"I won't be running away, that's for sure."

Tyrone stood up, looking down at his face. "So why didn't you shoot Captain Easy, white boy? You had the chance. Ain't nobody gonna hear that little gun. You could sneak out, steal a horse, take your Yankee ass back to D.C."

"And what would you do? Cut my throat with my own knife?"

Tyrone laughed. "I never thought of that. Yeah. Easy, now, he loves to hang prisoners," Tyrone told him. "And he got no reason to hold you."

"Maybe I have information."

"What did you do with the cavalry? Ride and shoot?"

"And train and care for horses."

For a long time, Tyrone was silent. Then he said, "Your Congress just passed the 13th amendment that ends slavery. My, my, black folks in the south done gonna be free. Ain't that somethin'? Hallelujah."

"After the war, you'll all be free anywhere."

Tyrone held the knife to Mulligan's throat. "It won't mean nothin' except no one can own me, white boy."

"In Ireland, I ran with a group of assassins called the Whiteboys. We killed whites."

"Irish whites?"

"English whites. Informer Irish. Oppressive landlords and English soldiers. I understand your anger, Tyrone."

Tyrone shook his head. "No you don't." He peered out the tent. "You stay here," he said and left. Mulligan sat in the chair, wondering when it would be time to kill Captain Easy.

He deserves it for shooting his own man, Lieutenant Smith, Mulligan thought. *And no man slaps me and lives.*

Michael Mulligan also knew he had been lucky for too long. He might not live to see the South surrender. Tyrone entered the tent after a short officer with white hair and a clipped silver mustache. Mulligan saw some compassion in the officer's eyes.

"This is Colonel Falkner," Tyrone said.

"You are Major Mulligan?"

"Yes, Colonel Falkner."

"I hear you met General Jeb Stuart and that you know horses."

"He asked me for advice about his horse, Colonel."

"And so will I. Come with me."

"I can't walk very well."

"Boy, get him a crutch."

"Yessir."

Tyrone left the tent and came back with a crutch.

"What a hellish war," Colonel Falkner said. "I do believe God has abandoned our cause. Maybe secession was a mistake. I was against it, and I refuse to let slaves bring in my crops."

"And yet you joined the Army of Northern Virginia."

"I did. Follow me."

Colonel Falkner led Michael Mulligan to a corral where he saw bony horses gathered, some running back and forth across the lot.

"We are expecting some supplies, including rations, rifles, and what hay and oats we could save. Captain Easy denies it, but General Sheridan has invaded our state and led a scorched earth policy. I never thought I'd live to see Americans killing Americans."

"Nor I, Colonel. As for your horses, they need better feed…and I doubt they are ready for the noise and confusion of battle. See that horse, there?"

He pointed to a white horse tied to a railing. It was trying to scratch its stomach with its rear hoof. "That is my horse," the colonel said.

Michael Mulligan ran his hands over the horse, feeling its stomach, and examining the hooves. "This animal has colic. You need to purge him or he will die."

"I don't have anything to give him."

"I know a few home remedies…anything to clean out his stomach and intestines."

They were talking remedies for colic when Captain Easy rode into camp, followed by four soldiers. He dismounted and walked quickly toward Colonel Falkner. Tyrone watched from the distant tent. Mulligan lifted his left foot to the railing.

"Colonel Falkner?"

"Where is your salute, Captain Easy?"

"Sorry." The captain saluted. "We found the bodies of Captain Reynolds and his men, some partially buried. They are all dead, Colonel."

"That is tragic, indeed. We need all the men we can muster."

"Niggers were picking over the bodies."

"You see any Federals?"

"No. We shot a few of the niggers," Captain Easy said.

"Why? They didn't kill Captain Reynolds and his men. Now they'll try to kill us. Send a unit to give our soldiers a proper burial. Mark each grave."

Captain Easy hesitated. "What about him, Colonel?"

"What about him?"

"He's a prisoner of war. We can't afford to keep prisoners...so I suggest we hang this Yankee right now."

"It would give you great pleasure, wouldn't it, Captain Easy?"

"It would."

"I am taking Major Mulligan with me to Richmond. He knows horses and we need every resource to stop this invasion. Get ready for battle, Captain. You are dismissed."

Captain Easy stepped back, his mouth tight. He saluted Colonel Falkner. "Yes sir."

When he left, Michael Mulligan said, "Colonel, how do you know I'll help your cause?" The horses moved like ghostly phantoms in the corral.

"You won't help the cause, but you will help horses because you love them. Captain Easy is an ugly man who thrives on war, but we'll need him to fight Grant."

That afternoon with Tyrone driving the team, Michael Mulligan left in a wagon for Richmond, the capital of the Confederacy. Tied to the wagon, Reginald Taylor's horse trotted behind. On a fresh mount, Colonel Falkner rode as an escort with a few select soldiers. They occasionally saw black men and women on the road, often ignoring them, a few breaking into spirituals. Tyrone stared ahead holding the reins.

"I'm glad you got the colonel, Tyrone. I do think Captain Easy would have strung me up."

"Not if you put a bullet in him."

"Then Colonel Falkner would have to hang me."

"Maybe I shoulda just let that happen. Two white folks gone."

"Don't I treat you with respect, Tyrone?"

The young man didn't answer.

They rode on. When they saw Richmond, Michael Mulligan realized the full impact of the Union advance. The city had suffered hits from artillery shells, and Mulligan saw shattered buildings and broken ruins. A patina of green covered the head of a decapitated statue. Specter thin Rebel soldiers marched in the streets layered with dust from pulverized stone.

"My God," Colonel Falkner said. "My God."

They passed a hospital. Colonel Falkner stopped.

"You'll stay here, Major Mulligan. Have that leg attended to and then you'll feed and care for our remaining horses. Don't try to escape."

"Understood."

Tyrone helped Michael Mulligan from the wagon and into the hospital which had sustained little damage. Mulligan carried his bedding with Reginald Taylor's journal.

"Here," Tyrone said. He handed Mulligan his knife. "Maybe you can stab Jefferson Davis."

"I hope to see you again, Tyrone."

"You will, probably digging out the rubble. That sentry will show you where to go."

Tyrone jumped back up unto the wagon. Colonel Falkner exchanged salutes with Michael Mulligan and then they rode down the crowded street. Mulligan heard distant guns; the light had drained from the sky so the landscape appeared dust-colored.

"I'll take that knife," the sentry said.

"Take it. But I'll need help up the stairs."

Later, Mulligan sat on his bed, feeling his leg and foot throbbing again. Then he heard a gasp. He looked up. Abigail Donahue stood in the doorway, wearing the same nurse's uniform. For a long time, they didn't speak. Her face was thin and he saw how time had aged her. Mulligan searched her passive face for any acknowledgement.

"Good afternoon," he finally said.

"Good afternoon, Mr. Mulligan."

For just a moment, Michael Mulligan imagined the old Nurse Abby of Gettysburg leaping onto the bed, her fingers undoing his buttons and lifting her baggy nurse's dress to reveal she wore nothing underneath before they commenced furiously copulating while still alone in the hospital room.

But that was only a fantasy as they faced each other.

"Shall I call you Abby or Ellen?"

"My name is Ellen. I tried to write to you but the mail during war time is…is unreliable."

"Of course. I sent many letters."

"I imagine you did. You look older, Mr. Mulligan. Michael."

"So do you…Ellen."

"We have all suffered." He couldn't tell if she was looking at him, her eyes flat and empty of expression. "How did you arrive here at a Richmond hospital?"

"I am a prisoner of the Confederacy," Mulligan said. "Again. And you?"

"It's a long story."

"Tell me."

"Not now. Are you seriously hurt?"

"Just a damaged leg and foot."

"Good. Maybe you'll be part of a prisoner exchange."

"Speaking of that—how is Mr. Kavanaugh?"

For the first time, he saw an anxious reaction in her dark eyes.

"Mr. Mulligan, I can't explain. Maybe when hostilities cease. I have to work another ward."

"Who is John Kavanaugh? A so called cousin? Brother? Husband? Lover, perhaps?"

"He is my husband."

"You could have told me the truth from the start."

"I could have. And since then, I have written you many letters in my mind."

"That's not good enough. I have been searching for you for over a year."

"I know you have."

"And never a single word. You have broken my heart!"

"Mine was broken long ago. If you love me, you will try to understand."

"Love you? I *do* love you, and if I could move, I would strike you!"

Ellen started to leave the room. Mulligan called out: "Do we have a child? Do we?"

Ellen turned to face him, her face drawn, her eyes suddenly moist. She was about to speak but something seized her and once again, he was staring at a mask of the woman he once knew as Abigail Donahue. "Good day, Mr. Mulligan," she said, and quickly left.

Another nurse entered. "I need to check that foot," she said.

As the nurse bathed and wrapped his foot and leg, Mulligan tried to catch his breath, thinking of this sudden chance meeting. What was Ellen doing in a Confederate hospital? Was she also a traitor?

"Where does nurse Ellen Kavanaugh work? What ward?"

"It's a ward for those with deadly wounds or contagious diseases like consumption. All the cases there are deemed hopeless. You know Ellen Kavanaugh?"

"In another world," Mulligan said.

The nurse, young and plain but with an efficient manner, stood by the bed, watching his face. "I won't ask any more questions, Mr. Mulligan. We are medical personnel. We serve the sick, regardless of what side they're on. Do you have any questions?"

After thinking, Mulligan said "No."

For two days, he stayed in the hospital, hearing the distant guns and reading parts of Reginald Taylor's journal. It had a style that brought back his cheerful if formal English voice:

"It is New Year's Eve, 1860, in New York, and there are glorious illuminations in the sky. Manhattan is bustling with energy and many carriages. There are so many people, and though I can't expect the Americans to speak like we English, the New York accent is harsh, even rude sounding.

The letter 'A' is universally pronounced like the 'A' in radish with an appalling nasality. I visited an art gallery but a painting of cavemen hiding in a pond from hungry dinosaurs is hardly suitable for serious art. There's a local tavern where the American poet, Walt Whitman, holds forth. One won't find a rhyme anywhere but the poetry is vibrant if at times indelicate. One serious note; with Lincoln's election, civil war seems inevitable. South Carolina has already seceded from the Union. The thought of that potential senseless slaughter fills me with dread, but I must cover it. I pray it ends quickly. How I miss Julia and the boys. In a few minutes, it will be 1861. As Whitman says, 'Allons!...come travel with me.'"

Reginald Taylor's eye witness account of Lincoln's inauguration resonated with Mulligan as he read:

"It was a splendid sunny March day, but one could feel the fear and danger, armed troops and sharp shooters posted everywhere. The Capitol Building stood unfinished. Despite threats, President Buchanan and President elect, Lincoln, arrived in an open carriage. Buchanan seemed pale and tired, Lincoln robust but somewhat awkward, in want of social graces. That disappeared with his inaugural address, delivered in a clear voice everyone heard. Though conciliatory, he argued that he had taken a sacred oath to defend the Constitution of the United States, and warned that a dismembered Union would lead to anarchy. The Rebels are preparing for war. A local journalist was so impressed with the risk of a bloody inferno threatening to engulf America that he skipped over Lincoln's speech and described

in detail the impressive inaugural ball and
what jewelry and fashionable gowns the
ladies wore as handsome couples danced under
gaslight."

Mulligan remembered the ballroom converted to a barracks with the commencement of the war. To his amusement, in the later part of the journal, Reginald Taylor referred to Mulligan as his "guide" and "splendid Irishman."

When he recovered, Michael Mulligan worked with horses, cleaning hooves, feeding them meager feed, watching for disease, but not training the herd as cavalry horses. Each day, the guns seemed closer and more buildings took hits. He saw soldiers marching and sometimes running in the streets. Like any city under siege, it seemed the whole population was slowly starving. At times, he glanced at the building where Ellen worked, hoping her face would appear in the window. She remained elusive. In his boot, Mulligan still carried the derringer with two bullets. Possibly the nurses knew about it, but at this point in the war, no one cared.

The end was clearly near.

In late March, Colonel Falkner rode up in a carriage and called to Mulligan exercising the horses. The colonel seemed older, his suit and white hat soiled. He held the reins in his old-looking hands. Down the street, Jefferson Davis's headquarters had escaped shelling.

"Major Mulligan, we have news Grant's army is getting closer. Things appear dire for our cause. We may have to evacuate, soon."

"I wish I could say that grieves, me, Colonel Falkner, but it doesn't."

"I understand, but you may have to take the horses out of danger."

"I could do that."

He sat on the carriage, watching Mulligan. "Where did you meet Nurse Kavanaugh?"

Mulligan was surprised. "At Gettysburg. I was wounded and she was my nurse. I guess she works for the Confederacy, now."

"As do you."

"I don't believe we are both prisoners."

"Maybe you are, Major."

"I have little to say about Nurse Kavanaugh, Colonel."

"I was told to inform you that yesterday, her husband died of consumption."

"Did Nurse Kavanaugh ask you to tell me this?"

"No. It was another nurse who thought you should know."

"Perhaps I don't care."

Colonel Falkner looked down the street at a warehouse. "We may have to blow that when the Federals arrive. I want the horses moved."

"I will see to that." After a moment, Mulligan asked, "Will I see her again?"

"I don't know, Major Mulligan. That may be up to you." A woman ran past them carrying a screaming child. "The first shot fired on Fort Sumter—a tragic blunder."

"That it was."

"I am working on a book, *The White Rose of Memphis*. I hope one day at a book launch, we can meet and discuss history and literature as fellow Americans and countrymen. I'll tell you about the Lost Cause and you can tell me all about Ireland."

"I would like that, sir."

"Good bye. I *do* hope we meet again, Major."

The colonel shook the reins and the matched team moved forward.

Michael Mulligan fed the horses, noticing that the rations of hay were growing smaller. He had grown used to the sounds of artillery, and even the horses seemed calm when shells hit the city buildings. He began thinking about Ellen, wondering if they would ever meet, and what would they possibly say. Wounded Rebel soldiers stumbled daily into Richmond.

With April 1st came the spring and a new desperation. Everyone knew the Federals were coming to seize Richmond. Outside the office of Jefferson Davis, barrels were placed for burning papers. Civilians watched from the streets as soldiers, some wounded, others exhausted and desperate, waited for evacuation orders. Michael Mulligan saddled Reginald Taylor's horse and drove the horses to a corral outside the city. No guards or sentries stopped him, though he still wore a Union soldier's cap. He left the horses in the care of two young blacks and the following day, rode toward Richmond, anxious to witness the end and possibly see Ellen again.

The evacuation continued. Citizens walked or rode carriages and horses out of town, while soldiers torched certain buildings. Mulligan saw government officials in front of the Jefferson Davis mansion burning records. Many buildings had lost their façades, revealing skeletal frameworks. A burning warehouse full of munitions suddenly exploded, killing nearby vagrants. Richmond had become a smoking inferno, the sky drained of natural color though the shelling had stopped. As Michael Mulligan rode toward the hospital, he was stopped by an elderly stooped black citizen.

"Uncle Lincum is coming," the man told him. "Uncle Lincum is coming."

Mulligan heard his name called and saw Colonel Falkner sitting in a buckboard.

"It's time to clear out, Major Mulligan."

"Not for me."

Colonel Falkner sat staring blankly ahead, gunmetal-colored smoke filling the sky.

"President Jefferson Davis has fled. I guess we are finally seeing the end of the Old South." He looked up at Mulligan. "Maybe that's good. We'll meet again, Major. I suggest you visit your old room in the hospital."

"Why's that?"

"You'll find out."

They saluted each other.

Colonel Falkner gently flicked the single horse with a whip and drove the buckboard down the road, pressed by hoards of people walking on either side, including women carrying babies. A few tried to climb on the wagon. Mulligan rode against the flow of human traffic fleeing the capital, passing stranded old people calling out for help. Because of the chaos, blacks and whites shared the same road.

In Richmond, looters broke into stores and buildings. Though still intact, the hospital was deserted. On the second floor, Mulligan found his bed and on the sheets, his knife and Union uniform cleaned and pressed. On top of the uniform was a letter addressed to him. Mulligan changed into his uniform and then sat down and read the letter. He was struck at seeing Ellen's beautiful handwriting for the first time:

"My dear Michael Mulligan,
As you read this, friends are taking me out of town. I am sorry I didn't communicate with you earlier but it was hard with hostilities. I should have told you I was married, however unhappily, to yet another Irishman. I think our affair, though wonderful, came about because of my awful situation with a drunken violent husband and the war, itself. You were wounded, as well. That doesn't mean I did not love you. I did. I still do. Now I believe we have survived. For some of us, I'm not sure that is good.

Before you hate me, I must inform you that when Mrs. Bachman sent me back to Washington, I was arrested and brought to Army headquarters. That's when I discovered my husband was a Rebel spy. They were going to put me in prison as an accomplice but then they gave me a choice: prison, or returning with my sick husband to spy for the Union. I sent back notes in code whenever possible to Stanton's office. I had little time for personal correspondence. When you showed up, I knew we could both be in jeopardy.

Michael, we are different people after all this time. I will leave my sister's address in New York, and when you are free, come visit us and maybe we can try again, even if our situation is altered. And no, I

did not get pregnant from our last wonderful
time together.

I love you and please forgive me if I
have hurt you in any way. I will forever
cherish the memory of our time together at
Gettysburg. War brought us together. I hope
peace doesn't drive us apart. Yours always,
Ellen Donahue (my maiden name)"

Michael Mulligan reread the letter and then folded the page
and slipped it into the envelope. With her New York address,
certainly he could find Ellen Donahue again, and even forward his
old letters. They might have a chance in a post Civil War world.

*War brought us together. I hope peace doesn't drive us
apart.*

He would certainly contact Reginald Taylor's widow and
send along Taylor's war journal in the hopes of publication.
Mulligan even imagined writing an introduction.

Michael Mulligan picked up his bedroll and walked toward
the street and his horse. Desperate citizens continued to evacuate
Richmond, some looters carrying what they could hold. Hundreds
of refugees passed under a broken arch. As Federal troops
approached the city, the cannons and bugles stopped. There
would be no waving of sabers or thundering hooves. Major
Mulligan would ride out to meet them and they would give him
another Spencer and then he would connect with General
Sheridan's brigade to hunt and trap General Lee's remaining
army.

JOURNEY

ON MAY 24TH, MICHAEL Mulligan visited the office of the British ambassador, Sir Frederick Bruce. The ambassador was a stout man with a bald head and a thick white beard. He sat behind an ornate desk, the window open on the street. They could hear the cheering crowds lining the D.C. streets and celebrating the war ending as wave after wave of soldiers passed. A British flag hung over the ambassador's desk. For all of Mulligan's life, that flag had been a symbol of oppression. Mulligan sat holding his Panama Planter's hat while the ambassador watched him with some impatience.

"I was about to watch the parade, sir," he said. "What can I do for you?"

"My name is Michael Mulligan. I traveled into Virginia with one of your countrymen, Reginald Taylor. We were—"

"My God!"

"Sir?"

"Mr. Mulligan!"

"Yes?"

"With Sheridan's cavalry?"

"Yes." He shook the ambassador's outstretched hand. "How did you know?"

"We've been looking for you for over two months."

"For me? Why? I haven't killed an Englishman in several years."

Amused, the ambassador explained with rising excitement.

"You see, we knew Reginald Taylor was writing about the Civil War, and he informed us he was joining you to find Sheridan's cavalry brigade as they tracked General Lee. He was hoping to be there for the surrender, if there was one."

"That's right."

"When Mr. Taylor's wife didn't hear from him for two months, she informed us and we began tracking you. General Sheridan's initial report indicated you never arrived, which meant you were dead, captured, or—or a deserter."

"I was captured," Mulligan told him. "When Richmond fell, I joined Sheridan."

"And we have a new report to that effect. Mr. Mulligan, I must say we were hoping you hadn't departed for California or New York. Allow me to shake your hand again."

They shook hands. Military music and cheers came through the window, and Mulligan heard the clopping of horse's hooves.

"Anxious to find her husband, Julia Taylor left for America in mid-April." Michael Mulligan could feel the ambassador's eyes on him. "This is quite delicate, but did Mr. Taylor survive?"

"I'm afraid I have bad news, Ambassador Bruce."

"I suspected as much. Tell me."

Michael Mulligan told the story of his trip to Virginia with Reginald Taylor, and the attack by highwaymen resulting in Taylor's death. Mulligan displayed Reginald Taylor's journal and three letters he had written to his wife but never posted.

"Could you give this to Mr. Taylor's widow as he requested? I have included a letter myself. It's so sad to give her this terrible news, but she must know what happened to Reggie—to Mr. Taylor—her courageous husband. He was a fine man."

Frederick Bruce took the envelope and journal.

"I shall be honored...and saddened."

"Reginald Taylor wanted his war journal to be published. I've read it, and it's a fine piece of work, Ambassador."

"Perhaps you could present the journal and letters to his widow yourself. She's here. In point of fact, Julia Taylor may be watching the parade as we speak. I could arrange a meeting for tomorrow. Perhaps at noon in this office?"

Michael Mulligan hesitated. "If you think that's recommended."

"I do. She will want to hear about her late husband from you. Where are you staying?"

"Hotel Whitman. It's a dump unfit for a lady to visit."

"I understand. Incidentally, why aren't you riding with the others?"

"I was with General Sheridan's cavalry, and he's not represented, today."

"On this glorious occasion, we should *all* be represented. I'll keep the Taylor material here for safekeeping."

"Good, Ambassador."

Mulligan was about to leave.

"Mr. Mulligan, another delicate question."

"Yes?"

"Do you know where Reginald Taylor is buried? We may want to repatriate his body to England."

"I can draw a map," Mulligan said. "Unless animals or grave robbers have disturbed the remains."

"Yes, of course." Ambassador Bruce stood up. "My thanks to you, Mr. Mulligan." He consulted a pocket watch. "And now—I think I shall view your splendid parade."

Michael Mulligan shook the ambassador's hand and left the office. Out in the street, the cavalry rode by as the crowds cheered and the bands played. The jubilation might dispel the gloom of President Lincoln's assassination the previous month, but Mulligan noticed Lincoln's somewhat sad cabinet members on a flag draped platform, their smiles frozen. Perhaps it was because Lincoln had not lived to see the May celebration and the disbanding of the Union Army at war's end. The gaiety all around him failed to lift his own spirits. For reasons Mulligan would never understand, large boisterous crowds often left him feeling alone and isolated. Soon, the army would release him and Mulligan could decide whether to make the long journey to San Francisco to see his son, or visit New York again and connect with theatre friends. He could also visit Ellen Donahue in New York. Was it possible to revive a dead wartime romance?

His days as a cavalry officer were over.

At the Whitman Hotel, he passed Jonas behind the desk, a fat man with bad teeth and stringy unwashed hair. Jonas always seemed to be laughing at some private joke.

"They can parade all they want, some Rebs are still fighting in the west."

"Maybe they haven't heard the news, Jonas. The war is over."

"It's over for some, maybe."

He climbed the stairs to his small room, with a bed and a sink. He was not far from Ford's theatre and the rooming house where Lincoln died in a similar cramped room. He lay on the bed and tried to nap, catching up on sleep lost when nightmares invaded his evening rest. Then he heard a loud knocking and opening the door, saw the round unshaven face of Jonas, now grinning and exposing his blackened teeth.

"I think you got a visitor downstairs," he said. "Mulligan, you old Mick, you might have a live one."

"What?"

"You got a visitor—a lady."

Jonas winked and walked down the hall. Moments later, Michael Mulligan walked down the worn carpeted stairs and into the dim lobby where he saw a slender well-dressed woman sitting alone, looking too elegant for the crumbling hotel. She wore a long flowing skirt without a fashionable bustle, her uncovered hair long and curled. Her dark blue eyes were round, luminous and bold. Other residents stared at her as she rose to greet him. Michael Mulligan bowed and kissed her gloved hand.

"No need to be so formal, Mr. Mulligan. You *are* Mr. Mulligan?"

"I am. And you are Julia Taylor."

"I am she. Ambassador Bruce found me with news I had anticipated. It is sad but better knowing what happened to

Reginald. Tomorrow, I shall be delighted to collect his journal and other effects."

"My condolences."

Julia searched his face. "May we adjoin somewhere to have tea or whatever you drink? I have so many questions…if it's not too much to ask."

"Of course."

They left the hotel and Mulligan found a restaurant with a well-lit tea room. Elegant couples sat, taking tea and coffee and having lunch. The celebration was ending in the streets. Julia ordered tea and Mulligan coffee. For some time, she didn't speak but stared at her cup, holding it in a dainty hand, her thoughts elsewhere. Then she stared at him.

"Mr. Mulligan. I guess I better hear all the details about my husband."

Once again, Michael Mulligan was back in that cold meadow charging the three surprised highwaymen, firing his Spencer repeating carbine, and then his horse was slipping on the ice, the sound of the horse's breaking leg like a gunshot, Mulligan suddenly on the ground staring into the barrel of an old muzzle loader. He would always remember the messianic face of Reginald Taylor as he rode next to the thief and fired point blank with the derringer, taking a rifle blast himself, the robber unaware that his own life would end within minutes.

"Reggie…Reginald, himself against violence, saved my life."

"You fired first. Why?"

"I knew what they were, vicious men who would stop a Confederate soldier, accuse him of being a deserter and shoot or hang him, taking everything he had, and Union soldiers they could claim were the enemy. I just knew they were evil."

"That's not very scientific," Julia said.

"It isn't. The Rebels who took me prisoner and buried Reginald confirmed they were tracking those very men."

"Well, that's commendable. And I am proud of Reginald for being so brave and saving your life. What a tragic end, however."

"I thought of him when Lee surrendered to Grant. It would have been a big moment for your husband."

"Indeed. He sent an article to England about Lincoln's first inauguration. Your war between the states kept him in America and away from his wife and family."

Mulligan caught an edge in her voice and thought of his son in San Francisco.

"I am sorry you had to come so far to hear such terrible news, Mrs. Taylor."

Michael Mulligan expected Julia Taylor to cry, but her gaze and voice were level. They ordered a refill on the tea and coffee and sat in silence for a few minutes.

"Mr. Mulligan, remember we were apart for over four years."

"Most people simply call me Mulligan."

"Okay, Mulligan. You must consider that Reginald and I grew apart in that time. He wrote regularly, of course, but it wasn't the same. I struggle to remember his voice. His twin boys have forgotten what he looked like and sounded like."

"How old are the boys?"

"Eight. They were nearly four when Reginald left."

"I see."

"Do you have any children?"

"One. A boy. He's 10."

"And you left him when the war was about to break out?"

To his surprise, Mulligan felt himself blushing.

"I did. I guess you have a point, Mrs. Taylor. Maybe you should have brought the boys to America."

"That wasn't an option." She met his eyes. "Of course, it is nice Reginald was fulfilling *his* destiny to write a book about the American Civil War."

"He was there for the first battle of Bull Run and there for one of the last, Cold Harbor. It was a bloody hell for nearly two weeks."

"He survived that only to die."

"I'm sure you're devastated, but I must tell you that I have never been predisposed to love the English. Your nation has been my enemy since childhood. I can honestly say I am proud to consider your late husband a friend."

"Well good, Mulligan. You speak well for an Irishman, I'll say that."

"You also speak well, Mrs. Taylor."

"I didn't mean to say that, exactly."

"I had good teachers, including cruel Anglo plantation bosses who taught me how to curse."

"Point taken, sir, and I *am* being rude. Sorry." Julia Taylor sipped her tea and then placed the cup in the saucer, again confronting him with sharp cobalt blue eyes. "You may find this insensitive of me, Mulligan, but part of the reason I came here, assuming I found Reginald alive, was to ask for a divorce."

"That would've shocked him."

"Indeed, but I needed a husband and a father to my boys."

"I understand."

"Do you? Good. Now to business. I will pay you well to take me to Reginald's grave. Ambassador Bruce can contact the mayor of Richmond regarding any legal requirements to exhume and transport the body."

Mulligan leaned back in his chair.

"It's too dangerous. Those three highwaymen are being replaced by bushwhackers, outlaw gangs still fighting the Civil War, using it as an excuse to plunder and kill."

Julia Taylor motioned to the waiter for the bill. "I'm aware of the danger. I know you are a brave man, Mr. Mulligan. I could pay for extra men."

He confronted her. "Listen, being a woman and traveling even with a group of armed men could make you a target yourself."

"Reginald wasn't afraid. I am not afraid."

"All the same—"

"I understand if you are reluctant. I will travel without you. How far is Richmond? A hundred miles, you say?"

"The grave is at a crossroads near Richmond. Julia?"

"I prefer you address me formally for now, Mr. Mulligan."

"Mrs. Julia Taylor, I don't think it's a good idea. Richmond is still in ruins. The Negroes are jubilant but I'm sure the whites still harbor resentment."

"Don't you have Federal troops in Richmond?"

"Yes."

"I'll take the risk."

Julia paid the waiter and left a tip.

"It is possible wild pigs dug up and devoured his body."

"That *would* be awkward, Mr. Mulligan. But this is a trip I have to make. Once I have Reginald's body, I'll ship him to England."

They stood up. "At least, you won't have to divorce Reggie."

Her expression didn't register his remark. Standing outside in the busy street, Julia Taylor gave Mulligan a card with her hotel. "I can be reached here if you change your mind. I'll be at the ambassador's office, tomorrow. Perhaps you could draw me a map to his grave. If we don't meet again, thanks for being Reginald's friend. It's been a pleasure meeting you and good day, Mr. Mulligan."

She shook his hand and walked across the dung-filled street, dodging a fast moving carriage. Mulligan watched her leave. Then he went back to the hotel and tried to rest. Guiding Mrs. Julia Taylor would be a job and would certainly pay well, but he wasn't sure if he could travel through that country, again, or even find the meadow where Reginald Taylor died. Something about Julia Taylor attracted and repulsed him. He didn't appreciate her intense direct stare and yet admired her strength.

But I shouldn't have made that remark about divorce, he thought.

He lay on the bed, running through options. Perhaps the trip to Richmond would not be that dangerous, but if they ran into a gang of bushwhackers, it would go badly. After a while, the voices in his head seemed to quiet. His sleep was disturbed by recurring nightmares of men charging through smoke and exploding with canister fire. Mulligan woke up, still tired. He left his room and walked through the lobby where men sat, some drinking from whiskey bottles. Jonas watched him from behind the desk, but said nothing. People crowded the sidewalks, many laughing and happy. Carriages and men on horseback filled the streets. A group of black singers sang on the corner, running through many gospel songs. Mulligan saw a tall stocky Indian man arguing with a white man in front of the restaurant where he had taken Julia Taylor. The Indian wore buckskin and had a black broad brimmed hat with a white feather. He also carried a knife and pistol in his belt.

"We don't serve Indians," the white man said. "Not in this restaurant."

"Why not? I'm a warrior. I have many horses and wives."

"Leave or I shall call the soldiers."

The Indian towered over the white man, but Mulligan noticed his manner was arrogant but not hostile.

"You don't serve Injuns? I bet you don't serve Negroes either," the Indian said.

"This is a white establishment. We don't accept Negroes."

"I don't blame you. I had to kill a few Negroes myself. And some Union soldiers. My people are *still* fighting."

He stepped forward. The white man backed toward the door.

"You stand back!"

Mulligan addressed the proprietor. "Why not make an exception? I enjoyed your tea and coffee, this morning. The war is over and we have a new birth of freedom."

The white man briefly glanced at Mulligan. "We have a policy, sir." He went back into the restaurant. Mulligan regarded the Indian.

"Their coffee isn't bad. My name is Michael Mulligan."

"Irving Watie," the Indian said. He did not extend his hand. "I don't expect much service in this town. You Union?"

"Of course." He hesitated before speaking. "Were you serious about killing Union soldiers?"

"Hell yes. I fought for the Confederate Cherokee Brigade. My cousin is Stand Isaac Watie and he's still fighting. Maybe I should join him and come back to burn this town to the ground."

"Why would Indians fight for the Confederacy? They had slaves."

"So did we. Your damn Federal government took our land *and* our slaves." Though there was anger in his voice, Irving suddenly smiled at Mulligan. "And I don't need your help, Irish."

"I don't believe you do."

Irving turned to walk away. Then he stopped and looked at Mulligan. "Something is stalking you, brother. Beware. Maybe you need *my* help."

Irving disappeared down the crowded street. Mulligan found another restaurant, and while walking back to his hotel, wondered about Irvin's last statement. At times, he did feel someone was stalking him.

In the morning, Mulligan visited the ambassador's office. He found him with Julia Taylor examining the effects of her late husband. She looked at him without smiling.

"So glad you're here, Mr. Mulligan," Ambassador Bruce said.

"And I am glad," Julia said tonelessly. "Ready to guide me?"

"Yes." Mulligan laid out his plan. "I think it might be good to leave with at least two other men. The road should be clear and the grave is not hard to find...assuming it is undisturbed. Rather than take Reginald's body back to D.C., I recommend taking the James River to Chesapeake Bay. There, you'll find passage to England."

"That was our plan exactly," the ambassador said, smiling at them.

"Then it's settled," Julia said. "I will rent a covered wagon and horse, a tent and some supplies, and we'll be off in say...two days?"

"That's about right," Mulligan said. "A buckboard might do."

"You have your own horse?"

"It's Reggie's horse," Mulligan said.

After a pause, she said, "Very good."

That afternoon, Michael Mulligan visited Fort Stevens searching for military men being mustered out of the service. Many would need jobs after the war. He also collected his mail, including a package from the Maguires in San Francisco.

Another letter was from a convent in upstate New York. In the military library, he opened the package and saw a letter from the foster parents of his son, written in Mr. Maguire's terse style. Everything was "fine" and "when was he coming back now that the war was over?" The package included a photo of the older couple and his son, boyishly handsome and grown, staring deadpan at the camera. Beneath books on warfare, Mulligan wrote a return letter explaining all that had happened to him and that soon, he would leave for San Francisco. There was news about a new transcontinental railway that would cut cross country travel by weeks. He praised his son on his growth and beautiful face, and promised to return soon.

"It's been too long, John, my dear son, it's been too long. Remember me."

He then read the letter from New York. It was from Ellen Donahue Kavanaugh:

"My Dear Michael Mulligan,
You will find me living in a convent for the Sisters of Notre Dame. I joined the order to dedicate my life to God, and heal the horrors of war through prayer. I will always remember our time together, and I must confess, I will miss the passionate side of our relationship, forged by war. But now, it is time for peace and meditation and good works. I will hold thoughts of love for you. Please understand, Michael, my love for you isn't gone, but it has changed and merged with a love of Jesus Christ and his compassion for humankind. Please write or visit. I would so love that.
Yours in Christ,
Sister Mary Ellen, (Ellen Donahue Kavanaugh)"

It was in the library that the Secretary of Military Records discovered him.

"Major Mulligan, so nice to see you again."

He sat next to Mulligan.

"Mr. Secretary. And how are you?"

"The war is over. Therefore, I am good, very good indeed." After a moment, he asked, "Did you ever find that Abigail woman?"

"Yes. In a Confederate hospital. I am, in fact, holding a letter from her. She is now a nun named Sister Mary Ellen."

"Really? How strange life is."

"But you knew her as spy for the Union."

The secretary did not avoid his eyes. "Maybe I did, Major, and maybe I didn't. It is now time to move on."

"I will, Mr. Secretary."

Michael Mulligan sat in the library for a long time thinking about Ellen's letter. Then he went to another office to sign papers and receive his severance pay, with more to come.

"Would you like a photo, Major Mulligan?"

"I'm not sure." He realized his son had no photo of him so Mulligan sat for a formal release photo, hat over crossed knee, his face composed and still for the camera. One day, the glass negative might cover a greenhouse.

As Mulligan left the building, he saw a familiar face.

"Caleb?" The young man stopped and looked at him, puzzled. He had matured and was no longer the young boy who carried the colors. "I met you at Gettysburg," Mulligan said. "Remember? We found Sallie, the bull terrier, guarding her fallen soldiers."

"I *do* remember you," Caleb said. His expression changed and Mulligan saw a sadness in his eyes. Mulligan noticed the dog wasn't with him. "Sallie was killed in battle at Hatcher's Run," Caleb told him. "It happened in February."

"I am sorry to hear that."

"Under fire, we buried her where she fell." Mulligan saw moisture in Caleb's eyes above the hard line of his jaw. "She was a great dog," he said.

"That she was."

After an awkward silence, Caleb said, "I need to check on back pay. Nice seeing you."

166

They shook hands. "Good luck, young man."

Mulligan was still thinking of the pug-nosed dehydrated dog licking water from his palm when he arrived at his hotel and found a note from Julia:

> *Mr. Mulligan, I have found two extraordinary people to accompany us. I have plenty of supplies, so it should be a pleasant journey. Please contact me soon.*
> *Mrs. Julia Taylor.*

He caught Jonas grinning at him.

"The lady is sending the Mick personal notes, eh? Better not disappoint her."

Jonas started to laugh. Mulligan gently squeezed the man's flabby throat. He could smell the cheap bourbon.

"Don't ever call me a Mick again," he said. "Or I will cut your throat."

Mulligan walked to his room. He reread Ellen's letter and remembered their wild lovemaking, trying to imagine the free spirit he knew as Abigail Donahue dressed in a nun's habit. Then he walked over to Julia Taylor's hotel, the gold lobby bright under the turning crystal chandeliers. A bellboy took him to her room and after a light knock, he entered and saw Julia standing by the window. She turned.

"I hired a marvelous Indian fellow who is good with a gun and knife, and he knows the country. I think it's important we hire oppressed people and give them a hand up. And I found a woman who wants to start an orchestra in Richmond. We'll have some classical violin music to entertain us. You like this arrangement, Mr. Mulligan?"

"Did you say 'an Indian fellow'?"

"Yes."

"Irving Watie?"

"Yes, as a matter of fact. You know him?"

"We briefly met. He fought for the Confederacy."

"Really?"

"And this woman—"

"A Miss Shelby Reed. Not a great conversationalist, nor particularly attractive, but she will fit in, I'm sure."

"Ma'am? Mrs. Taylor? We could run into a gang of bushwhackers on the road. We'll need more than an arrogant Cherokee and a woman who plays violin."

"Buck up, Mr. Mulligan. We'll do fine."

"This is not a pleasure trip, Mrs. Taylor. This is to dig up what's left of your husband's body and ship the remains back to merry old England."

Julia Taylor watched him, her expression passive and thoughtful. "I'm aware of that, Mr. Mulligan. If you don't approve, draw us a map and we'll leave without you— tomorrow at sunup."

Saying nothing, Mulligan walked toward the door.

"Mr. Mulligan?"

"Yes?" He saw her reflection in a large wall mirror.

"Are you all right? You seem bothered by something. Bad news from home, perhaps?"

He turned to face her. "My son is fine."

"Good. I was wondering where my plucky little Irishman went."

"I'm right here."

"See you tomorrow, Mr. Mulligan. We can discuss payment then."

Mulligan turned his hat in his hands.

"I got a letter from a former lover, today."

"A lover? Sounds deliciously decadent. You Americans are far more out spoken about these love matters than we British. I shall look forward to meeting her."

"She is now a nun in some convent, muttering prayers at the moon!"

Julia Taylor considered this statement. "That is too bad for you but good for her if she's found some spiritual fulfillment. Neither Reginald nor I were very religious."

Mulligan suddenly opened the door. "Good night."

"Sunup, tomorrow?"

Without answering, Mulligan left. In the street, he saw Irving.

"Hey Irish, they let you in to see the boss lady? I can't get past the door. What a way to treat a Cherokee warrior. I'm going to write them a letter of protest."

Michael Mulligan walked down the crowded street. When Mulligan entered the Whitman Hotel, Jonas was waiting for him.

"You better take your possessions and move now," he said. "I won't have this disrespect in my establishment."

"As you wish, Jonas."

"I'm sick of you Micks comin' around here. You'll find your bags under the stairs. And don't worry, I didn't steal nothin'."

"I have nothing to steal."

Mulligan found his military bag and suitcase. His Spencer carbine and .44 Colt remained in a rented locker. Jonas continued speaking.

"You just get out, you thick Mick."

Mulligan stared at Jonas who dropped his eyes. "You better be careful, you drunken piece of filth. I still have a knife on me."

"Just get out," Jonas said. "I've had enough of you Irish in my place."

"I thought I was the only Irishmen here," Mulligan said as he walked toward the door. A window in the door was broken and covered with a board. Mulligan stopped and turned. "What other Irishman came here?"

"Some young rogue off the boat. I could hardly understand him with his accent. Asked if you lived here. I told him 'Yes' and then he asked for a room and I told him 'No.'"

Mulligan looked around the lobby and up the dark stairs, and then walked into the street. It was twilight. There were a few rooming houses but he knew renting a room would be hard with so many revelers in town. He could possibly sleep at the stable where he kept Reginald's horse. He might knock on Julia's door and ask to sleep on her elegant white couch. Would that violate her English sensibilities?

As he walked, Michael Mulligan felt he was being followed. Passing a shop window, he saw the reflection of a young man following him. He turned down an alley and crossed a small park. Then he slipped behind a tree and watched the same young man, a cap low over his eyes. He waited until the man passed and followed him. At some point, the youth seemed alarmed, looking to either side, and then he began walking fast before him. As more crowds came toward Mulligan, the young man disappeared into the rush of pedestrians. Mulligan waited for his stalker to return but he didn't.

As Mulligan walked to the stables, he saw another man on horseback approaching him down a narrow alley. He couldn't see the rider's face but he nodded and touched his cap as he rode by. Mulligan said "Good evening" in Irish but the horsemen didn't respond. Then Mulligan continued down the alley to the stables where he found the proprietor, another Irishman.

"I wonder if I could bed down in an empty stall?"

"Love your horse that much, do ya?"

"Why sure."

"I'll need to charge you two dollars."

"Done."

Mulligan spread a blanket on the straw. He had his shaving razor for the morning. The sounds and smells of horses calmed him, and he could even sleep through a horse occasionally kicking his stall. As he slept, he heard a low warning nicker from his horse and opening his eyes, moonlight coming in the window, he saw a gargoyle face above him, black tongue protruding, the eyes bulging. Mulligan lifted his knife, about to slash the monster's face when it suddenly disappeared as if by magic, the body following and dangling over him.

"Behold," a voice said.

In the lamplight, Mulligan saw a young man, a sock in his mouth, his arms tied behind him as he hung suspended from Irving's arm. He made whimpering sounds.

"Shall I kill him, Irish? He was about to shoot you with this little girl gun."

Irving dropped a derringer to the floor of the stable. Mulligan confronted the terrified young man. "Why were you going to shoot me?"

He ripped the sock from his mouth. Irving dropped the boy on the straw covered floor, kicking him lightly.

"Yeah," Irving said, "what do you think you're doing sneaking around here?"

Sitting against a stall, the boy began to cry.

"Jaysus, don't hurt me, please."

Mulligan heard the accent and spoke to him in Irish.

"I don't speak Irish," the boy said. "We lost that long ago."

"Why did you try to kill me, young man?"

After a moment, the boy relaxed, catching his breath.

"I was on the dock at Queenstown and a man came up to me and asked where I was going. I told him and he showed me an article in the paper about a Michael Mulligan and an Englishman riding toward Richmond from Washington, D.C."

Mulligan squatted down and studied the boy's thin face.

"And they paid you to kill me?"

The boy nodded Yes. "One hundred pounds. Fifty pounds at first for me ma, and then the rest later after—"

"Who were they?"

"I don't know."

"Did they mention a brotherhood of Irish assassins?"

Mulligan's face was close to his as the boy rapidly blinked his eyes. "They said something about you being a traitor to your people."

"You're a wanted man, Irish? I knew there was something about you I liked," said Irving.

"How did you know what I looked like?"

"They had a photo. You were standing with another man, an officer, with a horse between you."

Mulligan remembered posing with General Elon Farnsworth shortly before Gettysburg.

"And how did they get that photo?"

"I don't know." Irving cut the ropes and the boy tried to cover his eyes in the light. "They know a lot about you."

"What shall we do with him?" Irving asked.

"You could scalp him or I could cut his throat." The boy started sobbing again and wet his pants. "Or we could let him go. What's your name?"

"Seamus O' Hara."

"Well, Seamus, we are going to Richmond, tomorrow. Maybe you could join us and use your little gun if we get jumped by bushwhackers. You'll be paid. If you decide not to join us, don't come near me again or I will kill you. My Remington derringer has *two* shots." The boy nodded, trembling. "Thanks, Irving. I guess I owe you something."

"There will be more," he said. "I know blood feuds. A rival Cherokee family killed all of Stand Watie's relatives...just because he agreed the tribe should leave Tennessee for the new Indian Territory in Oklahoma. How did he know the trek would kill so many? They will come after you again, Irish."

"Yes, they will...but not this week."

Unsteady and still trembling, the boy stood up. He began talking.

"By Christ, I wet myself. Look, I'm sorry. I won't try to kill you, again. I was born just before the famine started. Me da died of hunger, me ma tried to keep the farm going until some Scots moved in and took it and English soldiers after driving us off, and me ma was too weak to do the work the English finally gave us, and me sisters and brothers died or left.... so I had to leave for America when I got the chance, and when the man promised to give her 50 pounds, I...." Seamus looked around the stable. Michael Mulligan had stretched out in a stall, his hat covering his eyes. Seamus walked over to Irving, now placing blankets on some straw, his horse tethered nearby. "The voyage over was terrible, with people dying on the ship and—"

"I don't want to hear your sad story," Irving said. "Someday, I'll tell you about the Trail of Tears. Thousands of my people died. Sleep, white boy."

Seamus suddenly found himself in darkness when the lamp was blown out. In the moonlight, he found another stall. Gradually, he slept from exhaustion.

The next morning, they paid the proprietor and left for Julia's hotel, Mulligan stopping to retrieve his weapons. When they arrived, they saw the covered wagon pulled by two horses; Julia, in a yellow cotton dress, sat in the seat next to Shelby Reed, a round heavy woman with hair tried in a bun. She had thick glasses and protruding teeth. Michael Mulligan introduced Seamus O' Hara, trying to control his nervous horse.

"He tried to kill me last night, but has decided to join us. He'll need a rifle."

"I can supply one," Julia said, looking happy and confident. "The young man could use a meal. We have supplies in the wagon. Are we ready to depart?"

D.C. spectators in the early morning watched as the wagon driven by two women and trailed by three men left the city and headed toward Richmond.

What took two weeks in winter would take three days in the summer, and as they rode down the dusty well-traveled trail, Mulligan considered the possibilities of flash floods making the gravesite unrecognizable. He carried a compass and could put himself within 30 yards of the grave, but without the cross marker, it might be difficult to find the exact location to dig. Irving had ridden ahead and Mulligan rode next to Seamus. The wagon moved slowly before them, rocking slightly from side to side behind the swaying horses. Mulligan glanced at Seamus, bouncing on his horse.

"How are you supposed to contact these Irish people who want me dead?"

"Through my mother. She knows the one gentleman as a nice generous fellow. If I accomplish my mission, they promised to pay another 50 pounds."

"Does the 'nice generous fellow' have a name?"

"I think it was Sean."

"And what proof do they need?"

Seamus laughed softly to himself. "They did suggest sending a photo of your severed head."

"It might be hard to convince a professional photographer to do that," Mulligan said. "But I could make a fake head. Made quite a few for *Richard III* and *Macbeth*."

They rode on and stopped for lunch. Julia Taylor had bought sufficient supplies, including fresh meat, tea and wine. Irving had not returned. Shelby Reed ate quietly.

"I hope you can make some violin music," Julia said.

"Maybe later. Did Irving say his last name was Watie?"

"Correct."

Shelby nodded to herself, her expression passive.

"Some of the Cherokee supported Andy Jackson's Indian removal policy."

"Don't mention that to Irving," Mulligan said.

Shelby didn't reply. She took out her violin and played "Oh Suzanna," the lively melody making the lunch feel more like a picnic. Mulligan and Seamus drank wine while Julia sipped her tea and seemed quite happy, forgetting their grim mission.

"I just adore being English," she said.

After lunch, Seamus practiced with the rifle, missing his paper target even at close range. Then they moved on, meeting Irving at night. He had set up a camp with a huge fire.

"I think one of us should stand guard," he said.

"A good idea," said Mulligan.

After a meal of beef, potatoes and bread, they drank more wine and tea.

"I can't touch the wine," Irving said. "It makes me crazy."

"It makes me a bit crazy too," Seamus said, "and I love it."

As Shelby played her repertoire of Mozart and Stephen Foster, Irving took Mulligan to one side.

"I found some dead Union cavalry soldiers in a meadow near here," he said. "They were stripped down to their underwear."

"How do you know they were Union cavalry?"

Irving produced an army spur. "The thieves left this. And I saw horse tracks. One horse is missing a rear shoe."

"We'll have to alert the army when we get to Richmond."

Mulligan stood guard, but during the night, he heard an argument. When he walked back to the fire, Julia Taylor was pushing Shelby and Irving apart, the short heavy woman's face distorted with fury, the tall massive Indian dwarfing her.

"What's going on?"

"Irving's cousin, Stand Watie, is a traitor to the Indian people," Shelby said, her large glasses reflecting the firelight. "He sold out his own tribe."

"It was a done deal. There was nothing the Cherokee and other tribes could do...and you better watch your mouth, you ugly squaw, because he's *still* fighting."

"What's that supposed to mean, Irving? I'll shoot both of you."

"Please stop this at once," Julia said. Seamus took a drink of wine.

"Hell, we Irish have been killing each other for centuries."

The next morning, Irving was gone when they broke camp. The day was warm, a gentle breeze blowing through the trees. Shelby sat next to Julia, holding the reins, and Mulligan rode beside them.

"I hope we haven't lost Irving. We might need him."

"I hope so too," Julia said.

"I think slavery will remain a curse on this land, even though abolished," Shelby said. "And the treatment of indigenous people is just as bad. Stand Watie is the worst kind of traitor who joins the oppressors against his own people." She reached back and took out her violin. "But I admit, I did shoot my mouth off. Maybe I better stick to tea."

"We have to work together," Julia said.

Shelby played "Shenandoah" and Mulligan felt the melancholy music as he joined Seamus, staring at the road.

"I guess we'll all cross the wide Missouri, someday," Mulligan said.

"I could use another shot of wine."

"Wait until lunch," said Mulligan. "You need to practice with the rifle. I've seen bad shots in my day but—"

"I know. I can't hit shit."

Irving met them, sitting his horse in the middle of the road as the sun was setting. "I set up a camp," he said.

They settled and prepared food, Shelby and Irving eating in silence.

"I saw a band of Gypsies on the road," Irving finally said. "They were in costume, like some theatre troupe."

"Really?"

"That's right, Mrs. Taylor. Maybe they need a fiddle player."

Shelby said nothing. Seamus stood guard but was asleep when Shelby took his place. In the morning, Irving had ridden ahead and they continued down the road.

"We are close," Mulligan said. "The grave is near a crossroads. I *can* find the crossroads. I hope I can find the grave."

"Ambassador Bruce notified the Downey Mortuary in Richmond," Julia said. "I will need a paper from them before I can take Reginald home."

They heard many men on horseback approaching and Mulligan took out his Spencer. Seamus reached for his new pistol but dropped it on the road. Moments later, Union cavalry rode into view, Irving Watie riding with them. Mulligan met them, an officer blocking the road. He spoke in a rich resonant voice.

"I am Captain Robert Gingles Perky. Who are you? Identify yourself."

"I am Major Mulligan, recently of the Vermont cavalry. I rode with Sheridan." Mulligan produced his paper. "Why is my man riding with you?"

"We found him and he wouldn't show us any identification."

"This is my country," Irving said. "I don't need it."

"He's with us," Julia said.

"All the same, we need identification."

"I told them about the dead soldiers," Irving said.

"We've been plagued by bushwhackers on a robbing spree," the captain said. "I think they are former Rebs, and about 10 in number. We'll hang the lot if we catch them. Robbing and killing our soldiers will not be tolerated."

"Good luck in your endeavor, Captain," Julia said.

Captain Perky seemed amused. "You know, this road is dangerous for anyone, let alone two women, one man and a boy."

"I ain't a boy," Seamus said.

"And Richmond is a city of desperate people. Good luck to *you.*"

They galloped down the road with Irving. Mulligan sat his horse.

"I don't like losing Irving."

"Then we better proceed immediately," Julia said.

They moved on down the road, riding into a cloud of dust, black families now appearing out of the woods and converging on the road, individuals and families with children, one large group breaking into gospel songs. Shelby took out her violin and found the key, playing along until the walking black families disappeared. They passed white travelers on foot who stared at them in silence. When Mulligan found the crossroads, they left the main road and headed toward a row of trees and distant hills that looked familiar. Mulligan remembered the snow and ice of a country road, and picking their way carefully when the robbers appeared, but with trees and grass and flowers in full bloom, it seemed a different landscape. Heavy rains could obliterate the lonely grave.

"Are we close? This is rough terrain for the horses and wagon."

Mulligan looked at his compass. He dismounted and walked up a rise and stared across a meadow at some trees and a large boulder and then he saw a crude wooden cross, tilting to one side. He walked quickly, leading the horse, and moments later, stood over Reginald Taylor's grave. He turned toward Julia Taylor standing up in the wagon and motioned her forward. When Julia got close, she saw the cross and Reginald's name and stared at the grave, layers of rocks across the surface. Then she turned away, crying. Shelby gently put her arms around her. Julia cried bitterly, the tears rolling down her face like sweat. She closed her eyes.

"I'm sorry, I didn't know I'd do this."

"It's all right," Shelby said, slowly rocking her.

Mulligan saw the mound of earth and rocks and felt a sharp sadness. Then he knelt and gently pushed away the rocks and loose earth, knowing the grave was shallow, and saw the blanket Private Kennedy had placed over Reginald's face before covering the body. Seamus came with a shovel but Mulligan ordered him away. The earth had been hard, that cold late January day, but now the ground was soft and Mulligan worked with his hands, drawing in his quiet breath when Reginald's face appeared. Mulligan noticed that decay had not advanced, possibly due to the winter cold and a late spring. Mulligan touched Reginald Taylor's face, tan colored and hard to the touch. Tie still in place, the English writer might be napping, waiting for Mulligan to wake him. As Mulligan scraped more earth away, he saw bones showing through the leathery skin. There was a smell of death coming from the grave, faint compared to the rotting corpses at Gettysburg. Mulligan closed his eyes. Julia sat at some distance, regaining her composure.

"Damn," Seamus said. "Least he ain't no stinking bag of bones."

"Don't let Julia hear that," Mulligan warned.

Carrying a trowel, Shelby joined Mulligan.

"The body is slightly mummified," she said. "Maybe from the cold wind over the grave. That's good. But we need to get him to the mortuary before the real decay sets in. Don't want to disturb the nostrils of Richmond's citizens…or Mrs. Taylor."

"Right."

They dug around the body, cleaning Reginald Taylor's face with gentle swabs from a moist cloth, and Shelby left to get a shroud Julia had bought in D.C. Together, Shelby and Mulligan worked to free Reginald Taylor's body from the grave, the blood stains now earth colored, his clothes shredded. Mulligan carefully shoveled around and under the body and gently, they lifted and placed Reginald Taylor's remains in the shroud. Seamus stood at a distance. Shelby began pulling together the flaps of the shroud around the body, and started sewing them shut, working quickly with a needle and strong thread. When only the face was showing, Michael Mulligan called to Julia Taylor.

"Mrs. Taylor. Would you like to see Mr. Taylor's face before we close it?"

"Yes," she said. "I do."

She came forward and kneeled over the body of her husband, touching his thin brown hair and running her hand along his dead face. She began to pant but didn't cry. "Oh Reginald, my dear Reginald." Then she stood up and nodded to Shelby. "You can close it now."

Julia Taylor walked over to the covered wagon and leaned against one of the wheels while Shelby pulled the remaining flaps tightly over Reginald Taylor's face. Feeling a malaise, Mulligan walked toward her.

"I'm so sorry for your loss, but we found Reggie and he will now return to England. He was a good man, Mrs. Taylor."

"Yes," Julia said. "He was. Sorry to break like that, Mr. Mulligan. That was not very British of me."

"It's okay," Mulligan said. "You're in America."

Mulligan then began to shovel dirt back into the shallow grave, Seamus replacing some of the rocks. It was better if no one knew they had been there. The sun was warmer, and the breeze had died. Mulligan heard a chorus of birds singing. The shroud lay near the wagon, looking somehow out of place on such a pleasant day. He caught Seamus watching him.

"You still thinking about that 50 pounds for your ma if you kill me?"

"No. I had my chance. I was thinking about what should we do now, Major. Push on or camp here?"

"I'd like to wait for Irving. It's only 10 miles to Richmond, but a lot could happen in 10 miles."

Mulligan saw something turn in Seamus's eyes. Then the Irish youth drew his pistol as Mulligan drew his, pointing at Seamus's face.

"You better drop that weapon, young man," he shouted.

They heard a shot and turning, saw Shelby lumbering toward them, the rifle smoking in her big hands, a turkey lying flapping on the ground nearby.

"Blew that wild turkey's head off," she said. "Not bad."

Mulligan built a fire to cook the turkey, and then they talked over lunch, sitting in the meadow near the grave, the shrouded body now inside the covered wagon.

"We started with five people and I'd like to end with five people," Julia said.

"Do we really need big Chief Irving?" Shelby asked

"We will need his gun if we meet those bushwhackers."

"I got a gun," Seamus said.

Mulligan looked at Julia Taylor, sipping her tea. "What do you think? Wait for Irving?"

After a silence, Julia said, "I'd like to, but he could be detained with those soldiers for some time. These marauders could attack us here. Perhaps it's best we just get Reginald to the mortuary. Maybe we can meet Irving in Richmond."

"Then let's prepare to move out," Mulligan said.

"Mr. Mulligan?"

"Yes, Julia?"

"Those men who attacked you and Reginald. Are they buried nearby?"

"Not exactly buried."

"I found a skull hunting the turkey," Shelby said.

Julia Taylor shuddered. "Yes, I believe we should just move on."

They moved onto the main road and headed toward Richmond, passing groups of travelers. The crowds grew in number and Mulligan saw the press of people closing in on the solitary wagon. Their feet raised dust as they walked.

"Shelby, I suggest you display your shotgun to those folks."

"They look hungry," Shelby said.

Mulligan ordered Seamus to ride on the other side of the wagon.

"Let them see your rifle," he said, "since they don't know you can't hit anything with it."

They came to a hill and found a man and a woman with a young boy and girl standing in the road. To Mulligan, they could have posed for a portrait of hunger in the post-Civil War period, the man bent, his beard grey though he was still young, his face thin and gaunt, the woman heavy though undernourished, and the boy and girl in their early adolescence staring ahead with a gaze that saw nothing. The boy wore faded overalls and the girl, a single piece cotton dress. She was still pretty enough to earn her living with her body if her parents didn't have better luck. Julia Taylor pulled up the wagon.

"Good afternoon," she said.

"What you got in that wagon?" the man said. He held an old shotgun.

"My husband," Julia said. "He won't answer you, however."

"We're on our way to a funeral," Shelby said in nasal voice. "You need to move."

180

"Not until we get a look," the man said.

"Stand aside," Mulligan said.

The man stared at him, his eyes hollow, the cheeks sunken with hunger.

"That's a valuable horse you got, mister. Nice team, too. You a Union man?"

"That's no one's business," Seamus said, touching the butt of his pistol.

"Everyone is a Union man now," Mulligan said.

"Not if you're a farmer who had his barn burned to the ground and his crops and cattle stolen by Yankees."

Another young boy peered into the back of the wagon.

"They got something wrapped up," he said, "and cans of food."

The women reached toward the nearest horse.

"Hit those horses," Mulligan said.

Julia cracked the whip and the horses plunged forward knocking the woman to one side. Mulligan struck the farmer on the shoulder with the butt of his carbine and the crowd parted before the galloping horses. Shelby disappeared into the wagon and moments later, Mulligan saw the crowd converge on cans of food tossed from the wagon.

After a while, they slowed and stopped. Julia glared at Mulligan.

"Mr. Mulligan, I can't deny those people. You stuck that specter-looking fellow."

"He had a shotgun."

"Why don't we just give the next bunch the rest of our food?"

"They'll want to take and sell our horses and the wagon. We need both to get Reggie to Richmond."

Julia considered this. "I believe you're right."

"If anything happens, just keep driving. Don't worry about us."

"As you wish, Mr. Mulligan."

"There should be Union troops in Richmond."

They moved down the road. Shelby continued to throw out remaining cans of food to the crowds. When the food was gone, she took out her violin and played Mozart as they approached Richmond. More families appeared, some backing away when Mulligan and Seamus held up their rifles, and some not backing away.

"Those folks is *real* hungry," Seamus said.

"Seamus, why don't you ride back, a bit? If we get stopped, come on full bore firing away."

"Ain't you afraid I might be after hitting you?"

"I am a little afraid of that. You could fire in the air as a distraction."

Seamus held his horse and fell behind them.

Mulligan pulled a bandana over his mouth against the dust. The fields once white with cotton were burned black. Then they saw a man lying on the road, an armed man standing over him. He was tall with a narrow face and a hawk-like nose; he carried a bullwhip on his belt. Smiling only with his teeth, he motioned the wagon to halt. Another man with thin arms and a dropsical torso stood by the side of the road.

"Keep going," Mulligan said. "It's a trap."

"I can't run over that hurt fellow," Julia said. "I will stop, Mr. Mulligan."

"Run over the son of a bitch," he told her. "It's an ambush."

Julia stopped the wagon. They could see the wounded man bled profusely.

"We need your wagon, ma'am," the hawk-faced man said. "Just give me the reins and we'll get Joe here to the doctor in Richmond."

"Who shot him?" Mulligan asked. "Union troops?"

The man glared at Mulligan. "You don't need to know that," he said. "Now ma'am, I need you to step down from that wagon. Let's make this easy on all of us. My man is dying, here."

"He'll have to ride with us, sir. We can make room."

"I can climb in the back of the wagon," Shelby said, smiling. "Let me put away this fiddle."

She disappeared into the wagon.

"Put your wounded companion in the back," Julia told them, "next to my husband's body."

"Body? Take a look, Sam."

Drawing a pistol, Sam walked around to the back of the wagon and peered inside. "She's right, I see something wrapped up in there. Should I rip it open?"

"Don't you dare," Julia said.

Two more men suddenly rode down onto the road and leveled their rifles at Mulligan. They looked starved and rode emaciated horses.

"Let's just take the damn wagon," one rider said, "and the horses."

"That's unacceptable," Julia said.

"Unacceptable?" The tall man rested one hand on his bullwhip and looked at Julia. He began to laugh, and the others joined him. "Maybe we'll take you with us. I like pretty English ladies. We'll leave the ugly one." He regarded Mulligan. "You're making me nervous, mister. Drop your gun and get off that horse—now."

"Listen, my good fellow" Julia said. She reached in her reticule. "I can give you some money if you lack means."

She saw the sudden anger in the man's eyes.

"That's mighty kind of you, ma'am. Why don't you move over, my English Rose, and let me take the reins. Jack, take that man's carbine. If he resists, shoot him."

Mulligan slid the Spencer from the scabbard as the two mounted men advanced, rifles pointed at his face. They pulled down their hats against direct sunlight in their eyes.

"Forgive me," Mulligan said. "I am against killing, but these poor gentlemen think we're alone—and helpless."

"There *are* others," Julia said. "You will *not* succeed."

"I don't see nobody else, ma'am." The signal was barely perceptible, but the tall leader nodded to Jack who cocked his rifle, his horse nervously moving even as Mulligan spurred his horse, tossing the Spencer to him.

"Take it, Jack."

The rifleman tried to catch the carbine as Mulligan drew his 44. Colt and shot him in the face, the second rider pulling back on his startled horse and aiming at Mulligan when a second blast roared and Sam hurtled from the back of the wagon, his swollen face and upper chest full of buckshot. Mulligan shot the second horseman in the chest as Julia hit the horses and they bolted forward, rolling over the bleeding man on the road. Dismounted, Mulligan ran toward the lone remaining gunman firing at the retreating wagon. Then he turned to face Mulligan's raised pistol.

"Mister, we're sorry. We weren't gonna kill nobody."

"Seemed like you wanted to shoot me."

Unafraid, the remaining gunman stared at him.

"I seen you before. You're Union, ain't ya?"

"Yes. Drop the gun."

"We lost a war and it's getting bad, down here, Yank." He dropped the gun and looked at Joe's broken body. "We got a man down and we're hungry, you understand?"

One of the fallen men wheezed through his chest wound and then lay still.

"You got more than a man down," Mulligan said.

He aimed his Colt. Mulligan saw the tight firm jaw and the cold hatred in the man's eyes. "Go ahead, shoot. They're gonna hang me anyway. Shoot!"

"With pleasure." Mulligan hesitated "What's your name?"

"Former Private Carson of Captain Easy's Cavalry."

"Did you say Captain Easy?"

"That's right, Captain Easy. He is a sight, I will admit. You know him, Yank?"

"I do, and I'd like to put a bullet between his eyes."

"Not if he hangs you first."

"Is he the leader of your gang?"

Private Carson didn't have a chance to answer. They heard a distant rider and shots. A bullet took off Mulligan's hat. He hit the ground and Carson began running as Mulligan's horse reared and bolted down the road, bullets hitting the nearby rocks and the ground. The other horses also scattered in opposite directions. Yelling like an avenging Irish sprit, Seamus rode after the running highwayman, firing his pistol as Carson escaped across a blackened meadow and into distant woods. Mulligan stood and picked up his Spencer, but Carson was beyond range. He cursed.

"You crazy Irish son of a bitch, you almost killed me!"

Leaving the four dead men, Michael Mulligan walked a mile and finally found his horse grazing by the side of the road.

Mulligan checked the horse, tracing a bullet path that had plowed along the saddle but didn't penetrate the animal. He waited an hour for Seamus and then rode toward the city. Coming over a ridge, he saw the ruined smoking landscape, with broken facades of buildings and rubble-littered streets. He rode down a burned-out main street and finally stopped a passing stranger.

"Sir, do you know where the Downey Mortuary is?"

"Sure." The stranger regarded him with a quizzical expression. "Who died?"

"A friend from England."

"England? He's an English nigger?"

"No. He's white."

"Cause that's who works at Downey's—niggers. That cripple owner don't hire white people, but then what white man would work there? It may be the only working mortuary in town, but I know I don't want my body handled by former slaves. You a soldier?"

"Yes. I was mustered out."

"I don't need to ask what side. Downey's Mortuary is around the corner."

The stranger walked on. Mulligan guided his horse down the littered street. A group of black workers cleared rubble under the supervision of a white man on horseback. Mulligan passed the old hospital and then saw the Downey Mortuary. He tied the horse and walked inside. There was a chapel to his right and an office to the left with a long hallway leading to viewing rooms. In another room, organ music announced a service in progress. A tall bony man with a club foot suddenly appeared.

"Can I help you?"

The proprietor had a rich smooth voice coming out of a monster's body.

"I'm here for Reginald Taylor. His widow is also here."

"Yes, of course, Julia Taylor. You must be Michael Mulligan. Tyrone can show you."

He heard a familiar voice. "Major Mulligan has done arrived." Dressed in a suit, Tyrone stood in the doorway.

"Nice to see you, old friend," Mulligan said. He followed Tyrone down a long narrow hall covered with subdued yellow wallpaper.

"Glad to see you is still alive, Major. I see one of your boys didn't make it, and he's our first white man. Of course, he's as dead as any nigger...I mean Negro."

"You like working with dead bodies, Tyrone?"

"It's better than clearing rubble or making nails."

They entered a small quiet room where Julia and Shelby sat. Julia jumped up and embraced him; it was good to hold her. She looked up at him.

"So glad to see you. It's been a harrowing journey, but we are here."

"At last."

She looked past him. "Where's Seamus?"

"He went chasing after one of the robbers, but he should be here soon."

"You don't think anything happened to him?"

Michael Mulligan knew Seamus was a bad shot but he couldn't imagine Carson overpowering him while on foot, unless he used the bullwhip.

"I'm sure the thief is still running and Seamus is on his way."

Shelby sat, staring ahead. "I killed a man," she said. "I done killed a man."

"A man with a gun who would've killed you."

"It doesn't make me feel any better hearing that."

Julia sat down, her face covered with dust from the fast ride. "We are all exhausted. I can't believe how violent this queer country is, but I understand why Reginald loved it."

From the other room, they heard faint cries of "Yes, Jesus," over the organ music and clapping hands. Mr. Downey walked into the room, his gait rolling and rhythmic.

"We are getting Mr. Taylor ready for his journey. There will be a morning service, tomorrow and you can all give testimony. We can sing hymns, if you like."

"I can play some music," Shelby said.

Downey took Julia's hands. "I'm so honored you don't object to Negroes preparing his body. I will assist, of course."

"I'm sure Reginald would be proud."

"The local people can't imagine blacks and whites together, even in a cemetery. That is sad, indeed. We have a long way to go before Negroes are truly free."

"I would like to treat everyone to a nice hotel room with bed and a bath," Julia told them. "Perhaps we can do a little shopping before we leave."

"All the hotels have been demolished. There's a tent city, and an old armory has been converted into lodging. I have a few cottages on the property...mostly used by black people. We may have some rooms."

"Anything will suit us, Mr. Downey."

Shelby said nothing. Michael Mulligan felt a deep fatigue. Tyrone stood like a guard in the back of the room.

"We killed a few highwaymen, Mr. Downey, so you may have more work."

"The sheriff won't send those bodies here."

"Why not?" a voice said from the back of the room.

They turned and saw Irving dressed as a Union soldier. Michael Mulligan shook his hand, and then saluted.

"Well now, from the Cherokee Confederate army to the Union army."

"Captain R. G. Perky liked my work so I joined. The other highwaymen are either dead or about to be hanged."

Irving told the story:

"I tracked them to a campsite. It was easy since one of their horses didn't have a shoe on the right back hoof. They were sitting around a campfire eating and even had a bottle of whiskey. The captain ordered me to ride in and distract them. When I told the robbers I was part of the Cherokee Confederate army, they said that was good and to light for a spell. Then they asked for my money, horse and guns."

"Such humanity. And then?"

"I told them they were surrounded. One drew his pistol, so I shot him. The others didn't have time before the soldiers took them prisoner."

"And Captain Easy?"

"He's in custody. I will enjoy watching him hang."

Michael Mulligan could remember the venomous hatred in Easy's blue eyes.

"I might witness that myself."

Mr. Downey limped toward Irving and shook his hand. "It is terrible we have to kill our brothers. Sir, you are welcome to our ceremony for Reginald Taylor, tomorrow."

"He's our first white man," Tyrone said.

Irving's eyes went from one person to the next and he finally faced Mr. Downey. "I hate to say this but I can deliver another white man."

In a low voice, Julia asked: "Irving, where's Seamus?"

"On a horse out front." Irving removed his army cap. "We found him on the way back. Looks like he broke his neck riding fast under a low tree limb."

Julia turned away, her hands to her mouth. "My God. He was just a boy."

Shelby got up and embraced her. Then Irving walked over and hugged them both.

They took cottages on the Downey lot, though Irving retired to the army barracks. After a quiet discussion with the women in their cottage, Mulligan got up in the middle of the night and left his hot cabin, walking toward the James River. He had been plagued by nightmares from the war, and felt the stifling humid air and a need to cleanse himself. There was a full moon; he found a secluded bank and taking off his undershirt and dropping his pants, he waded naked into the river shallows. He could duck down and feel the cold water and then quickly dry off and dress himself.

He was still bathing when he heard a female voice. In the moonlight, Julia Taylor stood on the bank, wearing a white slip and thick shoes.

"Reginald loved your American poet, Walt Whitman. He said one could only read him naked and in a loud voice. Well, I don't have any Whitman, but with your permission, Mr. Mulligan, I should like to join you. If you're shy, you may turn your head but I don't mind. Surely a frontier man like you has seen many a naked Venus."

Julia lifted the straps to her slip and stepped out of it, kicking away her shoes and walking barefoot and nude toward the river. Mulligan always felt a sharp sense of wonder seeing a beautiful woman suddenly naked, though now, Venus was walking toward the water, not out of it. Moments later, they stood waist deep in the current, the soft blue-white light full on her small but firm breasts.

"Sure but you have a beautiful body, Julia Taylor."

"So do you. I don't think Reginald would mind us being here. I must warn you, though, I am not here for an amorous liaison."

"Who says?"

Mulligan slid his hands up her naked back and kissed her. She touched his hips. After a sharp intake of breath, Julia gently pushed him away.

"It has been a long time and I am flattered, Mr. Mulligan, but I must warn you—"

Then they heard the high pitched nasal voice of Shelby Reed. She stood nude on the beach, her body rotund in the moonlight, the pendulous breasts hiding rolls of fat.

"Hey, folks, here I am. Thought I lost you."

Shelby waded heavily into the river.

"Perhaps I better leave," Mulligan said.

"Don't you folks mind me," Shelby said. "Pretend I'm invisible."

"That's not likely."

"I do believe we have a *ménage a trois*," Julia said.

Mulligan waded to the bank and stood holding his clothes, letting the women view his body. "I should leave you ladies alone," he said. "I *am* a gentleman."

"That's too bad," Shelby said.

Julia laughed. Mulligan dressed and walked back to the cottage, leaving the two women in the river, talking under the full moon. Feeling cooler and with visions of Julia Taylor's nakedness, Mulligan slept well for the first time in weeks.

The following day, the double funeral service had long passed when Julia Taylor and Michael Mulligan waited on Rockett's Landing for the steamship. Mulligan wore tan pants and a formal jacket with boots and hat. Julia Taylor wore a new form-fitting skirt and blouse with a jacket, her bonnet a concession to an older fashion. To others, they might have appeared a charming couple embarking on a romantic vacation. The plain pine coffin sat on the dock with the luggage of other passengers. Mulligan remembered Reginald Taylor reciting Keats's "Ode to a Nightingale" in a quiet voice

Fled is that music:—Do I wake or sleep?

Julia appeared calm, resigned. "I do appreciate you coming with me the last leg of the journey, Mr. Mulligan."

"My pleasure," Mulligan said. "I will miss Reginald. And I feel bad about Seamus, so green and so young."

Julia had sent Seamus O' Hara's mother American money equivalent to 50 pounds with a note proclaiming her son a hero; if the mother wanted her son's body buried in Ireland, Julia would pay the cost. In a separate envelope addressed to Sean, Mulligan sent a photo of a severed theatre prop head meant to resemble him.

"What will you do now, Mr. Mulligan?"

"I don't know. I've seen so much death, maybe I should follow Ellen's actions."

"Your lady companion turned nun?"

"Yes."

"So you might enter a monastery for a quiet retreat?"

"Or check into an asylum," Mulligan said.

"I might join you."

As the steamer approached, Mulligan remembered the touching services and those who gave testimony, including himself. The journey and the deaths of others had brought them together. Seamus was buried in the yard behind the mortuary where he would lie with the anonymous black people of Richmond; while the others stood quietly, Mulligan saluted the young man who tried to take his life but became an ally.

"He was my Irish brother and so like myself at that age, so full of life and so naïve. I lament his early passing. I'd like to recite a story about an exiled Irish king going home at last." Mulligan then spoke the Celtic story in Irish, the mourners listening with respect though not understanding. He finished in English. "Rest in peace, Seamus O' Hara, and farewell."

Inside, they stood in a small chapel, Reginald Taylor's coffin draped with a Union Jack and resting on a raised platform.

"Music is mathematical," Shelby had said. "But out of that mathematical certainty comes sublime music that moves us. Richmond needs music for healing. I never knew Reginald Taylor, but his beautiful widow is a part of my journey and healing."

Then Shelby played parts of Mozart's Requiem.

Irving spoke: "I fought for the Cherokee Nation. I fought as a Cherokee Confederate. Now I will fight as a Union man. The Federal Government has a stronger medicine and the Cherokee Nation is gone. We must adapt. Many will not adapt and they will die. This journey to carry an Englishman that I never knew to his homeland has brought me a new understanding. Like Michael Mulligan, I also lament the loss of my young Irish brother, even if he was a bad shot."

Julia Taylor used her English eloquence to praise her husband and his vision and his courage, and to describe the violent land she had visited, and to mark her own pride at finding so much strength in herself:

"This odyssey has meant so much to me. I never thought I'd run over a dying man—even an evil robber—with a team of horses. I think Reginald, who saved Mr. Mulligan's life, would understand the necessity of such desperate action. I will miss him. His twin boys will miss him. His memory will not fade." Her eyes took in the mourners. "I shall not forget any of you."

She didn't break. Mulligan got up to speak. The naked pathos had moved him, and he wondered if he could deliver a eulogy that was fitting. He would remember always the small company gathered in the chapel before Reginald's coffin. He was aware of Julia's moist violet-blue eyes watching him intently.

"I didn't actually meet Reginald Taylor, I was assigned to him—or maybe he was assigned to me. He was English, my common enemy since childhood. But I found a rugged toughness in his gentle soul. I found a poet, like those he talked about. In fact, he nearly talked me to death. His words will live on. He will live in my heart. He will live in our hearts." After a pause, he spoke a sentence in Irish. Then he said, "I think this Irish saying fits Julia. Let me translate. She could whisper it in Reginald's ear: 'Sleep well, love of my heart.'"

Julia dabbed her eyes. To their surprise, Tyrone asked to speak.

"Please do," said Downey. "You are one of us."

"You all had yourselves an adventure and maybe learned something about yourselves. Well so did I. After Richmond fell, we heard the President was walking around town and the word went out to lynch him."

A shock ran through the group.

"Lynch him? The President?"

"Yes, but we thought it was President Jefferson Davis. When the black folk saw the emancipator himself, Abraham Lincoln, walking around the streets of Richmond with his few marines, they started to gather, praising the Lord and rushing to kiss Lincoln's hands. An old black man knelt at his feet and Lincoln lifted him up, saying 'Don't thank me, thank God who sent me as his humble servant. Enjoy the blessings of freedom.' I didn't accept all that singing and moaning for Uncle Lincum, but when he saw me, he seemed to understand and said, 'Don't let any white man call himself your master. If he does, grab a gun or a bayonet.' I had to laugh at that. Yessir, Mr. Lincoln, I will grab me a gun or a bayonet. I will be a slave no more. The crowd then pressed on him and his marines got real scared, so they went back to the Jefferson Davis house. I'm glad I was there. I'm glad I seen it. Yessir."

Touched, the gathered mourners applauded the dramatic testimony. Then they followed the casket to the waiting funeral wagon that would carry Reginald Taylor to the loading platform. They all embraced for the last time, except Julia and Mulligan. They had started the journey together in D.C. and they would finish it together at Chesapeake Bay.

On the landing, Mulligan could feel the breeze coming off the James River. Crews still worked to clear the river of torpedoes—mines that were deadly to ships. Julia stared at the bright water, thoughtful and silent. To Mulligan, she resembled an actress on the stage in a pensive moment, perhaps Portia in *The Merchant of Venice.*

"So Mr. Mulligan, where will you go from here?"

"I'm not sure. I have a lot of unfinished business."

"Your son?"

"Yes. He's far away. And I have to find a living. There's the theatre, but that's precarious. Or work with horses. You?"

"I have to confess I was not just going to ask Reginald for a divorce. I was also going to inform him that I fell in love with another man. And now?"

"And now?"

"After the recent events in your dangerous country, my Englishman may seem a bit stogy."

"He wouldn't bathe nude with you?"

"God no. Not in public." He could see her cheeks coloring slightly. "I hope I wasn't untoward in my actions, last night. I believe I shocked myself."

"It was wonderful," Mulligan said, remembering her small but firm breasts and curving hips and the triangle of hair as she waded into the river. "I wasn't expecting Shelby."

"Nor was I, though I did mention I wanted to bathe in the river. I saw you leaving. I followed you and she followed me."

"Perhaps it's just as well she arrived."

"We'll never know, will we?" She looked away across the river. "I could stay here, but I desperately want to see my boys back home." She glanced at him. "As you need to see your boy."

The steamship pulled alongside the floating pier and after deck hands secured it, passengers boarded. The coffin was stored on a deck beneath the bow. Carrying their bags, Mulligan and Julia walked on the upper deck. Well-dressed gentlemen posed and women in cage crinoline floated by them. Mulligan and Julia looked toward the ruined city.

"You think you might want to visit England? You could stay with me, Michael."

Her face was like an exquisite portrait that would haunt his dreams.

"That would be lovely, Julia. I know I can't see Ireland in the near future."

"More mystery?"

"And more danger."

"Of course." Julia suddenly smiled and closed her eyes against the warm breeze. "Maybe you should write a book."

"I will. But it will be a journal, like Reggie's."

Julia grew silent at the mention of her late husband's name.

"I met Reginald at a dance hall. He was a charming man, so intelligent, and he enjoyed my work so we started courting."

"Enjoyed your work?"

"As an exotic dancer. It paid the rent."

"Exotic dancer? Well, well, some mystery revealed from Julia Taylor."

"You're not the first man to see my breasts, Mr. Mulligan. I am not as prim and proper as I appear."

"I suspected that from the beginning."

They both laughed. Julia touched his lips with her fingers and then pulled away, averting her eyes. They stood on the deck watching the water as the steamer began to move down the James River. People on the bank waved. At Chesapeake Bay, Julia would board the ship that would complete the final journey.

"Perhaps one day, you could join me for an evening of theatre in New York."

"I would love that." From under the bonnet, her dark blue eyes seemed to engulf him. "I have grown fond of you, Michael Mulligan. I watched your face when we talked before our midnight swim. I know we will write to each other...and for years to come."

"We will."

Michael Mulligan smiled and started to gently touch her cheek when he saw one of the sailors running toward the bow. Another sailor was waving at the pilot behind his elevated cabin window. Mulligan walked toward the bow and saw a barrel tied to a log floating in the river. It lay in their path.

"Jesus, a torpedo," another sailor shouted.

Mulligan turned and ran toward Julia, her expression startled, her mouth lightly open, the eyes watching him.

"Julia!"

"What's wrong?"

Before she could speak again, he lifted her and ran toward the side of the steamer while other passengers talked among themselves, unaware of sailors running toward the stern. Then someone noticed the boat slowly turning and another passenger steadied himself with the sudden movement of the deck. A sailor shouted an alarm to back away from the bow. With Julia silent, her arms around his neck, Mulligan put one foot on the railing and launched himself over the side. They dropped toward the river. Seconds later, the ship's bow lifted, shattering with a loud explosion. Passengers were hurled to the deck or blown overboard. Moments later, the steamer sank from view.

When Michael Mulligan and Julia Taylor hit the cold water, he held her close, feeling the suction from the steamship pulling them down. Then he surfaced, Julia gasping for breath and holding him.

"I love you," he said, as the river current tore her from his arms, leaving behind her jacket in his hands. Then she was gone and Mulligan swam against the slow drag of the sinking ship. His boots filled with water and Mulligan slipped under. He struggled to the open air, and after some minutes with the cold river current carrying him, Mulligan began swimming toward the shore even as a new shoreline appeared. A woman floated by him, her dress spread wide on the waters. She reached out thick hands to Mulligan.

"I don't want to die," she screamed. "Save me!"

The woman suddenly disappeared, sucked down beneath the rushing water. Mulligan swam into a cove and finding the river bottom, walked stumbling toward the shore. He lay on the ground, panting, pressing the solid earth. A black man helped him up and Mulligan walked dripping toward the landing, soldiers running along the shore searching for survivors. The torpedo mine had destroyed the steamship, and many passengers went down with it. Mulligan frantically searched for Julia. With light clothing and being a good swimmer, it was possible she survived and came up further down the river. A piece of the ship might hold her up.

But he did not find her.

He walked to the Downey Mortuary; they had heard the news.

"She'll turn up," Mr. Downey said. "It seems even over, the war hurts us."

"I must telegraph the English ambassador."

Mulligan found a telegraph office open and wired Ambassador Bruce with the news. That night and most of the next two days, Michael Mulligan searched the river banks with groups of soldiers and civilians looking for survivors and bodies now washing up on the river banks. At night, he stayed in a small cabin behind the mortuary. His dreams were filled with Julia's panicked eyes.

"We haven't found her," Mulligan told Downey.

"I know she's tough enough to survive," he said.

The English ambassador sent a telegram: *Shocked to hear news. Keep searching. Will contact family. Ambassador Bruce.*

Even if Reginald Taylor's coffin was at the bottom of the river, Mulligan went out again searching for Julia Taylor, dead or alive. He remembered their last playful moments, the shy smile, his desire to kiss her, and then the sight of the torpedo mine in the path of the steamboat, the explosion and the plunge into the river. They had one last moment, holding each other, Julia's eyes on his face before the current took her and he went under.

For the first time, Downey's all black help was preparing the bodies of dead white people drowned or killed by the explosion.

"Guess we got a lot of northern whites," Tyrone said. "Don't mind black hands touching their dead white relatives."

"God does work in mysterious ways," Mr. Downey said.

Michael Mulligan continued his search for Julia Taylor.

Time passed. In June, Stand Isaac Watie surrendered, the last Confederate General to do so after winning the last battle of the Civil War. In July, Mary Surratt, Louis Payne and two others were hanged for conspiring to kill Abraham Lincoln. From a scaffold, Confederate officer turned highwayman, Captain Easy, cursed the Union seconds before the drop breaking his neck. Mulligan and Tyrone witnessed the hanging.

"People like that have to die for us to move on," Tyrone said.

The search and rescue teams had become recovery teams. Julia's body was never found. One day, a telegram came from Edwin Booth requesting Mulligan in New York for Booth's return to the stage. After the assassination of President Lincoln by his brother, John Wilkes Booth, Edwin Booth feared crowds might turn on him, though he was a strong Union man.

"If you need to leave, Mr. Mulligan, we will contact you if there is any news," Mr. Downey said. "You can't search for Julia forever."

Mulligan looked at the tall bent man with the club foot and a face that scared local children. Often they taunted him and threw rocks. "Thanks, you're very kind. I still have time."

"Julia was a loving person."

"She was."

Some days, Mulligan visited the grave of Seamus O'Hara and thought of their time on the road together, taking Reginald Taylor's body to a home he never reached. He thought of O'Hara's unusual fatal accident. He had been so young. One moonlit evening, Shelby met him in the graveyard and played her violin over Seamus's grave.

"I don't think he liked classical music," she said.

"No, I don't believe he did."

"Why did some survive and others not?"

"I don't know, Shelby."

"I miss Julia. I even miss Chief Irving."

"He's out on some military maneuver," Mulligan said.

"I'm glad his traitor cousin finally surrendered."

Mulligan felt an old longing sweep over him, a dark depression that often lasted for weeks. "You know, I feel Julia is still alive. I just feel it."

Shelby Reed didn't answer. One late afternoon as Mulligan walked along the James River, he realized he searched alone for bodies. The steamboat explosion was now old news. Richmond itself was rising from the ruins. Shelby Reed worked to raise money for a city orchestra. The South was promising representatives for Congress.

Perhaps he had to let the English woman named Julia Taylor go.

He walked among the shacks of Richmond's black population, living in squalor near the river. Two young men walked toward him, an old woman sitting on a mule. Michael Mulligan bowed politely. "I'm looking for a woman who was on that steamboat last month," he said.

The black faces regarded him, passive and secret. "A white woman? No sir," the old woman said. "Ain't no white woman here."

"I can be reached at Downey's Mortuary."

"The mortuary? I'll be sure to visit. Good afternoon."

The three black people quickly moved past him. Michael Mulligan walked back to the mortuary. In a week, another steamboat would take him to Chesapeake Bay and then New York. Before leaving he put an ad in the local paper asking for any information about Julia Taylor, presumed lost after the steamboat explosion. He also paid for an ad to appear in a London paper. On his last day he said good-bye to Mr. Downey, Tyrone and Shelby. Purple drapes framed a tall wide window.

"We've been on an odyssey indeed," he said. "I guess I'm doomed to keep wandering."

"You will find rest, someday," Mr. Downey said. "And we'll keep your horse for you. We call him Reggie. Mr. Taylor would approve."

"He would."

While waiting on Rockett's Landing, he saw the desperate farmer who had threatened them entering Richmond. His wife in a plain dress sat next to him, both staring at the river. Mulligan approached.

"I feel I did you an injury, sir. Here is a gold coin."

The man stared at him with pale eyes. "I don't take no charity, Yankee."

"It isn't charity. I struck you with my rifle and feel I need to make reparations," Mulligan said. "You saw a doctor, I trust?"

The man didn't answer but turned away, spitting.

"We need it," the wife said. She held out her hand. "You can pay me."

Mulligan gave her a gold coin. Then he became aware of a young black boy around 10 walking beside him.

"I hear you is looking for a white lady—fished outta the river?"

"That's correct."

"You got money, sir?"

"I have." Mulligan took out another gold coin. The boy, tall but thin, took the coin and studied it, turning it over in his upturned palm. The steamboat was about to dock and take on passengers. "Well? Where is Julia Taylor?"

"Sherwood Forest," the boy said. "You'll find her there. But I didn't tell you."

He started to leave.

"Wait, you got the right country, but not the right location. Where is she...and is she still alive?"

"She's alive...at Sherwood Forest."

"That's impossible...unless she joined Robin Hood and his merry men."

"Don't know no Robin Hood, but I know what I know," the boy said.

He turned and ran toward a black woman who was glaring at him. Mulligan could not hear what she said as they vanished into the crowds. Mulligan boarded the steamship and waited on the deck as they moved toward Chesapeake Bay and the open ocean. Chesapeake Bay was massive and wide. Boarding a second ship for New York, Mulligan began to see his whole life as a strange nomadic journey. He had been homeless for most of his life, and traveled across three countries: Ireland, England and America. Mulligan had always been a kind of refugee. The one woman he had left his country and society for had died. A second whom he loved in a different way, bearing him a child, had also died. A third he had loved and lost during a terrible civil war. Then there was Julia Taylor, widow of a brief male acquaintance, but somehow precious to him. There was the son he had not seen in five years.

"Someday," he said aloud to no one. "I'll just have to find a new home...or return to the old one."

On the first day at sea, Michael Mulligan found a map of Virginia and searched but didn't find a Sherwood Forest. What was the black child talking about? In his cabin he read *Leaves of Grass* by Walt Whitman and identified with Whitman's rugged spirit; he reread *Hamlet* knowing this would be Edwin Booth's major role and mark his return to the stage. Michael Mulligan looked forward to seeing his old friend. Constant friends had always made his nomadic life more pleasant.

Approaching the New York waterfront, Mulligan saw a young couple standing on the deck. "I could be wrong but I place your accent as from the great state of Virginia. Am I correct?"

"Yes," the man said. "Virginia it is. What's left of it. And you're Irish?"

"Yes."

"I hope the Irish Fenians invade England, someday. Where were the British when the Confederacy needed them?"

The young woman was clearly distressed.

"My dear, you need to be quiet about that. We are about to land in New York."

"Of course," the young man said. "The war is over, and so is our way of life."

"Is there such a place as Sherwood Forest in Virginia?"

"Not on any map," the young man said. "It's the plantation of President John Tyler. He called it that because he was a kind of outlaw. His former party hated him—a President of the United States who eventually supports the Confederacy."

Mulligan could feel the sharp wind from the New York harbor. Sea gulls flew overhead.

"Where is this Sherwood Forest plantation?"

"Next to Richmond, Virginia," the young man said. "Right on the James River."

In two weeks, still carrying Irving's telegram in his pocket, he arrived at Rockett's Landing in the early morning. Irving waited for him with Reginald's spotted horse, and together, they rode to a plantation called Sherwood Forest. While on maneuvers, Irving and his platoon had bivouacked at the home of President John Tyler, now run by freed slaves and the many

Tyler siblings. It was there that Irving heard about an attractive English lady in her mid-thirties pulled from the river by local blacks but now suffering memory loss. Tyler's servants waited on her. One afternoon, Irving saw Julia Taylor walking through the woods but Julia escaped when he advanced.

Michael Mulligan and Irving rode up to the large white mansion, extended with many additions over the years. The plantation had white oak and pine, and dogwood trees. Black servants watched them in silence, and black and white children played in the dust. A young black woman appeared, carrying chopped wood.

"The Tyler boys may pose a problem," Irving said.

"We'll get her out," Mulligan said.

A servant took their horses. Before the large door, an elderly black man stopped them. He was of medium build with tight curly hair turning gray.

"What is your business, gentleman? You can't come in the Tyler mansion armed." He glanced at Irving. "The Tyler family don't take kindly to Yankee soldiers or Indians, neither."

"I bet they like you," Irving said. "As long as you continue being a slave."

"I ain't no slave. After President Tyler died, I decided to stay on," the servant said. "Even after the war ended, I am still here," the servant said.

Michael Mulligan stated his business. "We're searching for an English lady named Julia Taylor who may have lost her memory. She is here, I understand."

"I don't know nothing about that."

"She may not know us," said Irving. "She didn't know me."

"Oh, she knows a lot of things," the black man said. He stopped, staring at them.

"Excuse me," Mulligan said.

Irving and Mulligan pushed the servant to one side and entered the mansion. Three laughing children ran down the hallway. They found Julia reading by a dead fireplace. She wore a cast off black dress with a white lace triangle at her wrists and throat, and when she got up, smiling, holding out her hand, her eyes revealed no recognition.

"Good evening, gentlemen. Or is it afternoon?"

"It is the late morning," Mulligan said.

"May I serve you gentlemen some tea?"

The gray-haired servant hovered nearby. "I tried to stop them," he said.

"Stop them from what, Jackson?"

"From breakin' in here."

"So good to see you at last, Julia," Mulligan said.

"That is my name. How do you know it?" She studied their faces. "You must know me."

"Yes. We do."

"You don't work for the Tyler family."

"No, we don't."

"They tell me I had an accident and lost my memory, but sometimes I remember things." She looked at Irving. "I think I remember this gentleman, here. I was walking through the forest. You scared me."

"My apologies. Irving Watie, Cherokee warrior."

"Hello, Irving." She turned to regard Mulligan. "But you?" She touched Mulligan's face, and closing her eyes, Julia began to nod to herself. "I remember the boat and this big Irishman."

"That was me."

"And then something happened."

"The steamer blew up. We hit the water."

"The water?" Julia stared at him for a long time, and Michael Mulligan felt unsettled as her eyes took in his features. "Sometimes I have vivid dreams and everything makes sense, and then I wake up in a dark room and remember nothing."

"Your sister will be at Chesapeake Bay to take you home, Julia."

"I have a sister, yes. Her name is—"

"Judith," Mulligan said. "Her name is Judith."

"Judith?"

"She made plans to sail here when she heard about the accident."

"You can't take her without no permission," Jackson declared. "The Tylers need to give you folks permission."

"Listen," Irving said. "I'm with the Union Army. President Tyler was a traitor who joined the Confederacy. We will take her out or burn your mansion to the ground."

Jackson said nothing, staring at Irving with red-rimmed but dark opaque eyes.

"They already tried that," he finally said.

"I have an order from the British Ambassador," Mulligan told him.

"That's fine. You still better talk to Tyler the Younger."

"It's all right, Jackson. These men are friends," Julia said. She approached Michael Mulligan, her eyes fixed on his face. "I think I *do* know you."

"You know me," Mulligan said. "We went on a journey to take your husband home."

"My husband?"

"Reginald."

"Yes. Reginald. Where is Reginald?"

"He died and his coffin sank with the steamship."

Julia stared ahead, her mouth working. "I had a nightmare about a ship sinking into the underworld." She pointed at Mulligan. "He died saving you?"

"Yes. Yes, he did, Julia."

She took his hands, her eyes moist. "You are—"

"Major Michael Mulligan—at your service."

"Master Tyler is gonna be real mad if he comes back and finds you gone," Jackson said. "He'll be real mad, Miss Julia."

"Yes, he will." Julia blinked rapidly and then faced Irving and Mulligan. "Maybe we better wait."

"We don't have time." Mulligan gave her two photos. "These children are your twin boys."

"My boys?" Julia examined the photos, holding them in both hands. Her lips slowly formed the names. "Max. Ben."

"Yes. Your sons."

Julia ran her fingers over the faces of the boys. Irving looked at Jackson. "Go get her things because we are leaving now."

Another servant directed Irving down the hall to collect what articles of clothing Julia had saved. Julia held the two photos and then stroked Mulligan's cheek, suddenly gripping his shoulder. "I always knew you'd come for me," she said, her voice breaking. "I knew. I just knew there was someone out there searching for me."

"You remember being in the water?"

"Yes—it was so cold and swift— and you were holding me." She kissed him. "I love you too."

Outside, they heard violin music, and Julia walked out on the porch, Jackson following. Mr. Downey and Tyrone had brought up a wagon with a team of mules. Shelby stood in the middle of the road, playing a Bach gavotte on her violin, children dancing around her. The two women embraced.

"Hello, Sister," Shelby said. "You remember me?"

"Yes. You are Shelby."

Julia then embraced and kissed Tyrone; Jackson stepped back, nervously glancing down the road. "This won't do, Miss Julia! You need to stop this before Master Tyler rides up."

"You be quiet, papa," the young black woman said. She had put down the wood. "She needs to leave and you best leave it alone."

Jackson was about to speak when Irving appeared carrying some clothes in a bag. Mulligan and Shelby escorted Julia toward the wagon when a middle-aged man rode up on horseback and demanded their identity. Mulligan told him. The man was thin with the familiar Tyler nose hooked into a beak, and thinning hair. He dismounted.

"We're taking her home," Mulligan said.

"This *is* her home. My slaves saved her."

"Your *former* slaves saved her," Mulligan said. "Which Tyler are you?"

"John, Jr. She needs to stay here until the mayor of Richmond makes a decision. And our doctor needs to give his permission. He has a place for her."

"We're taking her now, Mr. Tyler. She will have a personal escort."

John Tyler advanced on Mulligan. "You think you Yankees—surrender or no surrender—can come down here and order us around?"

Mulligan showed him the paper from Ambassador Bruce.

"Julia Taylor is a British citizen. And her sister, courtesy of the British government, is waiting at Chesapeake Bay. Now—we don't want an international incident, do we, Mr. Tyler? Besides, Julia needs medical care, and she needs her family. You will be reimbursed."

"I don't need to be reimbursed," Tyler said. He glared at Mulligan and then at Irving who palmed his knife. Unlike his plantation help, Tyrone was holding a rifle and watching him. "Is this how the Federal government works, an Indian in uniform and a nigger with a gun?" He stared at Mr. Downey slumped over the reins, the mules appearing asleep. "And that—that ape?"

"Don't forget me," Shelby said. She held up her violin.

"Or me, Mr. Tyler, an Irishman from the old sod. Now step away!"

Tyler didn't move. Julia walked up and took his hands.

"Mr. Tyler? John? I must thank the Tyler family for my rescue and care, but I have to go back home, now. You will be compensated by the British government for your service to me. Please, Mr. Tyler."

Tyler finally regarded Mulligan. "Do you have this ambassador's card?"

"Yes." Mulligan handed him a card.

"Take her," Tyler said.

"I hope no harm has come to her," Mulligan said.

"I am a man of honor," Tyler told him.

Julia said good-bye to the gathered children. Wrapped in a blanket, they drove Julia Taylor toward Hampton, Shelby sitting next to Julia, Tyrone sitting in the back holding his rifle, Irving and Mulligan riding behind the creaking wagon. By early morning, when they arrived at the Chesapeake Bay harbor, they saw a well-dressed young woman, remarkably similar in features, suddenly appearing out of the waiting passengers.

"Julia!"

Julia stared at the woman, blinking her eyes. For a moment, she remembered two young girls running through an English meadow. Then she focused on the woman's face.

"Judith?"

"Yes."

The two women held each other, sobbing. Michael Mulligan turned to Irving.

"Reginald won't make it back to England but his widow will." He looked at Mr. Downey. "Keep the horse, my good sir."

"We've made friends with the local children," Mr. Downey said. "Black and white kids love to ride him."

"If I come to New York, I'll track you down, Irish."

"Please do, Irving. Glad your cousin finally surrendered."

"So am I."

They said their good-byes. Moments later, Mulligan escorted the two sisters up the plank and to their cabin where they could sit and talk and revive memories of Julia Taylor's former life. Julia's memory returned stronger with each day. Their farewell came just before Mulligan left the ship that would take her to England. They had docked at the Port of New York where so many young Irishmen fleeing the famine had landed, and a few years later, got off the boat to join the Union Army and fight in the Civil War. Judith remained in her cabin. Standing on the deck with sea breezes blowing through Julia's hair, her face clear, her eyes the same sharp blue he remembered, Michael Mulligan imagined a romantic parting in a melodrama. Holding back tears, Julia shook his hand. "You must come to England, Michael."

"I will. When Reginald's journal is published, I'll be at the launch party."

"That would be fine. And you must write an introduction."

"I will do that. And you must come to New York."

"Or San Francisco."

"Or San Francisco."

Julia gently pressed her hand to his chest. "We've been on some journey, and none of it would have succeeded without you. Good-bye, dear friend."

Mulligan gently pulled apart the bottom of her glove and kissed her upturned right wrist and then her cheek. Julia closed her eyes.

"Good-bye," Mulligan said. "Our story isn't over."

"I don't think it is," Julia said.

He turned and walked down the plank toward the crowded pier and the New York City skyline.

BOOTH'S RETURN

JANUARY OF 1866, AND the Winter Garden Theatre, offering Edwin Booth's return to the stage as Hamlet, had sold every ticket. The packed audience waited, uncertain what was going to happen when Edwin Booth gave his first performance since his brother assassinated President Lincoln. There had been a few death threats.

Backstage, the celebrated actor sat in his dressing room, staring at his face in the mirror. Michael Mulligan sat near him. Both men had aged, particularly Michael Mulligan. At 45 years, war had added lines to his face. Booth applied a bit of clown white to the tip of his nose. Dark eyeliner accentuated the rich brown eyes.

"What a time it's been," Booth said. "Can you talk about Gettysburg?"

"No," Mulligan said. "It's too recent."

"I understand. I still miss those San Francisco days."

"So do I."

"We could've died in that neighborhood."

"I hear it's now called the Barbary Coast."

"Excellent name." Booth smiled and said, "We have heard the chimes at midnight, Mulligan."

"That we have, Sir Edwin, that we have."

"But no more drinks for me." Edwin Booth felt the leather cross gartering to make sure it wasn't too tight on his legs. A heavily marked script of *Hamlet* lay on a table. He had cut many of Hamlet's sexual references. Edwin Booth's Hamlet was a gentleman.

Michael Mulligan thought of taking a drink from his flask but hesitated. He saw Booth watching him.

"Do you still drink?"

"Of course. It makes others less boring."

Michael Mulligan didn't want to continue this topic, knowing why Edwin Booth had finally quit drinking. The actor ran through some scales and suddenly stopped. "How is your son?"

"Fine," Mulligan said. "He turns 11 this year. I plan to visit him, soon."

"You need to spend more time with him," Booth told him. "I can't imagine being away from my daughter, Edwina, for even a week. She's my connection to Mary Devlin."

For just a moment, Booth seemed moved. Yorick's skull sat in the corner of the dressing room, donated by a horse thief about to be hanged. They could hear the voice of Horacio, and moments later, an echoing wind sound and the elevated voices when the silent ghost appeared. Edwin Booth had a few minutes before entering the stage for the first time in nearly eight and a half months.

"I'm still a marked man," Mulligan said. "They might attack me while visiting my son."

"Or they could attack your son without you there to protect him. You need to connect with family. Mary died while I was out drunk. I will *never* abandon my daughter like that. Never!"

Booth powdered his face and turned toward Mulligan. They could hear the ghost scene ending. "Will you protect me, tonight?"

"No one will harm you."

"My brother *murdered* our beloved President Lincoln."

"He did, but John Wilkes Booth was a fanatic. Everyone knows you supported Lincoln. You're not to blame for what your insane brother did."

Edwin Booth remembered quarreling with his brother over Lincoln, and then hearing the news the morning after the assassination, and the subsequent cancellation of all engagements.

"I still haven't got my brother's body from President Johnson."

"Ask again."

Booth sat back in his chair. At 32, he was still relatively young with thick dark hair; before the assassination, he had performed Hamlet for 100 consecutive nights. Now fatigue and a profound sorrow filled the face in the mirror. For the first time, he was terrified of an audience. Did they still hate him for John's reckless horrid act? Would someone try to shoot him on stage?

"Speak the speech, I pray you," he said. "Did you admire John's acting?"

"John Wilkes cut a romantic figure and had tremendous passion," Mulligan told him. "But you have the poetry. Critics saw that when you all worked together."

"*Julius Caesar*," said Booth. "Ironic. I played the assassin, Brutus. My brother will always be remembered for his heinous deed, and Laura Keene knows she will be remembered for being on stage when it happened."

"Think about tonight's performance," Mulligan said.

"She cradled Lincoln's head in her lap as he lay dying."

"Someday, that might bring her some comfort."

They heard Horacio's words:

"But look, the morn in russet mantle clad

Walks o'er the dew of yon high eastern hill."

The stage manager appeared. "It's time, Mr. Booth."

Edwin Booth embraced Michael Mulligan and then joined the cast waiting in the dark wings to enter. Michael Mulligan always felt a rush of anticipation, waiting for the lights to come up on a scene. The air this night was electric. The seconds seemed to drag, the house dead silent, and then the lights illuminated King Claudius and his court. Booth was masked from the audience. Perhaps they even forgot for a moment why this performance would be historic. When Claudius finished with Polonius and Laertes, he addressed the still unseen Hamlet: "But now, my cousin Hamlet, and my son,—"

The couriers parted and the seated Edwin Booth appeared as if through magic, his dark eyes luminous in the stage lights. After a shocked hush, the audience suddenly rose for a prolonged ovation.

In the wings, Michael Mulligan was moved as Edwin Booth waited patiently for the applause to subside, and then he delivered his response to Claudius in a soft voice: "A little more than kin and less than kind."

The evil his brother did to his reputation vanished in an instant.

RETURN TO SAN FRANCISCO

THE TRAIN FROM SACRAMENTO pulled into the Oakland station. In a railcar, Michael Mulligan drank water, filling his dry mouth. He had seen so many changes crossing the open country, including passengers shooting at herds of buffalo, another attempt to destroy the plains Indians, but the San Francisco bay area had gone through major development since he had said good-bye to his five-year-old son and left on a ship for Panama and then the east coast, heading for war. Mulligan waited for other passengers to disembark. He rubbed his kneecaps, knowing the Maguires and his son, John, now 14, waited on the platform. When he left the station, he didn't see Patrick Maguire at first. Workers repaired damage to one building from an earthquake the year before. Suddenly, they appeared: red-faced Patrick, his wife, Elizabeth, and a tall awkward boy with thick hair and blue eyes. Mulligan tried to imagine the five-year-old boy he had left and match his face with the teenaged boy's face, now nervously looking down. Patrick, small and much older, his hair white, gripped his hand.

"Welcome home at last, Michael Mulligan," he said.

Mulligan then embraced Elizabeth, now grown stout.

"Hello, my dear boy. Michael—so good to see you at last."

Mulligan looked at John. "Hello. It's been a long time, Son."

The boy didn't answer but shook Mulligan's hand. Mulligan embraced him but the boy didn't respond. Patrick seized his elbow.

"We'll take the ferry to San Francisco and then the wife and I would like to attend the noon Mass at Mission Dolores. You and John can talk in the graveyard. It's a nice quiet place. We won't force John to join us, today."

"And the dead won't disturb us," Michael Mulligan said. "John, I haven't heard your voice yet. How are you?"

"Fine," John said, in a voice now breaking with puberty.

They boarded a double ended ferry with steam-driven, side paddlewheels. San Francisco had grown from a fishing village into a metropolis on the bay. The winter light was rapidly changing over the frigid bay waters. Sloops and schooners sailed by them, and they saw a distant four-master. Standing on the bow, Mulligan enjoyed the sharp sea breeze, and glanced at his son watching the water and city skyline while Patrick and Elizabeth sat on a bench, talking.

"We have a lot to catch up on," Mulligan said.

John nodded but didn't speak.

"I know I was gone a long time. There was the war and then—"

"The war ended in 65'."

"Yes," Mulligan said. "It did. I meant to leave right away but…I was sick for a while."

"You got shot?"

"A ball grazed my head, but I did sustain other injuries. There's a point where a soldier can have episodes of nervous fear…even terror, worse than physical injuries."

John didn't ask any questions, watching hovering sea gulls. Mulligan remembered a poem by Walt Whitman describing a ride on the Brooklyn ferry that somehow connected to future readers of the poet. Did Michael Mulligan and his son now mean more to the poet's meditations than they might suppose?

"Thanks to the new transcontinental railway, it only takes four days to get here. Did you get my letters?"

"Yes," the boy said.

They stood in silence on the bow, watching the approaching harbor and a wooden ferry station. Mulligan suddenly laughed. For the first time, John showed some curiosity.

"I was here in the early 50's when the so called Barbary Coast was really wild and dangerous. I had to rescue the actor, Edwin Booth, one night. I wonder if the area is still dangerous."

"I hear it is," John said.

Mulligan leaned on the railing and examined his son's profile. "You're becoming a young man, now. You got a girlfriend?"

The boy met his eyes and Mulligan saw the anger.

"The Maguires sent me to an all boys Catholic school," he said.

Mulligan decided to remain silent as the ferry docked at the wharf. They took a horse-drawn cab up Market Street toward Maguire's house in the Mission District. Mulligan saw more construction and repair work after the earthquake, and as they passed a large building, Patrick said, "That's Saint Ignatius where John goes to school."

"So you've turned my son over to the Jesuits, have you?"

"Yes, and it's about time you accept the One Holy Catholic Apostolic Church yourself."

"I'm a Celtic pagan," Mulligan said.

For the first time, he saw John smile. They stopped at an adobe church built in 1776, and the Maguires went inside for a late Mass.

"You can sit outside in the cemetery with your son, if you like," Patrick said. He whispered: "He doesn't know who you are after all these years, you know."

Mulligan and John sat on a bench facing a garden and many old headstones. Mulligan always found ancient graveyards and gravestones fascinating, but wondered how a 14-year-old boy would react. "You got out of Mass, at least."

"It's boring," the boy said. "Too much kneeling, sitting and standing."

"You like Saint Ignatius?"

"No. Too much work. When will I ever use Latin…or Greek?"

"Work is good. And where would I be without Latin? Son, I want you to do well in school. You'll thank me later if you go to a university."

"Thanks for your advice." The boy glanced at the gravestones and foliage.

"Listen John, perhaps after school, tomorrow, we could take the ferry across the bay and hike in the woods." The boy stared ahead, silently. "Or maybe not. We don't have to do anything, son."

"I have plans after school," John said. "I have friends, here."

"I understand." They sat quietly for a few minutes.

"Maybe we can do something if you want," the boy said.

"You really don't want to be here, do you?"

For the first time, his son responded quickly.

"I want to be here…but I don't really know why. I don't know you."

"Spending time together will help." Mulligan took out a toy half sun that fit with a missing piece. "You remember this?"

John looked. "No. It looks like a toy."

"It is a toy. I gave you half and kept half when I said good-bye on that pier, nine years ago. You have the other half?"

"No," John said. "I don't remember it."

Late that night, Patrick and Michael Mulligan sat up, drinking whiskey. A tiny statue of the Virgin Mary stood on the mantle. Jesus and his sacred heart watched from another wall. Above the fireplace, the portrait of Michael Mulligan, Civil War cavalry officer, dominated the room. In his bedroom, John was asleep.

"When you left, the boy cried and cried. He kept waiting for the war to end and his pa to come home. Then it ended and four years later, you finally show up. Were you waiting for the railroad to connect to Oakland?"

"Yes. And I had other problems. I was a little crazy, for a while."

They drank.

"I believe that," Patrick finally said. "He's not doing well in school."

"Maybe I can talk to him."

"He was after taking a China girl to a school dance and they wouldn't let him."

"The school?"

"Yes. A heathen girl wasn't welcome."

"The Chinese built the railroad."

"So? They still don't got any rights in California. Suzi's parents didn't want their daughter at a Catholic dance, either. Her father is Billy Chang, a big man in Chinatown."

"His first name is Billy?"

"They like them Anglo first names."

"How did John meet her in the first place?"

"Suzi Chang took the boys of Saint Ignatius on a goodwill tour of Chinatown. The mayor thought it was a good idea. The police chief thought it was good for race relations. Even Billy Chang approved. I guess John Mulligan and Suzi Chang got too close."

"Is the girl still around?"

"No, we put an end to that," Patrick said. "Her father sent her away to school. Suzie Chang is gone. And it's a good thing. Her brother threatened us...and John."

"Why wasn't I informed?"

"Didn't think it mattered."

"Didn't matter? A threat to my son doesn't matter?"

"We took care of it. And the girl's parents felt the same way. Of course, even Billy Chang got no rights in court. Don't have a Chinaman's chance," Patrick said, laughing. "And isn't John a bit young to be playing Romeo?"

"That's not the point. Patrick? You know about my enemies in Ireland? The whole point about my not being here earlier was to protect my son. I don't want *anyone* to know who or where he is."

"The Whiteboys are in Ireland."

"All the same, if there is *any* threat to my boy, Chinese or Irish, I will hear of it."

"All right. Done." Patrick lifted his glass. "To your health."

"Here's how and to your health." They drank.

"To a United Ireland." Patrick suddenly had tears in his eyes. "Good to see you, Michael Mulligan, even if you are a pagan."

After school, Michael Mulligan picked up John, dressed in a school uniform. The other boys watched as they left together and took another ferry across the bay to hike in the redwood forests and walk along the beach. Small waves lapped on the shore. John spoke little as Michael Mulligan narrated his history.

"Take advantage of school," he said. "I grew up with Irish Travelers and then was adopted by a director of a traveling theatre troupe. I knew Irish, Shelta, the Traveler's language, learned English, and even endured insults at Oxford. I also learned how to use a knife and a gun. Maybe too well. All survival skills are necessary, young man."

"Yes, I know," the boy said. He skipped a rock across the water. "I heard about the Irish Gypsies, the so called tinkers. I heard they are great thieves."

Mulligan waited to respond. "Are you suggesting I'm a thief?"

John watched him, perhaps expecting a sudden blow.

"No," he finally said. "I didn't say that."

"Stealing may have been part of their culture...because they were a repressed people."

"And we Irish are also a repressed people?"

"We have been. We still are."

"But not Michael Mulligan, soldier and scholar. Not Michael Mulligan, trainer of horses and absentee father."

Mulligan stopped. Sea gulls on the beach watched them.

"You got me there, son. I was an absentee father." He raised his voice. "Someday, you may want to know why."

"Can we go home?"

"Sure. I can leave tomorrow, you know. I don't have to stay here."

Without looking at him, John said, "Stay."

They didn't speak on the ferry back to San Francisco, nor did they converse in the horse-drawn cab. John entered the house and went to his room. Elizabeth worked in the garden, growing vegetables despite the cold foggy weather. Patrick was out. Mulligan sat in the front room, listening to an old clock ticking off the minutes and hours. He saw the formal military portrait of himself on the wall, but that was from another time. When Patrick came home, tipsy, Elizabeth fed them a meal of corned beef and cabbage. John said nothing at the table, ignoring his father's presence.

"I'm going to visit the Barbary Coast tonight," Mulligan said. "Track down some old friends…like Mary, a working girl. Thanks to her, I was able to find and rescue one of the greatest actors of our time, Edwin Booth."

"That place is a cess pool," Elizabeth said.

"She's right," Patrick said. "You be careful."

"I'm a Celt warrior," Mulligan said. "I can defend myself. And it's been awhile since I had a nice opium dream."

He could see John staring ahead, quiet but listening.

"You stay out of them Chinamen joints," Patrick said.

"And what if I desire a nice Chinese girl, working off her passage?"

"Michael, please," Elizabeth said. "Your son shouldn't be hearing such talk."

"I grow too bold. My apologies."

"For God's sake," Patrick said in a loud voice. "Set an example!" Patrick gulped his whiskey and water.

"But Patrick, I'm sure John doesn't mind hearing about lovely Chinese girls."

Michael Mulligan saw the fury in his son's eyes, his hands clutching a napkin, the knuckles tightening.

"Those foreign girls are sad," Elizabeth said. "Not even the Chinese deserve such treatment."

Mulligan nodded in agreement. "Maybe you're right. The Chinese have been exploited. The Irish were exploited after the great famine and when the Civil War began."

"We were. And you fought to free the niggers."

"Patrick," Elizabeth said. "Don't talk like that and lay off the whiskey!"

"Hey, you listen to me, both of you," Patrick said, pouring another glass. "We Irish were exploited, but not for long. The Jews own the country but the Irish will soon run it. And I mean Irish Catholics, not those English loving Protestants! We'll have an Irish Catholic President, someday."

"Not in our lifetime." Mulligan stood up. "I *do* need to walk around the city, see how it's changed. Care to join me, Son?"

"No."

"I didn't hear you."

"I said, 'No.' Are you deaf?"

"John, don't speak to your father like that," Patrick said. "Show respect."

"It's all right," Mulligan said. "Maybe tomorrow, I'll take a stroll along ocean beach. I've been away from the ocean for a long time."

Mulligan put on a bearskin coat and wide-brimmed hat and left the house. As he walked down the street, he could hear Elizabeth scolding Patrick. Mulligan carried his shillelagh with a knife in the handle, and he still packed a two shot derringer. He stopped and waited for John to leave the house and join him but the boy remained inside. Mulligan continued down Mission Street to Market Street and then Pacific Avenue, passing many of the old taverns and dark dens. Even the Barbary Coast seemed subdued. There was no tinny music, and fewer ladies on the street. The earthquake from a year before had struck the city briefly into submission. One woman approached him from an alley. "Want some, tonight? I like old timers."

"I'm young at heart, but no thanks. Do you know Mary?"

"I know a lot of Marys," the woman said.

A cold wind blew down the street. Mulligan described his old friend, prostitute and confidant from another time.

"That could fit anybody. But if you are talking that long ago, she's probably croaked by now. These streets ain't very hospitable, you know."

The woman laughed, harshly. Mulligan walked on, passing a Chinese opium den, tempted to join the addicts *drowsed with the fume of poppies* and free from pain. He ended at the beach facing the Golden Gate. Houses were appearing on unstable land reclaimed from the dark bay, and Mulligan wondered what a future major earthquake would do. After watching the bay and recalling his former life in San Francisco, Mulligan walked back to the Maguire home. The fog was often lighter in the Mission District. As he approached the house, he saw a police wagon passing with the night's prisoners inside. A young police officer approached him, his face spotted with freckles.

"A good evening to you, sir."

"And good evening to you, officer. You're Irish, I presume?"

"Irish as Patty's pig. I detect you're also Irish...possibly a real Irishman from the old country."

"That I am. I'm visiting. Name's Michael Mulligan."

"Officer Jimmy Quinn." They shook hands. "Picked up a little coolie bastard prowling your block. He should stay where he belongs, in Chinatown."

"What was he doing?"

"Watching the houses and windows. Maybe casing them for a future robbery. We had a bit of a scuffle. The yellow punk had a knife." He smacked a club into his palm. "And I have this."

"What was the boy's name?"

"Johnny Chang."

"Son of Billy Chang?"

"How do I know? How many Chinamen are named Chang? I think Governor Bigley was right, we need to stop this Chinese immigration. How long before we have Chinky police?"

"Oh, the sons of Erin will rule for now."

"That's right. Well, I'm off. Have a good night."

"And you, Officer Quinn." Mulligan entered the house and found John sitting on a couch by the window. Mulligan sat down. "You want to tell me what's going on?"

"Nothing is going on," John said.

He stood up.

"I'm going to put flowers on your mother's grave, tomorrow. Want to join me? It's Saturday."

"No," his son said.

"Why not?"

"Because I will only hear again how she died giving birth to me."

"You won't hear that from me."

"Good night," John said.

"Why was Johnny Chang in the neighborhood?"

"I don't know. Ask him."

"I will."

The boy disappeared down the hall. Moments later, a bleary eyed Patrick came into the front room. He blinked a few times.

"What's all this racket?" he asked.

"I'll tell you after I visit the police station," Mulligan said.

"Police station? What for?"

But Mulligan was gone. He walked to the neighborhood station and into a large, well-lighted room where police officers processed prisoners or prepared to go out on patrol. He came to the desk and faced a heavy-set sergeant with red hair and a brusque manner.

"And what can I do for you?"

Michael Mulligan gave his name and explained that an incident took place in front of Patrick Maguire's house.

"We know Patrick James Maguire very well, don't we, boys?" Another clerk laughed. "And what incident is that and who are you again?"

"Michael Mulligan."

"Well, it's a good Irish name, at least. And what does Mr. Mulligan want with us?"

"I'd like to talk to Johnny Chang."

A silence fell on the station. Another officer looked away. The sergeant leaned over his desk and glared at Mulligan. "You better be careful what you ask for, Mulligan."

"He was arrested in front of my house."

"And on Patrick Maguire's block. So what? We got Chinamen all over San Francisco."

"I want to know why he was arrested."

The sergeant stared at Mulligan for a long time, not blinking. His voice was soft but carried a threat. "Read it in the papers, Mulligan. Now if you don't mind."

"Why can't you tell me why Johnny Chang was arrested?

"You one of his dad's customers, Mulligan?"

A second office behind the desk smirked.

"Lower your voice, Sarge."

An angry woman suddenly appeared, demanding to know where her husband was.

"Sleeping it off," the sergeant said. "As usual."

Mulligan turned away from the desk and found himself face to face with a middle aged Chinese man in a fashionable suit. Though aware of his presence, the police and sergeant ignored the dapperly dressed Asian.

"Why are you asking about my son?"

"He was arrested outside my house."

The sergeant bellowed at them. "Okay, you two. Due respect, take it outside, Mr. Chang and Mr. Mulligan. We got more arrests, tonight."

They walked out onto a dark misty side street. A horse-drawn carriage waited at the corner.

"My name is Michael Mulligan."

"Father of John?"

"Yes. Listen, I realize your family and my family may have had some difficulty in the past, and I know about your honor code."

"Code? My people just want to become Americans and work. That seems to be difficult since the gold dried up and we finished the railroad."

"I know that. I have a code, as well. To insure my son's safety, I will do anything."

"Your son is in danger, Mr. Mulligan?"

"You know he is, Mr. Chang. I will do any favor or service."

Billy Chang watched his face impassively. When he spoke, his speech was measured and precise. "What kind of service?"

Mulligan shrugged. "Maybe you want someone eliminated."

Billy Chang showed no surprise. "Really? You're an assassin?"

"I have been."

"Are you armed now, Mr. Mulligan?"

"Yes." Mulligan exposed the blade in his walking stick. "I have a concealed derringer and access to other weapons. I fought in the Civil War."

"Impressive." Billy Chang leaned close and whispered: "Do you think you could eliminate that Irish cop, Quinn? No offense, but he's younger than you. And strong. He beat up my son with a billy club."

"I don't know if I would kill him, but perhaps he might endure a severe beating and a midnight swim in the bay."

Billy Chang quietly watched Mulligan's face and then addressed two large men who suddenly appeared behind him, speaking in Chinese and then English. "Wong Fook. Charlie Fong. Mr. Mulligan, here, has offered to hurt that Irish pig cop for me."

To Mulligan's surprise, the men laughed. Billy Chang also laughed. He finally regarded Mulligan, his expression quizzical.

"You Irish are a funny people," he said. "But I shouldn't be laughing. My son will need surgery on his nose and cheek bone." In the carriage window, Mulligan saw the boy's face appear, one side swollen and black. "Get back inside," Chang told his son. He again regarded Mulligan. "Mr. Mulligan, I have my own private army. I also run a respectable business in Chinatown. Unlike the so called 'Coolies,' I have some influence thanks to girls, gambling and opium for a premium price. I have excellent citizens for customers: the mayor, the chief of police, and even one bishop. You understand?"

"I think I do."

"Officer Quinn will soon have another beat...and it may not be pleasant."

The driver of the carriage called out. "We have to leave, Mr. Chang."

"In a moment."

"Mr. Chang, I thought your son was going to hurt my boy and—"

"Stop." Chang produced a letter. "Here. This is for your son from my daughter. Johnny was the messenger. I suppose we should have used the regular US mail, but we like to deal with our friends and enemies directly. Good evening, Mr. Mulligan. If I need your services, I will pay you a visit. If I can serve you..."

Billy Chang bowed, got inside the carriage and they drove off. Mulligan saw the note was addressed to his son who suddenly appeared before him.

"What the hell is going on?"

Mulligan handed him the letter.

"It's for you," he said.

John Mulligan tore open the letter and read it as they walked home. Mulligan suspected what it contained and felt his son's pain, but when Mulligan entered the house and went to bed, he wasn't ready to talk to his son about the letter or anything else. In the morning, he would find Emily O' Rourke's grave and pay his respects. It had been 14 years since she died and so much had happened, including a civil war.

The next day, Michael Mulligan left for the cemetery outside San Francisco. Emily's grave lay on a hill overlooking the distant ocean with a strong wind coming off the Pacific. The gravestone lay flat and weathered, with Emily's name and dates: 1830-1855. She had only 25 years, and a son she never knew except for a few minutes post birth before the fatal hemorrhage began. Mulligan looked at the simple plaque and tried to remember the shining face of the Irish Colleen, come to America for work as a maid and finding a man of the theatre. Emily had partially filled that terrible gap left by Maria Burke, and now, years later, he felt the lingering pain of this double loss fading. Other layers of reality including the war had filled those widening cycles of grief.

"Ah, Emily, I am so sorry."

His voice sounded strange to him. Mulligan was about to find an Irish tavern near the cemetery when he saw John walking toward him, slouching like the awkward teenager he was. The boy looked at the gravestone in silence.

"I'm sorry I never knew her."

"Only once," Mulligan said. "We are here only once so live and breathe and enjoy it."

John confronted his father. "What did you say to Billy Chang, last night?"

"That if he didn't leave you alone, I'd cut this throat."

"Spoken like a tough man," John said. "But no one talks to Billy Chang like that, not even the police chief. And maybe it's none of your business."

"You are my son. A threat to you is my business." Mulligan chuckled to himself. "Actually, I agreed to eliminate any of his enemies in exchange for your safety."

His son stared at him, uncertain whether to laugh or get angry. "Jesus," he finally said. "I can take care of myself."

"I need a beer," Mulligan said. "Molloy's is near. How about you? You can have milk or some ginger ale. The Irish invented it, you know."

The boy didn't answer, but followed his father to the tavern. A cold wind blew across the cemetery hill. John finally spoke.

"I wasn't threatened. The bitch said good bye and that's that."

"Such is life," Mulligan said. "After Gettysburg, I fell in love with a lovely nurse. Beautiful, she was. Then she left me for Jesus and entered a convent. Farewell the love that would last 'til doomsday."

To his surprise, his son found this detail amusing. They entered a small dark smoky tavern and sat at the bar. Mulligan ordered a beer and a shot of whiskey for himself and ginger ale for the boy. A fat woman passing by squeezed John's cheeks between her big hands.

"And ain't he a pretty boy?"

"Yes, he is," Mulligan said. He observed his son, seeing some of Emily's beauty in his face and along the hairline. The sharp focused eyes, however, belonged to him. "It will snow, soon, and I don't have much time. I have a stable of horses for rich folk, and a spring theatre season to run. You can come with me if you like, or you can finish school and meet me in New York after graduation. I can visit you every summer. What do you think?"

"I don't know. You could've come here sooner."

"It was a long journey to Panama and up the west coast. And I had other concerns."

"Such as?"

Mulligan swallowed the shot of whiskey and sipped his beer.

"I had some people after me in Ireland."

"Bad people?"

"No. They were my brothers but I abandoned them. We were called the Whiteboys and terrorized tyrannical English and Anglo Irish landlords."

"Why did you leave them?"

Mulligan hesitated. "I wanted to come to America, the land of opportunity."

"You killed people for money?"

"Usually for free," Mulligan said. "More often, a bad landlord was beaten or warned. But I think violence and intimidation are wrong. I believe refusing to work is the best Irish tactic against cruel and unfair plantation owners. If no one brings in the crop, they are finished. They have to make changes. Dead, they just bring in the soldiers and the war goes on."

John drank his ginger ale.

"So you left Ireland? Why not settle in San Francisco?"

"Because, son, those angry brothers of mine could find me and hurt you as well. I didn't want them to know you even existed."

The boy was silent for a long time. The conversation in the bar grew louder. Two men in a corner were arguing.

"Nice to know my father is so protective."

Mulligan didn't respond. He finished another beer with a shot and John drank a second ginger ale. Mulligan once again felt a sense of isolation in the crowded noisy tavern. He was slightly drunk when they left in a horse-drawn cab. An Irishman was the driver. Mulligan and John sat together as the cab moved forward in a light rain. Mulligan liked the sound of thudding hooves on wet pavement.

"I guess we are strangers and it's my fault, son. I'm sorry." He could see John watching him. "You like the Maguires?"

"They're all right."

It was raining heavily when they arrived at the Maguire house. Before they left the cab, Michael Mulligan gently touched his son's hand.

"You seem so young to be a Don Juan. God, you're only 14!"

"How old were you before virgins had to worry?"

"Ireland is a puritanical country, but I managed." Mulligan knew he must appear awkward and even shy as he struggled to find the right words. "There was an Irish lass named Maggie. This Suzi Chang girl? Son, you do realize the difference in cultures would have been disastrous?"

"I do."

"I hope she wasn't...you know...with child." John remained silent. It was his silences that disturbed him most. Mulligan suddenly laughed. "An Irish Chinese Mulligan might be a joy, now that I think of it. Any chance of that?"

John Mulligan faced his father, reeking of beer and whiskey, the boy's expression one of pity. "I'm not a pagan like you, Father, but a Catholic however lapsed. You should know better than to ask that question."

At first, Mulligan was surprised, and then he started laughing. "My son has a sense of humor," he said. "And he called me 'Father.'"

Michael Mulligan got out of the cab, and touched the big dray horse, wet from the rain.

"Strong animal."

"Has to be with these San Francisco hills."

"You treat him well, I see."

"He's my living," the driver said.

Mulligan paid him. "Good day to you, sir."

"Good day to you."

They entered the house and John started walking to his room. Then he stopped.

"Maybe before you leave, you could show me how to ride."

"I'd love that," Mulligan said. "I love horses."

"I know you do. I've seen your portrait."

"I guess that means you won't leave San Francisco with me?"

"Not this time." John Mulligan hesitated, his face turned away. Mulligan was beginning to interpret his son's pauses. "Regarding Suzi, we only fucked once under an overturned boat down by Fisherman's Wharf."

226

"Sounds romantic."

"It's been a nice afternoon, but I need to study for finals. Patrick may have some whiskey left."

"I don't drink every day, but if you're Irish, it's a good man's failing."

John Mulligan left his father sitting on the couch. Moments later, Patrick entered with a whiskey bottle and two glasses. "Cocktail hour," he said.

For the next two weeks, Michael Mulligan took his son to a stable surrounded by sand dunes that the city wanted to claim as a future park. They spoke little as John Mulligan rode a big horse around in a circle while Michael Mulligan called out orders and made corrections on John's style in the saddle. Thin and sinewy, John Mulligan was a good student, his brown hair lifting in the breeze created by the circular galloping.

"Be one with the horse," Mulligan said. "Relax. Anticipate the horse's moves and guide him or her. A mare can be just as difficult as a stallion."

Michael Mulligan felt more connection with his son, though they had little actual conversation, not speaking on the way to or from the stable.

Then as December advanced and the plains were threatened with heavy snow, it was time to go. They sat around the dinner table, John finishing his exams, Michael Mulligan speaking little, Patrick pouring drinks while Elizabeth served the food.

"I will be back in the summer," Mulligan said. John Mulligan said nothing, occasionally meeting his eyes over a plate of food.

The final morning arrived and Mulligan picked up his packed suitcase. Elizabeth had prepared a big breakfast and put more food in a bag. Patrick Maguire was unusually quiet, and John silent as they took a horse and buggy to the ferry station. Mulligan embraced Patrick and Elizabeth.

"If anything happens, let me know. I may bring a show here."

"Good bye, Michael," Patrick said. "One day, we'll have a united independent Irish republic."

"Yes, one day."

Elizabeth quietly wept as she hugged Mulligan again. Then he and John got on the bay ferry to Oakland where Michael Mulligan would take the train. They spoke little crossing the choppy white-capped bay waters.

"Will you be safe from the so called Whiteboys?"

Michael Mulligan turned to his son.

"I think so. But someday, I must go back. One can't run forever from one's destiny, Son."

They left the ferry and walked toward the train for Sacramento and then Omaha. A black porter was taking tickets and bags. Mulligan felt a pang of guilt and put an arm around his son.

"I love you, Son," he said, "though I'm bad at showing it."

"Thanks for teaching me to ride," the boy said. "I will continue. Maybe I'll join the cavalry after high school. I'll be just like you."

"That would be fine," Michael Mulligan said.

It was time to go. He shook his son's hand. "Good bye, John. I am so sorry we didn't meet earlier. I hope we meet sooner in the future."

"I hope so too. I am putting something in your pocket, Father. Take it out on the train. And write to me. I will do the same."

"Good."

Mulligan kissed his son on the cheek and quickly boarded the train. Looking out the window, he saw John Mulligan wave to him, actually smiling before he walked toward the bay ferry as the train began moving. Mulligan felt a deep prolonged sorrow. Why hadn't he decided to remain in San Francisco and take up another line of work, if only to be close to his son? Were they doomed to be forever separated?

He placed his suitcase over the seat and looked at the bag of food Elizabeth had prepared. Then he felt in his pocket and took out a circular object that felt like a half coin.

It was half of a toy sun. After nine years, the two pieces could fit together.

THE DEN

IT IS A BASEMENT ROOM down worn steps. A red light gives the room a reddish patina, touching the faces of those who occasionally sit up before reclining again. Smoke drifts though the dim light. Mulligan sees a bone-thin old woman staring at him, smiling, a single tooth visible in her upper gums. She is cackling. A red glow lights her thin gray hair. She motions toward the pipe and Michael Mulligan draws in the smoke. Soon, he will float down his own river, with no pain and no thoughts of the past war or dead friends or severed limbs or lost lovers.

He will not see the burning barn in Washington and hear the screams of the trapped horses. He will not see his son's resentful eyes. He will not see the face of the boy he shot during the New York riots—the boy with his son's name. He will not see Maria Burke dying on Grosse Isle. He will not see Nurse Abigail Donohue getting on the train that carries her away. He will not see all those people he loved fading from his sight. He will not hear the cannons.

Not today.

Mulligan takes another hit off the pipe. He suspects he will need more and more of the drug to feel the euphoria; one day, he may *cease upon the midnight with no pain.*

He peers through the gloom but doesn't see the emaciated old woman. He closes his eyes and when he opens them, a beautiful young Asian woman is watching him. She is naked, her breasts round and firm, her hips curving, the reddish light giving her skin a copper sheen. He imagines that sweet tight pussy waiting for his penetrating member. She leans over his prostrate body.

"Take a puff, my beautiful man. Suck on it. Then I will take your cock into my mouth. You will like that, won't you?"

Mulligan wants to answer *Yes* but closes his eyes, feeling the sweet lethargy stealing through his body. He dreams of a happy time, standing on the bow of a ship, his first love sleeping in their cabin, the blue sea beneath a blue sky stretching out before him. The air smells of fresh breezes and salt water as dolphins leap from the sea..

But something disturbs him. It is an English voice of all things. It penetrates his dream.

"I say, Mulligan, this is pretty low for you. I know you're a rogue and all that, but I never thought it would get *this bad*. Now I want you to get off that filthy bloody pallet and come with me. You are going in hospital, right this moment."

"Go away."

"The English have arrived."

"The English are my enemies," Mulligan mumbles.

"Not tonight. Or is it day outside this ghastly place?"

"What difference does it make?"

Mulligan sits up. Reginald Taylor stands before him wearing clean tan pants, shiny boots and shirt, his tie in place, hair combed, mustache trimmed. He is once again the jolly old Englishman from another time.

"You're dead," Mulligan screams. "I saw the bloody wound."

"You did. That was not my lucky day, I'm afraid. Now listen here. Focus on the moment."

"Leave me in peace—now!"

"You're not getting off that easy," Reginald says.

"Look—I never touched your wife."

"Oh I know all about that…bet you would've liked some of that English stuff, eh what? Don't blame you, old boy. Julia is a beauty."

"Reginald, I'm sorry you died but—"

"Stop blathering, man. Get up this minute."

Michael Mulligan tries to sit up. A red spot spreads on Taylor's white shirt. The old woman is crackling again. He becomes aware of slumbering bodies and pipes glowing in the low light.

"Don't destroy my pleasure," he croaks.

He reaches for his pipe but it is knocked aside. He doesn't know how much time passes, but Mulligan is aware of strong hands seizing him, and then they are somehow outside and cold air is brushing against his cheeks. Indoors, he sees a woman's face beneath a wimple, and feels a needle pricking his arm. He struggles but drifts away into zero consciousness.

Mulligan wakes up in a hospital, a cold draft blowing down the corridor, dull light filling the unwashed windows. Jesus is hanging on a cross. A nun holds a bowl of soup.

"Good morning, Major Mulligan." She offers a spoonful. "You will be in some pain and there is nothing we can do to stop that, sorry to say. You have to break the pattern. Take this."

He takes a swallow, feeling a dull ache through his body like the beginning of the flu. He is shaking.

"Sister, who brought me here?"

"General Farnsworth."

"He's dead. Elon Farnsworth is dead. He died at Gettysburg!"

"Correct. But John Farnsworth is alive. I believe Elon was his nephew. He heard about your opium addiction and decided to intervene."

"I don't know the man. He had no right." Mulligan is aware of leather straps holding his arms. "What the hell is going on?"

"An intervention. You will stay here for two to three weeks until you are clean, you will visit with Doctor Jones, and then you'll be released. If you wish to return to that filthy den, you may. But General Farnsworth who respected your work with

Elon's cavalry thought you deserved this one chance. Drink some more soup."

Mulligan grins. "Maybe you could grind up a little pill for me and slip it into the broth," he says. He wants to laugh, but sweat suddenly appears on his forehead.

"That is not part of the cure," the nun tells him.

Mulligan turns his head and vomits.

The early mornings are the worst when he wakes from nightmares and cold sweats to see the gray light outside the hospital window, his cells crying out for release from pain. Constipation turns to diarrhea. A tall gentleman, clean-shaven with burning eyes, informs him that when the addiction is broken, Mulligan will suffer bouts of depression.

"I'm Irish. We are always suffering bouts of depression. It's our dark Celtic nature."

"True," says the man who identifies himself as Doctor Jones. "I know you're a strong man, and it takes great strength to break an addiction."

Mulligan loses all sense of time. He hears people screaming in the hall. A nurse gives him bitter tea one afternoon and he feels better. It is hard to say just when the pain leaves, since he is pale and still trembling. Doctor Jones visits him.

"You weren't as bad as I thought. Any nightmares?"

"Waking or sleeping?"

"Both."

"I can't tell the difference."

"That's part of withdrawal."

"Doctor," Mulligan says, "opium is a blessing. You have *no* idea what I have seen."

"But I do, Major," Doctor Jones tells him. "I was a medic at Cold Harbor. I didn't treat many living bodies, however, only picked up bloated dead ones. Unlike you, I did not choose to blot out the pain with a drug."

"Good for you."

"That's only an observation." The doctor consults his charts. "I must make my rounds. We have a lot of interesting people, here, even a famous detective."

One morning, it is bright and sunny and he is walking in the garden feeling hungry, some of his strength returning. He has often sat in the doctor's office but they have spoken little. Dr. Jones has given him an assignment.

"Write a journal about the war. It might help."

"And confront that pain, that horror—again?"

"Yes. You might take away its power."

"I will start with a letter to President Grant. Today is April 9th."

"That date is significant?"

"It's the day Lee signed the surrender. Then I'll thank the President for his brilliant work as a general at Cold Harbor. We lost thousands of men in suicidal charges. Two weeks of slaughter."

"Indeed."

Dr. Jones has a calm way of focusing his gaze on him while writing notes. "What a terrible war," he says. "But you survived, limbs intact. You need to get healthy and carry on without a dependency on drugs or alcohol. Is there someone I could contact?"

"No."

"No one? It's not good to be a solo agent, Major Mulligan."

"I do have a son."

"Let me contact him. It's not shameful to have an addiction."

"I will contact him in my own time, Doctor Jones."

"Very well."

Michael Mulligan now sits in the garden. Other patients and nuns pass. If only Nurse Abby were here to heal him. He remembers their sensuous nights at Gettysburg. Then he sees an older man walking toward him, his beard thick, the head bald. The man holds out his hand.

"I am General Farnsworth. You served with my nephew, Elon."

"I did."

They shake hands. The general sits down. "How do you feel?"

"Like hell."

"Someone in your company saw you entering one of those dens, and alerted me."

"Who was it?"

"I'd rather not say."

"Tell me."

"Major William Wells."

"Why didn't Major Wells intervene himself?"

"He felt embarrassed. I guess he thought it wasn't his business."

"It *wasn't* his business."

"I decided to act. I owe something to Elon, and I know you rode together at Gettysburg."

"We did."

"How's the food?"

"Terrible. And no Irish whiskey."

"Not here." The older man smiles. After a moment, he says, "Joking aside, I am still a little concerned, Major."

"For me?"

"Yes."

"Why?"

"Next week, Dr. Jones is releasing you."

"Good. Looking forward to freedom."

"Here is my card. If you grow weak and need to return to that awful place, contact me." General Farnsworth doesn't move. "We have to recover from the war, Major Mulligan. Bind up the nation's wounds."

"That sounds like Lincoln."

"It is Lincoln. I was there when he died," Farnsworth says. "We have to live and heal the nation and make his death and my nephew's death somehow mean something." General Farnsworth suddenly stands. "I must be off. Keep in contact, Major Mulligan."

"I will, General. Elon was a brave man."

"He was."

"I'd like to kill General Kilpatrick who gave that fatal order."

"I understand your anger," the general says. "But we must forgive him and live our lives. The anger will only hurt you."

The old general salutes and walks away. Two nurses pass. Mulligan sits in the garden and takes a deep breath. Birds are singing in the trees. He begins writing in his journal: "Last night I dreamt of a pig sty in Donegal."

DEPARTURE

SOLDIERS WAITED ON THE Oakland depot platform for the troop train that would take them back east. John Mulligan in uniform waited with them. He also waited for his father. Once again, they would meet before journeys, but this time, it was the son, not the father, who was leaving. John finally saw his father, a little older but well-dressed and nimble, walking quickly toward him. Michael Mulligan had more lines in his face and his hair was turning white, but he still had a slender sinewy build. They embraced stiffly and shook hands.

"I'm sorry I'm late." Mulligan stepped back. "You look good, Son."

"As do you, Father. You never seem to age that much."

"But I am getting old. Sometimes my eyes bother me." Michael Mulligan watched his son with approval. He was a young man, now, his face handsome but rugged. "So my boy is now an army man?"

"And cavalry, at that, Father. Following in the old hoof prints, wouldn't you say?"

"Yes." There was an awkward pause. "It's been a while."

"Only six years. It was nine years before that." His father didn't respond to his tone. "I do have to depart momentarily," he said.

"I wish I knew you were leaving today. I might have got here sooner, John."

"I just got my orders. It wasn't deliberate."

"Of course. Sorry to hear about Patrick Maguire."

"He died drunk and happy."

Mulligan looked at the gathered soldiers waiting for the train, knowing he had only a few minutes with his 20-year-old son after traveling four days across America to meet him. His boy, still a stranger, had become a man.

"Where are they sending you?"

"President Grant is worried about Southern Democrats and the Ku Klux Klan in Mississippi killing Republicans so we are being sent to restore order. Then I may join General Custer in his Indian campaign."

"I know Custer. Don't join his brigade if you can help it."

"Why not? He's a Civil War hero."

"Oh, that he was. And he'll agree."

"You don't agree?"

"Custer was brilliant but too reckless and incredibly lucky. Bravery is one thing. Reckless disregard for safety is another. He lost a lot of men and horses at Gettysburg. Besides, I know he's going to die at the hands of the very Indians he likes to hunt."

Mulligan recognized the quizzical look he saw in his son's young smooth face.

"And how do you know that, pray tell?"

"I was a prisoner near Hanover and a young half breed boy, part black, part Indian—"

"Two marks against him in this country—"

"—stopped the Confederate cavalry as they were riding toward Gettysburg. He told two generals and a soldier how they would die, and it happened *exactly* as he said. He told me that Custer would die at the hands of his own people."

"The Indian people, I presume?"

"Correct."

John Mulligan noticed his commanding officer walking up on the platform. The train was set to depart. Then he regarded his father's striking if weather-burned face.

"Did he predict anything about you, Father?"

"Yes. He said I would die an old man, flea-bitten and waving my shillelagh."

John Mulligan began laughing. "I believe that. Father, you are amazing. Here we are not having met since I was 14, talking about a dark fortune-telling urchin."

"His predictions came true. Do not join Custer's brigade."

"I'll have little say in the matter." John Mulligan fought to control an edge in his voice. "You make me angry sometimes, but you *are* entertaining."

He could see the hard focus in his father's eyes. "You could have joined me in New York after graduation," Mulligan told him. "And I wrote letters."

"Yes, you sent me many letters. And you could have come to San Francisco, occasionally. I realize you're a big man in the New York theatre and have little time to see family in San Francisco."

"You're right. It was my failing." Mulligan adjusted his hat, averting his eyes. "I work with horseflesh too, you know."

"And I *do* appreciate those lessons in horsemanship. Here I am, in the cavalry, so I guess we are not so far removed."

The commanding officer was about to blow a whistle and direct the soldiers onto the train. John Mulligan saw the sadness in his father's eyes and felt a pang of regret.

"It seems we are always saying good bye, Father. Remember that time on the wharf when you left to fight the war? I was five."

"I had to fight."

"Then again on this same train station when you left to go back east? I was 14. And now at 20, I am leaving you."

"Most of life is saying good bye."

"I believe that." They embraced again. John met his father's eyes. "Well—you are something of a gypsy, right?"

"I am."

The commanding officer put a whistle to his lips and they heard a sharp blast. Young men fell into rank. A cold wind blew through the train station.

"I have to go, Father. I will write to you. Say good bye to Elizabeth for me, though we had our good byes."

"I will do that. You look good, John. So tall."

"Children do tend to grow."

"Good bye and be careful."

"I will." John hesitated. "What's wrong with your eyes?"

"They get inflamed. I feel sometimes like I have sand under the lids. No cure, but to irrigate them. Modern medicine isn't very advanced, I'm afraid."

John saw the line of soldiers entering the train. "It's time, Father." He embraced Michael Mulligan. "I'll remember your warning about Custer. He does appear a bit of an egotist."

Steam poured from the train.

"Take this," Michael Mulligan said. He handed his son a toy sun, two pieces fitting together. "Now this is *your* good luck charm. Take care. I love you, Son."

John Mulligan was unprepared for a sudden rush of tears which he quickly wiped away. He pocketed the toy sun.

"Thanks. I love you too, Dad."

With his duffle bag, he walked quickly toward the line of soldiers boarding the train. Michael Mulligan watched him go, remembering his own induction into the U.S. Army when the nation was divided against itself. Then he walked toward the dock, and the bay ferry that would take him to San Francisco where he would visit with Elizabeth Maguire, now a widow, and the one who had helped raise his son. At least Michael and John Mulligan had those few minutes on the train platform.

THE INDIAN WAR

MICHAEL MULLIGAN RODE HIS horse blindly through a white out in the direction of Fort Abraham Lincoln. It seemed he was traveling through a freezing wall of whiteness, causing his extremities to hurt. Mulligan knew that when his arms and legs and hands become numb, he was in greater danger. He also felt heat in his cheeks and forehead, and a dull ache that moved down from the crown of his head to his neck, now stiff and hurting. Mulligan wondered who would find him on this remote prairie. Then he saw strange pyramid shapes in the whiteness and heard startled voices. His horse began to nicker and shy from white phantoms converging upon him. Michael Mulligan recognized Indian voices and reached for his Spencer carbine but it had frozen in the scabbard. He felt hands grabbing him, and screaming words in Irish, felt himself spinning into a vortex, his own consciousness a dwindling point of oblivion.

He would remember little of the next two weeks except for wavering shapes and strange voices and the sound of a fire in the center of animal hide rising up to a hole at the top. Someone fed him a watery gruel, and once he woke up to see a painted mask with horns and long braided hair hovering over him, and then rough hands pushed a bitter cake into his mouth. The headaches and stiff neck continued, and when daylight filtered into what he realized was a tepee, his eyes squinted in the painful if low light. At night, he felt himself sweating with fever; dead women came to him in dreams: Maria Burke from Ireland and Emily O' Rourke in San Francisco. He saw Abigail Donahue Kavanaugh who became a nun, and sometimes at night, he thought he felt a young female body pressing against him, soft cool hands on his back and sides and stomach.

A bucket was left for body waste. Mulligan was too sick to care about privacy.

At some point, hearing the wind outside, Mulligan sat up and realized his clothes were gone. He no longer had a fever or a stiff neck but he was weak. An old Indian woman with a lined face watched him, speaking in her language. Pulling up a buffalo robe, he responded in Irish. Another Indian woman came into the tepee, young and slender and pretty with dark eyes. She was about 17 and spoke to him in her Indian dialect.

"I am Michael Mulligan," he said in English. "I need to meet General Terry at Fort Abraham Lincoln."

The Indian girl tended to him, but avoided his eyes. Only once did he see a warrior who held a club and stared at him, his dark face unmarked with war paint. By the third week, Mulligan could eat chunks of meat with the gruel. The old woman and the young girl still talked to him, but he didn't understand. Mulligan tried sign language. He drew a map and a picture of the fort. The women recognized the drawing and left. Moments later, Indian men came into the tent and stared at the crude drawing. They spoke to him and when he answered in Irish, this startled them. He drew more pictures of horses and himself addressing potential buyers. The warriors seemed to understand.

"Where is my horse?" he asked in English.

One of the braves pointed to the young girl, and they left. Throughout the next day, he could hear excited voices. The young girl came alone now, bringing food. She tended the fire and spoke to him in a light voice.

"I need my gun," Mulligan told her. He made a sign of firing a rifle. The girl frowned. Then she shook her head from side to side. "If you let me go to the fort, I can pay you. Money," Mulligan said. The girl didn't respond.

When the weather cleared, Mulligan woke up and found his clothes and bearskin coat in a pile. He looked out the tepee at an Indian village with many women and children; Sioux and Cheyenne warriors came into the camp, many of them armed. Mulligan had not seen so many Indian warriors from two different tribes in one place. He was quickly stopped when he approached a group of young braves, but then he pointed to the Indian ponies and they watched as he caressed them, searching for problems and speaking Irish to the horses.

"Good animals," Mulligan said, knowing they knew little English. "Fast and wild. But where is my horse? He had Arabian blood."

Then he saw an older Indian in buckskin, carrying an army Springfield rifle and knife and wearing a full headdress of feathers. The Indian was possibly the chief and he rode Mulligan's horse. When the chief dismounted, Mulligan called out and the horse approached him at a trot. Before he could touch the reins, warriors gathered around pointing their rifles at his face.

"That's my horse," Mulligan said.

"And you have life," the chief said. He gestured to the young girl who escorted Mulligan back to the tepee. "Her name is Yellow Bird in your language," the chief told him. He said something in Sioux and laughed; the other Indians joined him. Only one Sioux warrior glared at Mulligan as he entered the tepee with Yellow Bird. Mulligan suddenly felt dizzy and realized how weak he still felt. He let Yellow Bird feed him and lay on a blanket while the fire blazed, casting shadows on the tepee wall. The girl continued talking, watching him anxiously.

"I need to see General Alfred Terry," Mulligan said. "He commands the brigade at Fort Lincoln. You understand, Yellow Bird?"

He placed his hands on his thighs. The girl watched him and then with downcast eyes, slowly began to strip off her clothes. Her body was slender and beautiful in the firelight.

When she finally faced him naked, Mulligan saw tears glistening in her eyes.

"You're lovely, my sweet Indian colleen, but I can't stay here and I can't take you with me."

When he shook his head, she began to speak in a pleading voice and made a gesture of a knife being drawn across her throat.

"What will General Sheridan think, who hates Indians even more than Custer?"

At the mention of Custer's name, the girl pulled up her clothes hiding her body and staring at Mulligan. "Custer?" she said.

"He's at Fort Lincoln," Mulligan said.

Yellow Bird pulled on her clothes. "No fuck," the girl said. Then she spit and left the tent. Moments later, the Indian who glared at him entered the tepee. He carried a pistol and began speaking in an angry voice. Then he reached for his knife and grabbed Mulligan's hair.

"If Yellow Bird is yours, take her," Mulligan told him.

Mulligan heard a commanding voice outside the tepee and the warrior left. Then the chief entered the tepee, flanked by two men, both armed. One of the men was a Cheyenne warrior, and the other was a tall man with light-colored skin. He wore a fashionable vest Mulligan recognized from a New York store. Up close, he saw the pattern of wrinkles in the chief's face, with black eyes and thick braided hair. His voice was low and resonant and he carried no rifle, only a knife.

"I am Chief Red Horse."

"I am Michael Mulligan. I am honored to be your guest. Chief Red Horse, thanks for saving my life, but I need my horse and rifle."

Chief Red Horse did not respond immediately.

"Custer killed Chief Black Kettle. He will die for that. You are his friend?"

"No. He slaughtered a lot of Indian ponies," Mulligan said. "That I don't forgive."

The chief turned and spoke in French to the tall man who listened carefully and then addressed Mulligan in English. He had a strong French accent.

"You were spared because they know you as the man who trains and loves horses. And you spoke a strange language, so they know you are not like white soldiers."

"But I have been one. How is it you speak French?"

"My father was a French trapper, and my mother an Oglala Sioux. My French name is Pierre."

"Why is the chief riding my horse, Pierre?"

"The chief took your horse and rifle in exchange for giving you back your life. The Arapahoe girl was extra. She had no choice."

"Tell him I appreciate the offer, but I need to get to the fort."

Pierre sat without responding. "They are hoping you can get horses for them," he finally said.

"I could get horses," Mulligan said. "Montana has some great places to procure them. The U.S. army wouldn't approve, however."

"How soon can you get us horses?"

"Well, there won't be another sale for some time. There's a horse trader who rounds up mustangs for big shows. "

Pierre spoke to the chief who listened carefully. Red Horse spoke in French and Pierre addressed Mulligan: "Why do you want to go to the fort? To join the army?"

"No. It's to keep my soldier son out of Custer's battalion. I heard from an Indian boy with African blood that Custer will die at the hands of Indian people."

Pierre translated. Then he asked another question.

"Can you get us guns?"

"Guns, no. Maybe horses, but not until mid-summer."

After hearing the translation, Red Horse spoke in Sioux and French, and then got up and left the tent with his companion. "What is going on, Pierre?"

"Today, the Sioux heard they have to give up what you whites call the Black Hills and return to the reservation."

"That violates the Laramie treaty."

"*Mais qui.* What a surprise." Pierre stood up, avoiding Mulligan's eyes. "*Adieu, mon ami.*" He held out his hand. "I go now."

Mulligan also stood. "What about me?"

"They will decide," Pierre said.

"Wait. Why do you converse with Red Horse in French? You speak the Sioux language."

"I do, but we speak a different dialect. It is simply easier."

"Are they going to kill me?"

Pierre left the tepee. Mulligan, feeling weak again, sat down. The old Indian woman entered the tepee and sat opposite him, not speaking. Then she pointed to her mouth and said, "I know Custer. Yum, yum."

She was laughing harshly when two warriors came into the tepee and motioned for Mulligan to step outside. The air was cold and clear and there was much activity. Women and children were leaving the village and mounted warriors included lancers, archers and braves with rifles, their faces streaked with war paint. Mulligan was bound to a post. He called out to Pierre, mounting his horse.

"So—they're going to kill me?"

Pierre didn't answer. Mulligan watched as they evacuated the village. Carrying a rifle, Chief Red Horse rode up to him and said, "You tell Bloody Knife I will kill him. The Crows are traitors."

The chief rode off on Mulligan's horse. Moments later, though he couldn't hear the hooves in the snow, Mulligan saw a troop of cavalry riding down upon the village, many yelling. They tore down the tepees while riding, exposing no one inside. A soldier saw Mulligan and dismounted. "Well, what sport have we got here?"

Mulligan didn't answer. Moments later, a young officer rode up and dismounted. He was handsome with a stylish mustache and dark hair and wore a papal medal around his neck. Mulligan suspected before he spoke that he was Irish.

"Jaysus, what won't you find in an Indian village? And who are you?"

"Michael Mulligan, formerly a major."

"Hello, Major Mulligan, fellow Irishman. Captain Myles Keogh. Were those savages going to kill and cook you for dinner?"

As a soldier cut his bounds, Michael Mulligan told his story.

"I was sick and lost in a storm. They took me in. I did lose my horse...and my Spencer carbine...again."

"We can replace both, or at least the horse. What are you doing out here in this God forsaken frozen hell?"

"I had business in Montana. But now I must see General Terry."

"May I ask why?"

"You may...but I won't tell you."

"Good enough. Private, get this Irishman a horse." Keogh looked at the deserted village. "So they ran away again? General Custer will appreciate that. He's always trying to catch the cowardly buggers."

"I doubt they're afraid, Captain."

Keogh regarded him. "You may be right, Major Mulligan. How many fighting men were in the village?"

"Hundreds, maybe more—from the Sioux *and* Cheyenne tribes."

"They've united? I made arrangements in case I have an untimely demise."

"I think they spared me when they heard me speaking Irish and thought I was some kind of demon."

"Or angel. I never learned Gaelic."

"Thanks to the British," Mulligan said. "It's a great way to destroy a people—take their language and kill it." As they rode toward Fort Abraham Lincoln, Mulligan asked, "So you fought for the Pope, did ya?

"That I did. I fought a few skirmishes in Italy for his Holiness himself. Then Secretary Seward sends over someone to recruit officers for the Union Army. 'Mr. Keogh,' says he. 'You're the caliber of officer we are looking for.' 'Thank you,' says I. And now 11 years after the Civil War ends, here I am at Fort Lincoln in North Dakota."

"I lost my commanding officer at Gettysburg."

"So did I—but later. General Buford of Typhoid. Great cavalry officer."

They did not talk about the Civil War as they rode toward Fort Lincoln. Michael Mulligan saw some resemblance to himself in the garrulous Captain Keogh who did speak of other things, including a recent visit to Ireland.

"It was so nice to see Ireland again…and to return to America. Auburn, New York, is my home, now. Have you been back to the old country, Major Mulligan?"

"Not yet, Captain. Not yet."

Myles Keogh laughed. "I suspect there's a reason for that beyond money, but you can tell me why in your own time. You should appreciate this story. A private named O'Toole was shot with an arrow and they had to amputate below the knee. He asked for a shot of whiskey and while they cut off his leg, O'Toole barely made a sound. As they were taking him to the hospital tent, he said, licking his lips, 'Great whiskey. And how about taking off me other leg?'" Keogh laughed again at his own story. "It is sad that we have to exterminate the Indians."

"As the English once tried to exterminate us."

"Did you fight the English in Ireland, Major Mulligan?"

Mulligan did not answer.

After riding 30 miles through the snowy fields, they arrived at the bleak but functional Fort Lincoln. After a good night's sleep, Michael Mulligan finally sat in General Terry's office. He was a calm man with clean shaven cheeks, a mustache and long goatee. The bags under his eyes suggested he got little sleep, and Mulligan sensed failing health in the man.

"Major Mulligan. You have an impressive record," General Terry said. "I was also at Bull Run. I knew then it would be a long and bitter war. You have traveled a long way at considerable risk. What can I do for you?"

Michael Mulligan told him. "I want my son, John Mulligan, transferred to another command."

"I can't do that," General Terry said. "I could put him with Major Reno or Captain Benteen, but he'd still be under Lieutenant Colonel Custer's command. What is your concern?"

"Custer is a brave man. I saw that at Gettysburg. But he is reckless."

"Impatient to confront the enemy, I'd say."

Mulligan hesitated. "Let's say an Indian mystic told me Custer would die...with all his men."

General Alfred Terry had to smile. "I can't use that as a reason to spare your son his duties."

"Maybe I could do something for you."

"Like what?"

"In the Civil War, opposing cavalries had certain procedures. One man holds the horses while four others shoot. The Indians don't follow that procedure, and you will be missing one rifleman for every four shooting. Your mounts need to be exposed to gunfire. Indian women in battle will scare the horses by waving blankets."

"So they use their women to fight? Disgraceful."

"Why are you attacking the Indians in the first place? We have the Laramie Treaty."

"They found gold in the Black Hills and Custer made it public news. Europe has abandoned the silver standard. We are facing a depression, Major Mulligan. Gold fever has destroyed any treaty. If the Indians stay on the reservation, there will be no war."

"But they will *not* stay on the reservation. The Black Hills are sacred to them."

General Terry held a paper in his hands. "Here is an order from Washington. We are to proceed with military action against any hostile Indians." He met Mulligan's eyes. "Military action includes your son."

Mulligan looked out the window and saw a corral with many horses bunched together or running suddenly.

"Let me at least train your horses. Get them battle ready."

"I could allow that."

In the barracks, Major Reno and Captain Benteen played cards and drank whiskey while Captain Keogh wrote letters. Michael Mulligan visited the corrals and walked among the horses, the animals spreading out in a panic as he approached them. Then he stood in the center of the corral, and an hour later, a horse would break from the herd and nose him. Soon, other horses would approach out of curiosity. On the second day, Mulligan carried carrots and a bucket of oats. When the horses got close, he fired his pistol loaded with blanks and the horses bolted. An hour later, a lead horse approached him and ate oats and carrots out of his hand, and when Mulligan fired the pistol, the horse backed off, but didn't bolt. Mulligan was ready to continue when a stocky Crow Indian came to the rail.

"You see that house?" He pointed.

Mulligan saw the house on a nearby rise. "I do."

"That's General Custer's house. Him and his wife like their mornings. Stop firing off your pistol and disturbing them."

"I am trying to make the horses unafraid of roaring guns."

"Libbie Custer wants you to stop."

"Okay, I will stop. Who are you?"

"Curly," the Indian said.

"Your name is Curly?"

"Yes."

"And you fight for the U.S. army?"

"The Sioux are our enemies," Curly said. "Ask Bloody Knife. We hate them."

Curly left. For the next week, Mulligan walked among the horses, waving a blanket and getting them used to his presence, occasionally staring at the nice house where George Armstrong Custer lived with his wife. Often, Captain Keogh watched from the railing.

"By God, Major, but you got the Irish touch with horses. Maybe we should feed these horses some good Irish dark beer."

"That is a thought," Mulligan said. "We want them calm in battle."

"And you think there will be a battle?"

"I know there will be a battle. I saw warriors in that camp...many warriors."

"We are moving out in June. Perhaps you'd be so kind as to train my horse, Comanche. He's a beautiful animal."

"I would love to train him."

Michael Mulligan spent a week with Comanche, a large buckskin horse with a great heart. He was calm and unafraid of gunfire or other distractions, and seemed to enjoy training as another game. Myles Keogh watched with approval.

"Very good."

When the spring came, Michael Mulligan knew he would leave for Laramie and then a train going east. He did not want his son to see him when he arrived at Fort Lincoln, and discover he was interfering on his behalf. One day as the ground thawed, Mulligan was summoned to General Terry's office. Reno and Benteen were there.

"Let me get to the point, Major Mulligan. We know you seem to have a rapport with the Indian people. I have a plan. Perhaps you could track them and bring along a herd of horses...maybe 40 head or so. When the Indians seek you out, we could have Curly and his Crow scouts following behind. They could relay to us the Indian positions. Perhaps we could flush them out into the open and attack. Of course, there might be a risk to you but—"

"We want this to be a quick end to the war," Major Reno said. Captain Benteen remained silent. He had thick white hair, and Mulligan could smell the whiskey on this breath.

"Where is himself? George Armstrong Custer?"

"He had to testify in the court case against Secretary of War, Belknap."

"President Grant won't like that," Mulligan said.

"He won't. What do you think of our strategy?"

"Those Indians saved my life in a storm and nursed me back to health. I can't betray them."

"What kind of white man are you?" Captain Benteen said.

"An honorable white man."

"I understand your loyalty," said General Terry. "Might they surrender to you?"

"They won't surrender."

"No, they won't," said Major Reno. "They'll be too busy running. Let's go finish that card came."

"Good idea," Captain Benteen said. He looked at Mulligan. "I know you're a brave Irishman, but I think you've gone native, that's what I think. Keogh is a bit soft, also, but I know he'll fight when the time comes."

"As will I," said Mulligan. "As will you when the first volley of arrows decimates your ranks."

"I won't abandon my men which is more than I can say for the great Custer."

"Enjoy your cards. Save some whiskey for me, Captain."

After a hostile pause, the two officers left.

"You have made two enemies," said General Terry, not unkindly.

"What did that Custer remark mean?"

"We lost Major Joel Eliot at Washita. Captain Benteen feels Custer abandoned Major Eliot when he was caught by hostiles and killed, but I believe Custer didn't realize what had happened."

"I see."

"It's caused some morale problems."

Michael Mulligan confronted General Terry. "Regarding your plan, General, surely you don't think the Sioux and Cheyenne would not see the Crow scouts. They would suspect a trap."

"My officers, including Custer, find it hard to imagine the Indians uniting, let alone standing and fighting."

"Then go find them and fight," Mulligan said. "When the weather warms up, I am leaving. I have business back east. I'd appreciate the use of a good horse."

"You will get one. Incidentally, your son won't be here until July. I suspect we'll have this Indian war ended by then."

March was cold but in mid-April, Major Reno went on a scouting mission with Bloody Knife, a Crow Indian scout who kept to himself and refused to talk to anyone except Reno. Keogh went along and Mulligan decided to join them. He wanted to see the open country in clear if cold weather. They rode along Rosebud Creek where General Crook had fought against large Indian forces, and headed toward the Little Bighorn where scouts had reported a possible Indian village. As they rode along a ridge, Captain Keogh stared toward the endless prairie stretching out under an expanse of lowering bright sky. He had been unusually quiet on the ride.

"This is wide open wild country," he said. "We'll see the enemy from a distance."

"And they will see you. They could be on a company quickly," Mulligan said. "There is no secure place to make a skirmish line."

They came to a small knoll rising above the river and some trees, with open flat country spread in all directions.

"Well," said Captain Keogh. "If I die here, bury me in Auburn and erect a monument to my memory."

"I will do that," said Mulligan. "But you won't die."

"Even if they 'decimate our ranks' as you told General Terry and Captain Benteen?"

"Just some Irish blarney," Mulligan said, averting his eyes. He knew Myles Keogh was watching him and even smiling.

"I'm an Irish fatalist myself," Captain Keogh said. "And like all Irishmen, I don't discount predictions by mystics." He suddenly laughed quietly. "I had a dream where you were standing over my grave marker."

Mulligan didn't speak at first.

"Myles? Is there any way you can stay behind when Custer goes out on his next reconnaissance and destroy mission?"

"I have to do my duty as a soldier," Captain Keogh told him.

A cold wind blew over the prairie grass, and Major Reno ordered they camp for the night. As Captain Keogh and Mulligan sat around a fire, they heard two young soldiers splashing each other with water and laughing.

"God, some of these recruits are raw and young," Captain Keogh said. "They need more discipline. I think our Indian scouts are nervous. They believe a major battle is eminent."

"I know what I saw in that village." Mulligan watched Myles Keogh's striking face in the firelight. "Tell me. Is there no Mrs. Keogh?"

"By God, I love women," Captain Keogh said, "but never took a wife. Unfortunately, I got married to the cavalry. Someday, I hope to become a normal civilian and settle down in Auburn. And how about you, Major Mulligan?"

"Married once. I lost her. I also lost the love of my life but that's another story."

"I am sorry to hear that." They heard distant singing from Major Reno's tent. "By God, does he have no awareness of danger?"

"I suspect Major Reno likes his drink."

"As do I," said Captain Keogh. "But not while on duty." The captain fingered his Papal medal. "I've heard Reno was caught peeping in bedroom windows."

Mulligan chose not to reply.

In the morning as Mulligan stared at the river, waiting for the camp to awake, he found an empty quiver floating near the bank. Then he saw a human skull and fished it out of the water. He held it like Hamlet, staring at the empty eye sockets.

"Captain Keogh. Come here."

Myles Keogh examined the polished white skull. They saw a dark burn along the jaw, and a gold tooth gleamed among the others.

"Well, he was a white man. They burned his body and cut off his head. I suspect he was a prospector."

"How do you know he was white? The gold tooth?"

"Yes—which the Indians didn't pry out as a white man would."

When Major Reno saw the skull, he held it up and addressed his men. "These savages will pay for this. They will *all* pay."

They rode on and passed an Indian burial ground with many bodies wrapped and placed on elevated platforms.

"If Custer sees those, he'll knock them down," Captain Keogh said.

At another abandoned Indian campsite, Bloody Knife found hoof prints and stopped. "Plenty warriors have been here," he said.

"And now they're gone," said Major Reno. He took a swig from a flask.

Michael Mulligan dismounted. "But they *have* been here," he said, "and they will return."

Bloody Knife scowled. "I am scout and I will talk." He read the tracks on the ground. "I see many. The Sioux are a tribe of dogs and so they get the Cheyenne to help them. Even the Arapahoe who eat dog. Together—plenty warriors."

Major Reno looked across what the Indians called the "greasy grass. "And we are plenty," he said. "Let's go back."

Captain Keogh sat on Comanche, his expression grave. Michael Mulligan imagined the soldiers blinded by clouds of dust and gun smoke, arrows rattling through them, men and horses panicking, warriors with knives and clubs suddenly appearing out of the smoke. The company started toward Fort Lincoln, avoiding pools of quicksand along the river banks.

When Lieutenant Colonel Custer returned to Fort Lincoln, the day of departure came, and wearing his hat, white buckskin and shiny boots, he sat his sorrel horse at the head of the troops. A mustache and small beard disguised a weak chin. He did not sport the long curled yellow hair that others had described. Sitting his horse next to Libbie Custer, General Terry watched the proceedings.

"Your husband is not taking the Gatling gun," General Terry said.

Libbie Custer turned to him, dark hair parted in the middle, her eyes moist with tears. "General Custer does not need a Gatling gun. Not my Autie."

"I admire your confidence," General Terry said.

"I will defend my husband until the day I die, General Terry. And I hope to live a long time."

They left the fort and at one point, Libbie Custer had to stop. George Armstrong Custer stood in the stirrups and waved good bye to his devoted wife. Then the brigade continued, Major Reno and Captain Benteen guarding the rear. The band played "Garryowen." Michael Mulligan rode with Captain Myles Keogh and they spoke little for the first 25 miles. On the morning of the next day, Mulligan said good bye to Captain Keogh before riding toward Wyoming and Laramie. They saluted each other, and then shook hands.

"You come see me in New York," Mulligan said. "We'll have an exciting fall theatre season."

"Be careful of hostiles along the way, Major Mulligan."

"I'll speak to them in Irish," Mulligan said. "And Myles—you show them your Agnus Dei medal. It might be good medicine."

"Michael, my friend, I'll die if they get that close." Captain Myles had an expression in his face that Mulligan found unsettling. There was a different tone to his usually cheerful voice. "Bad things always happen to me in June."

"Not this June, Myles." Mulligan leaned over and stroked Comanche. "Take care of your master, my fine horse." Mulligan saluted Captain Keogh again and rode away as Custer's brigade advanced toward the Little Bighorn. Mulligan reined in his horse and watched the double column of mounted soldiers passing over a distant hill covered with brilliant wild flowers. Slowly, they vanished from sight. Captain Myles Keogh didn't look back.

Shortly after a patriotic July 4th celebration in New York, Michael Mulligan sat on a veranda. People were drinking and laughing. Mulligan glanced at a newspaper on the table and felt something turn inside. A producer in a white suit and fashionable Borsalino felt hat was complaining about the depression. "We need shows that entertain," he said. "Dancing girls. Spectacles. Maybe a minstrel show in blackface." Then he saw Mulligan's face. "What's wrong?"

Mulligan showed him the paper. United Sioux and Cheyenne tribes under Crazy Horse had annihilated Custer and his reduced company at the Little Bighorn. The following day, General Terry found the bloated bodies of Custer and his soldiers, all stripped and mutilated except for Custer—shot in the left chest and temple—and Captain Myles Keogh. In another part of the field, Reno and Benteen had survived a siege.

"I guess Custer didn't realize how many savages were waiting for him. Bad move," the producer said.

"Custer made decisions based on his own invincibility."

Mulligan took back the paper and read General Terry's tribute to the fallen soldiers: "Captain Myles Keogh was our wonderful Irish dragoon...he died within a circle of his men, fighting to the last...a charming fellow, so witty...he will be missed...."

Mulligan envisions the battle: warriors with bows and arrows, guns, spears and clubs, closing in on Custer's exposed desperate troops, some killing themselves. Major Reno, possibly drunk, sprayed with Bloody Knife's brains, retreating through dense woods to a hilltop, waiting for reinforcements from Captain Benteen. They meet and hear distant gunfire but light cigars and don't move.

God damn, Mulligan thought. He crumpled the paper in his hand, remembering Myles Keogh's smiling face and rich Irish lilt telling one of his many stories. Why had the Indians not scalped him or mutilated his body? Was it the Lamb of God medal?

"Farewell, my old friend," Mulligan said softly to himself. *To this favor we must come.*

Fireworks had melted from the sky. The producer was talking again. "We need to get rear ends in the seats, Mr. Mulligan, or we will lose money next season."

The band began playing "Garryowen." Mulligan thought he saw a band musician resembling Myles Keogh playing the penny whistle. Was Myles communicating to him from the other side?

A passing drunk saw the headline. He held a drink in one hand and single cherry by a stem in the other. "America has been here for 100 years. We'll kill all those heathen savages," he said. "You just wait. The U.S. Army will avenge General George Armstrong Custer. Those red devils will be hunted down and slain." He placed the cherry in his drink and bolted it down. "To Custer's last stand!"

"I believe the Little Bighorn will be the last stand for Custer *and* the Indians," Mulligan said.

"Maybe we could work it into a show," the producer told him.

"Buffalo Bill will beat you to it."

Michael Mulligan knew he would return to the battlefield, especially when he saw a photo of the one lone survivor from Custer's final battle: Captain Myles Keogh's horse, Comanche, shot many times but alive. Stuffed and mounted, Comanche would be displayed at the 1893 Chicago World's Fair; in future centuries, museum visitors in Kansas would see Captain Keogh's horse, Comanche, staring at them with glassy eyes long after the Little Bighorn battle of George Armstrong Custer and Chief Crazy Horse had passed into myth.

THE BOOK LAUNCH

THE AD IN THE paper stated: "Michael Mulligan, Irish American and Civil War veteran, will appear with Julia Taylor Braddock to launch *An American Civil War Journal* by Reginald Taylor. There will be a reading and refreshments."

Though it had been years, Julia Taylor still had a striking beauty, the silver in her hair adding a distinctive touch, the eyes a cobalt blue romantic writers loved to describe, the smile still sly and mischievous. A crowd was getting seated in the bookstore where they stood. She took Michael Mulligan's hand.

"Still as handsome as ever, Mr. Mulligan."

"But so much older, Julia, so much older. We've seen a few days since Richmond."

"We have indeed."

"My eyes aren't what they used to be, but I can still see your radiant face."

"Why thank you, Mr. Mulligan. You are kind. Welcome to London."

"My pleasure."

Julia glanced at the waiting audience.

"I'm so glad to finally launch Reggie's book." She leaned forward and dropped her voice. "Lionel, my husband, feels a bit awkward about it all. He's a police detective, not a literary person."

"I understand."

The audience at the bookstore was elegantly dressed, and horse-drawn carriages passed in the wide street. Copies of Reginald Taylor's book lined the shelves and lay spread on a desk. The cover was a photograph of war dead by Mathew Brady. Julia Taylor, slender, wearing a neck-high flowing dress, welcomed the crowd.

"It took some time for my late first husband's journal to finally see print, and I owe a debt to Walt Whitman's recent lecture on the death of Abraham Lincoln that brought back interest in those terrible years. I also owe a debt to Michael Mulligan who knew Reginald Taylor and was with him when he died. His introduction and my afterword complete a book which should have been longer. And now, Mr. Michael Mulligan, a major during the American Civil War, will address you."

Julia Taylor sat down. Michael Mulligan, wearing a wide crown hat and buckskin jacket and pants with scuffed boots stood at the lectern. He knew he created a dramatic "western" effect. At times, he felt his vision growing narrower, but he could still see rows of English faces, ladies and gentlemen in formal attire attending the late Reginald Taylor's book launch. He knew Julia was smiling, sitting next to her husband, a straight-backed stocky man with a mustache and short hair who seemed remarkably quiet for the expressive Julia Taylor. Mulligan wondered for a moment if any of his old Irish brethren with scores to settle lurked in the audience.

"Thanks for inviting me," he said. "Thanks for not joining the Confederacy during our Civil War." The audience of book lovers laughed. "I have a few former Irish cronies who may want to shoot me for leaving their cause against the English—no offense intended— so if shots ring out, don't be alarmed, they're after me, not you."

A nervous laughter followed. He could hear Julia chuckling while Lionel stared ahead, stoic and not smiling. Mulligan put on thick reading glasses.

"And now to our reason for being here, a manuscript by Reginald Taylor that I managed to rescue shortly after Reggie— Reginald— shot and was shot by a highwayman trying to kill me. Reginald did not survive. He was a brave man, and a good friend and a wonderful writer. He should have been my enemy, but it was my honor to know him. I will try to read some of his passages with Reggie's English voice, and then Julia will read a few passages. When we conclude, this remarkable book will go on sale."

After Michael Mulligan finished reading, a young Englishman raised his hand.

"This is most delightful and moving, Mr. Mulligan. Could you describe in your own words what happened that day you lost Reginald?"

"I certainly can. And I can describe in detail the odyssey Julia and I went through to get his body home. Reginald never made it back to England. He is resting on the bottom of the James River, so America will always have a part of England, if you will."

He could hear a murmur of approval from the audience. Mulligan told the story of that tragic conflict with armed robbers, from the first shot to Mulligan's horse breaking a leg to Mulligan suddenly on the ground—Reginald Taylor firing point blank with a derringer at the remaining thief who then shot him. He described Reginald Taylor's death and his final words. The audience listened in a profound silence.

"I guess Reggie will never get that knighthood he wanted. Is the queen here?"

There was more laughter. Another young man raised his hand. He had a green shamrock tattoo on his neck.

"Mr. Mulligan," he said, speaking with an Irish accent. "You joked about Irish cronies coming after you but I *am* curious. You've been away from Ireland for some time?"

"I have."

"How do you feel about the recent murders in Phoenix Park, Dublin? Officials Thomas Burke and Lord Cavendish were stabbed to death by the so called Irish Invincibles fighting for Irish Home Rule."

Michael Mulligan looked at the young man's clean shaven face, seeing an image from his past.

"I don't know much about that tragic incident," he said. "So I can't answer your question."

"Will Home Rule come to Ireland?"

"I hope so," Mulligan said. "We should rule our own country."

"Would you take up arms for the cause?"

A few people began to heckle the young Irishman.

"This is a book launch, not a political meeting," an older man shouted.

Lionel Braddock glared at the young Irishman.

"I'm a bit old to fight a revolution," Mulligan said. He sat down.

Then Julia Taylor spoke, telling of their journey toward Richmond with a diverse crew: Michael Mulligan, the widow herself, a young Irish boy named Seamus who couldn't shoot, a female violinist, and a former Confederate soldier and Cherokee Indian named Irving Watie.

"Seamus did not survive, I'm sad to say. But when I lost my memory after a mine hit our steamship and I plunged into the river, it was Irving Watie who found me, and subsequently, Irving and Mr. Mulligan who rescued me. Otherwise, I'd still be in America on the John Tyler plantation." After a pause, Julia said, "Any questions?"

Some patrons raised their hands.

"Mr. Mulligan, did you know Custer?"

"Not well. He was brave, perhaps too brave. I lost a friend at the Little Bighorn, Captain Myles Keogh. Custer made some big mistakes."

"Libbie, his widow, calls him a hero."

"General Custer certainly dressed the part. I agree that Custer distinguished himself during the Civil War, but Sitting Bull and Crazy Horse had another viewpoint."

"Surely you don't justify the Indian massacre at the Little Bighorn."

"I think I understand it."

The Irishman stood up and spoke in a loud voice.

"Five men were hanged for the double murders of Burke and Cavendish. An informer gave them away. How would *you* deal with informers, Mr. Mulligan?"

Michael Mulligan faced his inquisitive countryman.

"I think we all know how Irish secret societies deal with informers."

"Have you ever been a member of an Irish secret society?"

"I heard they don't exist."

Lionel approached the smiling young man. "That's enough," he said. "Move along or you'll be arrested."

The young Irishman tipped his cap and walked outside. By day's end, all the books were sold. Lionel sat in a corner, quiet but vigilant.

"We must talk before you leave England," Julia whispered.

"We will," said Mulligan.

"Alone. I think my husband is frightfully jealous…of you and even Reginald."

"Really? Why not just do some sightseeing tomorrow?"

"Superb suggestion," Julia said, taking his arm.

Lionel approached them. He was smiling, and relieved the book launch was over. "Very nice," he said. "Superb presentation. Wild story. Solid book."

"Let's hope an American publisher agrees."

Lionel faced his wife. "Shall we, dear?"

Lionel took his wife's arm and they walked toward the crowded street. Michael Mulligan lingered behind with many of the guests asking questions. The outspoken Irishman entered the store and cornered him.

"Mr. Mulligan, you should know that Irish revolutionaries like the Fenians are still fighting against the British oppressors in your former country. You might consider returning to your homeland and using your soldier's skills to help the Irish Brotherhood."

"At 62?"

"We could still use you. You're famous as a great fighter. You fought in the American Civil War. How about fighting in ours?" The young man smiled. "Have a pleasant day, Mr. Mulligan. I'll be in touch."

"Wait. Who sent you, and do you have a name?"

"No one sent me. We are fighting against England's unfair laws…and my name is Patrick."

"Patrick. Of course. Good day, Patrick."

"Good day, Mr. Mulligan. You know, as an American citizen, you could help us. Possibly we could help you in the future. Your enemies would become our enemies."

"I didn't know I had enemies."

Patrick smiled. "Maybe not in England. Listen, a few Irishmen in the movement may be traveling to America, soon."

"To work? To hide?"

"Among other things. Here is my card if you need to contact me."

Patrick left the bookstore. Mulligan followed him and saw Julia waiting.

"To be Irish is my fate," he said, watching the River Thames flow. A sudden shift in the wind brought a sewer smell. A lone folksinger sang "Barbara Allen" accompanied by a mandolin.

"Our phaeton awaits," Julia told him. Moments later, they rode in a coach toward Chichester where Julia and Lionel lived.

"We have a lovely basement room for you, Michael," Julia said. "And we can take you to Liverpool for the return voyage."

Mulligan listened to the rhythm of the horse's hooves. It would be a long ride.

"And someday, you and your husband can visit me in New York. We have electric light along the Great White Way."

"Sounds delightful."

She smiled at him. Mulligan was aware of Lionel occasionally glancing at him with cold impassive eyes, but suddenly, he spoke.

"Mr. Mulligan, I must apologize for that Mick ruffian who was so rude. We have our police for those people, I assure you."

"No problem, sir," Mulligan said. "I did hear of the Phoenix Park incident."

"Two Irish thugs stabbed one of their own, Thomas Burke, and Lord Cavendish who happened to be walking with him. Two men murdered in broad daylight."

"Can we change the subject?" Julia asked.

"Our guest was insulted, dear. Besides, Mr. Mulligan, you're an American now, not an Irishman. Why would you want the Irish to have Home Rule?"

"As they say, '*Sein Fein*,' or 'for ourselves.'"

"England is doing just fine with Irish affairs, thank you. Besides, Home Rule could be Rome Rule with the Pope taking over."

"That is frightening, Mr. Braddock."

"We English believe in order. That Irishman was taking a bloody liberty."

"We live in strange times," Julia said. "Darwin says we descended from apes. Marx tells us making money is bad."

"Both bloody fools," Lionel said.

They stopped once to change horses.

After a late dinner, Michael Mulligan paced the basement room that had been hastily converted to a bedroom. There were discarded chairs and lamps in the cluttered room, but a street level window faced a garden. A hunting rifle was placed in a rack on the wall. He could hear the cook and her assistant working in the kitchen next door. Michael Mulligan wondered if Patrick was right, that perhaps he should return to Ireland and join the Irish Brotherhood. Then all might be forgiven.

But I could not kill anyone, he thought.

He heard light footsteps on the basement stairs and Julia entered the room.

"I hope that Irishman isn't some advance guard out to attack you."

"No. But he had a point."

She sat on the bed. "Tell me what's happening with the others."

"There's little to report. Irving retired from the army and lives on a reservation in Oklahoma. He never writes. I hope he's not drinking. I assume Tyrone works at the mortuary. Shelby is playing second violin with the Richmond Symphony Orchestra."

"And you?"

"I live my quiet life. Keep a journal. Produce shows now and then. Work with horses."

"And see your son?"

"Not as often as I should. Where are your boys?"

"Ben is in the army and Max is training to be a horse doctor like you. They are 25, now."

"My God, how time has passed."

"We have grown old and boring," Julia said. Twilight filled the basement window. "Lionel is a good man, but not as exciting as you. And I must confess, I never felt so alive as when we were in constant danger, bringing Reggie home. Of course, we lost his body."

"But his work lives on," Michael Mulligan said.

"Thanks to you."

"And thanks to you."

Julia met his eyes and suddenly kissed him. "What would have happened if Shelby hadn't interrupted our nude bathing in the river that long ago night?"

"The possibilities are endless."

Julia laughed. She lightly tapped his forehead and Mulligan gently pressed his hand just below her throat.

"Oh dear," she said. She put her hands over his. "I still remember what you said to me when we surfaced after the steamboat blew up."

"So do I."

She kissed his fingers. "I better go."

Julia turned and walked back up the stairs. He called to her. She stopped and turned. "Yes?"

"When you came to retrieve Reginald's body, you said you had fallen in love with someone else and you were going to tell Reggie if you found him alive."

"Yes."

"What ever happened to that English lover?"

"I don't remember," Julia said.

She left the basement room.

For a week, Julia and Lionel took Michael Mulligan sightseeing in London and paid a visit to Oxford. Mulligan saw the university buildings, again, and the Bodleian Library, ancient coats of arms on the ceiling. He stood in the Divinity School and stared up at the vaulted ceiling, remembering old classes in theology which meant nothing to him, sitting among young wealthy English boys who always saw him as an outsider despite his connection to a former professor and his attempt at mimicking their affected accents. He remembered their voices:

"I say Jeremy, that Mulligan fellow seems a bit crude. I believe his father sold a farm to send him here."

The other boys laughed and Mulligan stared at them, smiling cheerfully. They knew enough not to confront him. He often left his dormitory room at night to visit the horses in a nearby stable.

While Julia waited, Michael Mulligan made an inquiry at the desk, addressing a well-dressed, middle-aged librarian, his thin hair parted in the middle.

"You once had a professor, here, one Tyrone Mulligan. I suspect he's gone by now. Do you have any information on him?"

"And you are?"

"Michael Mulligan. He was a mentor and father figure."

"Same last name? I guess he was. I can tell you he retired in Oxford and, sorry to say, he passed on 15 years ago. He was giving a public reading, in fact, and collapsed. Professor Mulligan is buried just outside of town. I can give you the address of the church cemetery, Mr. Mulligan."

"That would be very kind. What about his daughter— Maggie?"

The librarian checked the records.

"We have a listing for a Margaret Mulligan. She traveled with his acting troupe."

"That would be her."

"I assume this was not professional but illegitimate theatre." The librarian read the record and finally looked up. "Deceased," he said. "Evidently of smallpox in 1850, the year the famine ended. One child, a female, born in 1837, whereabouts unknown." When Mulligan remained silent, the librarian said, "Margaret would be a kind of sister to you?"

"That would be correct."

"So sorry," he said. "My condolences."

"Thanks."

Mulligan left the library and rode to the churchyard. Julia waited in the horse-drawn carriage as Michael Mulligan found the dirt-covered, leaf-strewn grave. An older woman wearing a cloak and hood watched him, and then hurried off. Mulligan caught his breath. Then he knelt and wiped away the dirt and leaves until he saw the name of the man who had given him a new life, free from the road and part of the road. He remembered their farewell in Dublin. Faces appeared in his memory and he was moved. Why had he never searched for Maggie? Where were Connor and the child? Under Tyrone Mulligan's name was a quote from Shakespeare: "This above all: to thine own self be true."

"So Tyrone Mulligan—you died performing to the last."

He touched the name, following the letters with his fingers. When he returned to the carriage, the coachman sat stoically, and Mulligan stroked the two bay horses. He looked at Julia who read his expression. "Are you all right?"

"Yes. I just wish we had met one more time. He was kind to me."

Mulligan got into the coach. Julia directed the driver to the train station for the ride back to Chichester. Mulligan could feel Julia studying him.

"You seem a bit pale."

"I saw a woman wearing a cloak and a hood that hid her face."

"And that's unusual?"

"Every culture has an angel of death," Mulligan said. "Maybe it's a dark angel of revenge, and maybe it's a bright angel bringing peaceful release. I think for me, the angel— always a woman wearing a cloak and a hood— is a dark angel bringing punishment for all the lives I have taken."

"Some you killed in self-defense."

"And some—evil though they were—as an assassin. One day, that angel will be coming for me. I have a lot of bad things to account for."

"You don't think you've done any good in the world?"

"Not enough good. Maybe it's because I learned too early how to kill so well."

"You were born into a hostile world," Julia said. "And maybe that woman knew Tyrone Mulligan."

"That's a possibility."

Julia began laughing. "I hope my angel of death is a handsome young man with a hard body willing to give me one last fling before oblivion."

Mulligan glanced at her profile. "Julia, sometimes you shock me."

"Good."

They passed a slaughterhouse on the way to the station and Julia covered her nose. That evening after dinner, Lionel took Michael Mulligan to target practice at a police range.

"This is a fine Swiss revolver," he said. "Citizens can't own them but criminals do."

They fired at paper targets. Lionel was a good shot, and he examined the pattern of Mulligan's bullets around the bull's eye.

"Not bad, I'd say. Not as good as my pattern, but not bad. Guess you never took lessons from Wild Bill Hickok?"

"Never did," Mulligan said. "My choice of weapon is the Spencer carbine."

"I imagine you were a fine soldier," Lionel said. "Techniques and equipment have improved since those days."

With the passing week, Mulligan began to feel restless, and knew Lionel was anxious for him to leave. Julia often sat with him in their quiet garden.

"We can take you to Liverpool," Julia said.

"That would be fine, but not necessary."

"I insist."

One night, Lionel looked at him over dinner and chuckled.

"Those Irish. One intrigue after another."

"How so?"

"James Carey will be leaving soon under another name. I think he's bound for Cape Town."

"Who is James Carey?"

Lionel smiled and winked at Julia.

"Well, I'm not supposed to discuss police business, but he informed on the men who killed Thomas Burke and Lord Cavendish."

"Cavendish's murder will push back Irish Home Rule for another ten years."

"Good. We believe Lord Cavendish was in the park by chance. Thomas Burke, whom the Irish considered a traitor, was their target."

"So Mr. Carey is making his escape?"

"Yes. Frankly, I despise the man, since he gave the order to kill Burke, and then turned in his own gang. I do hope Carey posing as Mr. Power makes his escape. Good riddance."

They finished the meal. Mulligan drank his wine and caught Julia staring at him, her eyes boring into his.

"You have something to say, Julia?"

"Not at all," she said. "Here's to Mr. Carey's safety."

"Yes indeed. Cheers," Mulligan said.

Lionel wiped his lips with a napkin. "Mulligan? This information about Carey is confidential," he said. "Don't share it with anyone."

"Lionel, your secret is safe with me."

Mulligan could feel Julia watching him, even when he looked down and reached for another piece of bread.

"What happened to your girlfriend who became a nun?"

"Well, Julia, I knocked on her convent door and was told Sister Mary Ellen had left the order to join a radical group of artists."

"What's this, Mulligan?"

Michael Mulligan told Lionel about Abigail Donahue who nursed him after Gettysburg, became his female companion, and then spied for the Union.

"Though a free spirit and thinker, she eventually converted to Catholicism and joined a convent."

"Bad luck for you, Mulligan."

"There's more. Her current lover is a Marxist Jewish woman."

Lionel gagged and dropped his spoon. He began laughing. Julia watched her husband's shaking upper body. "It isn't *that* funny, Lionel."

"I'm sorry," he said, dabbing his eyes. "You lost your girl to a Jewess, eh?"

"A Marxist follower of Sappho," Mulligan said. "I'd say it's the bad luck of the Irish."

Lionel snorted once. Then he took a deep breath. "Sorry for laughing, Mulligan."

"It's all right. I heard she became a morphine addict, but I have no proof."

Mulligan took another bite, and then realized Lionel was staring at him.

"Opium is the worst," he said. "It will destroy us. You ever take it, Mulligan?"

"I was a soldier," Mulligan told him.

A week later, Julia and Michael Mulligan took a train to Liverpool, Lionel staying behind to follow an important investigation. Like teenaged lovers, Mulligan and Julia held hands in the rocking train car.

"God, it has been a while, hasn't it? Seventeen years. Seeing you again makes me wish I could take something from you and preserve it. I guess memories will have to do. We went through a lot—and I suspect we'll never meet again."

"I hope we do meet. Come to New York. Bring Lionel."

"I will. And I will keep you up to date about Reggie's book. You will get some money for the introduction."

They arrived at Liverpool, the weather wet and driving overhead. Mulligan found a tavern in a waterfront hotel and they had a quiet meal of beef stew called Souse, and talked about their adventures in America. Julia ordered a second glass of wine.

"Are you happy, Julia?"

"Yes. Or at least I'm content."

"And you are content being Mrs. Braddock?"

She stared at him. "Yes. Why?"

"Just asking."

She smiled and brushed back a lock of her hair from the face that was aging but still handsome. "I am not immune to the masculine charms of others...but my husband is a police detective, you know, an officer trained to discover other people's secrets." She took Mulligan's hands, meeting his eyes with a direct focus. "I don't need another man, and Lionel's not a bad lover. I've trained him well, though he's squeamish about some things. I think he now finds you an amusing old adventurer."

"Old? How unkind."

"In other words, you are a friend and not a threat."

"I *am* a friend." Rain beat against the window. Mulligan took a drink of his beer and returned Julia Taylor's direct stare. "And I would never threaten you."

"I know. But I was talking about a threat to Lionel's male ownership of his pretty but independent wife." Julia caught herself. "God, what am I saying?"

"I don't know. What *are* you saying?"

"I am not a loose woman."

"No one said you were. You know, marriage is a kind of servitude. You give the man sex and maybe children for his protection, name and a ring."

"Listen to you," Julia said. "Women have little say in the matter, though Lionel doesn't consider you a romantic threat."

"Not a romantic threat, eh? He won't say that if I rent the room upstairs for an afternoon and hotel workers describe your cries of love as you came for the second and third time."

Julia watched his face. She didn't blush or smile. Then she gripped his hands. "Only three times?"

They didn't speak in the small furnished room facing the harbor. It had a low ceiling and a single crossbeam above their heads. Silently, Julia undressed and lay face down on the bed, Mulligan stripped and slowly moving over her body. He kissed her back and then gently turned her over, kissing between her thighs, searching with his lambent tongue. They heard sea gulls calling outside as they moved together, Julia's cries muffled as Mulligan kissed her, feeling cool air on his naked back and legs, staring into her face, then kissing her mouth and throat, thrusting just before her final moment. Then they lay still. Suddenly, she pushed him on his back, kissing his chest and stomach. She stopped and raised her head. Her eyes seemed to engulf him and her voice was low: "I want a taste."

They finished and briefly napped in each other's arms; then Julia got up and observed her body in the mirror. She pursed her lips. Mulligan appeared behind her.

"That was lovely," he said.

"But my breasts do sag, a bit."

He ran his hands up her belly and cupped them, gently touching her nipples.

"They are still lovely."

"And I have extra fat around my once narrow waist."

He ran his hands down her sides and over her hips. "The more to grab," he said.

"You have a paunch, yourself." She leaned back against him. "Too bad Dante Gabriel Rossetti just died. Maybe he'd paint me."

"I bet he would."

He kissed her neck and Julia closed her eyes. She turned to face him. Then she reached between his legs and drew in her breath.

"Oh dear," she said. "I better give Lionel more training."

They kissed again. Red light from the late afternoon sun filled the room.

When they finally left the seaside hotel and walked to the ship leaving for America, Julia was smiling, holding his hand and arm. Mulligan would carry the memory of their lovemaking, the taste of her body and the touch of her lips staying with him.

They walked through the massive harbor, passing the iron Albert Dock, searching for the wharf that led to Mulligan's ship. A group of men, women and children walked before them speaking in Russian. The women wore long dresses and head scarves, and the men wore heavy coats. Many of the men had thick beards, and Mulligan saw a yarmulke under one man's lifted hat.

"A lot of your people came here during the famine," Julia said.

"True."

They found the four-masted ship; when he kissed her on the misty dock, Julia felt like crying but remained calm.

"My God," she said. "I'm an adulteress. I should feel guilty. Why do I feel so happy?"

"Because you make me happy. Because I make you happy. Write to me," he said.

"I will."

"We must meet again."

"If Lionel dies before me, maybe I'll hunt you down, Mulligan. We'll grow old together."

They embraced, both knowing it was probably for the last time. They didn't speak again.

As Michael Mulligan walked up the plank carrying his bag, another man passed him leaving the ship, and for a moment, Julia thought she saw Mulligan pass an envelope to the young stranger who wore a cap low over his eyes. As the ship was pulling away, Mulligan stood at the railing in the twilight, waving good bye. Julia felt a glowing love for this aging Irish adventurer; she would cherish their brief final moments together. When she turned, Julia thought the passenger leaving the ship seemed familiar. Had she seen a tattoo of a green shamrock on his neck?

"You Irish son of a bitch," Julia said, but she couldn't contain her laughter.

She walked toward the train.

On the ship, Mulligan went for a walk on the deck as they left the harbor. He saw four men standing at the railing and caught the lilt of Irish accents. They glanced at him.

"Good day, gentlemen," he said.

"Good day to you, sir," one of the men said. "Me name's John Walsh." Then the man called Walsh introduced the others.

"Let's hope we all have a safe journey," Mulligan told them.

"Across the Irish Sea," one of the men said.

THE CELTIC CROSS

IT WAS JUST AFTER two O' clock in July of 1888 when Gettysburg officials unveiled the Irish monument. It was a Celtic cross listing three circled companies of Patrick Kelly's Irish brigade. A beautiful sun blazed above an Irish harp. An Irish wolfhound lay beneath the cross, mourning his dead master.

John Mulligan had left his two children back in San Francisco, and searched the field for his father, Michael Mulligan. He could have been waiting for a stranger. As officials described the terrible three day battle of 1863, noting it was a Confederate Irish soldier who had designed the Irish monument, John Mulligan felt no sense of reconciliation with the man who had fathered him. It was awkward to feel betrayal, still, at the age of 33.

But he did fight on this field that day, John thought. *What a slaughter it must've been.*

If the crowd expected the ghosts of Union and Confederate dead to rise on the Gettysburg field and demand recognition, it didn't occur. It was a pleasant warm day. The reddish cross in a small grove of trees faced quiet woods. As two veterans from each side joined the mayor on the platform and the band played

"The Battle Hymn of the Republic," John Mulligan wondered if he would even recognize his father. How much had age changed him? Then he saw a gentleman emerge from the crowd and walk toward him. He was tall and straight with thick white hair, his weathered face lined; a darkness gleamed in the eyes that made John Mulligan think of a character out of literature: the vengeful Heathcliff. Though now 68, Michael Mulligan possessed a striking handsomeness; he was dressed in the current New York fashion: dark pants, Norfolk jacket, Derby hat. John Mulligan tried to remember that awkward first meeting as adults when he was 20 years old, or the sad farewell at the Civil War's beginning when he was a child. Perhaps the conflict between the states had become a marker for them both.

The two men shook hands.

"So nice to see you, Son."

"So nice to see you."

With eyes averted, Michael Mulligan tipped his hat to some passing ladies, elegantly dressed. John decided to remain silent.

"I trust the twins are fine?"

"John Jr. and Kate are doing well, Father."

"Good."

"Thanks for asking."

"I enjoy your letters."

"You could write more."

"I could." Michael Mulligan examined the monument. "Nice job, it is. Then again, war is an obscenity. Why celebrate it?"

The two men found a bench and sat down. John Mulligan glanced at his father, searching for words. The latter had removed his hat.

"I assume this is sacred ground?"

"Sacred? *Cursed* is more like it. As for the Irish Brigade?" He didn't finish the sentence.

"Are you ever coming to San Francisco?"

"I could bring a show there."

"A show? The twins would like to meet their grandfather."

John saw a brief moment of pain in his father's eyes.

"Of course," he said. "How's the wife?"

"Making clothes. Watching the children."

Another speaker was holding forth in an oratorical style that seemed dated after Lincoln's eloquent sparseness. For some reason, John remembered a day at the beach. He was a boy chasing his father with a piece of seaweed when the man turned sharply and John ran into the surf. The tide caught him. Strong hands seized his ankles as the tide retreated. John was still spitting sea water when he caught his father observing him.

"You look good, John. Handsome as ever."

"You don't look so bad yourself."

"I feel ancient." He gazed across the peaceful battlefield. "I often wonder why some people survive and others don't."

"I guess you knew a few who died?"

Michael Mulligan nodded. "A few. I uncovered and collected many bodies."

"For the National Cemetery?"

"Yes. Some I couldn't identify." They watched the milling crowd as the speaker described the glories of war.

"War does make for nice speeches," Michael Mulligan said. "And empty words."

John noticed a scar along his father's temple. When he spoke, it was a man choosing his words carefully.

"In 1852, I met Thomas Meagher in San Francisco. He had escaped exile to Tasmania. I was an exile myself."

"That I don't doubt. Why?"

"I'll get to that." John waited patiently for his father to speak. "Meagher, now. Silver tongue he had. He liked to talk, ride horses and drink. I had rebuilt the Jenny Lind Theatre after an earthquake, and started producing shows. When the war broke out, he let me know the Union Army needed someone good with horses. I guess it's better I didn't join Meagher's Irish Brigade. They were slaughtered at Antietam and Fredericksburg. Meagher, sword in hand, had his horse shot out from under him. From behind a stone wall, Irish Rebels shot down their Union Irish brothers."

Michael Mulligan stopped and stared at the grass. Then Michael Mulligan met his son's eyes. "I could've died *there*."

"But you fought *here*—at Gettysburg?"

After a pause, Michael Mulligan said, "Yes—with a unit that's forgotten."

"Tell me about it."

"Not now."

"Why not? You have a silver tongue, yourself. You left a five-year-old child with friends and ran off to fight, so why *can't* we sit and tell stories of glorious charges uphill into Rebel guns?"

Michael Mulligan didn't answer. A wind blew through the trees. The speaker had concluded his speech, and John felt himself growing hot and edgy.

"Sorry," John said. "I shouldn't be talking about all this after so long."

"You have a right. I asked you here."

"I was surprised you did."

"Did the Maguire family care for you well?"

"Very well. But I often wondered what had happened to you. Now and then we got a bulletin from the front or a portrait. Then when Lee surrendered, I thought—"

"Thought what? That I was rushing home? Can you imagine what those three days were like at Gettysburg?"

"I've read the history books, Father. I can!"

"Ah yes, the history books. A man with a broken leg watches a grass fire started by hot guns burning toward him, and when he dies screaming, the historians capture his pain so well."

John Mulligan closed his eyes, knowing he had to let the drama of this meeting play out. The band began to play as the crowd dispersed. Michael Mulligan stood up and motioned to his son to follow. As the two men walked, John asked a question: "What happened to General Meagher?"

"They wouldn't let him recruit for a new Irish Brigade. Then he became governor of Montana, got drunk one day and fell off a boat into the Missouri River. He drowned," Mulligan said, with finality. He stopped and listened to the small band.

"Play 'Dixie'," he shouted. The band members finished and Michael Mulligan shouted again. "Play 'Dixie'. Even Lincoln requested it. Let's not forget, men from *both* sides died here!"

The piano player glared at Mulligan. "I don't play that Reb music."

Michael Mulligan got up on the stage. "Then play 'The Irish Washer Woman'. You may know it as 'Garryowen'. Custer loved it."

Following the piano's lead, they broke into the familiar Irish tune. Michael Mulligan threw off his Derby and began dancing, his arms straight down at his sides, his legs moving and kicking like a younger man's. Piano, horns and fiddle carried the lively melody. A few in the crowd gathered and smiled at the amusing spectacle. Some boys clapped. John Mulligan watched his father dancing an Irish jig with a rising maniacal fury and then looked away. Color touched his cheeks. Once again, he had lost his father to a distraction. He heard a man's slurred English voice.

"Is that respectful? We're here to honor the dead."

"And you're dead drunk," a fat man said.

"So are you."

Michael Mulligan's boots rang on the wooden platform

"The old bugger can dance, though," the fat man continued. "The bloody Irish are good at two things: drinking and dancing. Can't fight worth a damn."

John Mulligan confronted the two men. "That's my father," he said.

"Is that right? Well, your old man's better than any dancing nigger I ever seen in a minstrel show."

The two men laughed. John Mulligan watched the fat drunk and before he lifted the flask to his lips, struck out at the florid face. Blood spurted and he felt the second man hitting him in the back. Michael Mulligan jumped down from the stage and separated them; with a backhand blow, he struck the second man to the ground. The fat drunk knelt, a handkerchief to his bleeding nose. "He hit me," he screamed. "I'm bleeding!"

"I fought here and I have a right to dance here. And you better stay down," Michael Mulligan warned. "Let's go, Son."

As they walked away, the piano player began "Dixie." They hurried across the open space, the crowd parting for them. In another part of the battlefield, Michael Mulligan found a flat rock and sat down. John was panting from excitement.

"What was that spectacle back there?"

"You got angry watching your father dancing an Irish jig, and you hit a fat drunk."

"No, I mean why were you dancing like a—"

"Like a what? People show grief and respect in different ways. For God's sake, we're Irish, Son. We're both a little crazy. Sit down. I need to tell you something about this place."

"Haven't we already heard a speech about Gettysburg?"

"I mean, this rocky field. To the north, Pickett had done what the Irish did before—led a disastrous charge across open ground into cannons and guns. He lost an entire division. But here, near Devil's Den, General Judson Kilpatrick ordered Elon Farnsworth to lead his cavalry against some Rebel foot soldiers. They had cover. Look at this ground—uneven, with trees, fences and ditches, terrible for horses. General Farnsworth knew it was suicidal. We had won the day. Why lose more men? Kilpatrick, may he roast in hell, insisted no cavalry could be defeated except at sea."

John gazed across the rocky field at the distant woods. He could imagine hidden sharpshooters firing into the halting cavalry, and for a moment, heard the screams of dying men and horses.

"I rode behind Elon. I had trained his men and horses. That day, Farnsworth, saber in hand, fell on the hillside, shot to pieces. He didn't shoot himself as some claimed. My horse went down, blood shooting from his snout. I hit a rock and woke up in a Union hospital, screams of men all around me. An oil lamp cast a ghastly light over the sick and wounded." John stared at his father's drawn tight profile. "I never forgave Kilpatrick for that order. He was foolhardy like Custer. I understood what Pickett felt for Lee. Anger. Disgust. All those men and beautiful horses—slaughtered."

John touched his father's knee. "At least that took you out of the war."

Michael Mulligan looked into his face, suddenly appearing older.

"It didn't. That month, they sent us to put down the draft riots in New York. We had to shoot other Irishmen who wouldn't fight to free slaves and hanged every Negro they could find. God, weren't we once slaves ourselves? I shot a boy with your name."

"That is ironic."

"Then I fought at Cold Harbor. *Another* slaughter, this time under Grant. When Lee finally surrendered, I was a mad man. I could not go back to San Francisco and produce shows and embrace my ten-year-old son. I just couldn't do it! I had seen too much death. Maybe if your mother was alive, I might have, but she died giving birth to you."

For just a moment, John expected the old man to cry, but he didn't.

"Do you blame me she died?"

"You know I don't, but I was wrong. I should have come home. You might have healed me."

"I lost you at five. Met you briefly at 14. Then discovered you at twenty. A lot of lost years, Father. You don't think *I* needed healing?"

"You did. I'm sorry."

John Mulligan stood up and walked some distance. The fields beyond were empty of fallen soldiers. A group of men took pictures of each other with a new invention, the portable camera. Michael Mulligan stared at the Slyder farmhouse, now a historic site, and he remembered Abigail, the nurse who dressed his wounds and touched his body. He was still thinking about that lost love when John turned and approached him.

"In 1866, Mark Twain appeared in San Francisco to talk about his trip to the Sandwich Islands. The Maguires took me."

"Twain? Brilliant writer."

"And wasn't I impressed to see my father's name on the program? Mark Twain's lecture produced by Michael Mulligan and Company!"

"I have a knack for finding talent, John."

John turned away, not wanting to think his missing parent stood in the wings watching the humorist work while he sat in the audience with the elderly but kindly Maguires. Before he could speak, two policemen appeared.

"Were you the gentleman dancing on the platform, back there?"

Michael Mulligan tipped his hat. "That I was, officer."

"We have two inebriated fellows who claim you assaulted them."

"Two? Against an old fellow like me?"

"I assaulted them," John said.

The two policemen were young but not impolite. The taller of the two looked at John Mulligan. "Did you, now?" He then addressed the older man. "I am Officer Sullivan. Could you explain yourself, sir?"

Michael Mulligan told the story.

"He's a bit of a dancer, you know," said the shorter policemen. He had an Irish flavor in his speech. "I used to know the jig, myself. What sort of work do you do?"

"Produce shows for Broadway."

"Do you know Edwin Booth?"

"Worked with the man. Great actor. Tragic what his brother did."

"And here at this celebration of the Irish Brigade, you're after askin' the band to play 'Dixie'?"

"Let's not forget, a Confederate Irishman designed the monument. I also spilled blood on this field," Michael Mulligan added. "Irish blood."

"Those two drunks were disrespectful," John Mulligan said.

The two policemen considered this. "What do you think, Officer Murphy?"

"They *are* English."

Officer Sullivan shrugged. "Well, I guess we can let her Majesty's drunks sleep it off. Good day."

"I might enjoy a show with dancing girls if I visit New York," Murphy said.

"You will be my guest," said Michael Mulligan, offering his card.

As they walked away, John smiled and glanced at his father. "Well—and isn't my father a star, himself. Mulligan the Great!"

"And we have more to discuss. Would you like to take a ferryboat ride?"

"Sure. And where, might I ask?"

"Up Lake Ontario to the Saint Lawrence River. There's a place you should see: Grosse Isle."

"Where the famine ships landed?"

"Exactly."

John remembered an old photo he had seen of ragged people standing on a barren hill beneath a tall Celtic cross. Michael Mulligan reached down and lifted something from the ground. In his palm lay a minié ball.

A week later, they rode a silent paddlewheel, and John Mulligan felt as though they were floating magically across the lake. Only when he walked to the stern of the large boat could he hear the paddlewheel turning in the water. He felt happy traveling with his father who smoked cigars and pointed out the sights. Perhaps they were catching up on all the years lost. He had read about the coffin ships landing at Grosse Isle with Irish emigrants sick or dying or dead. After turning up the Saint Lawrence River in the afternoon, they sat on the deck, watching the riverbank slide by soundlessly. The river would narrow near Quebec City.

"So you landed at that terrible place?"

"In 1847. Like Meagher, I was wanted in Ireland."

"For what?"

"Stealing an Anglo Irish landowner's beautiful wife."

John regretted the question.

"You met my mother in San Francisco!"

"Yes. In 1852. This other woman's name was Maria Burke."

"Perhaps we better not discuss this."

Michael Mulligan drew on his cigar. "I want you to hear the truth. After all, I did have a life *before* your mother and *before* San Francisco."

"I find it odd you never talked or wrote about my mother."

"Emily O' Rourke was a lovely woman. I will talk about her and answer any questions you have. But first, you need to hear about why I left Ireland, why I came to San Francisco, why I left."

John saw people on the bank waving at them. He didn't wave back.

"I know why you didn't come back. The war."

"True."

"So what happened to this mistress? What was her name—Mary?"

"Maria. She died of ship fever."

"Of course. Ship fever." John Mulligan found himself asking, "In your arms?"

"Yes." Michael Mulligan stood up and gripped the railing. "Let's discuss this later. Shall I bring you a drop?"

"A strong one," John said.

When they arrived at Quebec City, they disembarked and had dinner at a fashionable restaurant. Elegantly dressed tourists and French-speaking citizens seemed everywhere. The city had a quaint decorum John found missing in American cities. Over dinner and wine, Michael Mulligan continued his story. He described being a stable groom and horse trainer and how he fled Ireland with the wife of a tyrannical Anglo Irishman named Nathaniel Burke.

"Burke loved the famine. It gave him a chance to starve out the Irish peasants. Plenty of grain sailed down the Liffey and the River Shannon, going to England. No Irishman could afford it. Maria and I took a boat to Quebec with plans to settle in San Francisco. Maria took sick with Typhus. When we arrived at Grosse Isle—she died." Michael Mulligan stopped. He took a breath. "I buried her and I stayed on to work. God but I wanted to die. I felt doomed to live. I only left when the island closed down."

John looked up from his meal. "So this Maria Burke was the love of your life?"

"I left my homeland and my fellow Irish for her. And if I go back and find Nathaniel Burke still alive, I'll kill him."

Though astonished at this remark, John sipped his wine. "After all this time?"

"We Irish always take revenge for the death of a family member."

"You blame him?"

"Yes."

"You took another man's wife!"

"He was evil. Burke betrayed his people—including me."

"I see." After a pause, John said, "Tell me about Mother."

The old man leaned back in his chair and spoke in a quiet voice. "Emily was an amateur singer and actress—very pretty—and after a proper mourning, I knew it was time so I courted her."

"Proper mourning?"

"For Maria, yes. In San Francisco, our theatre was doing well so your mother and I had three lovely years together. After she died in childbirth, I raised you alone. Then the southern states seceded and I left for war." He met John's eyes. "I believed in the Union free of slavery. The Maguires were good people, trustworthy, and I sent them money. I wanted the best for you. After the war—"

"I think we know what happened *after* the war." John carefully put down his fork and knife. "Tell me, did you *ever* love my mother the way you loved this English rose, this 'Mistress Mine'?"

"Watch your tongue!"

"Did you?"

The answer was immediate: "No. Not in the same way. But I *did* love your mother."

"You loved her but you weren't madly in love with the woman who brought me into the world. This unfaithful English wife was your *true* mate?"

"She wasn't unfaithful to me."

"*How* am I to understand all this?"

"You can continue hating me. *Or* you can accept the fact I was a bad father and let me be a devoted grandfather."

"Isn't all this a bit late?"

"Maybe so."

"I *can* accept you were a bad father. Did you abandon any *other* children?"

"None that I know of."

A man in a frock coat and black pants appeared at the table. He spoke halting English with a French accent.

"As proprietor, I must ask you people to keep your voices down. Be aware, *s'il vous plait*, we have other customers who wish to dine in quiet."

"My apologies," Michael Mulligan said. "We Irish are loud."

"If we want to argue, that's our business," John said. Michael Mulligan spoke.

"Allow me to buy the best house wine for any diner feeling discomfort."

The tall maitre d' bowed. "Very good, sir. *Tres bien.*"

They finished the meal. John felt the old bitterness despite the fine food and the strong wine. They left the restaurant and walked around Quebec City until they found an expensive hotel.

"I guess your theatre business *is* doing well."

"Well enough. We've had some disasters. There was a dreadful *Richard III* recently. Someone smuggled a donkey under the stage who brayed when Richard screamed, 'A horse, a horse, my kingdom for a horse.' The audience loved it so we considered leaving it in every night. The actor quit and sued us." After getting keys to their room, Michael Mulligan looked at his son, studying his face.

"What?"

"You know, I wasn't in San Francisco when Mark Twain appeared."

"Good. That's a comfort."

"I heard it was a great success."

John watched his father's face in the yellow light.

"You never talk much about your father."

"He was shot in the back by one of Burke's landlords."

"My God."

"We have a violent history, Son."

"Did you kill him—the landlord?"

"No, someone else did...but I wanted to. That's another story, son, and I *will* tell it. Right now, I'm tired. See you in the morning."

Restless, John Mulligan walked around the Canadian city and went to bed near dawn. The next morning, exhausted, he met his father for breakfast and then they took another small ferry across the Gulf of Saint Lawrence to Grosse Isle. There was a bitter wind coming off the water. For the first time, neither felt a need to fill the silence with talk. As they came within sight of the barren island where so many Irish died, John could see his father's composure slip. He seemed to tremble and displayed an uncharacteristic nervousness. They left the group following a tour guide and walked to an old church. A service was in progress and they heard a choir singing hymns. A vast cemetery lay beyond the stone church.

"This way," Michael Mulligan said.

They walked past the singing worshippers into the small churchyard dominated by a huge Celtic cross. One of the many scrawny island dogs slipped away as they entered. In moments, Michael Mulligan found a sunken grave he had dug himself 41 years before. On the weathered granite stone, the name was barely legible: Maria Burke, 1822-1847. Listening to the plaintive music and reading the name of the long dead woman, John Mulligan felt a surprising sorrow. He saw his father's face in profile, the mouth open, the eyes moist. Here was the man who had left his son to return years later like a pirate, free from responsibility.

"You know, we could clean up that headstone," John said. "Pay someone to recarve her name."

"That we could."

Perhaps Michael Mulligan finally recognized the little boy he had abandoned in San Francisco, the elderly Patrick James Maguire taking the crying child from his arms. Then he stared at the headstone and saw Maria's face and felt his lips tighten.

"My God," he finally said.

John touched his father's shoulder. "It's all right, Father. You loved her."

THE PLANTATION

ELDERLY IRISH FARMERS ON the Sligo-Roscommon border remembered the Nathaniel Burke plantation as a place of titled English and Anglo Irish landowners fox hunting while peasants starved in the fields and bogs and along the roads. When the public works finally began, the famine had weakened the labor force and few survived. Some local Irish escaped and those remaining collaborated, taking whatever work the landlords gave them, even evicting other farmers behind in rent.

Many knew the story of the Irish stable hand that ran off with Nathaniel Burke's English wife, and they felt a vindication that one of their own had cuckolded an infamous Anglo Irish landowner. Nathaniel Burke survived with Scottish workers, finding another wife who bore him a son, and even gained some fame in England for a book on flowers sketched in his elegant hand.

As the Irish moved back to reclaim the land, the Burke plantation grew smaller, the stables reduced to a single weathered stall. They saw the difference in Nathaniel Burke, Jr., a man who didn't want to own land and who gave away money to shelters, public works, even the arts. Nathaniel Burke grew senile at 70

285

and his son moved him to a Galway nursing home. While the farmers planted flourishing potatoes and raised sheep, they expected the son to take over the old Burke plantation, but the mansion sat empty and the land around it remained unattended, weeds growing wild in fields that once produced rows of green plants.

"Someone bought the old Burke place," a farmer said.

They had taken shelter in a shack and smoked clay pipes while heavy rain fell.

"Did Burke's son ever say who?"

"No, but I hear it was an Irish American."

As they watched the empty house in the rain, they speculated how this mysterious Yank would use his land.

"Maybe Irish Yanks don't know how to farm. We'll see a resort for rich English."

But the Burke land lay fallow and the house sagged into a ruin; local boys broke windows and rotting timbers produced a ghost mansion.

"And who is after buying the old place?" asked Father O' Connor, the local parish priest.

The son—tall, thin with regular features—only shrugged. "An Irish American who once worked there."

"And does this mysterious Irish Yank have a name?"

"I can't give you that information," Nathaniel Burke, Jr. said.

"Is he young? Old?"

"You'll know that when he claims the place."

The buyer didn't return. The Burke plantation crumbled, the unplowed ground itself swallowing the leaning old house, too dangerous now for occupancy. At times, the farmers heard that Nathaniel Burke's son had joined an Irish Brotherhood that wanted a United Ireland free from British rule, and now went by his middle name, George. A new century approached and Ireland was changing. Often, George would leave a secret meeting, watching for British thugs hiding in the streets, and wonder when the Irish American would return. He knew the senility that darkened his father's final months had ironically saved his life from the absentee buyer. George still remembered the day he returned to the old house to collect and donate some of his father's elegant furniture when he saw the tall white-haired man standing in the open door.

"The house and land won't be for sale until next month," George told him. "If that is what you are after."

"I am. Thank you," the stranger said. "And where's himself? Nathaniel Burke?"

Though the stranger had an authentic Irish accent, there was a sound of America in his speech.

"My father is very ill. I'm afraid he's lost his memory and is residing at the Galway nursing home. I am Nathaniel Burke, Jr."

The man stared at him. He wore round spectacles and had a strange cast to his eyes. "Nathaniel Burke, Jr.?"

"Yes. I prefer to be called George. And with whom do I have the honor of speaking?"

"Just another expatriate Irishman and Yankee Civil War veteran."

"And your name?"

"Connor Shaw."

"Shaw?"

"I once tended your father's horses. He had some nice stables."

"Long gone, now."

"So I see."

George studied the older man's lined face. He could sense danger in Connor Shaw, despite his advanced age. "Well now, why don't we make an appointment and discuss business in a week? Maybe you could tell me about those old days."

Shaw nodded and admired a spread of green fields. A band of sheep grazed in the distance, a rock wall lining the meadow. A thin old man in a black coat passed on a bony horse, and he stared at Shaw. Shaw watched him as he rode his horse to a crossroads and disappeared.

"Beautiful country," Shaw said. "Maybe someday the Irish will own it."

"I certainly hope so...and may we govern well"

George Burke felt no fear when the older man shook his hand, but that afternoon, he went through his father's massive tedious ledgers and journals, researching the story he had heard from servants growing up about a rebellious Irish stable hand that ran off with a landowner's wife. Even as a child, he saw a gloating malice in the eyes of servants telling the story. Her name was never mentioned by Lord Burke. She was not directly mentioned in the journals where even the marriage to his late mother was simply a footnote. His father's handwriting was elegant:

Sold a good mare for breeding. Getting married as I need a new wife. Famine seems diminished. I guess the Irish peasants will be happy, those wretches that remain. Christmas, 1850.

A new wife indicates there was a former one, George thought. He knew the local Irish would never reveal anything about the family history. They would only tip their caps and spit.

A month later, a deed was signed and money exchanged hands, much of it going to Irish charities or the movement for a United Ireland. Connor Shaw booked passage to America without making any plans to take over and revive the Burke plantation. George accompanied Shaw to the quay at Queenstown. Crossing the bay in a small boat heading toward an island harbor, Shaw kept silent. Finally, George spoke.

"Mr. Shaw? I have to ask you a question."

"Ask."

"I went to visit Father, recently. He's unable to recognize me, of course. They tell me he won't last the week." He expected the other man to comment but silence followed. "While there, I saw a man who used to work for him named Devlin."

"Devlin?"

"Yes. He is still coherent but very old, ravaged by drink. Poor man, he was terrified."

The dock was busy with traffic, and Shaw glanced at the ship that would take him back to America. "Terrified of what?"

"Of a man come back for revenge."

Connor Shaw was clearly surprised, and George felt a tinge of fear staring into the elderly man's troubling gray eyes.

"Devlin was terrified of you," George said.

"Me? I'm an Irishman come home to do business."

"Maybe so. I grew up with a suspicion that my father had married before he met my mother and that an Irish stable hand took her to America. I know my father was hated by the local farmers. Some of them still hate me."

"And why is that?"

"I think you know why—Mr. Michael Mulligan."

"Mulligan? Sounds like a horse thief."

"Did you know Devlin?"

"Everyone knows someone named Devlin." The other man glanced away. The guarded demeanor vanished and George saw an old warrior, sad and resigned. "Devlin was a spy and a coward, always doing your father's business."

"Devlin said you were staring at my father and for a moment, he thought you might smother him except a nurse arrived." The older man's expression was hard to read. "Who were the Whiteboys?" George asked.

"Devlin told you about them?"

"Yes. Who were they? Assassins?"

"They never existed, Mr. Burke. It's all a myth."

"I see. Well, Devlin was terrified and sounded pretty convincing to me."

Mulligan confronted him. "I'm Irish, Mr. Burke. We avenge wrongs to a family. In fact, I could even wipe out Burke's surviving seed—you."

"I'm not afraid."

"I saw that. Maybe you're not a true Burke."

"And maybe as Irishmen we should unite. Wouldn't *that* surprise the British?"

"It would. I'm through with revenge, Mr. Burke," Mulligan finally said.

The two men stood watching the agitated bay waters; a light rain began. "Shall we lift a pint, sir?"

Michael Mulligan nodded. They retired to an ale house and sat across from each other while musicians played and sang old folk songs in Irish. Outside was the harbor where so many Irish had left Ireland forever.

"Mr. Burke. You don't take offense. I admire that."

It was over beer that Michael Mulligan told the story of Nathaniel, George's tyrannical father, about Maria, his first wife, and about Mulligan's trip to America that ended with Maria's death. George sat in rapt attention, hearing a tale of sorrow and violence connected to his family history.

"So that was your revenge, stealing my father's bride?"

"No. My problem with your father started before I knew Maria existed. I was sixteen and traveling with a theatre troupe when I heard my father was shot by a Mr. Boyle, a landlord for Nathaniel Burke. I vowed revenge…but Boyle didn't die at my hands."

"The Whiteboys?"

"Perhaps. Then I found myself taking care of your father's horses, and I met his lovely bride. I knew what the famine was doing to the Irish peasants. I could continue fighting against the Anglo Irish landlords and landowners…or I could follow my heart and leave Ireland."

"With my father's bride? He must've been outraged."

"I'm sure he was." Mulligan looked at George. "I could've cut his throat. Of course, if I did, you wouldn't be here."

"I have to put this into some perspective, Mr. Mulligan. Continue."

"We left for Canada and you know the rest."

"I heard of Grosse Isle. Terrible place."

"Maria—a beautiful woman whom I never forgot—died there."

For a moment, both men were silent. George Burke sipped his beer.

"You survived Grosse Isle *and* the American Civil War. It's amazing you're here!"

"And now I'm leaving."

"You'll be back to claim the estate?"

"No. I want it to rot—to fall apart."

"Why not build something, or start a school, perhaps?"

"For Socialists? Romantic Fenians?"

"You could do worse."

Michael Mulligan leaned close to George's smooth face.

"Listen, a word of caution. The emancipation of Ireland has to be slow."

"Slow? We've waited 800 years."

"True. But I think George Bernard Shaw and the Fabians are right. Just like General Fabius, one has to wait, pick one's battles, and *then* strike and win. There will be more blood spilled, for sure. There will be a Republic of Ireland, one day, though maybe not in Belfast and certainly not in our lifetime."

"I'm not so sure it will take that long."

"I hope you're right." Mulligan finished his beer. "I'm off."

"Come back. The grounds will be waiting."

"Perhaps for my son or his children. Not for me. I have enemies."

"Certainly no one in the Burke clan will harm you."

"I left my brothers," Mulligan said.

"The Whiteboys?"

"Yes, though perhaps enough time has passed—and I can still be useful."

George Burke was surprised. "Surely you're not killing people now, Mr. Mulligan."

For the first time, George saw a smile on Michael Mulligan's face.

"Killing people? My God, man, I'm seventy!"

On the stage, the singer hit an emotional high note and patrons clapped. "That's a powerful song from our tragic history."

"You speak Irish?"

"I do. It's about a mad king turned into a bird." Mulligan closed his eyes and recited:

"Swifter than the wind in glens/Once the figure of a champion,

A legend now and a madman/ Your exile's over Sweeney— come home."

"Lovely," George said.

"He never returns."

They left the tavern and walked toward the waiting ship. Many houses were built into the hill above the bay. "I will look in on the place from time to time. There's the problem of squatters."

"Don't bother. Let it fall apart."

"I shall explore this Fabian group."

"Do so. The English shoot Fenians."

"Don't forget, we Irish can shoot back."

"I fear it may come to that. And of course, once we win our independence, we'll have a civil war. If that doesn't destroy us, the Catholic Church will. The Irish, Mr. Burke: a strange contrary race."

"I fear you're right." The two men shook hands. "I'm sorry about Maria," George said. "I am sorry about your father and I'm sorry what my father did."

"We're all sorry," Mulligan said. "Good-bye, then." Mulligan glanced back at the city, feeling the harbor breeze. The many houses built into the hills were blurred, but he saw again the hills of San Francisco and remembered the faces and voices of those he had lost, the men and women and the five-year-old son he told good-bye on the eve of the Civil War. George was surprised to see a tenderness in Mulligan's expression. "This place was called Cove when I joined a theatre on this very pier. I was a boy."

"When the queen graced us with her presence, the famine still raging, the English decided to rename the town in her honor," George said.

After a silence, Mulligan waved good-bye and walked up the plank to board. Nathaniel George Burke, Jr. watched Mulligan's ship sail out into the Atlantic.

When Nathaniel Burke died, his polished marble stone proclaimed Nathaniel Burke a "friend of the English." Father O' Connor objected to a Catholic burial service assuming Nathaniel Burke was Protestant and a member of the Church of Ireland. George Burke insisted his father was indeed a Catholic and wanted a Catholic burial.

"He hid his true faith."

"Even so, how could a fellow Catholic evict his brothers and allow his own people to starve during famine times?" the priest demanded.

"That was a long time ago," the son said, "and don't you think it's time for some healing?"

"Healing, you say?"

"Didn't the Savior himself believe in healing?"

When the dead man's son gave the parish a substantial sum, Father O' Connor agreed that it was time for healing.

———

"Tell us a story, Grandfather."

It was after the storm and now they were close to docking. John Mulligan still felt sick and went up on the deck as his 15-year-old twins—John Jr. and Kate—begged Michael Mulligan to tell them another story about Ireland. He had already told so many stories of Celtic warriors and old battles and the eternal Irish troubles with the English invaders. The old man's eyes had gone in the last two years, but his voice was still clear. He had the shifting rhythms and projection of a skilled actor.

"This is my last story. Then you children have to describe a house for me. And then—I will go home."

"Home? Where? Ireland? America?"

"Ireland, of course, Kate."

Michael Mulligan leaned against the bunk as the two children sat on either side. They had been annoyed by the ship's fleas and frightened by the storm at sea but now were well enough to be bored. He began: "This is a story of the ancient Fenians."

"Fenians?"

"Irish warriors like King Arthur's knights who rode out to right wrongs and enforce justice. To be a Fenian, one had to be a great fighter with bow and sword but literate, as well, capable of reciting Ireland's great epic poems. King Finn was the leader of the Fenians and had a noble son. He was a warrior and a poet. His name is spelled O.I.S.I.N. but pronounced 'Oh-sheen.'"

"Why don't they pronounce the words like we do?" asked John.

"I guess the Celts didn't have enough letters in their alphabet."

"Just tell the story," Kate demanded.

Mulligan continued. They could hear sailors running on the deck.

"One day, Oisin met a beautiful girl with golden hair." Kate and John giggled. "She was a queen," Michael added. "And immortal. She would never die."

"I know what happens," said John. "Oisin and the golden-haired girl fall in love."

"I told you this before?"

"No, but that's what always happens in fairy tales," the boy said.

Michael Mulligan lifted his hand. "But this isn't *just* a fairy tale."

"Do they live happily ever after?"

"No, Kate, they don't."

"All right," John said. "Let's hear it."

Michael Mulligan continued. He knew the ship was in the harbor and ready to dock.

"Oisin and Neeve, the golden-haired queen, fell in love and she offered him a chance to leave Ireland and live with her in a magical kingdom where no one grew old. He could hunt and fish and ride his horse and they could be together forever. Oisin agreed, and though his father wept, he left to live with his new queen. Now, time was all different, you see. One year in the beautiful kingdom might be 10 years in Ireland. After a great period of time when they never grew old and still loved each other, Oisin discovered he was lonely. Queen Neeve wasn't enough. Nor his horse and his hunting. No—he had to see those Fenian warriors, again, and see his native Ireland after so much time. Queen Neeve begged him to stay. 'That world is gone. If you leave,' she said, 'you will no longer have long life. You may *never* come back.' Oisin insisted that he would return, so Neeve warned him: 'Never touch the ground in Ireland. Stay on your horse, or you will die a hideously old man.' Oisin laughed. 'I will stay on my horse. I will return.' He left and rode his beautiful steed over mountains and across the ocean—to Ireland."

The two teenaged children stared at their grandfather. The ship was creaking. They saw a distant light in his cloudy eyes that disturbed them.

"I am like Oisin," he said. "I want to go back, but when I touch Irish soil, I will not return to America. I will stay in Ireland—forever."

"We'll stay too," said Kate.

"You *will* have a place, Yanks though you be," Michael Mulligan said.

The boy was silent. Michael Mulligan gently rubbed his grandson's hair, and then continued his story.

"Oisin returned to Ireland and rode across a burned-out land. Castles had decayed. The people starved and fought among themselves for bread. Invaders had cut the trees. He saw bogs and swamps everywhere, and even the green hills of Ireland had disappeared with the advance of many wild goats and sheep, quick and hard to catch. His friends were gone. His father was gone. When he asked about the Fenians, people laughed and told him that was a legend from long ago and probably false. Ireland had no Irish warriors like King Arthur's knights to protect the weak. The people stared at his strong stallion and Oisin knew they were hungry, so he rode away. He did not want to kill fellow Irishmen, even when thugs with guns laughed at his shield and broad sword. Did he steal the pretty horse from a circus? Sure but he must have been a queer sight, a golden warrior from another era riding through a waste land. Oisin knew it was futile and decided to return to the magical kingdom and his golden-haired queen. On the road, he saw a young boy trapped under a huge rock with his mother crying out for help. Oisin reached down to lift the rock in his strong hand and the sudden weight pulled him from the saddle. He touched the Irish soil and then—"

John lowered his eyes. "He died?"

"Oisin turned into an old man—hundreds of years old. The gorgeous horse reared and vanished. The mother took her boy and jumped back from the shriveled mummy on the ground."

John, Jr. remained silent. Kate began crying. John Mulligan came into the cabin and saw his distressed children.

"By God, Father, what are you telling them?"

"The story of Oisin."

"It's depressing don't you think?"

Staring ahead with sightless eyes, Michael Mulligan shook his head.

"Not at all. I have a new ending. You see, even as the young Oisin fell toward the soil of Ireland, knowing what would happen, he saw golden haired Queen Neeve standing before him, her arms outstretched. His body would shrivel and die, but their spirits would be together—forever."

After a silence, John grabbed his two kids. "Hit the deck. We're docking!"

Later, Kate helped her grandfather maneuver the plank linked to the dock.

"It's Ireland," he said. "I can smell the ocean and the green fields. I began here and I will end, here."

The next day they traveled to Galway and found a comfortable inn. Swans floated on the River Corrib flowing into Galway Bay. Michael and his son walked on the beach while the children played. The sun was setting. "Galway Bay really is beautiful. Someone should write a song about it."

"Someone will. Son, have you sent a note to George Burke?"

After a moment, John smiled and said, "No—but I'm sure I will. I doubt there will be any house left—if there ever was one."

Michael Mulligan drove his shillelagh into the sand. "Son, you don't have to doubt me. I have the deed."

"True, but after ten years, some squatters might have taken it. Why do the Irish just leave abandoned buildings to rot?"

"I don't know." They walked on. "You may have to scatter some of my ashes here, and take the rest and scatter them over your mother's grave—the children will appreciate that—*and* Maria's grave. That you can do alone."

Mulligan could imagine his son's face. "Father, for the love of God, you aren't going to die and I *won't* go back to that awful Grosse Isle."

"Remember your roots, Son. Ireland is still a colony of the English. Defend your people. Defend your country."

"America is my country."

"True—but we're here."

In another week, they would be in Ballaghaderreen, a small dull town after Galway, and it rained heavily. Michael Mulligan felt the cold piercing his bones, and at night, he dreamed of his ancient love, Maria. They were again taking an open coach across a famine-stricken Ireland, riding along dark silent roads toward Dublin and a ship to America. There they would begin a new life in a paradise where all men and women were free to work and love. In the morning, John played a penny whistle, entertaining the kids who were bored, again. The rain finally stopped.

"Shall we find this mythical mansion, Father?"

Mulligan turned toward his son's voice. "Yes."

"We have to tell him what it looks like," said Kate.

"That's right."

Before they left, John pulled his father into a corner.

"I heard from George Burke's office in Dublin. He hasn't responded since he got arrested in a demonstration."

"We'll have to give him a bit of aid, now, won't we?"

"I can't practice law here."

"I know. Advise him. He's your age."

"I hope he's smarter than I am."

That afternoon, the sky clear, they took a coach to the old Burke plantation. They rode along a narrow muddy road, past abandoned farms, arriving at an open field with low stone walls. The driver pulled up the horses. John stared out the window.

"Is this it?"

"There's a curse on this place," the driver said without being asked.

Michael Mulligan stared with clotted eyes toward the open field. "Tell me, Kate, what do you see?"

They got out and walked, Kate describing the scene: "I see an open field. Rocks. Tall grass. Rock wall. And over there is a house leaning over. I can see through it," she said.

"Someone took a few timbers," John said. "Sneeze and that structure will fall over."

"I see some wagons," said the girl.

"Wagons?" said Michael Mulligan. "Where?"

"In the field."

"We got a problem with Travelers," the driver told them. "Thieves and Irish Gypsies, they are."

The driver stayed behind as they walked toward the sagging structure. Michael Mulligan paused before the worn steps and the faded façade of the gutted mansion.

"Looks like Poe's House of Usher," said John, Jr. "I like the columns. Someone wrote on them."

"What did they write"

"I can't tell."

Nathaniel Burke did have some wonderful horses," the old man finally said. "But he was evil to his people."

"Is that why you left, Granddad?"

"Yes, Kate. A very romantic exit, you might say. Your father will tell you the story."

"Tell it now," Kate said.

"Perhaps in time."

The boy started up the rotten stairs, but Michael Mulligan grabbed him.

"Little John, the house is too dangerous. Son? Let's have it knocked down and have a big bonfire, shall we? Then we'll match my deed to the town records."

John Mulligan took off his straw hat and shook his head. "And what will I *do* with the land?"

"Lease it to farmers. One day, it might be a base of operations, or just a place to vacation."

"Vacation? Here?"

"You're close to Galway and Donegal up north. But first," his father said, "burn the old house in front of the town. Make it a big celebration. In fact, why don't you drive to town now and find a crew? I'll stay."

"To do what?"

"Talk to these Travelers. I speak their language."

"Shelta?"

"Yes. It was my first language."

"Let me stay," the girl said.

"Sure, Kate."

After hesitating, John decided to obey. "I'll bring back some food. What if it rains?"

"We'll stay with the Travelers," Michael Mulligan said. "Kate, would you like to sit in a covered wagon?"

"Yes," the girl replied.

As John drove away with his son, the driver warned, "Them traveling tinkers is dangerous, you know what I mean? They steal children. They've lived off the land since the famine days. I wouldn't leave your old da alone with them."

"I think he can take care of himself—and my daughter. He fought in the American Civil War, you know."

Later, Kate would describe approaching the line of wagons and ragged men with axes and one rifle greeting them, and how Grandfather spoke in a strange language and the men were surprised. A small wiry old man from the village greeted her grandfather. He had myriad wrinkles in his red face and a gruff voice.

"Well, well, the prodigal Mulligan returns."

"I am ready to face your wrath, Sean."

"I've waited years for this moment—to finally meet you face to face." Kate remembered the old man looking at her and then her grandfather and finally saying, "Welcome home, Mr. Mulligan."

They greeted each other in what Kate later discovered to be Irish. Then they talked about old skirmishes with the British. They shared food, and Grandfather talked about the mansion's history and even told the Travelers they didn't have to leave, which meant they would. She heard words in Shelta and Irish, and began writing them down using her own phonetics. One day, she would translate them and piece together what tragic history these men discussed, but she would never completely solve the mystery of her grandfather. At one point, she heard a change in her grandfather's voice, and looking up, saw tears in his pale eyes.

"Kate? That old man over there with the deep voice? He's a Traveler, a Tinker, a so called Irish Gypsy. Before I was adopted, I was one of them. We were hated. An Irish landlord named Boyle killed my father…shot him in the back."

He repeated the story in the language the Travelers understood, and they shouted out their anger.

"Grandfather? What happened to the man who shot your father?"

Sean laughed and said, "The fat Irish traitor who murdered your great grandfather was gut shot and left to die on a muddy road—but Michael Mulligan didn't pull the trigger. Not him."

"Who then?"

"Me," Sean said. "Mulligan got his revenge in another way by stealing Master Burke's lovely English bride."

Those listening voiced approval.

"You stole a man's wife?"

"They exaggerate, Kate," Michael Mulligan said. "I'm a gentleman."

Everyone laughed. Kate wanted to ask more questions but a girl from the Travelers handed her a cup filled with liquor that burned down her throat, and soon, Kate felt light-headed, staring into the glare of a campfire. The strange languages became a meaningless cacophony of tongues. Her grandfather took the cup and handed it to another.

"Don't be after drinking that stuff. As for my sad history, Kate, your father knows most of my secrets."

Someone put a blanket around her, and Kate closed her eyes.

That afternoon, musicians took out a guitar and fiddle and played music; a woman with long hair plucked an Irish harp. When the workers from town arrived, they dismantled the ruined mansion, a symbol of a slave era. They tossed the timbers of the mansion into a roaring bon fire. Local fire fighters burned a field of ragweed.

"It's to keep away the evil fairies," a fireman said.

The music continued and Travelers and Irish townspeople enjoyed a feast of lamb and potatoes. The Travelers put on a bare knuckle fist fight, two potbellied men, their greasy bodies gleaming in the firelight, slugging each other while the crowd made bets and cheered the pugilists. Michael Mulligan, his white hair flame-like, sat by the bonfire, feeling the warmth and imagining another time dancing with his lost love while his Irish American son walked among the townspeople and even tried conversation with the Travelers who only spoke English when necessary, and that hard to understand

Though blind, Michael Mulligan could see shapes and shadows on the periphery, and when he raised his head, he saw suddenly clearly a woman in black moving toward him, her face partially hidden by a hood. Leaning down, she pulled back the sides of the hood, revealing a young beautiful face.

"My God."

"Michael Mulligan. Hello, my dear one."

"You are here?"

"Of course, old boy. You've been on a long adventure, but now it's time to rest. You have people waiting."

"What people?"

"All your women, including me—and all those who went before you."

"Went before me?"

She touched his burning forehead and paraphrased words of an ancient poem:

"A legend now, your exile's over—come home."

When Kate opened her eyes, she was leaning on her brother's shoulder as he watched the celebration.

"Where's Grandfather?"

"He's talking to an old woman."

"Where?"

"Over there."

Then Kate saw the woman speaking to her grandfather in a voice she couldn't hear, and perhaps in a language Kate wouldn't understand. The woman resembled the old crones Kate saw in picture books. Her grandfather nodded, listening to the woman's voice. Suddenly, Michael Mulligan stood and found his son despite sightless eyes. They embraced one last time.

"Son? It's time."

"Time for what? Your party is going well."

"Time to go. I can feel them...all the people from my past. Myles Keogh. Reginald Taylor. Edwin Booth. Son—I see your mother."

"My mother? Here? Not likely."

"Emily is here. And Maria. I can see her. Maria!"

Mulligan's voice broke.

"You *can't* see," John said. He looked into his father's clotted eyes. "Sit down, Father. Rest."

"Dunne is done," Mulligan said. "Tell the horses." The old man began to sing in Irish and waving his shillelagh, gave a final yell, perhaps an ancient battle cry. The crowd gathered to watch his strange turning dance. Then he collapsed in his son's arms. John saw his children running toward him.

A week later when John Mulligan finally met George Burke on the Queenstown waterfront, Burke remarked it was rare that Travelers appeared anywhere without the inevitable missing wallets and pocket watches. What magic had his father used?

"We know so little about his early life in Ireland," John mused. "He knew horses, weapons and the theatre. He was a Traveler, a cavalry officer and maybe something of a scholar."

"The US army may have some records."

"I found out Mulligan was his adopted name. I don't know his real name. He told me he left a journal and some papers at Oxford."

"Oxford?" George nodded to himself. Passengers walked by on the dock. Ships with full sails crossed and turned in the bay. "You have a place to start a family history. Certainly your father was unique…meant to be different."

"Yes." John suddenly felt beginning tears for the man who had been a phantom for so long. "That he was. I'm glad we finally connected."

"I'm sorry we didn't meet again." George remembered standing in front of the Burke Mansion, the tall older man with gray eyes watching him quietly. "He could be quite intimidating, you know."

A ship waited to take the Mulligan family home. In the distance, John, Jr. and Kate stood waiting, each holding a suitcase. Some traveling actors were setting up a stage on the wharf.

"You know, it's ironic that he told the kids a story about Oisin and his death when he returned to Ireland."

"Ah yes, I know that old legend. I would've stayed in paradise with the beautiful Queen Neeve," George said. "Are your children upset?"

"I think they were prepared. One minute their grandfather was toasting the townspeople and the Travelers and the next, an old woman whispered something to him, and then he rushed toward me talking about the dead, including my mother. I caught him in my arms, babbling in English and Irish. He died before we reached the hospital."

"Who was the old woman?"

"Who knows? No one saw her except my kids. They insist she was real."

"Extraordinary."

"The next morning, John and Kate saw a white horse with a black mane and tail galloping across the burned-out field. I told them Grandfather's spirit was riding him."

"Maybe he was, John."

"As for his last request?"

"The local Irish Catholics aren't big on cremation, you know...but we got it done."

"That we did. Thanks." John looked at the man with graying sideburns whose father was so linked to his own. "Will Ireland ever be independent, George?"

George saw the dock and the narrow road leading to a bridge between two houses and imagined Irish rebels firing upon young English soldiers coming to quell an uprising. The English soldiers would fall and others return fire. The final battle for Ireland would begin.

"Home Rule will come one day, but it will be violent, and Ireland will probably never be completely free from strife."

"I sadly agree." He held out his hand. "So long, George."

"Good bye, John Mulligan. One day, we'll have our own country and we'll change the name of this harbor from Queenstown back to Cove. Safe journey."

With a light rain falling, John Mulligan sailed back to America with his son and daughter, carrying his father's remaining ashes in a small vial. One of the Travelers had agreed to scatter some ashes in a secret place known only to Michael Mulligan, but John knew where the rest would go. Crossing the sea at the beginning of the 20th century, he would tell his children of Irish myths and old battles and how all of Ireland's heroes were betrayed over and over, but the struggle would continue. Kate and John, Jr. seemed accepting after losing their colorful granddad. Kate held a notebook full of foreign words scrawled in her personal phonetic code, a record of her grandfather's last conversation.

"One fine day," John Mulligan said, feeling the roll of the ship, "we'll all live in a new world and salute the life to come."

CPSIA information can be obtained at www.ICGtesting.com
Printed in the USA
BVOW080201150513

320749BV00002B/296/P